2/10

"Fox c   e style
with t   uthors
try an   ology,
this m

                                              eview)

"A risi   good
hands.   H LEE

"Inter   s of
empe   . A
myth   sio

"Dani   history   and
sheer   ing
for th

                                              cus

"Danie   ar-
velous. . . . Definitely a novel—and a series—that should be on every
fantasy reader's radar."   —Fantasy Book Critic

By Daniel Fox

Dragon in Chains
Jade Man's Skin

Jade Man's Skin

Moshui

The Books of Stone and Water

Jade Man's Skin

BOOK TWO

DANIEL FOX

BALLANTINE BOOKS
New York

A Del Rey Trade Paperback Original

Copyright © 2010 by Daniel Fox

Published in the United States by Del Rey,
an imprint of The Random House Publishing Group,
a division of Random House, Inc., New York.

DEL REY is a registered trademark and the Del Rey colophon
is a trademark of Random House, Inc.

ISBN 978-0-345-50304-6

Printed in the United States of America

www.delreybooks.com

2 4 6 8 9 7 5 3 1

Book design by Mary A. Wirth

Not much lies within my gift,
but this does.

This book is for you.

You know who you are.

ONE

Dragon's Flight

one

*H*an flew, behind the dragon's eyes.

HE DIDN'T ride her, no. His body was somewhere else, below, and she would eat it if she could. Eat him.

As it turned out, though, she couldn't. She did try. But a little of him, the least little fragment of life that was himself sat somewhere within the enormity, the outrage, the cruelty of scale that was herself—and directed her just a touch, a veer away from what she most wanted, where she meant most harm.

HE HAD willfully cut her chains, and they were still bound together. That didn't seem fair, even to him. She was enraged past measure to have this puny passenger abiding in her head. Her thoughts were storms, if those were thoughts, if he understood her at all: banked like clouds but dense like solid water, more violent than the typhoon, churning and crashing together, flaring with a vicious light that meant no good to him or his.

She knew where he stood, and what he had done. He had cut her free, and watched her destroy the impertinence of ships on her waters—a whole fleet in shatters now, all their crews drowned or swallowed or clinging helplessly, hopelessly to turbulent wreckage. She had relished that, but he could feel the hint of doubt in her now. Had it really been her choice? Or had he pushed her to it, his little insolent hands in her head, nudging her anger, *using* her . . . ?

It was all for him now, that anger: a gift, his own. She brought it to him.

HE STOOD on the Forge, at the highest peak of that mountain-tip where it jutted from the strait, with the only people he cared about in the world: love and fear and respect, unequally divided. They all cared about the dragon, necessarily; they all feared her.

All his awareness was with her, in the air. In her mind, in her temper as she soared, as she spied, as she stooped like a hawk, like a queen condescending to pick out the petty ones she would destroy.

As it turned out, though, she couldn't harm him, or anyone in his shadow.

Not here, not now. Not yet.

Not quite.

two

General Ping Wen had immortal longings in him.

He had godhood in his eye, and the Jade Throne should be his road there. He had reached, reached twice at once, both hands, the one with a blade and the other with a flag; but the blade had been turned aside somehow, and the flag had fetched no friends.

The boy who sat the throne, the young emperor ought to be dead in his own folly. A boatload of assassins had found him and pursued him, and absurdly failed to kill him. The boy was camped out in the mountains somewhere, sending impertinent messages. And conscripting native miners to be his bodyguard, apparently. It was a wild fancy, almost a madness. An opportunity too, of course, but Ping Wen lacked means just now to exploit it.

He should have had an army. He had sent the signal across the strait to Tunghai Wang, to summon his invasion. That might have made other difficulties, as Tunghai Wang meant to take the throne for himself; but one general's claim was no better than another's, once the legitimate boy was dead. Ping Wen could have managed his own ascension, here on what would be his own island. Except that the invasion had not come.

Had there been a dragon, rising in the strait? The astrologers were certain; reports from the coast were confused and contradictory. Which was a strange way around, but much of the world was turned contrary now. As witness, a loyal general aspired to his master's throne and godhood, and thought it should be easy to achieve.

He thought he should have it by now. One way or the other. So many trained killers, and not one of them had reached the boy; so many shiploads of men, and not one of them had come ashore. A great fleet had been spotted, according to some. They were mostly those who claimed to have seen a dragon also, rising from the water and destroying all the boats. Others had seen a storm, no more than that, a darkness on the horizon.

Wilding or weather, he was almost sure that the invasion had been launched and met catastrophe. Almost. He couldn't be certain until he saw the wreckage or heard from Tunghai Wang; but the generalissimo should have trusted the signal. Whether that man was now dead in the strait or still stranded on the other side, seeing the ruin of his hopes wash up on every beach, Ping Wen wasn't able to guess.

Guesswork was for the credulous. When Ping Wen gambled, he did it on information. He had sent boats across the strait—manned by crews who did not believe in the dragon—to discover the true state of the rebels' forces and their surviving leaders. Any honest general would have done the same. Ping Wen had contrived to slip a few trusted men into the boats, to carry a minimum of news to Tunghai Wang if they had the chance; but the generalissimo must be a damaged man now, if he was not entirely broken. In many ways, his disaster should play well for Ping Wen, even if it did leave the emperor alive and apparently unchallenged here on Taishu-island.

Any honest general, of course, would also be sending messages to his emperor, urging the young man back into the proper protection of his army, the governing care of his mother and her council. Ping Wen sent daily, while doing everything he could to cement his own authority in the palace and across the island. The emperor would have to come out of the hills eventually; when he did, he would find himself in a subtly different world. For a while.

A short while.

Ping Wen clapped his hands for a scribe, and began to dictate another letter.

three

Li Ton sometimes liked to sit and count his losses. It helped to keep his purpose sharp; it gave a focus to his abiding anger, which might have whittled him down into a sour madness else. It might have let him die as he had lately lived, as a freeboot pirate, scum. Which would have been the last and almost the worst of his losses, if he had let that happen. He had lost so much already; he could not, he dared not lose his immaculate revenge.

HE HAD been a boy, and hopeful, and lost that. Well, but so did most men. Hope was not a likely survivor in the world.

HE HAD been a good soldier, an officer, and respected by his men. He had lost that. On his ship he ruled by fear largely and bribery a little, as any pirate captain must. He called it discipline, of course. Soldiers too lived under discipline, which was not easy— but a soldier can always run away. For the most part, his had not. Even as a young man he had valued that respect, and lost it.

HE HAD been a man of rank, high rank, known and trusted at the court. He had lost that. Any general's reputation shines only as brightly as his last battle, of course; any general can lose a battle for any number of reasons that are not his fault. Li Ton had lost an impossible battle and depended, perhaps gambled, on the emperor's justice when he returned to the Hidden City.

He had lost.

HE HAD been a man, a married man, a father; he had been a strong man, a whole man in his pride, marked only by the due scars of his service to the empire.

He had lost it all.

He had seen his wife and women executed, his children too.

His own skin he had seen emblazoned, treachery and cowardice writ large upon him, great black block characters tattooed with heavy needles while he struggled in his chains.

He had seen his manhood cut away, not by the skilled blades of the imperial castrators but the brute hack of an executioner. He might have died; he might have wished to die.

HE HAD lost that chance, and lost his country too: sent into exile, which meant a low and sordid death on some remote coast, broken and despairing and forgotten.

HE HAD lost his name.

HE HAD found . . . no, he had *been* found by Jorgan and raised up into something again, some semblance of a man who mattered. He had worked, and fought, and won himself a ship and a crew, a way to live, eventually a path to vengeance.

And now, apparently, he had lost all that. Jorgan was dead, Li Ton's ship was in the charge of the emperor's forces, his last unexpected chance to influence the way of the world seemed to be gone. Sunk, with the rebels' fleet.

ALSO, HE was an aging man and he had seen a great many terrible and wonderful things; many of them he simply didn't remember anymore. It was his own life, and he was losing the record of it.

THIS, THOUGH. This he was determined not to lose: the day the dragon came.

She might have been the death of his last hope, but she was a great and an appalling mystery, and he had stood in the stench of her and looked into her eye, and he would not lose that. No.

THE BOY Han had cut his own chains, willfully, just when Li Ton was hopeful that he could control the dragon. *Because* Li Ton was hopeful, therefore the boy had cut the chains.

He should have died for that. Li Ton had lost count of the number of times that boy should have died and had not. At Li Ton's own hands, most often. He was not a man who spared the weak or the guilty or the treacherous, and yet, for this boy he held his hand again and again.

Apparently, he was not alone.

They were on the Forge, Han had cut his chains, the dragon was free. There was nothing they could do but watch. She was like an emperor herself and all this petty world her court, the air her throne because it held her up; the sea her proper queendom because she soared above it. Until she dived, when all things were inverted: the sea her throne and the air her queendom, because she soared beneath it. Mortal man clung to that transitory skin between and was eaten, from above or beneath; or was broken, hurled from air to water; or was coldly left to perish in the desert vastness of the sea.

Oh, she was captivating: rapture in her liberty, beauty in her skin, deadly in her focus. Ferocity in her intent. She destroyed that fleet as Li Ton might have done himself, if he had chosen to, if he had been a dragon; and then—he thought—she came to destroy Han.

Li Ton took his first steps back down the path as soon as he realized that she was coming here. He thought they'd all be following him, tumbling down the slope in a desperate unavailing flight; but Han croaked at them—not in his usual voice, barely in a voice at all—"Tien, all of you, stay close."

"I'm not leaving you." That was the girl, Tien. "You come too. Come now . . ."

"No. Why run, where would you go? Stay close."

The dragon swooped low over the islet and Han was utterly motionless then, utterly straining. They were wrestling together, the dragon and the boy, on some ground that Li Ton could neither see nor reach.

Li Ton struggled only to stay upright. She was a dragon; it seemed as impossible to stand as it was impossible to run. What could any mortal doings matter, in the face of this? Her face?

He felt the gaze of her, impersonal and exacting. She looked at him, assessed him, dismissed him. Her frenzy seemed to be over, but he thought she would eat him regardless. Sooner or later. She was here for Han; the rest of them were incidental.

His doom, their collective doom came spiraling slowly down from her sky-throne to settle on the peak. Massive and dreadful, too dreadfully close. One great foot landed squarely on the furnace, where wood and charcoal still glowed furiously hot; she didn't seem to notice.

She was of a size to blot out the sun, a temple on a mountaintop. She drew awe from them, as a temple might, and demanded terror as a god might, visiting a temple. If those two together were not worship, Li Ton thought they came sufficiently close.

Worship, of course, was not sufficient for her. Not today.

She overhung them, menacing and beautiful. Unnameable colors shifted on her scales in sunlight, in the deep green dark of her eyes. Those eyes were captivating, in the worst way; a man could lose himself in that gaze. Briefly.

Her tail broke trees on the forest slope. He could hear their snapping, and the sudden flurried protest of the birds. That made him realize how quiet the world was, else. The fire had been a raucous thing, hissing and crackling; with that stamped out, he could hear his own tense breathing, the girl's too and her uncle's. The dragon that was so much larger, that could contain them all within the hollow of her armpit, he couldn't hear her breath at all. Perhaps she didn't breathe. What would an immortal need with air?

No matter. Her mouth held a more immediate interest now. What she would need with food was a question too, but that didn't stop her swallowing men.

She reached her long neck down and the reek of her overswept them all, sea sludge and salt decay. He might have gagged if he hadn't been so in thrall to the moment, and to her.

Her mouth opened. Her gape was vivid and immense. She had colors in her throat if you could see that far, if you could look past the teeth and tongue. Courage is often pretense; it was still possible to pretend—if only to himself—that he was a courageous man, when in truth he was only at the limits of what he could feel.

It wasn't him she reached for, yet. Perhaps that made it easier.

He was impressed with Han, a little, because the boy still didn't move. He was still fighting her, apparently. Or else he had lost all control, all contact with his body. Perhaps he only wanted her to get on with it, one quick lunge, one snap and gone . . .

SHE DID lunge, she did snap.

SHE MISSED him.

HER HEAD slammed forward like a snake in its certainty, and slid aside like a drunk man's fist that cannot find its aim.

She reared back, hissing, very like a snake; and the boy stood before her, very small, and said, "Don't. Not that. I think you've eaten me already, as much as matters."

The dragon must have disagreed. She tried again and missed again, and was seemingly as baffled as Li Ton. The boy apparently had some control over her, some access to her mind, even with the chains cut. That was strange—but he did still wear the iron cuffs and collar, even if the links hung loose that used to bind them all together. All that iron was etched with characters of control. They must still hold some measure of potency. And the boy was his, and—

No. The boy was not his. If anything, they were all the dragon's.

He thought they were talking, the dragon and the boy; he could hear it in the silence between them, in the stillness.

He thought perhaps he could hear a promise of safety, for this little time at least, in the slow iron creaking of the dragon's skin as she settled more heavily onto the rock, like a creature intending not after all to slay and go. He had attended enough parleys in the field, he could tell when the immediate threat went away and the serious talking began.

How do you talk to, how do you parley with a dragon? Li Ton couldn't imagine what was happening in the boy's head, or in hers.

SLOWLY, BOLDLY, Li Ton took one step back up the path, and then another. He was ashamed now to be the one farthest from the dragon. It had been the wise move, even the strong move in its moment; now it was wrong.

They were all exhausted. The boy was in the worst case, but there was nothing he could do for the boy just now. The girl and the doctor were both of them unused to hard labor, and to the fear and shock of war. He had been made for it, once. Then he was unmade, unmanned, in the emperor's punishment rooms; then he had been made again. He had laid muscle over damage, mind over muscle. He could work himself until he fell, and he very seldom fell.

The doctor was squatting on his haunches like a man at his uttermost limit, very close to falling. The girl was torn between caring for her uncle and running to the boy. While Li Ton would have claimed command anyway, he did think that he had earned it, if only by being stronger. Or more experienced, or right. He wouldn't say wiser, even now, but he did think he was right.

He went to them, to the doctor largely, and said, "Can you stand?"

To nobody's surprise, it was the girl who answered. "Of course he can stand, if he needs to," meaning *I will help him if you give me reason,* meaning *I would rather stay here,* meaning *I would rather be closer to Han.* All too obviously she expected him to order them away, back to the boat if they could get there, if the dragon would let them go.

Even here, in a dragon's dreadful shadow, he found a hint of pleasure in surprising her. "I think we should go closer to Han. Stay close, as he said. I thought it was boy's talk, bravado; but look at her," as though either of them, any of them was doing anything else. "She came to kill, to kill *him,* and she couldn't do it. Now they're . . . negotiating. I think. I think he's inside her head. We need to stay inside *his* head, in his sight," where he would— perhaps—hold them in the compass of his will. So long as he chose to. The boy had no reason to love Li Ton; which meant that Li Ton had a fine reason to stay as close as possible, within a dragon's swallow of Tien.

The doctor seemed beyond words, beyond understanding. The night's labors or the morning's dragon or both together had drained him entirely. He offered no resistance, no effort either as they raised him to his feet and took him forward, step by slow shuffling step.

Old or young, vigorous or exhausted, it would be hard to do anything but shuffle into that shadow, under that glare. It was Han she watched, but she was aware of them all; each of them stood separately under her claw, however close they clung. He could see her claws, iron-gray blades carving great gouges in the rock of the Forge. He thought he could feel the stone groaning under the weight of her. He was astonished that his own bones could hold up under the weight of her awareness. How Han could survive her full attention, let alone resist it, struggle with her, deflect her purposes . . .

Well. It defeated him, but he could accept that. He could accept this, the need to squat in the boy's lee. If any of them survived this it would be her choice, inhuman and immeasurable—unless it was the boy's.

Han turned his head to find them, so suddenly it drew a gasp from Tien, a wary frown from Li Ton. Perhaps it was the dragon entirely in his head now, and working him? That was how it looked, entirely.

But he sounded more like Han the boy now, even giving orders: "Tien, all of you—go back to the boat. Tell the fisherman to take you away from here."

"Where shall we go?" That was the doctor asking. Tien was bereft, and Li Ton had not asked any man for directions since he was the emperor's general, since he was betrayed.

"It doesn't matter. Taishu, or the mainland. Inland would be better." *Because the dragon is a creature of the sea,* he meant, *and I don't know how much or how long I can control her.* "Or there are other lands, beyond the empire. Li Ton will see you safe." That was not a prediction, it was an instruction. The boy's eyes were not the dragon's, no, but they had something of that hammer-hard implacability. He had been weak before or frightened, hurt or overwhelmed. Now he was compelling.

"What about you?" Tien had found her voice, though it was thin and tremulous, as she was.

"I stay here."

"I want to stay with you."

"No," he said, and there was no arguing with him. That was the deal, evidently: himself and the dragon to stay here on their own, until something was resolved. One way or another.

Li Ton could picture one way, which was the boy swallowed whole. He found it impossibly hard to picture any other. What, did Han imagine he could fly out of here on the dragon's neck, ride her like a plaything, like a horse?

It almost seemed a shame to lose him now, but there was no

challenging this. Even Tien realized; she only said, "How, how will you find us?" Meaning, of course, *how will you find me?*

"I'll find you," which was no answer at all, and yet it seemed to satisfy. Perhaps it meant *the dragon will know,* which was not a re-assuring thought at all.

The dragon's eyes moved to follow them, but he thought they were pushing now, wanting them gone. She might want them gone from the boy's thoughts too, but he didn't think she could have that. Tien was like a splinter in the boy's eye, forever sharp; and every time he looked at his hands, Han must remember Li Ton. Even now, the boy's fingers were rubbing at the raw scar where his thumb had been.

Jorgan had tossed it into the forge-fire, Li Ton remembered. Any last lingering ash of it, any nub of bone would stand under the dragon's foot now. That seemed . . . appropriate.

four

Chung took the message from the general himself, from his hand. It came with a scowl attached, as though the general anticipated the same response to this as to the dozen that had gone before. If he did, he was probably right.

Chung had carried several of those messages. Which the general knew. It was never a good idea to let the lords of life come to know your face. Chung's mother had told him that, when he was chosen to serve in the jademaster's palace. He had listened attentively, he had tried to be wise; he was sure the jademaster could never have picked him out from any line-up of the kitchen staff.

But things had changed, one extraordinary night. The jademaster had been displaced by the emperor, the palace had filled with soldiers and servants and officials, and it was suddenly so much harder to stay out of notice and out of trouble. Impossibly hard, it seemed, for Chung.

Now the emperor was gone too, and the soldier who sat beside the empty throne and governed in his name, General Ping Wen, knew Chung's face well. And what Chung meant to him was messages sent but not replied to, or not satisfactorily; and it was all too easy for a great man to blame the messenger.

This particular great man was said to have executed an entire squad of soldiers because they had claimed to see a dragon and so lost sight of an enemy boat. Ping Wen had not believed in their dragon, and so the men had died. Now almost everyone believed in the dragon, even perhaps Ping Wen, but the men were still dead.

If Chung was grateful for one thing in this new life, it was the yellow sash he wore, that said he was the emperor's own man. It wasn't true, not quite, but it said so none the less; and even a general could not touch an imperial runner. Which was definitely something to be grateful for today, to judge by the depth of the general's scowl.

There was this also to be grateful for, that he could put the general's message into his satchel and back away, bowing, shuffling his soft boots across the wonderful floor, leaving the great empty throne and the great man on his footstool; and when he reached the door he could turn and trot out into the air, and the guards there would simply stand and watch him go.

Across the courtyard to the imposing gate, which couldn't impose on him. More guards here, and he could ignore them all— gratefully—and run out onto the road.

The Jade Road they called this, or they used to: running as straight as a road might, from the harbor to the mountains and the mines. These days, as often as not it was called the Palace Road, because so much traffic came and went from the jademaster's palace here to the vast site in the foothills where they were building the emperor's new Autumn Palace, a second Hidden City.

Where most people believed the emperor was living now, and were wrong.

Chung knew.

OF COURSE Chung knew. How could he carry the general's messages, else?

HERE THE road was always busy, like a fish-dam in a stream. There was no city wall, no gate, but the general's soldiers funneled all the traffic into two queues, coming and going. They searched wagons and interrogated peasants at their own unhurried pace. Assassins had come after the emperor, and had barely been defeated; of course the authorities were more alert, more wary now.

Quite what the soldiers searched for so assiduously, though, once they'd seen that no assassin was hiding in the wagonback; quite what questions they asked—and why they would believe or not believe the answers—Chung couldn't fathom. He knew what things they kept. He saw them piled by the roadside, the piles growing as the day passed. Quite how a rice pot or a string of garlic might be contraband, how a bolt of silk might pose a risk to the emperor's person, he chose not to speculate. It was wiser not, with their general in the emperor's throne-room, if not quite yet on his throne.

Chung himself was neither searched nor questioned. The imperial sash was good for that; he could trot straight by the queues, straight through the roadblock. Something to be grateful for.

The road beyond was still full of soldiers, but none of them was interested in him. An alert sergeant or an officer might even move a troop out of his way, not to delay an imperial messenger. Mostly, the men held the crown of the road and Chung ran easily around them.

Soldiers never ran. Going out to the palace site or coming back, they idled as much as they were allowed to. If they had civilian conscripts with them, the civilians carried the soldiers' bags.

Chung was safe from conscription too, but they weren't taking palace servants anyway. City workers, rather, laborers and clerks. Breadwinners. Nothing was easy anymore, and the levies made it harder. Chung might be untouchable, but he wasn't blind. Nor deaf. The general seemed to be deaf to the general complaint, unless his stool at the throne's foot lifted him too high to hear.

Chung thought someone ought to tell him, but nobody would. With the emperor in the mountains, who could criticize his general?

Only one name came to mind, and she was in the mountains too.

He had a stone in his boot, a sharp pain in the ball of his foot. One more thing to be thankful for: that he could sit on the side of the road with his legs overhanging the ditch, shake out the stone, and then sling the boots around his neck and have done with them for now. Like the sash, his running-boots with their emphatically yellow lacings marked him out as a messenger, untouchable. But Chung was a boy of the lower town, who had never seen a pair of shoes before he was brought into the palace as a scullery lad. Who wore shoes, except for mandarins?

He hated them. At their best they were a definition of discomfort, tight and hot; and they were seldom at their best, either rubbing up blisters or else attracting stones. Or both.

He was knotting the laces together to make a handy sling when he felt a buffet on his shoulder: "You, boy! Up, and come with us. And carry this . . ."

A large pack, dropped by his side. A soldier, just beyond the pack: just a random trooper spotting an idle civilian and seizing the chance.

Chung stood, so that his sash came into clear view.

The soldier was twice his age, perhaps, but that meant he had the wisdom to blanch, to step back, to lift his hands in apology. He might have done more, might have dropped to his knees and kowtowed, because an insult to an imperial messenger was an insult to the emperor himself and a man might die for that; but Chung just smiled and turned away, trotted on barefoot and grateful.

IT WAS hard work on a hot day, but he'd never minded work and he'd learned to love the sense of moving on. A person on the road ahead became a person on the road behind. The land unrolled like a banner of silk horizons at a puppet-play; only the sea never seemed to shift, those times that he could see it, those times he turned his head as the road rose.

It was a joy to be away from the palace, away from walls and doors and a formality that was like another door always closed in his face, but that was not what put lift in his feet and power in his legs. It was a joy to be heading for the hills, the high hills and what waited there, that even the general barely knew about and did not understand. That was a promise and a lure, but not a reason for the pulse of contentment he felt at every pounding step and every sweat-soaked breath.

This was where he was made to be, this narrow ribbon world, this rolling treadmill that only rolled because he ran, he kept it moving on. Running, he was at the core, he was the steady beating heart of what was true.

HE CAME to the spur at last, the junction on this road that had no junctions before the emperor came this way. This was what emperors did, apparently: they brought changes, choices, risks. Chung's life had been quiet and easy and monumentally dull until the emperor came. Then even in the palace there was danger, even to a kitchen hand; and now—

NOW THE soldiers and their wagons, their conscripts, their horses and mules and all else turned aside, to follow the new road that last mile or so to where the new palace was rising slowly on its hill. Chung had been there, he had seen the great workings, the mud and the labor and the endless spread of the encampment around. No doubt the emperor must move there soon enough, or else go back to the city, with all his court in train and Chung too.

But not yet. For now Chung could follow the Jade Road a little farther, where it climbed into the foothills; now he could leap the ditch and run through tall grasses and into the shadow of the en-croaching trees.

There was a path, but barely so. It looked little more than a hog trail winding through the forest, muddy in the valley bottoms and hard to find on the high ridges, easy to lose. The mud was cool and welcome to his feet, though, the heights were a challenge and an achievement.

One valley and another, yet one more: and at every ridge there were two or three watchers idling beside the path, wearing little and apparently doing less. Hard bodies, hard eyes. Sharply green in the shadows, those eyes would track him remorselessly, though their hands waved him on. It wasn't the sash that passed him through this scrutiny. They knew him, so they let him by; no reason else. This path led directly to the emperor, who was in their charge. They took that charge quite seriously, although they were new to it. General Ping Wen had sent his own men, day by day more senior, to learn just exactly where the emperor was; word in the palace said that every one of them had been turned back. Those who had drawn weapons and tried to force their way by had been found next day on the road, too hurt to walk.

Officially, the general was said to be increasingly anxious at the emperor's staying somewhere so remote, in the hands of people not known to the court. Privately, he was said to be furious. Personally, Chung had seen hints and edges of that anger: enough to worry him, perhaps, if it weren't quite so impossibly presumptuous to worry about the welfare of the emperor . . .

The general was officially concerned only for the Son of Heaven's safety; and nowhere, truly, could be safer than here. No man could be safer than he was, in this hidden valley with lethal guards on every height around. Chung had tried to explain that to the general, the time he'd been called on to describe and then to draw the route from the Jade Road to the emperor's camp. That was one time he'd seen the general angry, because he was no good with words, nor with a brush and ink.

That was also the day that he'd seen a soldier's anger utterly eclipsed by a mother's. The empress had been there too, and oh, she was scathing. He thought that her vicious contempt was simply a by-blow, that her true fury was aimed at her son; but Chung was the one at hand, and he had suffered for it, and might have suffered worse. An imperial sash was no defense against an empress. Blessedly, she had remembered in time that her contact with the emperor depended on him and those few like him, messengers who were trusted. Trust was a fragile commodity in the hills just now. Let her execute even one of the emperor's runners, and she would be unlikely to see another.

Wise in her age, even in her temper, she had understood that; and so he had preserved his head, this long at least. There were other dangers on the road and in the forest, but nothing felt so risky as a palace empty of its emperor, in the heat of the summer of his absence.

NOW CHUNG came down into the last valley, near journey's end. He stopped at the bitter river to wash, to cool his skin and startle his tiring body into one last effort; then he kicked on along the river path, to the settlement at the head of the valley.

The clans were mining folk and they guarded their valleys jealously, from one another more than from the world beyond. The world beyond generally had better sense than to trespass. Here, though, a simple compound had outgrown its own palisade, sprouting tents and ruder shelters like fungus around a tree stump.

Not all the inhabitants were clansfolk. A mixed group of men and women stood in a circle on the only open ground, down at the river's edge. As Chung emerged from the trees, a voice greeted him: "Ha! Where's your cleaver, kitchen boy?"

He stiffened, and sighed; pushed a hand through dripping hair; tried a smile, knowing it would fail. "Not now, Shen. I have a message for the emperor . . ."

"Of course you do. Why would you be here else? No kitchens for the scrubbing, and you're not much use otherwise, except for running. Will you run away from me?"

He was a short, stocky young man, a soldier, stripped now to his trousers. He didn't have the lean scarred hardness of a miner. What he had instead were fighter's muscles, slabs and cables beneath his oiled skin.

"If you'll let me by, sure, I'll run. If you want me to." There were fighters, and there were runners; never the two should meet, if the runner could only get a head start.

"I don't want you to run," the soldier said softly, working his shoulders. "I want you to fight. Will you fight, kitchen boy?"

He wasn't really offering a choice. He stood between Chung and the compound, and the circle of his friends was re-forming around them both, to make an arena. This wasn't the first time. Chung's hand lifted involuntarily toward a seamed scar on his lip, where Shen had left his mark at their first encounter. Shen saw, and smiled. A point to him, if this had been a game played for points.

It wasn't. It was played for blood. Around the circle people were betting sweets and trinkets, duties, whatever they had to gamble with. Chung knew how few of them would be betting on him.

"The emperor won't be happy," Chung said, "if I go to him with blood on my sash."

"Take the sash off, kitchen boy. It buys you nothing here."

He knew that, but he'd had to try. He lifted it over his head, along with his satchel and his boots; a woman took them from him with a glance he couldn't read. One of the clanswomen; there were no women in the army. He ought to know her name, but he was never here long enough to learn them all.

"If I go to him hurt, I meant." And he hadn't quite meant the emperor, but Shen knew that.

"Oh, I won't hurt you. Much. You'll still be able to run. That's all he cares about."

That was neither true nor relevant. Chung ignored it. "I'm *tired*, Shen . . . !"

Shen grinned. "Then I'll just knock you over quicker, won't I? Don't beg, it's boring."

He had emphatically not been begging. He was angry now; which of course was what Shen wanted, but there was nothing he could do about that. He chided himself for being weak even as he made a darting move forward, as Shen's hands came up swiftly in a defensive pose, as the circle fell into silence.

Near silence. There was the sound of the river behind him, but he could ignore that. There was the sound of his own breathing, and he could ignore that too. Shen's breathing: that mattered. And Shen's feet as they slid through the grass, that too. A master of the art might claim to hear the creak of his joints, the groan of his muscles as they worked. Chung was no master; he had no hope ever of mastering Shen.

He backed off and they circled each other slowly. Shen's foot lashed out in a high kick; Chung blocked that with a forearm, and the fist too that followed it. And countered with an elbow to the face, except that Shen's face wasn't quite there to be elbowed. His knee slammed into Chung's thigh and made him stagger, almost knocked him down.

He went back instead, far enough—just—to duck the follow-up kick and make a snatch at the ankle as it fell away. And astonished himself by catching it: only with a half-hand grip, but enough to drag Shen off-balance, enough to follow with jabbing fingers to the belly that the young soldier had no time to block.

That knocked the air out of him, stilled him for a moment; just time enough for Chung's favorite elbow again, aimed at the throat and not quite making that, driving hard into Shen's shoulder.

Which should have been good enough, but somehow wasn't. Chung saw Shen's face twist in pain. What he didn't see was Shen's left hand, slamming upward under his chin.

After that, he saw nothing at all for a while.

WHEN THE world came back to him, when his eyes opened, he saw a dizzying blur that resolved itself slowly into Shen's face, upside down and grinning.

Then there were Shen's hands, holding something, a water-skin. Tipping it, squeezing . . .

A hard spatter of water in his face: Chung sat up suddenly, spluttering, mocked.

Then the laughter stilled, all of a rush. There was a strong arm under his to haul him to his feet, and that was Shen's as well; and right in front of them, pushing through the circle, there was Mei Feng. The Lady Mei Feng, the emperor's favorite and only choice of concubine, the small force of nature that ruled this compound and the imperial heart together . . .

She was, predictably, furious.

"You, Chung. Why are you here?"

"I, uh," touching his hand to his lip and finding blood, again, "I brought a message, lady. For the emperor."

"Don't *call* me that! You know my name. But why are you *here*, fooling with this fool Shen—again!—when you have a message for my lord?" And then, when he shrugged, when he obviously had no answer, "And you, Shen—what do you think you're doing, knocking him unconscious? Again? When you knew, you must have known, he was here with letters for the emperor?"

Shen shuffled his bare feet in the dust. She snorted roundly at both of them, snapped her fingers for the satchel and set off back up to the compound; and paused before she'd gone half far enough, and turned back, and said, "At least get yourselves cleaned up, both of you, before the Son of Heaven sees. You know he'll want the story if he finds his own runner covered with blood and dust, and he won't be happy when he hears it." A pause, just long enough for the world's heart to beat once, and she went on, "It's past time you learned to defend his messages better than that, Chung, getting knocked flat every chance. Perhaps we'd best keep you here longer, send someone else to the court and let Shen work on you some more?"

Chung grinned dizzily, and never mind the blood on his teeth. "Yes please, lady."

"My *name* is Mei *Feng*," but her own smile broke out at last, backed with an exasperated wave. "Go. Wash. Find clean clothes. Both of you. Then you come and speak to my lord, Chung, he'll want to know how things are at the palace, and in the city."

"Yes, lady," but he said that to her retreating back, so that she could pretend not to hear it.

Then Shen's arm was around his shoulders, and, "Did I hurt you?"

"Of course you hurt me," wincing, feeling his jaw for soreness. "Did I hurt you? At all? It'll be okay to lie, if you feel like it . . ."

"No lie. You got me right in the gut, and I wasn't ready for it. Nor the shoulder, either. Yes, that hurt."

Which was triumph for Chung, who had barely managed to lay a hand on Shen the last time they'd sparred, which was the last time they'd seen each other. In the palace, he had no one to train with; he was diligent in exercise and shadow-boxing, but it was never the same as having a solid body to work against. Preferably this particular, this very particularly solid body that he leaned against now, that half held him up as they made a slow path down to the riverbank.

This was the body that had hurt him badly, maliciously, when Shen was a palace guard where Chung was only a servant, when Shen was newly come from the long march with a year of brutalities at his back and Chung was an innocent, a fool with a hot temper and a stupid pride.

When Mei Feng had seen them fighting and saved Chung's life and Shen's as well, with some brilliant improvisation under the nose of General Ping Wen. As a result of which, Shen had been co-opted into the emperor's personal service, to train his guards in ways of fighting hand to hand; and Chung had been co-opted body and soul by Mei Feng, to be her personal messenger.

Her slave, Shen said, which was another reason to learn how to hit him.

Her spy, Chung thought, these days. It was the emperor's sash he wore and the emperor's messages he carried, the emperor he would speak to when he made his report; but it was Mei Feng who listened, dictated, demanded, instructed. If she had slaves, they numbered at least one more than one, and that one extra was the Son of Heaven, who was as delightedly devoted as Chung so fiercely denied himself to be, whenever Shen accused him.

Bare feet in cold water, that was good, as he sat gratefully at the river's edge and let them dangle. Rough fingers pressing on his neck, digging into his shoulders, working the taut strings of his body with a savage intimacy: that was another kind of good, cruelly good, as he leaned back into the groaning, painful pleasure of it. These same hands, that had so delighted in hurting him the first time—well, they did still hurt him, and it was still deliberate, and now at least some of the delight ran the other way. Chung had been remade, from the outside in; the changes had reached his head and heart and belly, and were insinuating themselves deep into his bones.

He closed his eyes and tipped his head back and found Shen's shoulder exactly there to support it, which put Shen's ear right here next to his lips, where he need only whisper to say anything he wanted . . .

There was nothing he could think of. Head to head, skin to skin, that said it all. These same brutal hands were an adjunct, the river in the valley: good to have, but it was the jade in the mountain that mattered.

They had talked to each other, he and Shen: awkwardly, reluctantly, because they had that one thing in common now, that they were alive by Mei Feng's courtesy when they might both have been stupidly, pointlessly dead. And because she had decreed that Chung too must learn to fight by Shen's odd northern methods; if he was running her messages, she said, and her lord the emperor's also, he should be able to defend them. And because it was hard to sweat and hurt and learn at another's hands and yet not speak to him, not want to know who he was, this swift young man with the black stare and the sudden laugh, the inaccessible skills and the deep shadows at his back. And because . . .

Because of this, in the end: because one young man and another could slip their clothes off and wash a fight away, shuck all the evidence of difference, be nothing more than two bodies in the stream with no intent to harm, no wish in the world.

five

Jiao was not made to be a teacher.

Her patience was a solitary art, the patience of the hunter to squat all night by a trail, waiting for the one clean kill. It was a skill long practiced, an aspect of herself. She had none for other people when they were awkward or idle or slow.

Her restlessness went with her patience, hand in hand. She was a woman who appeared with the evening star, killed if she had to and kissed where she could, and was gone by dawn. She was a creature of the road and the shadow, fugitive as wind; she didn't linger. That she had stayed with Yu Shan as long as this—well. He was Yu Shan, and she was interested.

Even being here, in a dead-end valley far from the road, walled in by mountains, sleeping in the same bed night after night: even this she would accept, because of him. Because of her interest in him. It came from her, as ever. She wasn't vulnerable, only engaged.

And closeness to him brought her close to the emperor, insanely close, which was also interesting. And dangerous, but risk was spice in the pot, fire in the night and welcome. It would bring another kind of danger in the city, where she might not follow unless she chose; she had seen politics and ambition before, and was not interested.

But for now they were here, where dangers came with steel blades and hard fighting, and she was happy.

Except that they were trying to make a teacher of her, and she was bored.

Down by the river, Shen taught his colleagues—imperial soldiers and mining clansfolk, group by mixed group—how to fight bare-handed. Up here, in a forest clearing hacked out for timber, she was meant to teach the same groups how to fight her way on bad ground. It was the emperor's idea, which meant it was probably Mei Feng's. Soldiers or miners, they thought they could fight already, and they were mostly right. With their own skills added to Shen's added to hers, they should be formidable. She and Shen were opposites, a pair. Where he taught them to duck, she taught them to bite; where he taught them to kick, she taught them to back away.

When they were prepared to listen. They had grown up with clan wars, or else they had matured on the long march from the north; they thought they knew how to be vicious, relentless, entirely the killer.

Group after group, it was her task to show them they were wrong. Didn't these people *talk* to one another . . . ?

Apparently not. One more time, then: her long steel tao blade, her body—tough as a root but tired now, tired in the worst way, tired of doing this—and her honed experience against one of these implausible clan boys. Implausibly young, implausibly strong, implausibly swift and supple. She could be tired of that, too, but he came at her hard and fast and she didn't have time. Their blades clattered and sparked. He was aggressive and confident, cocksure; he'd learned nothing from watching the others. She backed across the clearing, always giving ground, faltering under the simple weight of his blows until at last his foot stumbled over a stump hidden by new growth. Even then he didn't trip, but his eyes glanced down instinctively; in that moment of distraction she slammed the hilt of her tao into the side of his head.

Possibly a little harder than she had to.

He fell very satisfactorily, like a hammer-felled ox. No cause to worry. They weren't Yu Shan or the emperor, these kids, they didn't heal miraculously from blows that should have killed an ox, but they did have remarkably strong bones—thick skulls, she liked to say, that needed lessons pounded into them—and powers of recovery that were honestly not quite human.

As witness, this lad was stirring already. He did have the grace to groan, but she thought that might just be to gratify his teacher. She held him down with one booted foot on his shoulder and addressed the gathered circle of her pupils.

"You fight on whatever ground you have to, but be aware: bandits will always choose ground that works to their advantage. And use it. Sometimes it's easier to go backward. You look like you're retreating, in fact you draw them on, into—"

She broke off as another figure appeared at the edge of the clearing. Another of these clansfolk, but a face Jiao didn't know; and she came not from the compound but the forest. A volunteer, then, unless she was a messenger. There was a thin but steady stream of them trickling in, the young and the jadeless and the dispossessed. As word spread through the mountains—the emperor here and recruiting from the clans, offering something new—so they came, nervous and curious and hungry.

And hopeful, and extraordinary, and a little bewildered. This one lifted her eyes—green, yes—and said, "Please, they told me on the ridge-height to come this way . . ."

Actually they'd probably told her to follow the river, but newcomers tended to keep to the trees. It was no easy matter, Jiao knew, to walk openly into enemy territory, and these clans had been fighting one another for generations. It had been no easy matter to establish this as a valley of truce, let alone to make them all settle together. Having a leaven of imperial soldiers helped, but not enough.

Still, none of them had killed each other yet. And the more clans were represented, the more dilute clan loyalty became, the

easier it would be to build a new loyalty. They had someone to follow, who was the emperor; they had someone to resent, who was
herself; someone to admire, perhaps, who was Shen. They'd sweat
down into a reliable crew soon enough.

She said, "Yes, and welcome. Why have you come?"

Looking for the emperor, looking for a new life, they had a
dozen ways to say it but it was always the same thing, not to eke
out their days in ever more strenuous working for ever less stone.
This one, though, she looked shy suddenly, perhaps she even
blushed a little; her voice was firm enough, though, as she said, "I
was looking for my clan-cousin, Yu Shan. I heard he was with the
emperor, so I came to see . . ."

Jiao's mouth worked a couple of times, soundlessly, before she
managed a reply.

"Yes. Yu Shan is here. I can, I can bring you to him . . ."

So could anyone in her class, so could anyone in the encampment, and her lesson was barely begun; but she abandoned it and
them, all her curious pupils, as she steered this girl toward the
compound.

Her mouth was oddly dry and her mind was oddly dizzy, but
one thing at least: she was no longer bored.

six

*M*a Lin had been a woman of substance once. She'd had a home, a reputation, a family. A husband and three daughters, all her own. No son yet, but he might yet come. It had been a good foundation, something to build a life upon.

Now her husband was dead, and she had trodden in his spilled body. One of her girls was gone: little Meuti, who had chosen not to live after she saw her father killed and her big sister ruined. She had stopped eating, and would not walk. They had carried her, turn and turn about, most of the miles from there to here, but she had grown lighter and easier day by day, and at last there had been nothing left to bear. So they buried her instead, and her absence had been a harder thing to carry and still was.

The home was lost and left behind, the reputation far forgotten. All Ma Lin had left was two daughters, and one of those was broken beyond measure.

Jin the eldest had always been most useful, but she was gone inside herself now, into bad country. Silent and unreachable, she needed telling when to eat and when to excrete. Some days, she needed washing.

Blessedly, Shola the other daughter—youngest now—could do all that and more. She had become her sister's keeper, bossy and tender and determined; which left her mother free to worry for them all, as was proper.

MA LIN was a practical worrier, practical in everything. If anyone would be found sitting on the temple steps, looking out over the strait toward Taishu, empty-handed, that would be her daughters, not herself.

"Watch for the old fisherman," she said. "He knows where we are. Perhaps he will come again."

Or perhaps it would be the dragon who came again, let them watch a wonder. Or perhaps it would be soldiers bringing terror, but Ma Lin didn't think so. She thought most of the soldiers had been on the boats, when the dragon broke them. The temple was a mile's walk from the road, a good mile through trees and over broken ground; there was no path anymore, and the soldiers were strangers in this country. They wouldn't know it was here; and if they knew, they wouldn't care; and if they cared, the Li-goddess whose temple it was, she would protect a mother and her girls, refugees under her roof.

Wouldn't she?

Ma Lin was no theologer. She waited warily for the goddess, worried about her children, even while she walked the mile or more to the road.

Went cautiously, never quite the same way twice, not to leave a track through the undergrowth; and lurked at a vantage-point still within the trees' shadow, where she could see the traffic both west and east.

Mostly the traffic she saw was soldiers. These were the destroyers, the men who had rampaged through Santung and ruined everything good that was hers. They enraged her and terrified her both at once, and she trusted neither her rage nor her terror. She crouched in her shadows and watched them pass, and waited.

If the road was clear of soldiers and a farmer came with his mule-wagon or a peasant with his burden, she might slip from cover to beg mutely at the roadside. She was luckier with peasants than farmers; the poor beg best, most profitably from the poor.

When it was women on the road, she did not beg, but offered: her hands, her back, her wisdom or her skills, whatever might be useful to them.

Mostly, almost always she was turned away, but seldom without a blessing. Food was wealth and trade goods; everyone carried something in a bag or a pouch or a pocket. Ma Lin might come away with a handful of rice or a lump of sugar, dried mushrooms sewn into a scrap of silk, perhaps a pot of preserved vegetables. Really the offer to work was just another way to beg, and they all understood it.

When she had strained the day's luck or the gods' generosity as far as she dared, then she would pack up her worry and her goods and turn back into the forest.

And not go directly back to the temple and her daughters, no; but walk through the forest and bless all the gods for a peasant childhood, before her man Tojo found her and took her to Santung. She knew at least some of the leaves that could be eaten, some of the roots and mushrooms. She had found a whole grove of bamboo, where fresh shoots could be cut almost daily. They got by, her and her daughters.

Still, nothing stopped her worrying. She worried most about the hospitality of the goddess: sure the old fisherman had not meant for them to stay and stay. Every day, she thought she should speak to the women on the road, see if she could beg a roof in exchange for work. Shola could work too, carry water and scrub floors; even Jin could be induced to simple chores. The temple could not have been so clean for a generation.

Today, perhaps, she would find the courage to ask. Why was it so hard to ask for shelter, where it was so easy to ask for food?

Because food is a meal, her own sour voice replied to her, *where shelter is a commitment. Giving out is easy; taking in is hard.*

Trusting is hard. Promising another meal tomorrow, that's hard too, when you might need it for yourself.

Even so. It had to be done, she had to ask.

Maybe today, this time.

Here came a woman on her own, a rare sight on the road. Now would be the time. If the woman wasn't too scared by the sudden eruption of a lean and desperate figure from the trees' shadow, begging, clutching at her . . .

Not to beg, then, not to clutch.

Ma Lin had washed her dress last night, and bound up her hair in a cloth this morning. She looked as respectable as a woman could, who had only this to wear and only cold water to wash in.

She walked out of the forest as she might have walked from one stall to another in a street market at home, when she had a home, when there were markets in the street and a little money, time to spend and things to buy. Almost idly, more interested than purposeful, and not quite directly toward the woman as she came: just heading for that point where the two of them must meet if they both only kept going at the same pace.

The woman might have faltered, but only briefly. Ma Lin was deliberately not staring, barely looking at all, only from the corner of her eye. Also she was trying to look harmless but healthy, fit to work but not intimidating, which was a difficult trick to bring off.

They did arrive more or less at the same place, more or less at the same time. In fact the woman on the road was first and might have scuttled on if she were nervous, but chose not to, chose to wait.

And then was first to speak, made Ma Lin nervous; said, "I have been looking for you."

Ma Lin might have run then. If it had been a man, certainly she would: hopelessly, pointlessly, but still she would have run. Like a desperate bird, away from the nest: down the road, perhaps, or across the road and over the ditch and into the abandoned paddy.

But this was a woman in her middle years, and they were neither of them built for wild chases. Ma Lin stood very still and said,
"You do not know me."

The woman didn't blink. "I think you are the priestess at the
temple." And then, in the face of Ma Lin's stupefied silence, "Did
you think we don't talk to each other, hereabouts? Or listen to our
husbands either? A woman alone, always seen on this road, asking
for alms . . . This is our country, we know who comes and goes.
And why. We do not trouble you at the Lady Li's house, we who
left it neglected for so long; but you have come there with your
children—we know!—and we are glad. Here, I brought you this."

This was a basket of woven bamboo, heavy with fresh noodles,
in a sacking bag that held a pair of cabbages and garlic too. Ma
Lin said nothing. But she took the bag.

The woman said, "Come here in the mornings and there will always be one of us who comes to you with something. For you, and
for the Lady."

She meant *a gift to you is a gift to the Li-goddess,* which was an
appalling suggestion, but Ma Lin's tongue cleaved to the roof of
her mouth; all she had was a vision of her hungry daughters, and
a way to see them satisfied. If that meant an equal balance with
terror, what an outraged goddess might choose to do—well, let it
fall on her and her alone. She could pray for that, at least.

She could not speak but she nodded, and turned and walked
away into the trees.

No foraging today. She had food, unexpectedly; more, she had
security, a promise she could believe in.

If there was a price to pay, she could confront that. When she
must.

She wanted to be with her daughters.

Straight through the forest, then, with not a thought to confusing her trail. The women knew where she was. It was odd, perhaps, but that made her feel more protected than exposed.

Her shame was great, but she was trapped now, seized by generosity. She could see her daughters fed, and all she had to do was play the priestess. How could she walk away, how could she walk her daughters away from what they most needed?

The goddess would . . . simply have to endure it.

Ma Lin wanted to be with her daughters.

Urgently.

THROUGH THE forest and on, her thoughts as broken as the ground she scrambled over, her anxieties shifting like the thin stony soil beneath her feet, every step exposing another, deeper worry.

And so over the last rise and here was the headland, with the creek below and the strait beyond; and here was the temple, with its feet settled into a hollow and its roof standing proud and clear, the paintwork blistered and faded but the dragons at the sweeping upturned gables still glowering protectively over the building, while those on the ridge stared out to sea.

They had the best view, but the temple steps offered a good second best, and there she found her daughters, neither one of them empty-handed. Shola was talking cheerfully as usual as she washed seaweed in a bowl before laying it out to dry on a stone in the sun, and as usual she might as well have been talking to herself. Perhaps she was: she was a sensible girl, and had likely long since given up on any hope of an answer.

Jin was washing too. Perhaps she liked to ape her younger sister. She had another bowl of water, and a line of idols taken from the temple and set orderly along the topmost step. One by one, she was meticulously bathing them, as though she were a little, little girl and playing dolls.

seven

*M*ei Feng was laughing at him.

She kept her face as still as a painted silent statue and not a muscle in her body was moving except that her eyes went from one to another politely as they spoke; and yet, he knew, inside she was laughing. Hugging her sides, rolling on the floor, breathless with the pain of so much pleasure.

The emperor was amused, perhaps, but fascinated more. He watched them as eagerly as he might have watched the sparring of a pair of fighting crickets.

A pair of fighting crickets with Yu Shan between them, slashed and slashed.

He had not thought, ever, to find himself here and like this.

These were the high hills of his home, and still he had not thought. Settled on the margins of clan territory with no thought of mining now, with other things entirely on his mind—and with someone else entirely in his bed—he had not once stopped to think about his clan-cousin, except as a regret left far behind.

Even when the young of other clans started to filter into the valley: even then, he had not thought.

But of course she had come, what did she have to keep her in his absence? A promise broken, a heart as empty as the slopes they tried to mine. Likely she would have come anyway, just for the adventure of it. When she heard that he was here, with the emperor—

Well. She had come.

And had found him, but found Jiao first. And it was all very bad indeed, and no amount of jade in his blood could save him from their barbed tongues as he sat between the two of them, as they slashed and slashed.

Deferentially, because their chief audience was after all the emperor.

Deferential fighting crickets, yes.

Even their silences were vicious, and apparently entertaining. Mei Feng's eyes were dancing with delight, stepping lightly.

Yu Shan himself hadn't spoken for a while. What could he say? Everything was true, and impossible, and appalling.

At last he stirred, he shifted, he stood.

Mei Feng arched an eyebrow, just the one.

Height gave him air, a little, enough to breathe; enough to speak, a little.

He said, "Majesty . . ."

And faltered, under the combined weight of so much cynical amusement. Even the women in question, he thought, even Jiao and Siew Ren were enjoying this, beneath their steel edges.

He took another breath, and tried again.

"Majesty, you wanted Guangli the jade carver fetched here from Taishu-port. Someone should go to fetch him. With your permission . . . ?"

"Not you," the emperor said briskly, immediately. "We want him, yes—but we want you too. You know these mountains; we want you all the more. We want you to show them to us." Whether *we* meant *the throne* or *Mei Feng and I*, it was impossible to tell. In any case, it was a distinction without a difference. The two were inseparable, by imperial decree. Perhaps the three of them were inseparable now; certainly the emperor showed no signs of letting Yu Shan go.

Instead he said, "Jiao shall fetch the jade carver. She knows the man, and can protect him on the road. And help him with his tools, and—"

"I am no man's donkey!" Jiao burst out.

Interrupting the emperor: who scowled and said, "You are my donkey, if I choose."

Jiao's eyes rolled in her head, but her tongue was not so loose; she said, "Of course, majesty—but not Guangli's, not now. Please. I want—"

It was the emperor's turn to interrupt her, seemingly. "What *I* want," he said testily, "I want my jade carver fetched here, whether he wants to come or no; and I want to see the mines where the stone is dug. And I want you, Yu Shan, to show them to me, because you know them well; you can show me your own family's mine, yes. And your cousin Siew Ren is the same clan, she knows that valley too, she can come with us," and he glowered deliberately at Jiao as he said that, daring her to protest again, "while you, Jiao, go to Taishu-port and bring your friend Guangli."

It all made perfect sense, and it pleased none of them except perhaps Siew Ren, who produced an acid smile and, "Thank you, majesty. I will be happy to show you my home. And to remind Yu Shan of where he comes from."

"What he left behind," Jiao observed.

"In order to bring a great gift to the emperor. Which you tried to steal. But now the emperor has come to us, and has taken Yu Shan into his service, his *personal* service, and . . ."

And Siew Ren sounded so smug, Yu Shan was flinching already, even before Jiao said, "Indeed. If the emperor wants him, of course the emperor must have him. And if Yu Shan wants to be taken into the emperor's most *intimate* service, to join the ranks of those few, too few that his majesty was able to bring with him, then he knows just what needs to be done, and I will be happy to oblige . . ."

Her hand caressed the tao at her side, though even she didn't quite dare to draw a blade in the imperial presence; her eyes lingered purposefully, affectionately on Yu Shan's groin.

And there was a smothered choking sound, which was Mei Feng desperately trying not to howl with laughter; and the emperor had his good cheer back, apparently. "Even you, Jiao, might find yourself too slow and your blade not sharp enough to, ah, geld Yu Shan against his will. Or mine."

She snorted. "I was fast enough to catch him in the forest, majesty. And he was wise enough to stand very quiet, against my blade."

"Yes, but he has grown since then. Learned more. And so have I. It would be interesting—but no. Thank you, Jiao, don't trouble yourself."

"No trouble, majesty; it would be a pleasure. And it might stop people fussing back at the palace, that you weren't properly served out here . . . ?"

The emperor's lips twitched into a smile. *People* meant his mother, largely, as he knew. She was one of the reasons why he kept refusing to go back. The ubiquitous eunuchs were perhaps another.

He said, "Nevertheless, we will retain Yu Shan as he is, I think, intact. And we will see you again when you have fetched Guangli and settled him in."

Thin-lipped and distrustful, she said, "Of course, majesty," though it was Yu Shan she was looking at, him she was absolutely not speaking to. She didn't so much as glance again at Siew Ren.

And then she was gone, suddenly and unacceptably: she who had been his shadow and his shelter for all these many weeks, the sharp heart of this new life he was building, steel to his stone.

Gone, and he wanted to go running after her, and could not: because there was his emperor who had forbidden it, and Mei Feng who would laugh aloud at last if he dared to do it anyway. And . . .

Gone, and here instead was his clan-cousin, who had been safely tucked away—he'd thought—in his previous life, to be mourned over and cherished in memory and not considered here. Not ever to be imagined in the same place as the emperor, under his interested eye.

Let alone Jiao's.

But Jiao was gone and Siew Ren was indeed here, small and dark and still a delight to him, despite Jiao and despite her own glowering temper. Still a slender reed with so much hidden strength in her; even in that she was the opposite to Jiao, who wore all her strength and experience openly on her skin, in her raking muscles and her scars.

He couldn't look at Siew Ren now, seemingly, without thinking of Jiao. It used to be the other way around.

He found it hard to look at Siew Ren at all, when she had such fierce contempt on her face. He turned to the emperor for help, which would have been unthinkable a month ago, would have appalled the whole court today if they could have seen it; but nobody could be formal here, there was no kowtowing and the emperor's face was something you might dare to look upon, even something you might look to as one young man might simply look to another when he needed to.

"If we left now," the emperor said, "could we be at your home before nightfall?"

"Of course, majesty." He was emperor; if he wanted it, it could happen.

Mei Feng snorted. "What, you can push mountains aside and fold inconvenient distance together, can you? Or does he have to do that himself?"

"It's close enough to walk in a few hours; and nobody will prevent us." Ordinarily, one clan member trying to sneak through other clans' valleys? That wasn't simply slow, that was suicidal. But these were not ordinary times; Siew Ren and others had come here untroubled. And besides, he was emperor. Who would trouble him?

Yu Shan would sooner have had Jiao on his other side, even so.

Lacking her, he was still sure he could bring the emperor safely through to his own valley.

And what then, introduce him to the family? *Mother, Father, this is the emperor, he wants to see our mine . . . ?*

Apparently so, yes. The emperor was on his feet and ready to go. Mei Feng gripped his wrist two-handed and hauled herself to her feet against the imperial solidity, grinned at him in celebration of the impertinence then looked at Yu Shan with more of a scowl, as though he could and should have been more discouraging.

Indeed, she said so, more or less. "We need to arrange things here, choose people to come with us, sort out what we need to take . . ."

"Why?" The emperor looked honestly bewildered. "People here will be fine without us, they can do what they normally do, which has little to do with us. We can go with Yu Shan and Siew Ren, we don't need anyone else; and what do we need to take? A change of clothes, for when we get wet. No more."

"*Little to do with us?* Chien Hua, all those people out there are here to protect you, no reason else. What they normally do is train themselves and one another for that purpose, while they watch the ridges and the forest and the river, while they risk their *lives* to be sure that assassins aren't sneaking up on you again. And what, you want to shrug that off and leave them all behind, go wandering off into the hills with just a handful of us?"

The emperor thought about it briefly, and nodded. Emphatically. "Yes, I do. They can carry on training without us; Jiao's the only one they'll miss. And we'll only be gone a night or two. I don't want to march with an army, Mei Feng. I want to walk with my friends."

He was acquiring a taste for freedom, Yu Shan thought. The farther he came from the court, the fewer restrictions there were on him—and the fewer people there were around him, the more he wanted to cut loose altogether.

Probably, they should not let him; but probably they could not prevent him.

There was a compromise, of course, and Mei Feng found it. Not an army, but he consented to half a dozen guards, a mix of imperial soldiers and clansfolk. And with that many backs to carry, of course, they could take more than a simple change of clothes . . .

By the time the expedition was organized to her satisfaction, it was almost too late to set out—which might have been her plan, but if so it was frustrated by the emperor's impatience and the abilities of jade.

"Night comes early in the mountains," Mei Feng urged.

"Yu Shan and I can see as well in the dark as we can in daylight. All these mountain people have cats' eyes."

"I don't."

"You," the emperor murmured, "have been sharing my bed, lying skin on skin with me; and holding my hand when I am wearing my rings; and rubbing up against jade a hundred ways, a hundred times a day. I think I could leave you in a cave in the middle of the mountains, the middle of the night, and you would see well enough to read, if you could read. You find your way around our hut without a lamp, without a hesitation."

She shook her head.. "There are so many gaps in the walls, the moonlight floods in, that's all."

"Stupid," he said, slipping a tender arm around her. "New moon, barely a sliver yet, and it's been all cloud the last three nights. Your eyes are changing. Everyone's changing, just from being here and mixing with the clans. You most of all, though. Being here and mixing with me . . ."

Yu Shan wasn't sure, it seemed very fast; but she was never far from the emperor's side. Perhaps he fed her some of his own food? Or perhaps she didn't need to eat jade. His sweat was hers, his saliva, his seed. Inside her. Perhaps there was enough stone in him to make a swifter difference in her.

The soldiers, though, who were barely arrived in the mountains, who had barely begun to mingle with the clansfolk, sharing food and sleeping quarters and tentatively, transiently sharing beds . . . No. It wasn't that easy. The touch of jade was a life-gift; if you weren't emperor—or, perhaps, the emperor's beloved—then it had to be hard-won through years of closeness, years of sweat and hurt and toil in the dark, hacking stone from narrow twisting seams. Hoarding it, breathing its dust, scabbing green where a sharp edge of stone had cut you and you hadn't noticed until the stone-grit that got everywhere had worked its way into the cut and stopped the bleeding and now you had stone in your blood. Yu Shan wouldn't have it easier than that, something that one man might casually pass to another, no.

He thought they would be leading soldiers by the hand, if they were still on the path at sunset.

The emperor would lead Mei Feng by the hand in any case, whether it was dark or not.

Yu Shan might have led Jiao the same way if she had let him, which she would not; but this was a trip without Jiao, with Siew Ren instead. Who used to lead him by the hand often and often, away from all paths and up into the forest, her slender fingers imperious and teasing and delighted. He didn't think she would want to touch him now. Unless she wanted to seize him with hands like manacles, never to let him stray again.

Not sure what he wanted, he was none the less entirely sure that it was not this: the way she stayed close but cold, close enough to watch but not to reach; the way her eyes avoided his except when they did the other thing, when they sought him out, challenging and contemptuous and betrayed. The way she would not speak to him, except when she did and that was worse.

The way the emperor had trapped him with her, sending Jiao away. On the path he felt that absolutely, arranged to the imperial satisfaction. Yu Shan and his clan-cousin were the guides, side by side; the emperor and his consort followed, while their guards ranged before and behind. Perhaps, to the casual eye, the two couples had enough distance between them to ensure privacy, but that was nonsense. The emperor's hearing was jade-sharp. He could hear a whisper in the next valley if he reached for it; Yu Shan knew. And the emperor knew that, of course, and played with it.

And knew that the same was true the other way, that Yu Shan could hear him. He played with that too, telling Mei Feng how pretty Yu Shan's cousin was, how fresh, how desirable . . .

At one point, Mei Feng asked acidly if his majesty desired her for his concubine, as no doubt Yu Shan would be pleased to make the arrangements . . . ?

That won her no more answer than a laugh, or at least a laugh with a kiss for sweetener. Unkissed and not at all laughing, Yu Shan gritted his teeth and walked on, his clan-cousin just *there*, at his shoulder but out of reach, a stormy silence in the corner of his eye.

YU SHAN heard hard challenges and soft replies at every ridge and valley-head, where the vanguard met another clan on watch. Again and again he heard someone crash away downslope, a runner gone to tell the elders *the emperor is here!*

He and Siew Ren followed warily, knowing how hard this was for everyone. They were watched, stared at, but not challenged. It was as if they were carried on the wash of something greater; he could hear it at his back, that stillness and silence where the emperor came walking.

Farther down would be the elders, as many as could be swiftly found or gathered; it might be just one family from one mine-head, all that the runner could reach. Whatever their authority— or lack of it—these people couldn't simply let the emperor pass by. There had to be a formal greeting, a stuttering welcome to clan lands. If there wasn't quite kowtowing, it was only because court manners were unknown in practice and bewildering in reputation. There was a lot of kneeling in the mud, lowered heads, averted eyes.

The emperor needed a swift technique in gracious brushing-off, and didn't have one. He had to stop, to speak to the senior there, to ask about the valley's mines, the jade, how rich the seams and how hard, how tight the workings.

Jade was perhaps the only thing he could speak of to these remote and nervous strangers; stone they could always talk about, to anyone. Especially perhaps in these days, with the veins so thin and spare, fresh seams far to seek and never as good, never as promising as they were wont to be.

And so time passed, in one valley and the next, and there was no hope of reaching Yu Shan's home by sundown if they ran all the rest of the way. They might as well take their time, then, linger, talk to everyone. Maybe stop the night in this valley, with this household, where they would surely be most fearfully welcomed; or maybe one more rise, one more ridge, stay in the next valley over . . .

DARKNESS CAUGHT them on a height between one valley and another, that sudden plunge of sun behind a mountain peak that left light in the sky but none pooling in the valley bottoms, where they would actually need it. Yu Shan and the emperor might have gone on comfortably, and the clansfolk with them, but not—as he'd predicted—the imperial soldiers. Mei Feng kept her own counsel, what she could see and what she couldn't.

Downslopes were more perilous in the dark, and so were clannish watchers who would see only shadows moving through shadow, and might well shoot before they challenged. Safer now to wait for dawn, in this high hinterland between one clan's ground and the next.

They climbed off the path and found a shelf where leaf mold softened rock still warm from the day's sun. A rainwater pool refreshed them, and everyone shared what edibles they had; it made an odd meal, but satisfying. The emperor seemed to enjoy every mouthful.

"Shall we gather wood for a fire?" he mumbled, cracking nuts between his teeth.

"Best not, majesty. I'm sorry," as his face fell, child-like in its disappointment. "It would be a struggle to find dry wood, and one of us might wander too far and get into trouble, and—"

"What he *means,*" Mei Feng murmured, slipping her arm through the emperor's and making as if to whisper in his ear, though her voice carried happily to all of them, "is that it would be wonderfully stupid to hold back here until the light comes, but to make a light of our own that might draw all those wicked wary guards we were trying to avoid . . ."

It was astonishing sometimes, the liberty he allowed her. Here, in this small group of friends, he only smiled and put an arm around her neck and kissed her. "You be my warmth, then," he said. "How shall we sleep?"

They were barely enough for proper watches, except that better than half of them were touched by jade, at least a little. A night without sleep had never been a trouble, even when he was a boy alone at the mine-head. Tonight, back in true mountains after far too long away, Yu Shan couldn't imagine sleeping. His bones were thrumming. If mountains had a heartbeat, the slow pulse of jade in their veins, that same pulse was alive in him like a silver wire sliding through his marrow: never quite painful but eternally cold and sharp, all shivery edge and threat.

The emperor showed no signs of sleepiness either, but Mei Feng was dozing already with her head conveniently cushioned in his lap. That should hold him at least for a little while if they were disturbed, if trouble came. At least long enough for Yu Shan to get ahead of him.

In the meantime, there were stars overhead and the night forest all around; and they were both of them young, the emperor and himself, and a long night of talking stretched ahead, and he could be strangely excited about that—

—EXCEPT THAT there was his clan-cousin too, *here* was his clan-cousin too, on her feet and twitching, restless with unhappiness.

"Walk with me?" she said. Which used to be an invitation to delight, but not tonight. He looked to the emperor and almost hoped
for a refusal, an imperial command, *you stay here with me*—but
instead there was a wave of the hand, a casual dismissal, and of
course he had to go.

HUMAN FEET turn naturally uphill, and here in the mountains
there was always somewhere higher. Sometimes they had to scramble and that was good, it meant they could stop walking awkwardly beside each other and go single-file; just once, the first
time, he turned and crouched and reached down a hand for hers.
Old habit, remembered pleasure, yearning, forgetfulness: she was
still who she was, he forgot that he had changed, and Jiao was
nowhere in his head at just that moment.

Jiao must have been still very much in Siew Ren's head. His
clan-cousin didn't move at all for a moment, and then very deliberately didn't take his hand; she stretched for a different grip,
clambered up another way, came to the top of the boulder and
walked on without even looking at him.

They walked, they climbed independently and together, and in
the end he said, "Siew Ren, if you don't want to talk . . ." Touching was something else and he knew it, he'd been stupid, unthink-
ing; but if all she meant to do was reject him, stony silence over a
cold shoulder, he thought he might go back to the emperor.

She spun around, fierce in starlight, and said, "No, I don't want
to talk. I want *you* to talk. I want you to say what's happened to
you, what you've done to yourself. Look, it's still summer, you
haven't been gone so long; but you've come back someone else in
Yu Shan's skin. Hardly his skin, even," stumblingly, "even the way
you look is different. What have you *done* . . . ?"

He opened his mouth to tell her, knowing before he took breath
that it was hopeless, a waste of breath, he couldn't begin to explain what had happened to him except for the one thing, the jade
beneath his tongue, the little nodule of stone that her own tongue

might have found out if they had still been as they were before—
but then it didn't matter because actually she wasn't looking for
answers, she wasn't actually looking at him at all anymore.

Looking past him, rather: staring, rather, with an expression
he'd never seen or thought to see on her face, hers especially. Of all
the women in the world, she was not the one to be utterly awed
and utterly frightened. She'd faced the emperor with hardly a
twitch. And these were their own known mountains, there was
nothing to terrify her here. Even a war party coming down high
over the hill to avoid the watch, she might see the danger but she
wouldn't be afraid. She certainly would not be awed. She wouldn't
stand there with her eyes as wide as her mouth, caught in cold silence on a hot night.

Besides, he'd heard nothing: not the scratch of metal on metal,
not the hissing whisper of a foot softly laid in grass, not the least
hint of anything beyond the normal sounds of the forest in its
night. He still didn't. Between the birdsong and the occasional
crash of a late monkey in the canopy, the rush and burble of distant water, the sough of wind and his own breathing and Siew
Ren's, there was nothing. He was sure.

And then he turned, and—

OH. THAT was—not nothing, no. The opposite of nothing,
rather: an entirety, an engulfing.

HE WAS vaguely, heedlessly aware of himself stepping back, because he dared not stand so close; reaching his clan-cousin and
stopping there, because he dared not leave her to stand alone.

Feeling her take his hand, like a promise that he would not leave
her; she would prevent it.

FEAR AND awe, yes: caught so perfectly between the two, he had
no thought of leaving, any more than he had any thought of going
closer.

ON A rock above their heads, against the twisted shadow of a twisted mountain tree burned a tiger.

It stood as still as they did only more so, magnificently still, still as the rock beneath its vast paws. Except that it was a living, liquid thing, still only because it saw no occasion to move.

Jade tigers, they were called. Stone tigers, sometimes. This one might have been stone itself, true jade just for that moment, if god or man could have cut jade into an absolute of tiger, the essence of it, sight and touch and power. If he could have touched it, Yu Shan was sure of harsh fur and a hot body, skin and muscle and bone beneath, the imperative of movement imperiously contained.

Its eyes shone: two chips of jade, exactly the green of the deep-sea stone, exactly the green of the emperor's eyes and his own. More than that, its fur shone green between the bands of black.

It . . . considered them, seemingly. He thought those eyes saw what he had confessed to nobody, the chip of jade in his mouth; he thought they saw how far the stone had penetrated. He thought the tiger was a jade-eater too, or else it was born in the mountain's heart, born of the stone, jade in its blood from the beginning.

He thought he might die from not breathing.

Sometimes he wondered if he could die at all, but not now; now he wondered how he might dare to go on living, having seen. Having been seen.

The tiger leaped down like moonlight pouring from a jug, a vivid flow immediate in movement and immediate to halt. When it had landed on the path before them, it was entirely still again.

Then its whiskers twitched, it opened its mouth and breathed out. Yu Shan smelled the deep smell of the mines, jade and dust and air that was sodden with stone. He had missed that. The tiger's eyes said *yes,* as though something had been understood between them.

And then it had turned and was leaving, leaping away, and was gone; and its absence was a sudden aching hollow in the world that the night could rush into, rush and rush and never hope to fill.

Siew Ren clung to his arm two-handed, like a monkey on a rope. Eventually—because one of them after all did have to say something, do something, change the world, or else they would only stand there forever in the same bewildered daze—she said, "Do you, do you think that was an omen?"

"I think it was a message," which might be the same thing, if an omen was a message from the gods. "I just don't know what it means."

She nodded, her cheek against his shoulder, and they were quiet again, still again.

"Was it even real?"

"It was real. See, it left pug-marks on the path," an enormous spread of paw and striking deep where it had landed, so much weight behind it, how could it not be real?

"Yes," she said, "and its breath smelled of forest pools with the sun on them—but if it came from the gods, that still doesn't mean it's real."

He knew stone tigers were real, even if he'd never seen one before. The mountains were full of stories; he had stroked the fur of a skin, it almost seemed long ago now, in the jademaster's palace. Even so, he understood her doubts. If a god were involved, it could be real and real and still not actually exist, not now be padding through the forest with the rumble of hunger in its gut and a weary ache in its bones.

He found it hard to imagine, tired. Sleeping, that was hard too; it was either there or it wasn't, he couldn't see it in any other way. Not vulnerable, turned away from the world, adrift.

Hungry wasn't hard at all. He thought it might have swallowed them both, quite neatly. If it had done that—well, he thought they would both be really dead. That was real enough for him.

He didn't say so, quite. Only, "I don't know how to tell the difference, between something that's real like we are and something that's real because the gods sent it."

The notion itself was unreal, that the gods would send something to him. To them. She had seen it, or at least smelled it, differently; perhaps it had been two different messages, both equally incomprehensible?

At least Siew Ren seemed not to be hating him just now. That would return, no doubt; her anger had simply ebbed, in the face of something infinitely greater. Something shared. Something for Yu Shan to be grateful for, except that that seemed like a monumental impertinence: neither jade tigers nor gods would stoop to interfere with mortals simply to hush a quarrel or smooth over a betrayal.

He assumed not, in any case. Perhaps that was impertinent too, and he should just be grateful.

CONFUSED, HE settled for being in a hurry; she was pulling at his arm, hurrying already.

Hurrying back down the hill, back to the emperor where he sat with Mei Feng cushioned against him, in the circle of his arm but not at all asleep anymore; and when they said what they had seen, the emperor nodded and said yes, him too. Mei Feng too. And no, they had no idea what it meant, only that they were both sure that it meant something.

eight

At least the pirate had sea-sense and common sense together; his sense of self-preservation encompassed everyone aboard.

That did not stop Old Yen resenting him. This boat might be a bastard, but she was his own bastard, and had been for a long time. He had refused to let any of his sons take her over, even at the cost of losing them as crew; he loathed to lose command of her now. Especially to a strong man with a dark soul and shadows at his back, more of a bastard creature than the boat had ever been.

If there weren't other people with their lives in the balance, he might have resisted Li Ton, at whatever cost to himself. He didn't believe even a pirate captain could have sailed this boat well enough to make a landing at the Forge, let alone brought her out again whole. He didn't believe he could have done it himself without the hand of the Li-goddess to guide him, to smooth the waters and raise the hull; he wouldn't have attempted it, if he didn't believe wholeheartedly in her kindness.

But there was the girl and her uncle, and there was young Pao too; any of those might have died, to teach a simple brutal lesson to the others.

Also, of course, there had been the dragon.

Old Yen had seen her distantly, rising and swooping and rising again. Pao had seen more from the masthead, and called down more than he cared to know.

And then she had come here, to the Forge. Seen from below she was a mighty terror, a shadow like ink against the bright paper sky, blotted of all color. She flew without wings—*on the wings of her will,* as the storytellers had it—with a slow sinuous motion like the flow of spilled ink while her head turned this way and that, surveying all that lay below her.

Surveying Old Yen and Pao in the boat there, precariously huddled against the sheer rock of the Forge.

He was utterly certain that she saw him in person, specifically. Saw him and dismissed him, he hoped, he prayed: why would she care about one more mortal man, so long as his boat was not out upon her waters?

But she seemed to grow in the sky as she came lower, as she spiraled lazily in the air above the Forge, as she stretched out her legs and the claws glinted darkly and she came down; and for a little while there he really did think that owning a boat was offense enough and she was coming down to destroy them.

He told Pao to swim for shore but the boy wasn't listening, or couldn't move. He wasn't sure that he could move himself. His limbs were tired, awkward, useless things; his body was a trap, dull and heavy, beneath contempt. Her contempt, as he stood within her shadow.

And then the dragon wasn't interested in them after all, or not yet. She settled on the island's peak, where the smoke was rising. Old Yen couldn't guess and refused to imagine what business she had with the pirate or his passengers, why the smoke should summon her.

He didn't at all imagine that it could end well, for any except the dragon.

EVEN so he stayed, and the boy with him. His goddess wouldn't be pleased if he abandoned innocents, marooning them on this island where nobody came, giving them over to the dragon's uncertain care. He would have fewer qualms—no, he'd have no qualms at all—about abandoning the pirate. That man was responsible for everything dreadful that had happened here, the slaughter of the monks and the dragon's release. It would be nothing but justice to leave him with the bones of his victims and no help else. If he wanted a reward, he could look to the dragon for it, and hope not to find it in her belly.

The goddess might disagree, though, even about that. These were her waters, in many ways the dragon had been her prisoner; she would frown—he thought—on anyone's being left to those untender mercies. The guilty too could look to her for succor. Even if it came tempered with justice, that would be her own and not Old Yen's. Neither the dragon's.

Pao stayed because there was nowhere to go, if the boat wasn't leaving. That's what Old Yen assumed, at least. The boy crouched high in the bows, turned away from him and the island both, not to see if the dragon came down to eat them.

Who came, in the end, were the pirate and the doctor and the girl.

Not the boy with the chains and the crippled hand. On the way here, Old Yen had wondered if he had a crippled mind as well, he had behaved so oddly. Perhaps they had bought the dragon's favor, with his life? Old Yen was sure that the pirate at least would leap at such a bargain.

They came down in a little group together, like conspirators, struggling over the rocks. The pirate even helped the others when he had to, and they accepted it, when they had to; then he whistled across the water for the sampan.

Old Yen fetched them himself, giving Pao just a little more time to find his courage.

Himself, he felt emboldened. A dragon had passed across his sky; more, she had looked at him directly. What should he fear now?

He said, "Where is the boy?"

"The boy will not be coming."

Old Yen stopped plying his oar, right there in the slack water between boat and rocky shore. "Why not?"

For this he was ready to fight, unless the boy was dead already. It would be a fight he would lose, of course; but then they would all be losers, because the pirate could not take his boat over the rocks. He thought—he hoped!—the man would realize that, and not fight.

In fact it was the girl who answered him, who dispelled any need for fighting. "Han told us to go." She sounded desolate but determined.

"Why so?"

"Because he and the dragon are . . . bonded, in ways I can't explain." Not ways she didn't understand; it was apparently his understanding that would fail, if she tried to lay them out. Well, he could believe that. He had seen the boy, and he had seen the dragon. There was no bargaining there. "He thinks we'll be safer if we're gone," the girl went on, "he says we must go . . ."

The pirate had fetched them here; would a cripple boy send them away?

Perhaps, with the dragon's shadow at his back. The pirate was nodding. "Believe it, fisherman. The boy has some hold on the dragon. Not much, but enough perhaps to hold her off, while you take us to safety."

"And what of the boy, then?"

A shrug. "Perhaps he can keep her away indefinitely, without us to worry about."

"And do what, live here? Live how?"

Another shrug. Li Ton had no answer. Nor did the girl: only a silent, obvious, impossible wish for things to be otherwise. It was her uncle the doctor who said, "One man could live here, if he was careful about it. The monks had gardens, I saw those, and there must be game. Small game. Han is no fool. He could survive . . ."

For a while, perhaps, if he was lucky. He didn't seem to have been very lucky so far in his life.

"You could bring him fish?" the girl suggested. Meaning, all too clearly, *you could bring him fish and eggs and rice and meat. And greenstuff that he's not smart enough to grow. And me . . .*

With the dragon abroad, Old Yen thought that no one would be bringing anything to the boy. No one would be sailing to the Forge, or anywhere else in the strait. He was kind; he didn't say so, yet. Also, he didn't want her plunging off the sampan to hide up somewhere on the island until the dragon left.

He said, "I'll take you back to Taishu."

"No," the pirate said. "Not Taishu. Not Santung, either. Anywhere but the city."

"Why so?"

"If we go to Taishu, we lose the boat. If we go to Santung, we lose the boat." He meant, clearly, *I lose the boat,* but he was right either way. The emperor's men on Taishu, the generalissimo's men in Santung, either would seize command and mastery of Old Yen's boat as soon as he brought her into harbor. The emperor needed all the fleet he could achieve, to provision and protect his empire, his little island; the generalissimo had just lost all the fleet he had. "I need to speak to someone," Li Ton went on, "and General Ping Wen may not be so easy to reach a second time. Also, he might not be so pleased to see us back. Tunghai Wang will see me, I am sure, so we will go that way. I am less sure that I will want to give him what he asks for. I want to keep this boat and you to sail her, fisherman, since my own *Shalla* has been taken from me. You must know somewhere we can put in undisturbed, close enough to reach Santung, far enough to be safe."

Old Yen did what he had to, to survive. He had been a fisherman all his life, for his own sake and his family's; now at last there was only himself to consider. Himself and his boat. He had been a faithful subject, plying back and forth across the strait in the emperor's cause, because the risks of cooperation were always fewer than the risks of refusal. Now apparently he was enlisted in the ranks of the rebels, for the selfsame reason. Old Yen could worry about that, because the rebels' triumph would be the emperor's despair, and Mei Feng was with the emperor. Worrying was all that he could manage, though, and it was probably useless. Nothing he did was likely to affect the outcome. One man with a boat was not so much.

And yes, of course he knew a place on the coast where he could bring them privately to land.

He knew many such, but he had one particularly in mind.

It FELT strange to be watching the sky for something other than weather; it was hard to remember that he must watch the water too, that she was as likely to rise as to fall.

Impossible not to watch, although there was nothing he could do if the dragon came.

Nothing but pray, at any rate, and he was doing that already.

He did that anyway, his simply being on the water was a prayer; his boat's hull carried the characters for "hope" and "luck" and the goddess's blessing, cut deep into the wood below the waterline. He had asked a priest to write them on when she was beached one time, long ago; the cutting he had done himself, and renewed it himself every storm season.

More, his every glance, his every move at sea carried an awareness of the Li-goddess, her generosity, her benevolence. He could not look at a horizon without seeing her hand cupped in protection; he could not taste the salt wind without feeling her kiss on his lips. All of that was prayer, a constant muted undercurrent.

Today, though, he prayed aloud. Surprised himself, almost, with the steady monotone growl of it as he chanted like a dutiful monk in appeal to his goddess to watch over them, as he kept peering back over his shoulder like a doubtful fisherman in case the dragon took wing in their pursuit.

For a long time he could still see her, as motionless as a temple roof-dragon, where she coiled squatly on the peak of the Forge: an outline, poised and deadly. And blessedly holding still, not uncurl-

ing in outrage at the impudence of a boat upon her waters, not flying lethally arrow-straight to send them down and down to her
former prison, to the deep.

But she dropped below his skyline, and then he had nothing to
trust but prayer; his eyes were no use anymore where she might
come striking through the underwater, invisible to watchers.

He could not, he dared not distrust his goddess, but neither
would he take her for granted. He was dutifully anxious, then, although she sent a helpful wind on his quarter and a smoothing sea
that even his bastard boat could scud across like a young cat over
short grass, head high and delighted.

The pirate was just as watchful, staying close beside him at the
stern and calling the boy Pao to his duty if the sails slacked even a
little, interrogating Old Yen about the landing-place he'd chosen,
even while his head kept turning just as often as Old Yen's did to
scan the sky behind them, and—even more uselessly—the dark secrets of the sea.

THE SUN covered its track across the sky as the boat covered its
track across the waters, and no dragon came from above or below.
Nothing threatened, even the weather stayed kindly; Old Yen almost faltered in his praying as the coast rose like a wall ahead, like
a limit to worry. Almost. It was his song now, though, settled in his
bones. He worked his oar to the rhythm of his chanting; it was his
prayer that brought them home.

That brought them actually into a deep shadowed creek, just
around sunset. For Old Yen, at least, it was sunset. There was still
light enough above to make the temple stand out on the headland.
Old Yen smiled privately as he spoke to the pirate, as he nodded
across the creek:

"There is a path, that you will see come morning. That will take
you to the road, and the road will take you to Santung."

"Come morning, the road will take us all, I think. To be certain.

I might leave the boy. There is work enough aboard to keep him busy, and I don't believe he could sail her single-handed."

Nor could he defend her single-handed—but Pao was a sensible lad, with a gift for avoiding trouble. It was Old Yen who had dragged him into this; who had no recourse now but to nod easily and say, "Will you object if I go up to the temple there, to give my thanks to the Li-goddess?"

"I thought you had done that, all the way over. But go if you want to, go now. Ask the priests if the goddess has any food she can spare us."

There were no priests at this temple, and Old Yen doubted that there was any food to spare anywhere within forage of Santung. Even the goddess might be going hungry, even in her busy places. Old Yen liked to make little offerings from the boat, as though all the sea were her temple; even he hadn't had much to give her recently, bar fish heads. Which might have made a soup else, but he was perhaps a little tired of fish-head soup.

Still, he thanked the pirate politely, as though he did need permission to leave his own boat; he took the sampan and poled ashore as though he cared not a whit about leaving his boat in that man's charge. He didn't offer to take any of the others. The boy would have to learn to deal with the pirate, at least until the pirate wasn't there. The other two, the girl and the doctor, were not his concern. Let them make their own devotions in their own way, if they were devout at all. He supposed the doctor must be, or how else would he bring about his cures?

This, now, this was a devotion in itself for Old Yen: this climb from the little strand to the clifftop. There was a path but it was steep and hard to find in the thick light, muddy and slippery underfoot, always a penance. Today, exhausted by nerves and wonder on top of too much work, feeling every year of his age, he had to pause halfway. And looked down to see his boat solitary in the channel, picked out by lamplight in the cabin and at the stern, and thought a little about each of those separate lives below, and how unlikely it was that they had all been brought here together.

And turned and went on up, knowing that at least he was still on the track of his life, serving the Li-goddess and sailing the strait; and came to the top of the cliff at last, aching and grunting, glad to be alone.

And stood for a little while looking at the sun as it fell again, that last little way to a farther horizon. Dull red fire was swallowed by darkening glistening quenching waters, as though the dragon had been repossessed by the goddess. That thought made him search for the Forge but there was nothing now, not the least touch of light on its peak to tease his eyes into wondering whether or not the silhouette of a dragon still showed.

With the sea dark and the sky darkening to match it, Old Yen turned at last toward the temple where he would light a lamp and make little offerings—the best that he could manage, better than fish heads but only slightly—and stay awhile just to speak to the goddess, to tell her about his day and his anxieties about tomorrow and his granddaughter and the world . . .

AND STOPPED, because a light already showed in the doorway, in this place where no one came except himself. There was no priest, no nun; rumors and fear kept local people away. Briefly he thought the rumors must be true after all, the goddess herself did indeed visit her own house here; he thought she had come for him.

Then a shadow moved between the light and the door and, briefly again, he thought his own suspicions were right instead, the temple was used as a shelter for thieves and smugglers, outlaws. Spies, perhaps. He wasn't the only man who took the emperor's men to and fro across the strait. He had brought them to this same creek, indeed, though never to this holy place. Another sea-captain might have suggested the temple as a roof, shelter, a base to return to; or the men might have found it themselves, empty and apparently abandoned . . .

Except that, even to old and tired eyes at this most confusing moment of the half-light, that shadow was no man, be he thief or spy. No woman, neither. Just too *short* . . .

And then he knew, he was sure he knew who was here, where they ought not to be. And he ought to tell them so, tell the mother at least; but it was the little girl who stepped out onto the broad top step and stooped to pick up something, a basket he thought, and called back over her shoulder as she did so, "We have greens here, Mother, and cold rice, and vinegar. That's good, Jin likes—"

And then she must have seen him in the corner of her eye, although he didn't think he'd moved. Perhaps she only sensed his watching, felt the weight of his gaze. She turned and peered into the near-dark, and called a little uncertainly, "Hullo? Have you brought us food, too . . . ?"

And then her mother was there, swift and anxious with a lamp in her hand, the other arm around her little girl and her voice sharp, "Who's there? Come into the light, let the goddess see you . . ."

That was a bluff, but a good one. Anyone come this far from the road, lingering uncertainly, likely they'd be no more than a gawping peasant drawn by whispers; likely her command would make them run. Which she would want, far more than a man standing in her light, on her threshold . . .

Old Yen was that man, and likely she would not want him either, but he went anyway: across the thick tussock-grass to the temple steps and up those, four and four; so that they met in the doorway, on the threshold, both of them knowing it was not hers and she had no right to it.

He said, "You should not," and again, "you should *not* be here."

His fault, perhaps; he had sent them here, the woman and her two daughters, when they found him on the strand below. But only for a night or two, he'd meant, and then move on. They couldn't treat the Li-goddess as a landlady, her house as common boarding . . .

He'd thought that was obvious. He did still think so. What was she, a priestess, to linger like this? What were her daughters, votive offerings?

Someone thought so, apparently; more than someone. She said, "I know; but the people hereabouts bring us gifts of food, and the temple gives us a roof. Should I take my daughters on the road, in the rain, to face their hunger?"

"If you had done that, the goddess would have led you somewhere safe."

She smiled wryly, an expression he was used to on others' faces. "I feel safe here. I don't believe the goddess will turn us out. We take care of her house, at least, and burn incense when the people bring us some."

He could smell it, indeed, like prayer in the air, and still didn't think that was enough. It was for the goddess to say, of course, not for him—but it was hard to step back from indignation, to settle his soul to the notion.

He stepped inside, and yes, this was not the temple he had left last, filthy and neglected. There was lamplight rather than starlight, not a hole in the roof; there was nothing underfoot but the proper planking of the floor, well scrubbed; there were all the idols in their niches in the walls, gleaming bright in the writhing smoke from incense pots and joss sticks everywhere.

And there was a bed improvised in one corner, quilts and comfort; and there were the two girls as well as the woman, and still none of this felt right.

Perhaps he only wanted his old ruined temple back because it was his own, by right of long observance? Perhaps he resented her for making this place more properly a place of worship, and so less his own . . . ?

Perhaps. He did resent her, that was sure. And resented himself for bringing her here, across the creek. At the time it had been a necessary kindness, but now . . .

He looked at her, and at her daughters. She seemed brighter, better fed, more confident of her right to a place in this world. Before, she tried to send her daughters into safety even at the cost of her own; now, he thought, she knew she needn't do that. She had perhaps always been a fighter, but now she expected to win.

The little girl had caught some of that from her parent, unless the parent had caught it all from her. Small and fierce and determined, competent because she had taught herself to be, she was stripping green leaves from their stalks and washing them in a bowl in the corner, while she watched her mother, while she listened.

The elder girl, Jin, was still bereft of sense, but didn't seem so hollow as before. Whatever her story was, Old Yen had thought her irrecoverable; maybe not. She sat on the floor before the altar, bobbing and bowing before the particular idol that was there because Old Yen had set it there long years before, though it had never been this clean and cared for. Briefly he thought that she was praying, before he remembered that she had no voice.

And then she turned her head hard to look at him, and her mouth opened, and she spoke in a voice that should never have come from a girl's mouth, could never have belonged there. It was rich with salt and threat, like the drag and stifle of weed in the shadow of a rock in deep water; and she said, "Fisherman. Tell the dragon, the strait is mine. Tell her that if she will not be my prisoner, she may not be my guest."

And the girl's mouth closed on that dreadful voice, but its presence still hung in the air between them, between them all.

TWO

Her Water's Voice

one

*W*aking alone; standing and stretching alone, unwatched; stepping out of his rough shelter and still being alone. Going naked to the stream to wash, and then running all down its tumbling length until he plunged into a sea-pool at the bottom, shrieking like an idiot as the surf broke over his head just because there was nobody to see him, nobody to hear. Sometimes he could feel like king of the world. King of his life, his little world, this island.

He'd never been alone before, in any way that mattered. His family, his master Doshun, Li Ton and the crew of the *Shalla*—always there had been someone to overlook, to claim his time and assign his space and keep him under their control. Now here he was, marooned. No one actually knew for sure that he was here; only a handful could guess at it.

One man in the world, perhaps, could come to the Forge to see. And that man was in Li Ton's hands now, where Han had been before him. Under the pirate's eye, sailing the only boat the pirate had. The fisherman had greater worries than Han to occupy his mind.

Besides, Han didn't need worrying over. He had this whole island, all the Forge to himself; he was doing well. King of the world.

AT FIRST he'd thought he would never manage on his own. When the dragon left him, he thought it was a death sentence, slow and cruel. A boy alone with a crippled hand on a rock of ghosts, an island of slaughtered monks—how could he live?

Obviously, he thought, he wasn't meant to. She couldn't kill him directly, but she could strand him here and let him die.

No, he had stranded himself, hadn't he? He'd sent everyone else away, to save Tien. The dragon had only let it happen. Then she'd flown away and left him, and he would starve to death if he didn't fling himself off a high cliff first, or die of simple solitude for being all alone.

That first hour, when he realized the truth of it—that she was unbelievably gone, and the boat was gone, and they were neither of them coming back—he had run madly down to the old broken jetty in case there was a miracle, a boat somehow that he could somehow use; and then back up to the peak again in case of another miracle, some distant sight of the fisherman coming back to rescue him, with Tien at his side.

And then through the monks' old ruined settlement, calling pointlessly, screaming almost, because the monks were all still dead and their burned bones lay where he had scattered them.

Perhaps Tien had slipped away from the others, on their way back to the boat; perhaps she was in hiding somewhere on the island, waiting for him to find her?

Or perhaps the old fisherman had sent his boy to swim quietly back to shore and hole up until the dragon left, to be Han's boon-companion in his exile?

Or perhaps he would find the monksmith's ghost here, where they had burned his body. That should be frightening too, but what did Han have to fear from an old man's shade, when he had stood in the dragon's mind? He wasn't brave, and all summer he had gone directly from one terror to another, again and again. Nothing could be more frightening than the dragon, though. Now that she had left him, he thought perhaps that nothing would ever frighten him again, because nothing could come close to matching her.

Except that he was frightened of being on his own, apparently. He would have welcomed the old man's ghost, if only he could find it.

No ghost in the ash and ruin of the monks' compound, only a sudden eruption, half a dozen black chickens battering the air with shrieks and wings and lifting dust as he stumbled through them where they scratched at the grass together.

He ran on, through the wild gardens and the steep tangle of trees behind, and came to a clifftop and didn't jump, no, though he did almost go over anyway before he knew it was there. Grabbed at a creeper and saved himself right on the brink, and stood for a little with his heart pounding and the sweat cold on his skin and the fall in his eyes, the long plunge to the water and then farther, all the way to the bottom where her chains lay, where she had lain herself until he cut them . . .

. . . CHICKENS?

THE MONKS must have kept chickens, and fed them too. Not for weeks, being dead and so forth, but that didn't matter much. The birds foraged for themselves, in the open and among the trees, but still lingered around the compound.

They wouldn't let Han close enough to catch one, though he made a private diving idiot of himself in trying, again and again. Meantime they laid eggs, sometimes, that sometimes he could find; and he laid traps, each more intricate and hopeful than the last, as thoughts of spitted chicken blazed brighter and brighter in his head with every day that passed meatless. He could smell it, taste it, he could feel the grease of it on his fingers and the shreds between his teeth. Only not the warmth of it in his belly, because he couldn't—quite—get it there.

He had the fire ready. The moment he'd realized that he might yet live after all, which was the moment after he hadn't quite gone over the cliff-edge, he raced back up to the firetop and salvaged still-smoking charcoal from the crush of the dragon's footprint. He'd kept it alive in a firepot since, fed it twigs and moss and more charcoal, blown it into constant sullen life, dull and red and waiting. Sometimes he thought his stomach was the same, that dull red burning ache of ever-present hunger.

Not that he was ever truly hungry, or no more so than he always had been. The monks' gardens were full of greens and onions and garlic, long beans and curious roots, between the rampant overgrowth of summer weeds. In a few short days he'd learned to be a farmer. And he'd found their low stone storehouse, full of grain and dried fish. He made congee daily over a slow fire, and was probably as healthy and as well fed as he'd ever been; only that his belly ached and grumbled, waiting for the promised meat that he could never quite lay hand on. It wasn't only chickens. There were other birds in the woods, and creatures that scuttled and slithered through the leaf mold, and any of them, all of them might have been edible, if only he could catch them.

He slept dry or dry enough, first in that same storehouse, then in a roomier shelter that he made for himself close by. He didn't like to go into the old compound, because there were still bones mixed with the ash where someone had built an inadequate pyre and tried to burn the monks. Some of the bones were bound together by scorched dried flesh and tendons; the skulls still had skin of a sort. They were dreadful. He thought they stared at him, with their hollow eyes. He thought they screamed at him with their silent gaping twisted jaws, their blackened teeth; he knew they had good reason. He had been one with the men who killed them, and one again with those who scattered their remnants, searching the dead pyre for wood that would still burn. He hated both those memories, the one cold and the other fresh; his life had turned and turned again around those nights and the days that followed.

And now his life—which meant Tien, Li Ton, the dragon above

all—had left him here, solitary at the last; and he had learned that he could live this way, doing no harm to anyone, having no effect. For a little while he had mattered in the world, and it had all been terrible. Now he was nothing: neglected, abandoned, alone. That was something to rejoice in, except that he missed Tien. She was safer without him, though, and so he should be happy.

And so he was happy, with no one making demands and no one to be responsible for. No one to watch him, laugh at him, worry over him. No one to see if he threw himself into the surge of the sea and only barely made it back to the rocky shore, no one to be scared or scolding. No one to rub his hair dry and push their fingers through it after, threatening to take a scratchy comb to the tangles. No one to share his tension as he snuck up to his latest chicken-trap and his disappointment when he found it empty, no one to be disappointed in him.

He did better, with no one else around. He did best alone, and he'd had to be marooned like this to learn it—

—EXCEPT, OF course, that he never was alone. Not quite. Any more than he was quite entirely here, marooned on the Forge.

SHE HAD left him, unbelievably, when he was exhausted and numbed and close to surrender, overwhelmed within the great spaces of her mind. She had lifted into the sky and left, not tried to eat him after all. She was gone: and yet she was a silence somewhere in the back of his head, a stone-cold voice that never spoke, a weight that dragged at his thoughts like a pebble thrown into a sheet of silk, distant and potent and inescapable.

HE? HE was a thread caught in her claws, a tangle of weed around her neck, a tickle in her throat, an irritant. A negligible presence, something she carried because she could not shift it, something she struggled to ignore.

REMOTELY, THEN, he did still fly with her. Some little part of him was awed, perpetually full of wonder.

REMOTELY, THEN, she did still stay with him. Some little part of him felt the impact of her constant regard and was in perpetual terror, perpetually trying to stand against it, not to be eaten from within.

two

*I*t was entirely the wrong way around, for Guangli to be laughing and easy on the road while Jiao was increasingly uncomfortable. It was against the natural order. He was a jade carver, an aging man with a sedentary occupation, a heavy belly, a comfortable house and a settled life that the emperor's word was fetching him away from. She was an outlaw, a pirate of the road, unencumbered and dangerous and free. This was her proper habitat and she should be rejoicing in it, she should be making a triumphant parade of herself, and . . .

And she was scowling and kicking dust like a sulking adolescent, while he smirked and prodded at her temper and marched along like a lad half his age, delighted to be out on the emperor's highway with his discomforted companion. He was a mean-spirited old man and she was torn by honest doubt and worry about someone who mattered to her deeply, and . . .

"Tell me about this clan-cousin of his, then," Guangli said, not at all for the first time, "who has kept him from coming with you."

"It was the emperor," she snarled, through gritted teeth and not at all for the first time, "who prevented him. He asked to come," and never mind that he had asked to come alone. Guangli had no need to know that.

Guangli might have divined it, to judge by his snort of laughter. "Who is this girl, then, that he's so eager to escape her and yet fails so profoundly? Is she so very dangerous?"

She's half my age, and she's been his seductive playmate all his life. Also, she amuses the emperor. So yes, she is so very dangerous . . .

Quite why it mattered so very much, when she had come and gone through a dozen dozen men's lives and beds and never hurt too badly over any of them, that was a question she would have found hard to answer. And yet, it did matter. Extremely.

Which was why Guangli's teasing mattered, immediately, now; why a long and cynical friendship stood suddenly in the hazard, because he couldn't see the risk. Because he thought it no more than funny that she had lost her heart to a stripling, to a boy: when he of all people should have understood how much deeper it ran, like a vein of stone running all through her, twisting, lethal . . .

He might have learned just how lethal, because her temper was on a short chain and due to snap. Only there was a sound behind them, a sound that she hadn't heard for a while. That had her stiff and still, turning to look although there was nothing to be seen yet around the bend in the road; gesturing to the old man to be silent, seriously, and to get off the crown of the road, get off the road altogether, get behind her and if that meant get into the ditch then it meant *get into the ditch!*

Thankfully, he was wise enough to understand how very much she meant that. Awkward under the load of his tools—wishing no doubt for his former apprentice, for Yu Shan, even as she was wishing for him too, as she had been all this damned journey— he stumbled over the verge and down, to stand sandals and feet and calf-deep in muddy water without the least real notion why he should, except that she had told him to.

He could hear it too, surely, the slurred steady rhythm of shuffle-running feet. Men in number, under discipline, under an urgency. It meant soldiers, necessarily. On this road, soldiers were nothing new but never in a hurry. Something had changed, then; and on this road, between the one palace and the other, any change must engage the emperor.

The absent emperor. This might be revolt, rebellion, an army uprising. More likely it would be his mother sending troops to fetch her wayward son: he might not come back for his generals, but for her, surely, he would come as he always had . . . ?

Those were all the options Jiao could think of, in that little time she had for thinking. Here came the advance guard now, banner-men and troops, sweating hard and trotting steadily, at that mile-eating pace that she knew trained men could keep up all day. She could do it herself, if she had to.

The banners had a lot of yellow in them. So did the men's uniforms, scarves flying free in the breeze, tassels around their spearheads. Not the pure yellow of the emperor's own guard, but close enough. Too close. Any man on this road could claim to be on the emperor's business, but few declared it in their clothing. She could do so herself, but she'd sooner keep that quiet; which being true, she stepped back off the verge and joined Guangli in the ditch. Better to look like peasants, better to pass entirely unnoticed by anyone this proud or this important. Who could command soldiers and dared assert such close imperial connections? His mother, again; his generals, perhaps.

And here came a high-wheeled carriage pulled by men, and that too was decked out with yellow streamers; and perhaps she and Guangli both should be kowtowing like real peasants, but she really needed to see this. Whoever it was in that carriage, they must be going to the new palace site, and the emperor would want to know.

Someone wise in the ways of the court might be able to read what the banners signified, this much yellow and that much blue; she was mystified. All she could usefully do was count the men and hurry back to the valley in the hills . . .

Except that the carriage stopped when it reached her, which made her lose her count entirely.

The carriage door had a sliding screen; it was a man's hand that slid that screen aside, a man's face that peered down at her from the shadows. Not the empress, then, she could tell the emperor that much. His mother wasn't come herself in search of him. This could still be an envoy.

Except that the man looked entirely too haughty to be anyone's envoy but his own; indeed, he looked thoroughly out of temper. Which gave her a clue, perhaps, knowing as she did how many messages had been run from the valley to the city and back.

He said, "You, there. Where are you going?"

She kept her head low like a terrified peasant, and made the vaguest possible gesture, *along the road, highness, that way . . .*

He said, "No. Don't try to fob me off. Whom do you serve?"

He wouldn't be satisfied with anything but a direct answer; he wouldn't be satisfied with this, but none the less she said it. "We all serve the emperor, highness."

"That is true, but would he miss you, if I took your heads now? Both of you?"

That brought her head up, no more dissembling. She met him eye to eye and said, "I think he would."

"Yes, I thought so too. Where would you actually be going, if not to him?"

Guangli put his silence aside, to forestall her own answer: "To the new palace, of course, lord. I am a jade carver, and I thought there might be work. The woman is my bodyguard: unusual, I know, but she is an unusual woman. And she is right to say the emperor would miss my work, if I were not there to make it."

"No," the man in the carriage said again, and she was increasingly certain who he was. "Nice—but no. The new palace is not ready for its decoration, and no jademaster would let a skilled carver wander the island unsupervised."

"Alas," Guangli said, "the supply of jade has been . . . interrupted, since the emperor came. My master has seen none of any quality for too long; he thought perhaps it was being intercepted, diverted to the new palace, to await the emperor's pleasure. And so he sends me, to please the emperor more."

"Almost credible, old man—but, still, no. If you lie to me again, I will take your head in earnest. I think you know where the emperor actually is, and are going to him."

It was imperative, she thought, to save Guangli's head. And her own. She bowed low, and said, "Highness, we do. This is his favorite jade carver, and his majesty has sent for him."

"Indeed. Why does his majesty want a jade carver?"

"He is in the mountains, highness, among the mines. Perhaps he has found a stone he wishes to see carved. I was only sent to fetch the man."

"And to lie to your superiors if necessary, to see him safely there? I understand you perfectly. Very well, go your way. And tell his majesty that General Ping Wen has come to visit him; and is waiting at the site of the new palace, but will not wait for long. If his majesty does not come to me there, tell him, I must come to him. However hard he is to find. Tell him there are matters of great importance to discuss. Do you understand me?"

"Highness, I do." And had foreguessed him, his name at least, which pleased her.

WHAT PLEASED her more, he clapped his hands and started his whole procession moving again, lifting the weight of empire from her shoulders. For a moment there, she'd felt as though the whole edifice had been looking at her, through him: assessing her place, her contribution. Her inadequacies.

She never felt that way when the emperor looked at her. Despite his rank and his extraordinary body, despite his astonishing eyes, despite his undeniable allure, when he looked at her she still only saw a boy. A boy's curiosity, a boy's amusement, a boy's hope.

His empire had been missing all this time. Apparently his general had it, in the pocket of his sleeve.

Had it, and had taken it away.

She counted the hundred soldiers he had in his tail, and waited until the last of them had moved on, shuffle-shuffle out of sight.

Then she helped Guangli up out of the ditch, and set them both to following rather faster than they had been going before. No danger of catching up with the general again, even her long loping pace couldn't match that short shuffling relentless run, even if Guangli could have kept up with her; but she thought the emperor should hear this sooner rather than later.

If that meant that she saw Yu Shan sooner rather than later, well. That was incidental.

three

Li Ton had seen cities in ferment, and cities in torment; he had seen cities in ruin. More than once, he had been the instrument of that ruin. Fire and sword, the walls broken and the fields sown with salt. He was used to marching with the stink of smoke at his back, the wail of women in his ears, the wet chafing weight of fresh blood on his clothes.

He had never quite seen anything like Santung as it was now, twice defeated, under occupation by a hollow sour army that would shatter at a blow if anyone could land one. Soldiers and civilians both looked to the sky with dread, and found it empty, and saw no comfort in that. All they knew to do was wait, it seemed, until it would not be empty any longer. In the meantime, they had no idea how to live, day to day or with one another.

THE FISHERMAN had been strange last night when he came back from the temple, was strange still this morning, silent and distracted and somehow not afraid of the right things, of Li Ton or this walk into the city, nor of the dragon in the air. Something had scared him for sure, but it wasn't guessable.

Nevertheless, Li Ton wasn't leaving him behind, with the boy and the boat. It was Li Ton's boat now, and he meant to keep it.

The boy was properly frightened of Li Ton, and would do what he was told: rowing the rest of them to land and then returning to the boat to scrub decks and mend sail until they hailed him ashore again. Something might come that he could not deal with—men

with boats or intrepid swimmers, a tidal surge, a dragon—but Li
Ton was a practical man, and only ever demanded what was possible.

He might have left the doctor, who was no kind of sailor. If he
met trouble anywhere between here and Tunghai Wang, though, it
was likely to be with the remnants of Tunghai's army. His own
face, his own name would mean little or nothing, whereas the doctor had been well known on the long march here. Soldiers were
sentimental about anyone who took care of them in their need;
healers or whores were equally cherished. The doctor might see
him safely through to the generalissimo if his own resources
failed.

He might have left the girl, but he didn't trust her with the boat.
She wanted to get back to her own boy, to Han on the island; she
might persuade Pao that the two of them could sail it well enough
together. He didn't think they'd get as far as the Forge, and he was
utterly certain that they would lose the boat and themselves on the
rocks there if they did, but the young were often idiots. It would be
a shame to let them throw their lives away when they might yet be
useful to him; it would be folly to lose the boat like that, to a girl's
sentiment and a boy's susceptibility.

So he took the girl and the doctor and the fisherman too, to the
beach and the road and the city.

THEY MET peasants and farmers on the road, if there were any actual difference between the two. Li Ton had never been sure. To a
soldier they were all alike, mud-grubbers whose food would keep
an army marching, though it had to be taken at the blade's edge.
To a ruined man, to a beggar much the same, except that the food
had to be wheedled or stolen from them, when he had no blade.
And to a pirate the same again, land-bound, as vegetable as rice
and roots. Whether they owned the land or only worked it,
whether they were owned themselves, paddy by paddy: no difference.

Certainly there was no distinguishing them on that road, that day. They were all afraid of him. And with reason. There were soldiers on the road too, coming and going, with wagons that were mostly empty. Supplies must be running low and pickings would be few, on land that had been picked and picked already. One lesson that abided, from Li Ton's time as a general: an army should keep moving, whatever the cost. Once it stalled, for winter or weather or bad country, for any reason at all, that was when trouble came. Not hunger alone, but hunger usually first. He'd always hated sieges; a siege could be as hard on the soldiers outside the wall as it was on the citizens within.

This, now, this would be worse. A siege of sorts, yes, only with water in lieu of a wall: unbridgeable water, a surging sea that had already swallowed one fleet of men.

A surging sea with a dragon to guard it.

Tunghai Wang's men would likely be hungry by now. There had been too many of them before the dragon, and they had been here too long. No wonder the peasants were afraid.

Even so, hunger was likely the least of Tunghai's troubles. The generalissimo had ridden this far, all across the empire on a chasing wave; stalled at the last, his men lost and his armada too, what should he do now? Creep back to the capital in defeat, and try to claim a missing throne in an empty city? He would never survive the journey. One of his allies would slay him, the others would challenge for his place, and the whole rebel army would splinter and scatter. Lucky if it didn't destroy itself entirely, the men all fighting one another, this regiment against that, one general against another until perhaps there was only one survivor, a new generalissimo and no army left to lead.

No wonder then if even the troops were edgy, passing strangers on the road. Li Ton could never look like a peasant; no more could his companions. And Tien was a girl, young and pretty. To a squad of soldiers, any squad of soldiers Li Ton had ever known, that could be enough. It disturbed him, almost, that it was not: that the

soldiers looked, touched hands to hilts, muttered among themselves and hurried on by. Under orders, perhaps—*no more rape,
no more killing, we need the people now; who else will feed us,
who else will build more boats?*—but even so it worried at him like
a needle in the flesh. An occupying army should be prouder: swift
to challenge, hard to pass. He was still a soldier in his heart, and
he would have had these men flogged, their captains executed for
showing their own doubts and fears so openly.

Which would not have helped the army, he understood that. It
was too late for discipline, which meant it was too late altogether.
This was an army broken, and he was quite surprised that Tunghai Wang still had charge of it, still breathed.

IF HE did, of course. If he did. The common soldiers would speak
to Li Ton no more than the peasants would, those few times he
tried to stop them on the road. Perhaps he should have held back
and sent one of the other men. Or the girl. There must be news,
and these people would know it; gossip ran like rain in a gutter,
through any city with an army in it. Filtering truth from terror was
an art, but he had a lifetime's practice at it. If someone would only
speak to him . . .

Apparently not, but a voice did hail his little group at last, or
one of them at least:

"Doctor!"

Tien's uncle had been bewildered all day and perhaps for days
on end, still not caught up with his change of status. Not a doctor
at the moment, not allowed to be—barely more than a hostage, indeed, a creature of some use to someone else—he still reacted to
that title.

Came to a startled halt and turned around; gazed a little
blankly at the soldier staring back; waited.

The soldier said—quite rightly—"You won't remember me,
doctor. But I was sick on the march, months ago, and you gave me

a tea that broke the fever. Blackwater fever, all my troop was down with it but I was the lucky one, I came to you . . ."

And now the doctor clearly did remember, as they all do, the disease if not the patient; he smiled behind his beard and his sheltering hand, said, "More wise than lucky, perhaps. Asking help when it is needed is the prerogative of wisdom."

Li Ton thought it was a survival instinct, and didn't say so.

The soldier said, "I made sure my friends all came to you, after." *All those that lived* was understood. "But why are you here, doctor? We missed you, from your tent; word said you had gone with the fleet to Taishu, and were lost . . ."

Are you a ghost? his eyes said, though they were trying hard not to believe it; and to be sure he looked not at all ghostly to Li Ton's eyes, only tired and dirty and afraid.

"I went to Taishu," the doctor said, "and am back."

Which was as good as to say *I am a ghost,* and he knew it, and didn't apparently care; or else he did it deliberately. Perhaps just to assert his own mystery, perhaps just to frustrate Li Ton. For sure it did that, because the soldier paled to a sickly color and hurried away before he could say anything useful, anything at all.

Still, even his departing back left one thing unsaid but apparent, that the doctor was remembered among the troops, that his face could still be useful.

AND HERE at last was the city. No wall, no gate: a town built on wealth alone, buying good relations with its neighbors and ultimately protected by the emperor's own word, his jade-port, where the stone came in from Taishu. As a pirate, Li Ton had been drawn in; as a soldier, he despised the complacency and felt small pity for the ruin that it was.

Over the ridge of the river valley, and here was where the army camp had ringed the city, where the doctor and the girl and himself had all found one another. All through Han, who was stranded now, with his dragon for company. If the dragon hadn't eaten him already, or carried him off. Li Ton hadn't forgotten Han; he still hoped the boy might make a useful piece in this game, for later play. He was another reason to hold on to the fisherman.

The camp was empty now, abandoned, a mess of poles and fabric flapping in the breeze, cold firepits and foul latrines and rotting heaps of trash. A city of flies and rats, that had so recently been a busy city of men encircling a city of the dead.

"Where are they all?" Tien murmured.

Dead, but he didn't say so.

"Let's find out," he said instead, and led the way down into the tangle of lanes and broader ways that made the city proper.

THEY WEREN'T all dead, of course. Tunghai Wang could never have built or assembled enough boats to take his entire army, in the short time he'd had. He must have meant to ferry back and forth.

Perhaps he did still mean to. Certainly there were men still busy on every beach, building another fleet. Perhaps there were even the soldiers to man it, or would be by next year, when it might be ready. Some of those squads on the road had raw recruits with them, who must be local conscripts. As local as they could be, when Tunghai Wang had ordered the slaughter of every man and boy in Santung . . .

The city itself had a population again, but never a natural one. There were men, soldiers, everywhere: doing nothing, as soldiers will, only idling in gangs at street corners, tossing coins and knives and words around as though none of them mattered, as though nothing ever could.

And there were women: the soldiers' own and the city's survivors, those who had lacked the sense or the luck to flee. They were busy, busy, always in a hurry, if only to be out from under the eyes of the men. They scurried from door to door, traded briskly in murmurs, vanished into shadow. Or they went slowly, strug-

gling under burdens—a sack of charcoal, a rope of kindling—to
show how weak the hungry are. Or how desperate, some of them,
who crept out to beg from the soldiers, knowing already what that
would cost them.

Men, women, everyone watched the sky in glimpses, all the
time. Down at the docks or the beaches, Li Ton guessed everyone
would be watching the water too. Not going too close, not willingly taking a punt across the harbor.

The same must be true too on the other side of the strait; he
wondered how Taishu would feed itself when no one dared take a
boat out to fish. Freeing the dragon might have saved the island
and doomed it, both at once. Which meant, of course, saving the
emperor and dooming him too. Not that the boy would starve, but
he would truly be an emperor without an empire. Let him style
himself as he chose, it was over; Tunghai Wang could forget him
and go home. So could Li Ton.

If he had a home to go to. If he was allowed to leave. The generalissimo didn't worry him unduly, but he needed to get that far.

He'd have asked for directions or escort at the gate, but there
was none: no gate and no guard on the road, no apparent watch.
That wasn't Tunghai's discipline, that was the heedlessness of a
broken force, men whose officers cared no more than they did.

Officers whose men were let rabble in alleys or linger on street
corners, coldly eyeing every passer-by who was not one of themselves. And here came Li Ton with the fisherman in his train and
the doctor too, and of course Tien. Of course they attracted stares
and interest. He had hoped to do no more than that, but he hadn't
anticipated the slack despair that overhung the city. He'd left an
army in good heart under a strict master; what he'd come back to
was—well, not that. Not an army at all, by any definition he was
used to. Just too many soldiers, in fear of something they couldn't
fight. Wanting something they couldn't express, something else,
not this.

And here came people who didn't belong among them, and

none of the men was young, and the girl was pretty; why in the world would they not call out, not follow? When they had nothing else to do, when there was nothing in the world to prevent them, when there was a dragon in the strait and everything else was just waiting?

"OHÉ. FREEBOOTER."

Did he look so much like a pirate, that they could read that at a glance? Was it burned into his bones now?

Maybe it was in his walk, a seaman come ashore. What did they know of the sea, these men who had walked ten thousand dry and dusty miles to reach it? It blocked them from journey's end, the battle they had come for; it spewed dragons, and ate their fellows. That was all they'd had the chance to learn. Maybe they thought all sailors were pirates.

Maybe they were right.

Freebooter was an insult none the less. Li Ton didn't care, except that it meant they hadn't recognized his face: hadn't tagged him as one who knew the generalissimo, an important man, not to be mocked. He wouldn't care about that either, mockery could hurt him nowhere that mattered; but if they didn't know him, there was small chance they would help him to Tunghai Wang.

Even so, he turned around at the call. There were five of them: peeling themselves away from the wall now, spreading out as they came toward him. Li Ton's own companions pressed more closely together at his back. That said it all: confidence on the one side, fear on the other.

Rightly so, on both sides. Old men and girls should fear such as these, who had every reason, every reason in the world to be utterly confident, to swagger as they walked, to press forward as though a crowd parted before them.

Every reason but one, perhaps. Even now, trying to be impressive, they couldn't help watching the sky. They had their own fear, these men, but that only made them more dangerous.

It would be deadly to run, which was why Li Ton had stopped. It would be deadly also to wait, to let them set the rules; which was why he stopped them with a question.

"Where can I find Tunghai Wang? Can you conduct me there?"

A moment's stillness, a sudden bark of laughter, and, "Perhaps. What, do you have a ship to bring him, pirate? He would be glad of that, he would welcome you for that. He has lost all his own."

They had found drink somewhere, these men. They were not quite drunk, not yet; but still, they had been drinking. Enough to loosen words on their tongues, to slacken discipline, to make them more dangerous still.

He said, "I have a boat under my command, yes. And have served him before, and he will be looking for me to do so again. Indeed, he will be waiting to hear from me now. Where in the city—?"

"Ah, there's no hurry, captain. Captain pirate. He's good at waiting, the generalissimo. It's all he has to do now, with his men so very dead. Did you see them, from your ship? All the dead men? Some of them come to shore, you know. Those the dragon didn't eat. They come floating in on the surf, and we get to pick them up and try to guess who they were before the little things started to eat them. Will you sell us your girl, pirate captain, sir?"

"No," he said calmly, keeping his voice easy and his hands a long way from his weapons. "No, I won't do that. Will you take me to the generalissimo? He knows me well, and will be grateful if you do."

And will be angry if you don't, if you delay, if you cause me trouble. He still had hopes that they would understand that and be appropriate, but those hopes were ice in sunlight, chill and slippery and vanishing.

"Give us the girl, then. She is our price." The spokesman said that proudly, almost, a herald before the court. Dictating terms, looking for surrender.

"No, then."

He bowed and turned, and made to usher the others down the street, *walk, don't run, but walk swiftly;* and heard the scrape of steel leaving a sheath, heard a low grunt, found his own sword already in his hand as he kept on turning, all the way around to face them again.

Walk, don't run. Walk swiftly. He set the pace by walking backward, as swiftly as a man may. They came at him, all five of these men, blades in their hands and a grimness born of this city and their own desperation. Their own captains, their own general couldn't halt them now.

Li Ton had seen this before, in men either terrified or frenzied, after bloody battles either lost or won. Each time he'd stopped it with swift deaths and slow executions, first to stall and then to crush the spirit that drove it, before it could infect the entire army.

Each time before, he'd had squads of men at his back, if not a regiment. And the emperor's authority, that too. Here he was one man alone, and he thought the entire army was likely infected already.

He cursed Tunghai Wang silently for letting his soldiers come to this, sordid fighting in a ruined city. Aloud, he cried, "My name is General Chu Lin," just in case it was still remembered.

One laughed, one spat. Not one of them hesitated. They really did mean this.

Pity: he would have liked to see how matters fell out, with Han and the dragon. He would have liked to see the end of the emperor too, this boy whose father had ruined him: the boy's head on a pole, yes, he had worked for that a little and would have liked to see it. Even if it meant Tunghai Wang on the Jade Throne. It wouldn't last, if the man couldn't hold one small army together in the face of catastrophe, but he didn't care about that.

Logically, he should simply hand over the girl. Why not? She was nothing to him. Except that Han wanted her, and that could still prove useful.

Except that if he died here, nothing that he'd hoarded could prove useful anymore.

It was too late now, to listen to that voice of sense. If he gave her over, they would shove her into a doorway for later and still come on to kill him and the other men. They had that death-look about them, fixed and slightly vacant; they reminded him of his crew, on a hundred brutal adventures.

He wouldn't have backed himself against any five of his crew, either.

One on one, yes, against any of them; that was why they followed him, why they were his crew, because no one of them would ever dare fight him alone.

Li Ton stepped back, and the men came on.

He stepped back, and the men came on.

He stepped back and stumbled, and one of them rushed him.

And died noisily, messily skewered on Li Ton's tao as he came rising up from one knee. He had gone down explicitly to draw one to him, because they did so much remind him of his crew: mean, yes, and vicious with it, killers to the core but really not too smart.

Four to one. If those four had all rushed him, right then, he might perhaps have killed another but would certainly have died himself.

They hesitated, though, glanced from one to another—and he rushed them.

Rushed one of them, at least. The way they'd spread themselves out across the street, the others were too slow again. He had time to reach the startled soldier and bully through his hasty defenses, give him no time and no chance at all, leave him sprawled and bleeding and audibly choking on his own blood, not quite dead yet but surely dying.

Three to one, and it wouldn't get any easier than this. They were drawing together now, covering one another. Giving Li Ton time enough to get back to his companions, and he'd counted on that too, but it would do him little good. Or them. They were a hindrance, nothing more; he'd sacrifice any of them, all of them, to save himself.

Three to one, and those three alert now, angry now but coldly so, three ready blades glinting in sunlight and he still didn't like the odds, wouldn't back himself.

Backed away, then, with the others behind him; watched the blades and the men who held them, watched them advance; waited for the rush that must be coming.

WHEN IT came, it was behind those three.

A whole other group of men, who must have heard the clash of steel and come running; they boiled out of an alley-mouth and saw the bodies in the road, saw their comrades, saw how one man faced them down. Tried to face them down, at least, with blood on his tao.

Saw the girl too, perhaps.

And understood the fight, entirely what kind of fight this was; and came joyfully running down the road to join in.

Nine to one.

No chance. Li Ton wasn't sure how much the original three welcomed this new company, but for sure they wouldn't fight among themselves. Not until he was dead, at least, and the other men with him, and the girl available for fighting over.

He gave one desperate glance up into the sky, in hopes of making them pause one moment longer, for fear of a dragon; at the same time, he made a sign behind his back, which any of his pirate crew would have understood immediately.

These people? A fisherman, a doctor and a girl?

Nothing.

He had to turn his head to scowl at them, to shout "Run!"

At nine to one, it couldn't make things worse than they were already. If it only bought a minute, well, who knew? Maybe the dragon might really come.

No dragon.

What came instead was a rush of feet and a curdling cry, that guttural noise that men make to urge themselves on, not to hold back under the eyes of their brothers.

Li Ton sighed, and turned again. Perhaps he could stall the rush a little, buy time for the civilians to get a little ahead, if all nine of those blades were greedy enough for a fight . . .

Not even that: the gods he failed to believe in wouldn't grant him even that much grace, to do a good thing before everyone in his story died.

Some of the men came at him, and there were screams and hurtling blades and he was screaming too as he blocked them and battered back, screaming with a mix of battle-rage and fury. If they had sides at all, they were on the same side, these men and he. He was just as keen to see the emperor dead, and he was just as afraid of the dragon. He had come to Santung to help, perhaps. And they would kill him now because he had a girl with him and they wanted her. She had traveled with them for months, helping her uncle the doctor, but apparently that didn't matter now, or it simply wasn't remembered.

Men were running past him as he fought, chasing those behind. This was a fight, but that would be a slaughter.

War broke old bonds, but tended to forge new ones. Under the dragon's shadow, he supposed, all bonds shriveled to nothing.

Stamp, block, swing. Scream. What else to do?

Kill this man with a backhand slash that takes his throat out. Barely fetch it back in time to block that thrust; there would have been sparks, perhaps, if his tao hadn't been so gory-wet already. There was blood running down the handle, making it hard to grip, even between sharkskin and calluses . . .

He gripped it two-handed, clenched his fists tighter than he liked, swung and hacked in a frenzy—and then turned and sprinted after his companions, because there might just be something after all that he could do.

IF IT wasn't too late already. They'd made it farther than he'd expected, to the steps of a temple, but no god was stepping down to help them; and that was the doctor that lay sprawled and broken on the steps there, while his niece and the fisherman stood above him with knives in their hands, trying to hold four soldiers at bay.

Four soldiers who were laughing at them, teasing them with little thrusts that never quite followed through.

The doctor wasn't dead yet, but he would be soon enough. Li Ton could see how much of his blood had spilled out over the white steps.

One of the soldiers was too slow to hear Li Ton coming. The tao took him in the side, cut him half and half, bought Li Ton time enough to scoop his free arm under the doctor's shoulder and drag him higher.

The doctor screamed, thin and breathless. There was more blood, coming from his belly.

The soldiers gathered in a group, at the foot of the steps. No temple sanctity, no god's anger was going to hold them back.

Li Ton tried to lift the doctor bodily, but the man flailed and fell back boneless, his mouth guttering air as his belly gouted blood. Not dead, not quite, but he couldn't live.

Living, he couldn't save them if he couldn't stand.

Li Ton made his choice, and swung his tao.

AND CAUGHT the head by the hair, even as Tien shrieked beside him; and held it up high in one hand and bellowed, "What, does none of you know this man? Does no one recognize the doctor who kept you all healthy on the long march, all this way?"

There was a stillness, a shock that gripped them all, that gave them pause enough to look.

One man grunted; another said, "Aye, that's him. That's the doctor. He mended my arm, when it was broke so bad . . ."

"It is," Li Ton confirmed, "it's the generalissimo's own medic who never scorned to treat any of you or your women, anyone who came. He might have taught us how to resist the dragon. His niece here knows his secrets; she owns his tent and his medicines now. I don't know if she will consent to stay. Perhaps you should pray that she will, unless you prefer to pray to the dragon."

He gave them a moment, during which none offered to come up the steps and kill him; then he went on, "If one of you will run to Tunghai Wang and tell him that I am here, Chu Lin who was general under the last emperor and a friend to Tunghai on the battlefield and in the court, that man, I may ask the generalissimo to spare that man's head. That one man. Go."

Another frozen moment, where they were so hot and frantic in their thinking that they couldn't move at all; and then, inevitably, they all turned and ran together, racing one another. It might even come to blades between them. Li Ton didn't care. He turned his back and marched up the last of the steps to the temple door and found a priestess waiting for him, waiting to welcome them all inside.

AND REALIZED that he was still carrying the doctor's head, and that the girl was staring at him, at it, at him again as though she could barely tell the difference, they were both so dreadful.

She did, somehow, manage to speak; she said what was most obvious, "You, you killed him . . ."

Li Ton shook his own head wearily, even as he dropped the other. "No, girl. He was dead already. I used that, to save you."

Which wasn't entirely true, but close enough. He didn't imagine that any of them was actually saved, was safe; there was no bar on the temple door, and the building had clearly been ransacked once at least already. The men had run off at his word, but they could always think better of it and come back, slaughter everyone here, rather than face the generalissimo with their confession. He would.

Wherever he looked, there were nuns at work in the temple: scrubbing, painting, scraping at charred pillars until they were whittled back to clean bright wood. Men were hard to find, he supposed, but they seemed to be doing well enough without. They worked to the accompanying drone of a prayer, lofted by incense and intercut with strokes on a gong; even that voice was an octave too high for any priest.

If the soldiers did come back, they could enjoy their slaughter. Here were victims enough, and no one to stop them. Li Ton was done. Not tired, but weary to the bone; he'd done enough, too much, and nothing worked. He never came close to anything that he could value. Even his revenge would be a cheat if he took it now, acted out against the wrong emperor.

Which would not stop him if the chance arose, but the taste of it was sour in his mouth already, in anticipation.

The public area of the temple was a wooden gallery around a central courtyard. There were idols of many gods scattered through the gallery, but one great statue sat apart, facing the courtyard with the chanting nun at her feet, wreathed in smoke. He didn't recognize the goddess. He could ask the fisherman, if that man hadn't gone ahead to drop to his knees and burn joss before the statue.

He could ask the shaven-headed woman at his side, who had offered that unequivocal welcome at the door, who had not blanched even at the head that he had carried within. More usefully he could ask her to take care of Tien, who had no apparent idea what to do with herself: who stood deliberately alone, separate from himself, and stared down at where her uncle's head had rolled half into a corner, where it lay in the shadows staring out.

Li Ton was the last person who should talk to her, the last she would allow. Leave her to the nuns; he shouldn't need to ask.

He stepped down into the courtyard, thinking that perhaps he might light a stick or two of joss himself, he might kneel beside the fisherman he cared so little about in order to thank this goddess he didn't know for the protection he did not believe that she had offered him—

—AND HIS way took him past another nun who was cradling a child in her lap. It looked sickly, or at least as though it had been sick; but it opened its eyes as he passed and spoke, spoke to him, in no voice that any child should ever own.

"Speak to the fisherman," it said, and that voice—oh, that voice!—was all rocks and tidal suck, tongued with those weeds that drag pirates all down to a dreadful death in the sea they're all afraid of, "be sure that he tells the dragon, she is not welcome in my waters."

four

"hien Hua?"

"Mei Feng." He always knew she was serious when she used his name. Whether his solemn response was a sign that he took her just as seriously, or whether he was only teasing—that, she wasn't always certain of.

"Do you think you could—well, not grin quite so broadly when you see Yu Shan with Siew Ren, or with Jiao?"

"Or with both," he said, and he was grinning in the darkness, she could hear it in his voice. She wanted to thump him.

He was emperor of the world, and she did thump him.

"Ow," he said, quite unconvincingly. And then, "Why should I not grin? I think it's funny. I think it was you who taught me how funny it was. I know it was you who almost swallowed her tongue from trying not to laugh, the day Siew Ren showed up."

"Yes, lord—but time passes, moods change, and I don't think it's funny anymore."

"I do," he said stubbornly. And, "Time passes, moods change, people come to an accommodation. It's only funny because they keep resisting. How many women did my father keep? And Yu Shan stumbles over two, and cannot make them happy . . ."

Mei Feng wasn't prepared to guess how many of his father's women had actually been happy. She saw no need to pierce his smug self-content, so long as he remained content to keep just the one woman himself. When that changed—well. She hoped to deal with it better than her friends were.

"He doesn't know how," she said, still struggling to introduce him to the idea that not everyone saw the world from the peculiar perspective of a dynastic throne. "None of them was expecting this. Yu Shan's torn down the middle, Siew Ren is still angry, and Jiao—"

Jiao was the one who worried her most: because she was twice their age, and seemed to hurt twice as much because of that. And she had perhaps been hurt twice over, though she'd never admit it. She was the only one of them not to have seen the jade tiger. Of course she saw that as an omen. They all did. Only, Jiao saw it as an omen against herself. Yu Shan had been alone with Siew Ren when they saw it: how could that not be significant?

Mei Feng had been alone with the emperor when they saw it, but she didn't think its significance had anything to do with them.

Well. There was nothing she could do just now about Jiao, except try to stop the emperor's mocking. He didn't see the harm, but it was one of his charms that he would listen so carefully and let her teach him. She was his tutor in the world, as he was hers in the palace.

And it wasn't all lessons, explanations, worry. Sometimes they could just be quiet together. Or the other thing. He seemed to be thoroughly awake now; she thought they might be very noisy together, soon enough.

She did have another question for him, but later. Over breakfast, perhaps. He wasn't a greedy boy—at least, as boys go, or emperors—but he did tend to linger over his breakfast.

"Lord?"

"Mei Feng. What have I done wrong now?"

"Nothing, lord," with a swift reminiscent smile, "nothing at all. Except that I think you should eat more congee, and not so many eggs."

"I like eggs. And I am emperor."

"Yes, lord, and your farts are most imperial. But the ducks are not laying often at the moment, or else we are not finding them; and other people also like eggs, although they are not emperor. Also, congee is good for you."

He smiled at her, in that sated way that suggested he might like to be sated again later, not too much later, if the opportunity arose. Ping Wen was waiting for them at the Autumn Palace site, and really, they ought to go today; but let someone else tell him that, or else she could tell him later. Not too much later, but just not immediately now.

Instead, "Lord, why did you ask Guangli to come here?"

"You know why. He is my jade carver. I am here, the jade is here, he should be here also."

"Is that all?"

He frowned. "Isn't it enough?"

Not for Jiao. Not to justify sending her away, making her miss the tiger, making her lose ground so far. She needs to feel it was important that she went, more than just your whimsy . . .

"Of course, lord. Never mind. When shall we go to see General Ping Wen?"

He made a face. "Tomorrow?"

"You said that yesterday."

"I could say it again tomorrow?"

"No, lord. We need to do this. He won't go back until we've seen him. Make him wait any longer, he'll insist on coming here, and nobody wants that. I think we should go today. I'll tell people to be ready, shall I? In an hour?"

She might never have seen him look more petulant or less imperial. He could always be managed, though, if he couldn't be forced. His stubbornness was like his throne, all stone, too heavy to shift; but it stood on the softest of sand, no foundation at all— she blamed his mother, entirely—and that could be eaten away in patience, so that the whole edifice of his will would topple into the gentle stream that was hers.

ONCE PEOPLE were busy—arranging guards for the journey, sending scouts and messengers ahead so that no one would be surprised en route or on arrival—she went to find Guangli, where he had settled disconsolately into a hut.

Which he was sharing with Jiao, so no wonder he was disconsolate; but her bitter companionship was only sauce for his mood, not the root cause of it.

He felt as out of place, as uncomfortable here as Mei Feng had, her first days in the palace. She knew.

"Mei Feng, tell me. What am I doing here?"

She had found him squatting on his doorstep in watery sunshine, waiting for more rain. She valiantly resisted saying *you are avoiding work, of course, as you have done since you arrived*. Instead, she said, "The emperor wants you, and the emperor is here; and jade belongs to the emperor—"

"—and so do I, I know, but—"

"—and he means to stay out here, and there's no point shipping the stone back and forth to the city, it makes far better sense if you're here at hand."

Even she wasn't sure how much sense that made, truly. His expression was like flame on new growth, withering.

"Does it? Really? When the city is one day's travel from here, and holds a house that doesn't only offer simple amenities like dry beds and decent clothes and comfort, but also has the space and tools I need to work, and the stones I need to work on?"

"I think his majesty thought that if you were this close to the mines, new stones could be brought directly to you, or you could supervise their cutting, even, right in the mine there, and—"

"I don't think his majesty thought at all. He just had a whim, and snapped his fingers, and dragged me away to this forsaken ditch that doesn't have the courtesy even to pretend to be a mining valley. There's nothing I can do here, Mei Feng, and I want to go home."

It was another of his majesty's whims that had spared Guangli's life when that was absolutely forfeit to the law. She forbore to say so; instead, she seized on the one complaint she might be able to relieve.

"Is your hut uncomfortable?"

"The roof leaks," he said flatly, knowing this to be an evasion but following anyway because truthfully, what else could either of them do? "Jiao doesn't care, but it troubles me. And I am tired of sleeping—of not sleeping, rather—on a bed of ferns."

"His majesty sleeps on the same ferns," she said reprovingly.

"His majesty is young and magnificent, and I am neither. My bones hurt, worse in the mornings and worse yet in the wet. And I only have a journeyman's tools, which would only allow me to do a journeyman's work if I had any work to do, but I do not."

"We gave you stone! Everything we brought back from the mines . . ."

Almost everything. They had collected what they could, against a promise of payment later. Yu Shan had insisted that every man and woman from the mountains needed a little piece of jade, on their person, all the time. Crude stone, unworked, that didn't matter. They wore them as pendants mostly, against the softness of the throat.

The dust and sweepings the emperor had kept, for his meals.

All the rest of the jade had gone to Guangli, and he despised it.

"You gave me nothing. Nothing I can work with. Spoil, cracked pebbles, detritus. How am I supposed to work with pieces that come apart when I set an edge to them?" His hand made a gesture that started fierce and ended weary; his voice softened abruptly. "Not your fault, I know. You gave me what was there, what Yu Shan's people had dug. Good jade is rare, and getting rarer; but I have good pieces under guard, back in the city. Work to do, work the emperor will love. The dragon I am carving on his commission, that is not finished yet. Mei Feng, tell your lord, I want to go *home*."

Which was the one thing he could not do, of course, and neither could she. She could inveigle and manipulate and tease the emperor to his imperial heart's content, but even she dared not tell him what to do, or what he did not want to hear. They both knew it. Fetched at a whim, Guangli was here until that whim should turn against him.

Instead, Mei Feng said, "You should come with us today."

"What, where? Why?"

"To the Autumn Palace. We are going to meet with General Ping Wen," who actually would try to tell the emperor what to do, what he did not want to hear. That should be interesting. "You should come to see the site, to understand his majesty's plans. You might have ideas to contribute. We can tell the emperor that, at least," with a smile to be shared between the two of them, no farther. It came by nature now; she was learning all the arts of conspiracy, too quickly for her entire comfort. "You might rather stay there than here. The emperor wouldn't mind; it is his palace, after all. Going to be. We'll be spending more time there as the work progresses. Even now, you might think it more civilized. Less jungly. We can find you a tent that doesn't leak. And we could bring a wagonload of your things out from the city, if you wanted: stone, tools. Your own bed . . ."

For herself, she had far sooner be here in the valley compound. Small, enclosed, protected: it was like a village, where the palace site was a city even now, albeit a city of tents and men. Far too many men, packed far too close together and worked too hard: small wonder if they quarreled and fought for amusement. Even without the knowledge that any one of them could be a spy or an assassin, she could never be comfortable there. With that knowledge, she was nervous every moment, desperate to take the emperor away, and utterly unable.

Which was her remembered reason for being here: "Guangli," while he was still mulling over the suggestion, "I have a commission for you."

"You do?"

He was distrustful, thinking that she'd offer him some make-work, a trinket to be carved for herself or for her lord. Something to keep him busy and make him feel useful. Of course he was.

She nodded firmly. "We are told that one of the Lords of Heaven has an armor made of jade, yes?" She wasn't strong on mainland gods, but this was common knowledge.

"Of course. Lin Bao: it turned the serpent's tooth, when he went down into hell for his beloved."

"Yes, because he had modeled it on the serpent's scales, so it would not shatter at the strike. Guangli, is that actually possible? Could you make an armor out of jade, a scaled armor, that a man might wear?"

He shook his head instantly. "It would be impossibly heavy, he wouldn't be able to move. It needs a god to carry such a suit."

"My lord the emperor is a god."

Technically, at least, that was true; and it amused them both for her to remind him of it, now and then. More to the point, he was a man infected with jade from birth, who still ate jade-dust daily and wore stone next to his skin. He was strong past any mortal measure. And terrifyingly quick to heal, magically quick, but she still feared assassins and wanted him better protected in the world.

Guangli whistled air softly through his teeth. "The emperor . . . Yes, he could wear it. And lawfully too, the only man who could . . . Does he want it? I have heard that blades cannot cut him."

"That . . . is not true. I have seen him cut, and almost killed. *I* want this, Guangli."

"Will he wear it, though?"

"If I ask him to, and if he loves it."

Guangli's head was shaking again, more in thought than refusal. "It will be . . . cumbersome."

"No. You can make it better than that. Snakeskin is not cumbersome. The finer you make the scales, the more supple it will be."

"And the stronger, too. But you don't know what you're asking."

"Yes, I do." She was laying a challenge at his feet, something far
beyond makework. "Make my lord safe, Guangli. No one can, if
you can't. I will bring you the finest silkworkers from the city, to
make a tunic for the scales to be sewn to. Quietly, though. He is
not to know."

"No one should know, until it is ready. Until it is perfect. Interlocking scales, that will give like skin to pressure but lock against
a blow, resist a blade . . . Go away, Mei Feng, and let me work."

"Come with us, though? To the palace site?"

"Yes, yes. I must watch the emperor as he walks, see how he
moves . . ."

HE CAME like a muttering bearded demon in their midst, harmless
and eccentric, with a bag of rejected jade fragments on his belt
and a flake always in his palm, which he scraped at as he walked,
as he stared at the emperor's back and neck and arms.

"Mei Feng."

"Lord?"

"What are you grinning at?"

"Oh, nothing much, lord. Nothing at all . . ."

"I," reaching out a long arm and curling it around her neck,
"am emperor of the world," kissing the top of her head, "and you
will not lie to me. Will you?"

"Never, lord!"

"Good. What were you grinning at?"

"I was just, just wondering . . ."

"Mmm?"

"How tall you are, lord. How broad." *How much jade the
carver will need to make you a suit of clothes, and how he will
ever make it cling and move like snakeskin . . .*

"How wet, you mean," for there was a river that ran across their path and they had to wade it, and so they were all sodden from the waist down.

The waist in his case, at least, this tall unlikely northern boy of hers. On her the water had come higher, significantly higher, even though she had clung to his arm and almost floated over.

"My lord knows that his physique is magnificent, and I do like to look upon it," making a great show of doing exactly that, simply in order to make him blush. He would still do that, this great gauche awkward northern boy of hers; and now he had entirely forgotten his original complaint, and her present to him could go back to being a secret if she could keep it so, if she could trust the jade carver.

The jade carver and Jiao. No hope of keeping it secret from her, whether or not he kept within her hut.

Jiao was out there somewhere now, scouting ahead of them, not trusting the jungle any more than Mei Feng trusted the work site. Or so she said. More likely she didn't trust herself to walk peaceably in company, when Yu Shan and his clan-cousin were in the party. As they had to be, because the emperor wouldn't go anywhere without Yu Shan and Siew Ren wouldn't let Yu Shan go anywhere without her.

And then there were the emperor's bodyguards, half of them mountain folk, half soldiers from far away; they were hammering one another—quite hard, quite a lot of the time—into what seemed to be a single unit, almost a new clan. It wanted a name, perhaps.

For sure it wanted a captain, a leader, someone to take charge. Lacking that, lacking any voice of authority among them, they did more or less what they chose, individually or together. Which meant that more or less all of them were coming along, because nobody would agree to stay behind.

General Ping Wen had come to have a conversation with the emperor, and would find himself confronted by a circus.

Mei Feng was not entirely sure how that would go.

five

*T*ell me again, Chung, why you needed to be here?"

"I am the Lady Mei Feng's runner," as though that were simply and obviously something to be proud of. "Of course I must be here. What if she needed to send a message, what then? Could *you* run to the city?"

"Yes, of course. Any of us could."

Unhappily, that was probably true. They ran up and down the mountains, just for training. But, "Could you find your way around the city? Could you find anywhere at all, except the palace?"

Shen shrugged, and Chung felt a brief spur of victory. Too brief, too soon: Shen said, "Why would I need to? She never sends you anywhere except the palace."

"That's only when she's sending messages to the general; and the general's here, so . . ."

"That's my point. The general's here. What are you going to do, trot from one side of the tent to the other? He's come out here so they don't have to send each other messages. Which means she's not going to need you. So I repeat, what exactly are you here for?"

For the walk, he could say. Or *for you,* but that would only make Shen laugh the harder.

"Why," he said, "are you worried about me?"

Shen frowned and concentrated on his fingers, where they were picking a stone out of dried mud at his feet. Chung couldn't see quite what it was about that particular stone, but it was suddenly demanding a lot of Shen's attention.

"Yes," Shen said distractedly, "yes, I am. Mei Feng worries about the emperor every time she brings him here. No surprise, after what happened before. There are so many people: who knows where they all came from, and what they all want? And if she's right to worry about his majesty, then of course I have to worry about you. You don't need rebels and assassins to talk yourself into trouble, you can do it with any old random soldier. I've seen you, kitchen boy. Remember?"

"That was you."

"That's my *point*. You get into trouble and you can't defend yourself. Despite everything I've tried to teach you . . ."

Actually he could, against anyone but Shen, but this wasn't the time to argue it. Nor the place to prove it. He just smiled and said, "Well then, I'd better stay close to you, hadn't I? Let you defend me, when I talk myself into trouble. Maybe I'll do it deliberately, just to watch."

Now that he'd dug it loose with his fingernails, Shen seemed not to know what he'd wanted the pebble for. He tossed it in his hand, looked to toss it away, changed his mind and wrapped his fist around it.

Probably as well, not to fling it casually aside as he might have done in the valley camp. Here were people all over, who were almost sure not to appreciate having a stone flung at their heads.

It might be amusing, if Chung seized the chance to step in and defend him—but Mei Feng was almost sure not to be amused. Not here, not now.

They were in the middle of the new palace site, between the hill where the palace would rise and the vast sprawl of tents and huts that made the workers' encampment. Most of the men had been soldiers before the emperor made laborers of them: his own soldiers for the most part, that army that had fled the Hidden City with him. That had kept him safe for a year, for so many miles; that had seen him across the water and installed him here as lord

of this shriveled empire; that labored now to build his proper
home, and would no doubt defend him in it when the invasion
came, if it only held off that long.

So why did Chung—yes, and Shen too—feel as though they
crouched in the camp of their enemy?

Maybe it was only Mei Feng's nervousness transferring itself to
them. She had a right to be nervous; nobody could hope to check
that every man here was reliable. Nor every woman, either. There
had been a little flurry a while back, women with trays, *yum cha*:
tea and dumplings for the emperor and the general. Why bother to
assassinate with blades and risk and rumpus, when you could do
it with quiet discreet poison and slip away before anyone was even
dead . . . ?

The emperor should have a taster, perhaps. Jiao might just be
reckless enough to do it—but who would be reckless enough to
ask her? Her mood was lethal these days, there was no talking to
her.

All the way here she'd ranged ahead, alone. Even now she
wouldn't join the others, where they stood or squatted in a watchful ring around the tent where the emperor and the general were
meeting. Mei Feng was in there with them, and so were Yu Shan
and his new girl, if that's what she was, if that's what had so upset
Jiao.

Something, at any rate, had stopped her following them inside.
Whether it was the same thing that prevented her from standing
guard with her fellows, Chung couldn't say; but she was very conspicuously keeping herself apart.

This one big tent—this palace of a tent, silk-covered board
walls and a carpeted floor, chairs and a table and Chung didn't
know what more—stood at the foot of the hill, just outside the
palisade. When the emperor and Mei Feng stayed here, they had
another, grander yet, barely any longer a tent at all, inside the palisade. Apparently General Ping Wen was not entitled to presume

that far, or else he had chosen to display this little modesty, a hesitation before the gates of greatness.

He had at least found himself a little distance from the common splay, the rough accommodations of the men. Some had actual tents, or at least a share of a tent; some had rude improvisations, a length of greased fabric and a couple of poles. Some, many, did the best they could with less than that, branches and dried reeds.

There were paths all through the encampment, beaten by many feet many times over, giving it a semblance of order. Here men slept, here they washed, here they ate together. Here were the yards where wagons came, all day and every day, to offload what they brought: ropes and timber and iron, stone and sand, oil and charcoal and rice. Here were the smithies, making tools and pegs and nails, chains and hinges. Here was the path, almost a road, that led the men from yards to smithies to the palisade with everything they needed for their work within.

Within was not so different, except that the worn paths made a map around ditches and terraces, land cleared to build on. Out here the paths were the only clear spaces; they took their winding ways between chaos and confusion, too many men pressed too close, their dry clothes and precious few things stored in their cooking pots and woe betide any other man who came to steal them. There was always someone offsite, resting or injured or sick, and so free to watch over his things and his neighbors'. And there were always thefts despite that, and other quarrels besides, and so the emotional ground among the men was as crowded and messy and insecure as the ground beneath their feet, with very few paths that were clear and safe to walk on.

Nevertheless. The men did bind together, as men will, in cliques and clubs and gangs; and Jiao was out there mixing with them, crouching in a circle rolling bones.

She couldn't talk to her own people, apparently, but she could

roar and point and jabber, laugh and roll with strangers, chew
something unsavory and spit between her legs.

Jiao was in full land-pirate guise, dress and manner too: the tao
on one hip conspicuously balanced by the heavy knife on the
other, both blades flaunted here where the workers were forbidden
them. She swaggered, she cursed, she turned a shrugging shoulder
on those she had come in with; she muttered something that made
all the men in hearing choke on illicit laughter, that they struggled
manfully, failingly, to suppress. Some coarseness, then: some com-
ment about the emperor, perhaps, that could see a man's head
struck from his shoulders if he made it, if he was overheard. Or
else about the general his majesty had come to see. A man who
was not quite master could be doubly sensitive of his honor . . .

Chung wasn't comfortable here, with any of this. Those men
that Jiao was raucous with: conscripted once into the emperor's
flight, fighting their way all across the empire and losing all the
way, crowded at last onto this one small island with nowhere else
to run; conscripted again into this, building a luxury palace for an
idle boy while starvation threatened on one hand, war on the other
and a dragon overhead; they had no reason to be loyal, except to
save their own skins for one more day of labor. The mainland had
already risen in rebellion, and Chung wasn't the only one who
feared that the same might happen on Taishu.

If it was fear that kept the men obedient, then it was Ping Wen
they feared; the emperor himself was too remote. Certainly
Chung was afraid of him. He didn't suppose for a moment that
the general would remember either him or Shen, or care a whit if
he did remember; and certainly no one, not even he could touch
them while they stood in the emperor's protection; and even so,
Chung was afraid. He hadn't even seen the general today, and he
was afraid.

The general's personal guard ringed the tent, just as the emperor's did; they interspersed each other, more or less. And didn't

talk. It was why Chung's comrades stood so unnaturally still, or squatted so watchfully on their heels, hands on hilts; it was why he and Shen talked in such soft murmurs, why Shen was actually so anxious about Chung's being here at all.

Jiao was playing at bones with the soldiers who worked here, and it felt as though she were tossing chances with an enemy in overwhelming numbers, who might turn on her and all of them at any moment.

The emperor was in discussion with his closest and most trusted general, while their own people kept watch outside. It should be the easiest, the most comfortable embassage for both sides, all friends together; and yet, and yet. It seemed more like ne-gotiations for a truce, when neither side trusted the other for a mo-ment.

Maybe life in the valley was breeding paranoia and a taste for isolation? Certainly Chung wanted to be back there, himself and Shen, all their new-adopted clan and their charge the emperor too.

In the meantime, he was desperate for something to happen, to break the tension, to remind them somehow that they were meant to be better than allies: friends indeed, all one people under one throne.

And then the dragon came, and he could almost believe that he had made that happen, just by wishing it.

SHE CAME over the mountains, high and sudden, abruptly there: a discontinuity, a break, a line like a worm in the sky, alive and deep-ening, stretching.

Diving, coming down.

SHE FLEW without wings, writhing through the air; but he thought the sun darkened as though she did indeed have wings, as though she spread the wings of her will all across the sky.

He reached blindly for Shen and blessedly found him, so that they could lean into each other as they rose to meet this on their feet. They didn't kneel even to the emperor, unless he asked it of them; they should not cower before a dragon, who had less right to their lives than he did.

Less right but more power, simply to take them if she chose.

Others were not so proud, around them. Even some of the guards were screaming or cowering or scuttling away. As though running from the big red tent could save them. Chung thought that if she wanted to eat everyone here, she would do that, however swiftly or crouchingly they ran.

Nothing they could do down here would prevent her. He and Shen stood, hand in hand, and watched her come.

There was noise all through the camp. The tent doors flung back, and figures came striding out: the general, yes, and the emperor.

The emperor flanked by Mei Feng, by Yu Shan, both of them pressing close: far closer than custom or court manners could allow, but for once no one was watching. They came out, they looked around, they saw how everyone not running stood transfixed and staring upward; they glanced upward; they stood transfixed.

She came swooping low over the hill, and Chung thought she would strike like a sea-eagle above a silver glinting swirl of fish: slam down with taloned feet extended, snatch and seize and thrust into the sky again.

But in that last moment before she must come down, her head lifted and she rose like smoke on a windless day, coiling and twisting in the air. Chung thought she was dancing, but only because he had no other word for it. It seemed utterly personal, inward, a private expression of herself.

He thought perhaps she did it only because she could, after a long age of the other thing, when she could not.

A rough voice cut their silence, as it cut the screams that still tore through the camp: "Quickly, then. Away from the tent," that big bright attractor that must stand out in a sky-view like the sun reflected in a pond. "And take that *off*, have you no sense at all?"

And here was Jiao, whose voice it was, hurtling away from her bone-rolling companions, who were either cowering or fleeing, according to their tempers. She came straight to the emperor, ripped the yellow tunic from his shoulders and hurled it back inside the tent.

Left him his trousers, blessedly, but they had been scarlet once; faded and mud-splashed and soaked, they were nothing anymore, nothing to draw even a dragon's eye.

Presumably.

"There," she said, her hands spread against imperial skin and pushing, "sit there," where she'd sat before, where there had been a circle of men before they'd all run away. "Mei Feng, you with him, of course," because she wouldn't be anywhere else. "And you," snapping her fingers, wanting Shen, "or, no, both of you," Chung too, then, "you're no good alone. Sit with him, look ordinary. I want more, too: you and you. Make a crowd around him . . ."

"Jiao," the emperor said, quite mildly, "she's a dragon. If she wants me, I think she can probably sniff me out, don't you?"

"Perhaps," frowning, dealing with it, "but if she does, it'll be the jade she smells. Won't it? Just being emperor doesn't give you a different perfume from the rest of us."

Which was probably heresy, because the emperor was of course a god; but they had lived with him in the valley, some had fought with him, seen him sweat and bleed. Mei Feng said he farted . . .

Right now she said, "We could smear him with ashes, from the fire there?"

"If you like, but I doubt it would help. This isn't a jungle hunt. But whatever it is, Yu Shan will smell as strong to her, stronger, if it comes to sniffing." She turned to him, her orders as impersonal as they had been to the emperor: "Go, run. That way, away from here. Get into the trees if you can."

"I'm going with him." That was Siew Ren, of course.

Magnificently, Jiao just shrugged. "If you can keep up. So am I."

There was nothing more to do or say, apparently, except to snap at the general: "Take your own men about you, try to look no different and go that way," a nod of her head into the camp. "Look like you're running, like everyone else. In fact, run."

One last glance up at the still-rising dragon, and she turned to do the same. It was Shen—from where he sat, obediently next to the emperor, where he had pulled Chung down beside him—who called after her, "Jiao . . . ?"

"Yes, what?"

"What do we, um, *do*? If she, you know. If she comes down?"

She's a dragon, he was saying, *how do we fight a dragon?*

Jiao almost smiled for a moment. "No idea," she said. "Just— oh, do *something,* yes? Throw stones at her. Something . . ."

And then she turned and ran light-footed after Yu Shan, who was keeping steady pace with his clan-cousin when he could certainly have outsprinted her if he'd wanted to.

Chung looked at Shen; Shen gulped a little, and turned to the emperor.

"Um, if we have to throw stones, majesty, your arm's the strongest . . ."

"Which would only give away who he was," Mei Feng pointed out. "I think she'd notice, if he was standing down here hurling pebbles at her."

"If she's close enough to reach with a pebble," the emperor said calmly, "I think she'll be close enough to know who I am anyway. And if I'm who she wants," he added almost casually, "do you think I'm just going to sit here and try to hide, while she tears everyone else apart looking for me?"

"*Yes,*" in a fierce whisper from Mei Feng, "yes, you are!" And her small hands wrapped themselves around his arm, as if she could hold him still and quiet by simple determination, because for sure she had no other way to do it.

He just laughed, and shook his head at her; and then down the dragon came, and her grip on his arm was wholly different suddenly, a match for the way Shen leaned two-handed on Chung's shoulder, as if they were all equally breathless, all caught in that strange space between wonder and terror.

She came down in a slow spiral, and flew similar turning patterns over their heads, over the hill and all the sprawling camp. She quartered the ground like a kite, almost, head poised and staring down; but whatever she was looking for, she seemed not to find it. At least, she didn't stoop or snatch, she never came to ground.

They sat very still in her shadow, and she passed over them and moved on, drifting where she would in the windless air, lethally intent, except that seemingly her intent was not to strike.

She looked, she quartered, perhaps she charted this new build, this imminent city in the vast dark recesses of her mind. Then her long undulant body flicked, and she left them.

Left them all unharmed, unmarked except by the passing of her shadow. Which might be a mark that lingered, a lingering kind of harm, but it would need time to say so.

For now—well, for now, no one was moving just here, until the emperor slowly opened his clenched fist, and let a sharp stone conspicuously fall from it.

Mei Feng seemed to choke on an outrage of laughter, and hugged herself against his arm, face hidden.

Shen might not have been the first of the bodyguard onto his feet, but it seemed so to Chung: standing and staring after the dragon where she'd gone, and then reaching down an imperative hand for Chung to grip, so that he was hauled up to stand beside him.

There was nowhere else to look. They stared together at the eastern horizon, where a hair-slender shadow still ripped the sky, promising a spill of tumult from some atrocious world beyond the tear. Who knew what dark ocean the stars had to swim in, or what might leak through?

"Her shortest way to the sea," the emperor said, behind them.

Maybe so, though she didn't seem to be in any hurry. They stood and watched—and the emperor moved around to stand directly beside Chung, because Mei Feng couldn't see over any of them, and she grumbled—until none of them claimed to be able to see any distant living speck of her.

SLOWLY, SLOWLY the camp came back to some kind of life around them. Men dragged themselves up out of the mud, out of the ditches where they had groveled in terror, or out of the tents and huts where they had cowered. Those who had run came back, or some of them did.

Those who had been told to run, they came back, and the one who had told them: Jiao came back, with Yu Shan and Siew Ren together. Nothing looked any easier among them.

Presumably the general would be coming back too, with his bodyguard. Chung wished he could think that a good thing.

Somewhere in the camp, a man was shrieking that the dragon was their special protector; she had destroyed the invasion fleet, and was showing herself now to her chosen people.

Chung thought he had never heard anything madder or more stupid.

But that madness at least made them look at one another. Mei Feng said to Jiao, "Has he told you, what was happening in there?"

Jiao glanced at Yu Shan and said, "No." *Of course not,* her body said. "He hasn't told me anything. What?"

"Ping Wen wants to go to war with the rebels. On the mainland. And I think my lord the emperor," *my lord the idiot,* she seemed to be saying, "is planning to say yes."

"Of course I am," he said, mildly enough, but with that mild implacability of stone that need do nothing, that only has to sit there in the certainty of its decision while lesser forces break themselves against it. She glowered up at him—smaller by any measure, lesser by definition, stormy and unreconciled—and Chung felt a shiver like the first hint of an earthquake, that time when the sea had slipped wrongly out of harbor against its own tide and all the hairs on his arms had stood erect, just before the ground tore itself open all through the city.

*O*h, and are you too speaking for the goddess now, is that her voice you are using?"

"*No,*" Tien said with a shudder. "No, it is not. I speak for myself. But I want you to go. I think you should go. I think you have to go, when she tells you to. This is her house, and those are her waters . . ."

It was a strange reversal, but Old Yen did not want to go to sea.

Not even to escape this hissing confrontation, Tien and the pirate Li Ton snarling at each other right here in the temple courtyard, which was twice profane: once for the fight itself in a holy place, and once again for what they were fighting over, whether or not they should obey the goddess.

It really wasn't a question, as far as Old Yen understood it. Certainly it should not be a question here. In her house, as Tien said.

And yet, Old Yen stayed silent, and caught himself hopeful that the pirate would win the fight. He had served the goddess all his life, she was his second nature, the spirit that underlay his thoughts as much as she underlay the waters that he sailed; and yet he was afraid of her now, shudderingly reluctant, wanting not to be here.

And not to go to sea.

His goddess had always been private with him. Never secret— all the world knew him to be her devotee—but never ostentatious: he could talk as much as he liked about how she helped him find his way in fog or lifted him over a mud bank, and all that other people ever saw was good seamanship and local knowledge, never her hand at all.

He was accustomed to that and liked it, rather. Not for the praise it brought him, which he would shrug off discontentedly when it was offered, a coat that fitted ill; but for the sense of intimacy it left him with. What would she care, if no one recognized her touch? He knew it when it came.

Now she was speaking to him directly, and to others too. She borrowed the mouths of muted children but put her own voice within them, and it was nothing, *nothing* that he recognized. Or wanted to know, or to listen to.

He had excuses, one prime excuse, the dragon: she had allowed him to sail from the Forge to the mainland, but there was no reason to suppose she would allow him to sail back. There was every reason—wreckage on the water, bodies coming bloated to the shore—to imagine that she would not.

In truth, though, he was just a man who had heard at last the true voice of his goddess, and was appalled. And afraid. And wanted to be nowhere near her.

It would, of course, never be his choice whether he sailed or not.

He was beginning to think that it wouldn't be Li Ton's either.

The pirate was still trying to deny that.

"She didn't tell me to go," he said, blustering. "She said to tell the fisherman what he is to say to the dragon. Well, I have done that. When he is free to sail as he chooses, no doubt he will do as she says. At this time, he sails for me, where I choose. I see no profit in going back to the Forge, and no purpose in it. We will not go."

"You're afraid."

Of course he was afraid, they were all afraid; of course he could not confess it. "The command is mine, you little fool; that is what

matters here. Do you still not understand that? Have I not *shown*
you . . . ?"

He had not changed his clothes; he still wore the spatters of her
uncle's blood. Deliberately, Old Yen thought.

Her head came up, pride in sorrow; she would not be cowed.
Not in here, in sight of the goddess, where she was oddly certain
of her ground and Old Yen was oddly so very much not.

"That wasn't command," she said bluntly, truthfully. "That was
desperation. You needed my, my, my uncle," *my uncle's head,* but
apparently she couldn't quite say that, "to save yourself. Perhaps
you needed me too; you promised me to them. If I was under your
command before, *if* I was," meaning that she had never thought
so, "I am not now. Perhaps I will stay, and do what I can with my
uncle's medicines, with his teaching and his books; if I do, that
will be my choice. I still have a choice. You don't. You and he," a
gesture of her chin toward Old Yen, "you're under another command. She *spoke* to you—and what, you want to just ignore her?"

"I've seen fortune-tellers and their tricks before," the pirate said
unconvincingly, unconvinced.

"Do you think she'll let you sail anywhere else? On her strait,
with her message undelivered?"

"There is a world beyond the strait, girl."

"I know that. But can you reach it?"

In Old Yen's bastard boat, to sail against the will of the goddess? The dragon might bring storms, but tide and current were in
her hands, under her control. He half thought that the boat itself
would work against him. That was fancy, of course. But whether
it was the boat or the water or the goddess herself rearing up like
some sea-made monstrosity—now that he had heard her voice, all
salt and weeds and the grindings of rock in water, he could not see
her body except the same way, made of the water at its darkest—
something he was sure would stop them if he steered anywhere except toward the Forge.

The pirate snarled, which was answer enough to say that he agreed. Then, "Well, say we go. Say we deliver her message, what then? Do you think I will bring your boy back to you?"

Old Yen was still astonished that Tien wasn't looking to come herself, to be taken back to her boy. She shook her head, though. "Han will do as he chooses."

"Really? I think the two of you are on different sides, girl. I think he will do as the dragon chooses."

Old Yen thought so too. If the girl believed him, she did not seem broken by the news. Oddly tough she seemed as she drew herself up, as she almost faced him down, that stone-hard pirate three or four times her age and nastier than she could ever hope to be.

As she said, "He will come to me when he is ready, whether you bring him or not. And when he does, I will be ready for him. Whether the dragon comes with him or not."

It was magnificent, and it should perhaps have been the end of things, defeat for the pirate, capitulation. Something had happened here, more than the brutality of loss: something had turned inside her, turned or changed, transmuted. Perhaps it was the courage of community, being here in a house of women, under the eye of the goddess; perhaps she thought she was untouchable, with the strength to make her own choices.

Perhaps she was right.

HE WAITED for the pirate's word, and heard another voice instead.

Not the goddess again, no. The voice might carry her authority, but in a simple human sound: that nun who had met them at the temple door, who was not apparently a common nun at all but high priestess of this place.

Who had that dreadful child in her arms, mutilated and silent and full of dark promise, that voice just a stolen throat away.

She said, "You will be sailing, then? Where the goddess wills it?"

The pirate only glowered at her; it was Old Yen who had to say, "I think we will, mistress, yes." If the goddess's will could overcome the dragon's. Which had to be an article of faith with him, or he would never have the courage to put to sea.

She smiled and nodded, as though it were an accepted fact. "I think you should take this boy with you. He and his mother . . . only harm each other, the longer they keep together. She cannot forget what she did to him, she cannot live with it, and neither can he. In another place, there is no reason why he should not thrive; here he never will."

Old Yen looked immediately, without thought, to the girl Tien. She was a doctor, was she not? Or at least she had a doctor's knowledge, albeit much of it in books, as yet unlearned. And the child was clearly unwell, so where else, where better should he go?

But she was backing away, shaking her head, raising her hands in refusal. Besides, it was himself to whom the nun was offering the child.

If Old Yen took it away from here, perhaps the goddess would not use it again. Thus far, she had only used children in her temples.

If it could be taught or induced to speak, perhaps she would not use it; she had only used mutes. Thus far.

Old Yen did not want the child at all, in any way. If it had been a normal healthy boy, he would not have wanted it. A eunuch, cut by its own mother? No, and twice no. A mouthpiece for the goddess, for such an appalling voice? No, never . . .

And yet this seemed as inevitable as the other, that he and the pirate would sail again for the Forge; and no, Old Yen really, really did not want to go to sea.

THERE WAS a knocking then, thunderous on the door, and voices calling. The priestess rolled her eyes.

"It's not even latched," she said, as though this were some simple domestic house. "Those will be soldiers. They need to make a noise now, every time they come, to show how delicate and respectful they are of us."

And she thrust the child casually into Old Yen's arms, as though this were some simple domestic arrangement, and went striding to the high wood of the door.

SOLDIERS IT was, a full squad of them, striding in behind an officer.

"Well," said the priestess, "have you come to offer to the goddess, or to pray? She will be grateful either way, and take your gifts and words at equal value."

Was that as barbed as it sounded? Old Yen wasn't quite sure. But he was quite glad not to be the man who had to face this woman down.

Who was looking past the priestess now, scanning the temple courtyard and its open galleries around.

Who found Old Yen—a graybeard with an infant in his arms, an overgrown infant, silent and staring: probably an idiot, then— and ignored him entirely, looked straight past him.

And found Li Ton, necessarily, the only other man in the building and looking so piratical; and said, loudly and distinctly, making believe that he addressed the priestess when so clearly he did not, "Sister, I am here on commission from Tunghai Wang himself, seeking the eunuch Chu Lin."

That was not, perhaps, the summons he expected or would have sought; some words carry a weight beyond their simple meaning.

Still, he was too proud to deny his status, or his former name, when he himself had sent it to the generalissimo.

"You have found him," he said, mildly enough, "though I am more often known as Li Ton these days. That would be *Captain* Li Ton. Or General Chu Lin, perhaps, if you must. Thank Tunghai Wang for me, for his swift response to my message. What says he?"

"He says," the officer replied, gesturing his men forward, "that the eunuch Chu Lin is to be stripped and manacled, and taken to await his justice. Which will be swift to come, I think, but slow to linger. He is *extremely* angry."

LI TON gave up his weapons, and then his clothes. It was Old Yen's first sight of his body, with its block tattoos and its cruel maiming: his first sight of imperial justice and its residues on anyone. He wanted to turn his head away, and would not.

Which meant that he was still staring, deliberately at Li Ton's face rather than the appalling body beneath, when the pirate looked to find him.

And shaped words that Old Yen could read across distance, used as he was to reading Mei Feng's lips in a storm: "Be sure you tell the dragon," Li Ton mouthed mockingly, "she is not welcome in these waters."

WHICH MEANT *go on your own,* clearly. Or with the boy Pao, no more company than that. Pao was good to sail the boat, but Old Yen would certainly not take him onto the Forge, to face the dragon.

The dragon might come to them, of course, in open water. If she was still in a sinking vein. And he had nothing to set against her, except . . .

He gazed down at the child, weighing heavy in his arms; and saw solemn black eyes looking back at him, and a mouth that was closed and still, no way to tell if the goddess had any hold on it at all.

seven

"Again . . . ?"

The man on the scaffold was a bloody ruin.

To a swift or inexperienced eye, at least, he would seem so. Tunghai Wang was far from inexperienced, and just now in no hurry at all. Besides, the voice was clear, although it was pulled with pain. Not ruined yet, then. Good.

"Treachery," Tunghai Wang said, "has its price. If you have never learned anything else, you should have learned that. Before now, before this."

"I was never a traitor."

"You allowed the emperor to lose face; that is a treacherous act."

"He sent me to do the impossible, at which I failed. Unsurprisingly. That is not—oh, why are we arguing about this? It's an old story often told," and even this brief telling was costing him almost more than he had to give; fresh sweat was breaking through the bloody mask. His eyes were dreadful, glaring horrors, shrunken pupils shot red all around. "How did I betray you, Tunghai? Old comrade?"

"You sent the signal to launch the fleet. Didn't you?"

"Of course. As we had arranged, and as Ping Wen instructed . . . Oh, what, do you think I was responsible for the dragon?"

"I think you knew about the dragon, Chu Lin, yes. I think you sought to make your peace with the imperium. I don't know whether they captured you or whether you meant all along to sell yourself to them; you will tell us that, perhaps. But you gave yourself over, and then you gave us over to the dragon. You lit the beacon on the Forge, summoned our fleet, and saw it destroyed."

"Why . . ." The hanging man started, but stalled suddenly: losing his words or his breath or himself, somewhere in the landscape of his pain.

"Why would you do that, when you owe the empire a long revenge? I don't know, Chu Lin. Perhaps you thought you could take the boy and make a pup of him, rule the Jade Throne yourself from his shadow. Perhaps you thought you could take the throne in your own name, once you were inside the palace. Ping Wen has thought the same things, perhaps; he stayed loyal to the emperor in hopes of influence, but could not finally find a way around his mother. So he sent to me, and we came to an agreement. Now he is trapped on that island, and—well. Perhaps he has new ideas. Perhaps he thinks of that dragon as his protection. Did you and he collude, I wonder? Destroy my fleet, to then destroy the boy and divide the empire between you . . . ?"

He tried again, twisting on his ropes within the bamboo framework. "Why would I come back?"

"To build your powers on the mainland, of course. One safe on Taishu, holding the throne; one actively recruiting men, winning allies, stealing the empire from me piece by piece."

"Then why would I come here, why would I send to you? When all the empire stands open at your back?"

"Because you are a fool, perhaps? You thought I could be manipulated twice? Half my army is lost, but only half. No doubt you would see the remainder as a place to begin."

"No, Tunghai. If I wanted to betray you, I would see the Hidden City as a place to begin. You would have neither capital nor throne, and your army would dwindle between the two. But I did not, I did *not* come here to betray you. Nor did I anticipate the dragon. I wanted to use her, yes, but against the emperor, not you . . ."

"Well. We will see." A low table at his side held a dish of bamboo splinters; Tunghai Wang's fingers sifted them slowly. A point pricked the pad of one finger; he tutted and sucked it for a moment, patting lightly at his lips. "Do you know what will be done with these . . . ? Oh yes, of course you do. As you say, *again*. We are not the first, are we? My men report you have many, many scars beneath those handsome tattoos.

"Well. We will give you more. And then perhaps you will be more forthcoming in your answers."

"You can't change the truth, Tunghai, by torturing me."

"Not change it, no. But perhaps we can, hmm, dig it out of you? I will come back later, to hear whatever you would like to tell me."

WHEN HE did come back, there was more blood and a slaughterhouse stink in the air. Happily, he was prepared for that; a wad of perfumed silk in his hand kept his breathing clear and the worst of the maleficent odors from infecting his body.

The bowl on the table was half empty. The man in the frame had patches of weave in his skin, where those long splinters had been sewn in and out of his flesh.

His eyes seemed madder now, and his tongue was still.

Tunghai Wang considered him for a minute, and then went away without asking any questions.

The door closed behind him. A man rose from his corner and haltingly returned to work.

ON HIS third visit, Tunghai Wang did at last receive some useful information. A scribe was summoned, to be sure that nothing was lost. He had to sit uncomfortably close, to hear the broken, slurring whisper; his paper when he rose was spattered with blood and sweat and spittle mixed.

AS TUNGHAI Wang was leaving, already busy in his mind for ways to use what he had learned, his limping man asked if he might continue anyway. There might be nothing more to be had from the man on the scaffold, but his body could teach them much in its responses.

It would be a shame, he said, to waste such an interesting subject. A man once tortured comes to it differently a second time; his knowing so much already made the work at once easier and harder, and the torturer was very keen to pursue those separate courses. To the end, if he only had consent . . .

Tunghai Wang had meant to give his prisoner a swifter end, thinking him useless now, whether or not he had ever been a traitor.

If he had something more to yield up, though, even if it was another kind of knowledge . . .

He gave his inquisitor the nod, and went his way.

Between the Wind and the Water

one

*W*hen the dragon came back to the Forge, Han knew.

She did not, in any sense, try to give him warning. Nevertheless, he knew.

She came at night, flying above the low dense clouds that presaged storm, and he knew.

She coasted in, as silent as a creature can be whose natural elements are air and water, and he knew.

As it happened, he was asleep at the time, and still he knew.

EVEN IN his dreams, he shared a fraction of her mind, as she did his. He felt her coming, and woke; and ran swiftly up to the peak, and kindled a fire in the ruin of the forge.

Not for a beacon, to guide her in. She knew his whereabouts exactly, just as he knew hers. She could have found him in a fog, in her own fog from deep below. He could have found her in the ocean, except that she would have found him first.

It was a warm night already, sticky with pending violence. But fire is comfort and always has been, that's written on the bone; and he thought also that he'd like a little light, something to see her by, that was not the glow of her own green eyes.

SHE BROKE the clouds, shadow on shadow, and his head lifted. Her descent was slow and inexorable; he waited, as still in himself as she was the definition of movement, the flow of water, nothing in her that was still.

He saw her eyes from a distance, as others had seen them as they plunged. Tonight he was the one who waited and she was the one who came, but that gaze was just as deadly.

If her mouth was open for him, he couldn't see it yet.

He shifted marginally in her mind, just to remind her that he was there.

She landed, massively light on her feet, crushingly heavy on the earth. Her head swung toward him, and the fierce salt stench of her was as dizzying as that appalling eye as it blazed, but she made no attempt to swallow.

For a while, indeed, she did nothing, and neither did he.

Then, they talked. In his head, in hers: did it matter which? If there was a difference?

Either way, whichever way, it hurt. Her words cut at him like bitter cold blades, searing where they slashed; her thoughts were rocks and whirlpools, crushing and tearing and engulfing. It was hard to understand, moment by moment, how he could ever hope to survive this.

She herself was easy to understand: bitingly, viciously clear, in that tiny aspect of her being that brushed against his. The rest of her was utterly beyond his reach.

SHE SAID:

Little thing. I find I cannot leave you.

Did he hear it, did he feel it like thunder in his bones, did she write it behind his eyes or burn it directly—characters of icy flame!—deep into his mind? He couldn't tell. The words were there, and they carried her temper with them: a harsh indignant rage that could never be outmatched by the tickle of curiosity that came with it, how something as mean as him could ever be even the slightest nuisance to something as magnificent as her.

He said—or thought, or envisioned, offered up—the only honest answer he could make. There was nowhere to hide in here, in his head or in hers; nowhere to hide the truth. Deception was beyond him, somewhere else.

Great one. I hope you never do. When you fly, you carry me to wonder.

Flattery was beyond him too. He made no effort to cloak his dread of her, the horror that she was. It was only that the wonder, the majesty broke through; his fear could not stand for a moment, against his awe.

She said, *You are like a stone, small and muddy and sharp beneath my skin. I cannot shake you.*

She was like a flame in his head, if steel could burn, if mountains could diminish. He wished that she would leave him, he wished that he could let her go; he had tried, once, and yet they were still linked. He would like to live quiet and alone until Tien came back to find him, if she did. He would like not to live with this chilly connection. It was his obligation, he knew—and how would Tien ever come to the Forge if the dragon watched the strait unguarded, if he was not able to keep her safe?—and yet, and yet . . .

He was weak, and afraid, and in awe. He could hide nothing. What he had, she saw.

He said, *I think it is these chains I wear,* that he had broken but could not shed: cold iron around his throat and wrists, links dangling. Memories of the big smith, Suo Lung, who had lived in a slow sorrow and died abruptly, whose hammer had set these chains on him, whose scribing tool had marked them for the dragon. He could not shed those memories either, but he could turn away from them, or try to. *If they could be cut away from me, I think you could fly free.*

Hold still, little thing. I will cut them.

Claws she had, iron-dark and strong as stone; sharp teeth she had, she showed him.

No! He would not let her close. He was in her head; he could deflect her. Apparently, he could deter her. He refused it, and she didn't try.

I mean, he said, *if a smith could cut them from me, with proper tools. We could melt the iron after if we had to, have nothing of them left. What could control you then?*

Melt away all Suo Lung's scratches, betray him utterly, set the dragon free. Han thought it could be done. He didn't think it should be; he was sure that he should stay here, live out his life as the dragon's sole restraint. Fly with her, and turn her from the worst that she could do.

But. Weak, afraid, yes, and in awe of her already; he could not face her perpetual anger or the constant abrasion of himself. He would go mad, he thought, if he really tried to spend his life in management of her. Perhaps he was mad already, to think it was his proper task.

She said, *I have looked, little thing. I have found people who do that, who melt iron and cut at it with tools.*

She showed him, in her mind there, but he knew it already; he had been with her, fractionally, as she drifted over the island, where so many men were working to build he knew not what. A hill all dug over and laid out in terraces and foundations; a vast camp, and hordes of people running; a line of structures that leaked smoke, looking curious from the air but familiar from the shadows that they cast, with blocks of stone or iron close at hand. Those were forges, with their anvils and their quenching troughs. For certain there would be someone there to do this thing for him. Few people liked to see a boy in chains.

Even so: *No,* he said. *No, not on Taishu. There will be people on the mainland who can do it. I can find them.* If he freed the dragon entirely, she might make the strait entirely impassable. If he had the choice, he would not willingly be on the wrong side of the water from Tien. *But,* he said, *how would I get there?*

It lay between them, obvious and unmentionable, dreadful to

contemplate; he was almost surprised that she managed at the last to give it voice.

I could . . . carry you?

No, he said again. *No, you cannot. I cannot allow it. How could I trust you?* What, put himself voluntarily in the claws of a creature who only needed to squeeze, to pierce, to crush the life from him and she would be free already?

Or else to swallow him, of course. That too.

They looked at each other, caught either side of a quandary; she said, *I do not know, then. What to do.*

Can you find me a boat? he asked helplessly. *Let a boat come, if it will—but I don't know how you'd tell the men to sail it here.*

I will find a way, she said. Doubtfully. He was astonished to find her suddenly so vulnerable, where she was so immense; and then she lifted into the air and flew away, and he was astonished to find himself standing in the utter dark, because his little fire had failed and he hadn't noticed, because he had been seeing at least somewhat through her eyes.

two

Old Yen had walked into Santung with three companions. The doctor was dead; Li Ton was arrested; Tien was gone to play doctor herself, as well as she could among her uncle's things. Old Yen walked out of Santung alone.

No: not alone. Not quite.

To the edge of the city, to the height of the ridge he had an escort. The high priestess of the temple came, with several of her sisters. The city was as nervous today as yesterday, the streets were just as tense—but he stood in no danger from the soldiers, apparently, so long as he was accompanied by women, shaven-headed and unarmed. The generalissimo had issued a fiat: nuns were inviolate, no man was to touch them. Santung's punishment was over. It was his city now, and he meant it to flourish. Which meant that it must lie within the blessing of the gods, which meant that their temples and their devotees were sacrosanct again.

More, the soldiers had adopted these. Hungry for something other than blood, perhaps for a woman's face that didn't scream at first glimpse of them, they brought gifts to the temple, offered help in its restoration, came to pray at permitted hours although the Li-goddess was a stranger to them. In the streets, now, they bowed at the sight of a nun, gave words of respect and duty.

Old Yen walked among women, and was protected by them, but only to the city limits.

From there, all the long road to the headland and the creek

where his boat—he hoped!—lay waiting in care of the boy Pao, he had to walk alone.

No: still not alone. Not quite.

The nuns had carried the child until they stopped. The priestess took him then, smiled a farewell into his silent eyes and laid him gently in Old Yen's arms.

How long had it been, since he held—or held any responsibility for—a child of this size? Not since his own sons were so small, and that was long ago. Simpler times. They had grown, and quarreled with him, and moved away. His grandsons were being raised on the other side of the island; he saw them seldom. Mei Feng was the only grandchild he had contrived to keep, and now she too had been taken from him.

At this age, Mei Feng came to sea and hauled ropes with a will if not much science, and wanted to work the steering oar with her arms at full stretch above her head and her grandfather's hands around hers. This child—Old Yen still struggled to call him a boy—lay still and watched the world with vast black eyes like pits in his hollow face, and must be carried because he would not walk.

Or could not. Who could tell?

Old Yen carried him, and tried to be glad that he was all bone and skin, no meat, no grease. At least he was no burden . . .

No. At most he was no burden. That was all there was to say of him except the one thing, the appalling thing, what his mother had done to him in her extremity; and perhaps the other thing, extraordinary thing, if it were true.

This child was—

No. Nothing was that dependable, in a world so broken; but this child might be the key to his survival. His only hope.

And the survival, the hope of every man, woman and child who went to sea in these waters, that too; but start with him.

Start with this one journey, and see what happened.

The goddess had given Old Yen a message and charged him to deliver it. She would not, surely, send him to his death. He must have some protection from the dragon; this child, perhaps.

It was the nun's idea, but the nun was priestess to the Li-goddess, and so perhaps a tool, as the child was.

As the child had been, and might be again.

He hoped.

Did he hope? Was that a thing to be hoped for, that the child's mouth would open and that voice come again?

Well. He could survive it. He could not survive the dragon without help.

It did occur to him that protection was a passing thing. He had had the nuns' protection, for a while. He might have the protection of the goddess, but only for a while: for as long as it took to deliver her message to the dragon. That task complete, perhaps she would go away and leave him.

Him and the child both, duty done.

Dragon fodder.

Perhaps. He could believe it, of the owner of that voice.

Did he walk under her protection already? Perhaps. He didn't know what influence she had on land, but he met no trouble on the road. People hurried by, watched him as warily as he did them. No one spoke to him at all.

When it came time to leave the road, he might have gone first to the temple on the height; he did not much want to go down to the boat. He had never been so reluctant to set sail.

However strong the reluctance, though, he was more reluctant yet to enter that little temple. To see that other child who had spoken in her voice. The two together, who knew, who could imagine what they might not say?

He went straight down, then, to the little beach; and on the way saw his boat still at anchor, just where he had left her in the creek. And felt relief stained with that traitor reluctance that would almost rather have seen her gone and him helpless, stranded.

The boy Pao was on deck and watching for him, so he didn't even need to hail. The boy would punt over in the sampan, and they could raise anchor and be on their way immediately . . .

EXCEPT THAT there was someone else on the beach.

Pao was waving and pointing, conspicuously not hurrying ashore. There was a message in that: the boy did not trust the stranger, and wanted to stay safe—or keep the boat safe, or both—until Old Yen was satisfied.

Old Yen did not want to deal with a stranger. It would not quite be true to say that he would rather deal with the dragon—or the goddess!—but at least he was ready for those, as ready as a man could be. Here he was utterly unprepared.

The stranger was getting to his feet. He dusted dirt from his robe, though that was torn and shabby; he bowed low to Old Yen, who was not accustomed to such manners and besides had a lanky awkward child in his arms, and made a poor mess of bowing in return.

He was a young man, this stranger, and his head had been shaved, though not recently: a priest, perhaps? His robe was dark and simply cut, but the silk had been heavy—which meant expensive—before it was mistreated. Not a priest, Old Yen thought, after a day's close acquaintance with the nuns at the temple. Their dress was cut from coarse stuff, cheap. And ill sewn, self-sewn. This was . . .

Oh. A shaved head, dress costly but discreet . . .

Old Yen knew, before the man spoke.

"My name is Jung. Please, can you take me to the emperor?"

Old Yen had refused so many, surely it should be easier by now. He said, "I cannot, it is forbidden. We cannot feed the men we have. I am sorry."

"I am from the Hidden City," Jung said, "from the emperor's own palace. I was left behind . . ."

He and countless hundreds of his brethren. Not many had

made it this far in pursuit. Old Yen was impressed, and touched with pity, and still shook his head. "There is no Hidden City on Taishu. You must find some other way to live."

"I am a eunuch," Jung said simply, which Old Yen had already understood. "I have no other way to live."

He was a young man, thin and pretty. Old Yen wanted to say *go to the city, find a soldier who will offer you protection; he will teach you how to live another way.* But he wouldn't willingly send anyone into Santung at such a time, with tempers stretched paper-taut and everyone watching the sky, waiting for the shadow of a dragon.

He only shook his head again, said nothing.

Jung waited, as though simple time would erode a refusal; Old Yen waited for him to accept that same refusal, and go his way. He wouldn't beckon Pao until the man was gone. Squabbling over the sampan would be ludicrous. And awkward, with the child in his arms.

"Is the boy sick?" Jung asked, as if he had been following Old Yen's thoughts. Perhaps he had followed his eyes; a palace servant would be swift to pick up on subtleties of desire.

"Yes—or no, perhaps. I am not sure. He is . . . of your kind, but it was crudely done in a hurry, and he has not spoken since. Nor walked."

"Oh, he is too young! That should not have been done . . . Let me see."

Jung took the child, before Old Yen could think of refusing him.

They stared at each other, those two, unlike in everything but loss: the one lost in body, the other lost in soul. Then Jung lifted his head again and looked to Old Yen and said, "We belong to-gether. Eunuchs belong to the emperor: you know this, it is the law. You must take us to him."

IT WAS the law. Also, it was the excuse that Old Yen needed. Eunuchs did belong to the emperor, unequivocally. Some said they were a gift of the gods to the Jade Throne, to the god-on-earth, a mortal equivalent to those ghosts and spirits who served the gods in heaven. Some said it was politics, an earthly device to keep ambitious lords and generals in their place. If eunuchs were a sign of ascendency and godhood, then it followed that only the emperor might possess them. Therefore, if a man started to cut his servants or buy castrated boys into his household, it was a sure sign of usurpation, conspiracy against the throne. Of course the law must stand against that.

Old Yen wondered what had happened to the vast numbers of Jung's brethren: how many had been kept in the Hidden City under guard, how many were perhaps being herded along in Tunghai Wang's wake, in his wagon-train. Perhaps some were already installed in Santung, to serve the emperor-in-waiting. That man led a revolt against the throne, and meant to seize it; he would have no hesitation in seizing the emperor's discarded eunuchs. Possession of them would reinforce his claim, when he dared to make it . . .

The young man knew what was right, though. Old Yen couldn't send him to the usurper, after that cry of law. There was sweet relief in bowing his acquiescence, in waving and calling to Pao.

If he were honest, there was sweet relief too in handing over the child. Jung could watch him on the boat, all the way across the strait; Jung could take him to the palace and give himself and the child over into the emperor's service. No one could turn them away, and Old Yen would have no more responsibility for either.

If they made it that far, under the goddess's protection. Under the dragon's eye.

Old Yen's plan was to sail to the Forge and speak to the boy there, Han, if the dragon hadn't eaten him. Yes. Han could pass on what the goddess said. How could a fisherman speak to a dragon, anyway? Either from inside or outside her gut? That must be it, that the boy should be his intermediary as Old Yen was hers, the goddess's. Yes. Man spoke to man at the last. Let the immortals speak to each other through their servants . . .

PAO COLLECTED them all from shore, wide-eyed and wary, as a boy learns to be in time of war. Wary was good; Old Yen shared no secrets, and no plans. He told Jung to keep the child out of their way, either in the cabin or in the bows. There was warm sun on easy water, a pleasant breeze; the eunuch opted to sit high in the boat's beak, holding the child upright in his lap to show how the water sparkled, how gulls gathered and dived above a school of fish.

The boat behaved as sweetly as the weather, cutting through the low swell with a steady hiss, catching the wind just off the quarter and barely rolling, barely pitching as she scudded south. It was as though his goddess rode beside him—as she used to, as he used to believe she did—with one hand on the steering oar and one to lay a road by wind and water.

Had he ceased to believe in her companionship, her kindness? He wasn't sure, but he was deeply shaken. That voice, that terrible voice could never come from the image that he'd held so long, the tender generous soul he'd thought to be watching over him. No one could deny that she was watching, but nothing else was certain now.

At least she wasn't talking anymore. The child sat in the bows and stared forward and said nothing, although these were her waters. Old Yen blessed her silence, blessed this speed—although the wind more properly lay within the gift of the dragon, from whom he would never dare ask it—even while in all honesty he would sooner not be taking gifts from her, not now.

Even while he scanned the sky again and again for any sign, any hint of dragon.

THERE WAS none, and none, and none.

There was the Forge now, a tooth on the horizon. He worked the oar to bring the boat's prow a little closer to the line—not too much, because she made a leeway in any wind and there was current here too that he could feel through his hands, the tug of it that he needed to steer against, a long-familiar calculation so deeply worked into his life, a pattern so closely woven that he didn't think about it at all, it was all in his skin, in his muscles, in his bones— and called to Pao to ease the mainsail a touch.

Just then, the dragon rose.

He had been watching and watching for her, in the sky or else on the island. It was how he saw her last, aloft; of course he looked to find her where he left her. What fool would not?

He was most certainly a fool. All his life she had lain beneath his keel; had he forgotten so quickly that she was a creature of the sea?

He saw a strange swirl in the water that seemed at first to shoulder the swell aside, and then swelled like a wen beneath the surface, and then broke: broke around a rising rock that was no rock at all but her head looming high and high, mast-high above them, higher. Her great body must somehow have stalled tide and current both at once just as her will—perhaps—stilled the wind, because his boat lost all way at once, wallowing slack-sailed in the wash that ran off her.

It might only have been a moment that they stared at each other, boat and dragon. It seemed much longer. For himself, Old Yen closed his eyes. He saw no need to watch it as the wide gape opened, teeth and tongue reached down to swallow them.

He stood in the private dread of his darkness, and nothing seemed to happen. The dragon and the goddess both were silent, Pao and the eunuch too; even the boat was quieter than usual with no strain on ropes or timbers.

He decided to open his eyes again.

It seemed to take a while.

There hung the dragon, head in the sky, just as she had been, with her mouth agape; and whether she had stopped herself or whether the goddess had stopped her, he couldn't tell, but she seemed not to be swallowing them after all.

He thought perhaps she was going to seize the boat instead, and shake them out of it.

But still she waited, open-mouthed, and the boat seemed to be waiting too, and everyone aboard it; and at last, Old Yen did what the goddess and then Li Ton had sent him out to do.

He drew a breath and yelled up at the dragon.

three

*T*hey did, of course, have to come back.

Mei Feng had always known that, in her heart. It was the emperor who had resisted the idea, with the stubbornness of absolute rank, not seeing why he should ever do what he did not want to do; and she had clung with joy to that intransigence, for as long as ever it could last.

Then General Ping Wen had come, with his plans for war; and her boy-emperor fell in with him almost gleefully, which was so strange and—to be honest—such a disappointment, after so long living free of the court, living almost wild in the forest. So now they were back, too abruptly, too soon: back in what used to be the jademaster's palace and was the emperor's now until his new Hidden City had been built, which would take longer if he sent all the soldiers off to war.

She wasn't the only reluctant one. In the valley they had lived like a clan, all together, and most of them had learned to love it. She thought he had loved it too. But, *We can't plan a war from the jungle,* he had said—in Ping Wen's voice, frighteningly—and of course that was true, which was another reason why she thought they should have stayed.

Some few, the lucky few had stayed, if only to keep the idea alive, the emperor's retreat in the mountains. And to keep some of them out of the palace. Pirates and jade-eaters, say. The rest were back, and not his clan-kin now. His personal guard, most of them, which was still a fine thing to be, but different. And she? She was his concubine again, and nothing more. She could look out of her window and across the courtyard to his mother's wing, again; and he had deliberately put himself back under that woman's wing, she thought. If that wasn't entirely fair, well, she didn't feel like being fair. She wasn't obliged to be fair.

He had put himself even more into the hands of Ping Wen, whom Mei Feng liked and trusted no more than she did his mother. Less, perhaps. The empress would try to keep him safe and ineffectual; Ping Wen would do the opposite, make a hero of him, a leader and a warrior.

With faithful Ping Wen right there at his shoulder, of course, number two in the realm, just in case. She was painfully aware—who knew better?—that the emperor had no heir, and the Jade Throne could not be left empty.

Sickness, assassination, war: those were the means of untimely death available to an emperor. She could only think about it iron-ically, because thinking about it seriously gave her the terrors. Al-ready there had been assassins, and now he was planning a war.

Sickness—well, no. He was absurdly robust. It came with the throne, his vigorous good health and radiant charm and energy and such. At least, it came with the jade that made the throne.

So did strength, the simple strength of stone, and its endurance. He had taken a blade to the chest, and survived it; he could fight all day and exhaust all opposition and still want exercise. If any man, any one man was made to survive a war, he was that one.

And yet, people did die in war however good they were. Emper-ors, indeed, had died in war. Miraculous powers of recovery wouldn't stop a frenzied squad of soldiers hacking his head off, and there would be no coming back from that.

Mei Feng hated the thought of war in any case. She hated the actual war that had come so close, seizing Santung and sealing off Taishu. She had hated the little splinter of it that she saw, the as-sassins who slipped under the island's skin and drove almost to the heart of empire, the emperor himself. Fleeing and fighting, blood and death, she had hated all of that.

More than anything she hated this, that her idiot the emperor would leave this island, load as many men as possible into the ramshackle fleet that they'd accumulated, and sail over the strait to fight Tunghai Wang and his rebels. The very army that they'd been fleeing for so long, that had driven them here to Taishu, driven the emperor to her in the dragon's-breath fog.

She hated that he wanted to; she hated and dreaded that he would, that he was committed, if it could only be achieved.

He was speaking to the council now as if it were all his own idea. He said, "We know what happened to Tunghai's fleet, with so many of his men aboard. What's left of the rebel army is stranded in Santung now, or else it's in flight already. We will never have a better chance to strike. One blow, one battle and we can end this. Destroy Tunghai and all his traitors at a stroke . . ."

He wasn't even talking like himself, but the council listened to him regardless. Some were nodding their agreement: old generals, men who had fought and won under his father, who thought that winning was the natural order. Who would have fought at the Hidden City when the rebels first rose, would have fought and died and lost everything sooner than run, if they had had command.

The empress was wiser. It was the empress, of course, who had seized up her son and fled, dragging everyone else along in her imperial wake.

She said, "Have you inherited your father's folly, together with his empire?"

Her son looked at her, momentarily wordless. All the council waited for what in the world could follow. Mei Feng waited too, private in her corner with the tea-things.

"Your father," said the woman who had perhaps known him best, "was foolish often, when he was young. I had his own word for that. Even later he made mistakes, which other men would pay for. Battles were lost, though few remember those. He became invincible mostly by means of outliving all his enemies, or waiting until they were old and weak before he struck against them. It is an effective tactic, but the first essential is to stay alive long enough to employ it."

The simple scorn in her voice was like a blow. He did flinch, and Mei Feng almost wanted to cheer for the old woman. How strange was that, to find herself supporting the empress in an argument? With her boy? The empress was the enemy within the palace, whom they fought day in, day out. Until they left the palace.

Now they were back, and something had shifted. The world was new, and the old woman had acknowledged it; at last, she was actually right.

"That's what I say," he said, sounding almost child-like for a moment, urging his case against her implacability. "Tunghai is weak at last, and now . . ."

"Oh, and are you strong?" No one else could interrupt the emperor in council, no one else would dare; he didn't know how to override her, so he subsided, looking weak. "Do you have more soldiers than you did a month ago, are they more willing to fight?"

"More than him," he muttered, more and more the sulky boy. "We have more than he does!"

"And you know this how?"

"We saw the dragon destroy his fleet at sea, we have seen the bodies . . . !"

"Bodies, yes. The dragon, yes. The fleet? How many ships, how many men aboard them?"

His silence was her answer; she let it hang until at last, almost desperate, feeling it all threaten to slide away from him, he said, "We don't know. How can we tell? No one has been over the strait to see. At least, no one has come back. But it must have been the most of his army."

"Oh, must it so? Why not a scouting force, a probe, with the most of them held back for another day? How can you tell how many he has lost?"

"Because the dragon took so long to eat them."

That was a score for him, alas, and he had had the line from her. She felt the mood of the room sway, these men so easily persuaded, they wanted war so much, to redeem their mortgaged honors and ride in triumph home, all those long months of miles along the same road where they'd fled.

But the old woman wasn't done yet.

"Yes," she said, "the dragon. Why have we not sent more spies to Santung, to try again to learn the true situation there?"

Again she waited, to force it out of him.

"No one will go now," he mumbled.

"And why not, why don't you command them across?"

"Because of the dragon. They are afraid . . ."

"Their fear means nothing, but the dragon, yes. No boat can evade the dragon's eye, be it dark or day. If she will not let a sail by, then how can you mount this invasion, how can you have your foolish war? Will you tunnel to Santung? You cannot fly, unless the dragon carries you."

To that, he simply had no answer and offered none. There was no answer to the dragon. The skies were hers, and the seas too. He could command his invasion—no, Ping Wen's invasion, that he had so gleefully adopted—as often as he liked, as often as he could make men listen to him; blessedly, not he nor Ping Wen nor anyone could command the dragon.

ANOTHER BLESSING, someone came to take Mei Feng away from this: one of the palace eunuchs, sidling into the throne-room where the council met. That was Hui, who had given some time and attention to her when she was new to this life, when she needed training. She had a fondness for Hui, although he was the empress's man through and through; she thought perhaps he was fond of her too. It was her that he came to now, rather to her astonishment, among all these great figures. He dropped to his knees behind her, as though she too were a person of importance, and leaned forward to murmur in her ear.

"There is a person, lady, who begs an audience."

"With me?" It came out too loud; it turned heads. Now no voice would be quiet enough. The old woman at least could read lips, Mei Feng was sure of that. She gestured, then, *outside;* and bowed low to her puzzled lord and followed through the servants' door, behind a screen in the corner. Probably not a good idea politically, too much like an admission of her proper status, but right now Mei Feng might not even want to argue that. Making the emperor's tea hardly qualified her for responsibility and respect. Nor did quarreling with him in whispers in the night, in the suddenly awkward spaces of his bed, trapped by those same heavy curtains that used to offer such a welcome privacy.

OUTSIDE APPARENTLY meant literally outside, though it was raining. The eunuch had an umbrella to hold over her; there was none for her visitor. Visitors. In the public courtyard stood a bedraggled little group of three, not what she had been looking for. She had expected perhaps a message from the forest compound, where they had left some friends behind. Instead, here was a young and shaven-headed stranger, bowed shelteringly over a recumbent child: and—

"Grandfather!"

She should have hurtled, should have hugged him hard and could not, because that too would have found its way back to the empress. Which ought not to matter, never would have mattered until now. Now, though, when they slept hunched apart with their backs turned, when the emperor refused utterly to listen to her, he might slip back into old habits and allow himself to listen to his mother, to let her opinion influence his.

So no: under Hui's eye, Mei Feng swallowed her delight. She

must still have glowed; she might have bounced; her voice did rise indecorously, but only in that first squeal of joy. With that outside her, she could be moderate and duly deferential. She bowed courteously to the stranger, deeply and genuinely to Old Yen. She'd never really treated him with the respect he undoubtedly deserved, all the years she was living with him; she was a beloved child, and then she was crew, and both of those muddied the waters. Now she was—something else again, but distant from him, gone away. She could see him more clearly, and show him something of what she saw.

Also she could fuss over him outrageously, not to let him think that she had changed too much to bear. He always loved it when she fussed, he could be all gruff and weathered, as sweet and stubborn as his boat.

"Grandfather, *honored* Grandfather, whyever are you standing in the rain? What were my people *thinking,* to leave you so . . . ?" This, of course, to the man who was soaked through five nights out of seven, who thought nothing of sailing across the strait and back with a bitter wind sealing sodden clothes to his skin, who would barely think of this as rain at all, though it was dripping from his beard.

She might have been more honestly angry about the child, who looked sick, or at least too big to be carried about that way unless he was sick. But she was completely confused about the child, and the man who carried him. Who were they, strays that Old Yen had collected somewhere? Probably so, but he wasn't supposed to be bringing any more people over the strait. Why would he have fetched them here, and to her . . . ?

Come to that, no one was supposed to be sailing the strait anymore, under the dragon's watch. The empress had just been exulting about it, laying it like a piece in elephant chess to frustrate any invasion. For a moment there Mei Feng had forgotten that it ought to apply even to her grandfather.

She couldn't take him or any of them into the palace; protocol would forbid her. She wouldn't speak to anyone out here in the rain. Very well.

She signed them to follow, and led out of the courtyard and into the broad gardens behind. Hui shuffled along beside her, with the umbrella as his excuse. She kept him because she had to, because it would be a scandal else; she walked far enough ahead that the rain he kept off her would fall on him instead, his punishment for leaving her grandfather out in it.

She could not send him out of earshot, so anything said here would be passed on, directly to the empress. Hopefully Grandfather would understand the need, the absolute imperative to be discreet . . .

As they went along, though, Mei Feng remembered that she was not on terms with her beloved, that there would be no murmured, gleeful sharing of secrets in the curtained dark of the bed tonight, only the hard broad silence of his back. That, rather, she was at one with the empress for once. That, whatever Grandfather had brought her—strangers, a child, news in the flesh and otherwise—she might prefer to share it with the old woman than with the emperor.

That the old woman's network of spies and servants could be her friend, if she could find a use for it.

That was a revelation, and it needed time to think about. Not now: here was the bench already, where she and Grandfather had sat once before. At least, he had sat while she knelt at his feet. She couldn't do that today, in the rain and the mud with Hui watching. He had allowed it once, when she was new and foolish; now they were past that, she and he. But if she took the bench, at least Grandfather and the stranger could both come in under the shelter of its roof; and officially she was only a concubine, they needn't kneel to her. Which was just as well, as Grandfather's knees were not so good and the thought would probably not occur to him.

The stranger did just that, though, instinctively it seemed; and he took off his rice-straw rain hat so that she could see the stubble on his skull where a shave was growing out. Which explained those little hints of familiarity in the way he stood and moved and bowed: a shaved head was the swift sure way to lose a giveaway queue, if a man for example had to journey unprotected for many days before he could find a way back to his master. This man had been a palace servant, which was what the queue denoted, the intimate service of the emperor; which meant he was a eunuch, and had somehow contrived to come this far because what else could he do, where else did a eunuch belong, except in the service of the Son of Heaven?

And—

"Grandfather, where have you *been*?" Which was both a question and an accusation, if he was listening properly.

He said, "In Santung," in a voice she hadn't heard from him before.

"In *Santung*? Grandfather . . . !" That was more than she had expected, worse than she had imagined; it almost put the dragon out of her mind. She glanced instinctively at her eunuch servant under his umbrella. *He heard that. Saying you have been to Santung is saying you have been to the enemy; and he is not truly my servant at all, he belongs to the empress. What he hears, she will hear. Oh, what is the death due to traitors . . . ?*

The eunuch smiled thinly. "Lady, this rain blurs an old man's ears. I can hear nothing today."

Did she believe him? No, of course not; the smile was to emphasize the lie, to draw her into the conspiracy.

Did she trust him? No, not that either. Of course not. Hui had been the empress's man long and long before he was ever hers. Fondness could not outrank loyalty; it would not prevent betrayal.

But. Information was currency all through the palace, from top to bottom. The empress was weak just now, seeing her son in Ping Wen's sleeve and not her own. Anything she had, which they did not: that would be jade to the empress in her bitterness, in her determination. Anything she could use.

Information, say, about the state of things in Santung . . .

Let this go to the empress, then. Mei Feng had Hui's implicit promise not to bring consequences back to Grandfather. That would be the best that she could get from him, the most that he could offer; she did not think the empress would renege on it.

She didn't think so. No. The old woman paid her debts.

She said, "Tell me, then. Was it in Santung that you found . . . these friends you have brought to me?"

"Mm? Oh—no. Well, yes. Yes and no. Mei Feng, this is Jung. He is, uh . . ."

"He is a eunuch," she said quietly, "like my friend Hui here; and I think, like Hui, he must have been a servant in the Hidden City, am I right?"

Jung bowed. "Master Hui was too far above me to be troubled by my presence, but I watched him and admired and tried to learn. You see very clearly, lady."

"I see a queue shaved off, and a hard road traveled; I think you were not always so thin. Young, though, I expect you have always been young." Actually, he was older than her; she forgot sometimes, here at court, how young she was herself. And he was impetuous, unless he was desolate. Foolish either way, to chase so far after the emperor once he had been abandoned. Surely there were others like him, eunuchs left behind, finding other ways to live? Growing out their hair and learning to farm, learning to barter, learning that the world outside the wall was different and difficult but not impossible at all.

She said, "You are welcome here, Jung. You have made a brave journey to where your duty lies," and oh, when did she become so formal? She sounded like a shadow-empress in a puppet-play, mouthing phrases while the real action went on behind her, where she couldn't see. What the young man needed was a hot bath and a hot meal, clean clothes and a place to sleep, a place to call his own. Perhaps a hug. She couldn't hug him, but she could at least arrange the rest. "Master Hui here will see to all your needs and comforts, and the emperor himself will see you tomorrow. But the child? Did you find him on your way, and take him up as charity?" For sure, the palace could take in one more boy—but this boy looked broken. Was he deformed, perhaps, or simple-minded? Something held him slack and heedless in Jung's arms.

"No, lady. I carry him for Old Yen."

"And I for the Li-goddess," her grandfather grunted, just as swift to deny the child.

"Grandfather? A temple offering?" Sometimes a family had a diseased or crippled child and could not cope, would leave it to the nuns to raise and nurture. "Why bring him here?"

"Not . . . that. Not quite that. Mei Feng . . ."

He seemed stranded, on this difficult shore of words. She tried to help: "Did you find him in Santung?"

"The child, yes. In the temple. Not Jung, he found us later. But we brought the child here because we must, because he already belongs to the emperor."

What was he *saying* . . . ? It seemed as though she ought to know, but her only reading of it made no sense. This boy was small and thin and apparently crippled, but far from a baby; he couldn't be the emperor's child. Unless Chien Hua had been— well, precocious. And dishonest with her. Perhaps his mother had encouraged him? Emperors notoriously found it difficult to sire children. Supposedly the jade in their bodies poisoned their seed, so that a woman's body could not nurture it. A wise woman, a dowager empress might well think that an early grandson would be a boon, treasure stored in heaven.

If her boy were old enough, and willing. If the babe were healthy. Perhaps it had been deliberately left behind, abandoned . . . ?

Mei Feng still didn't believe it. He would have told her; she would have learned it in his touch, that he was not new to the pleasures of his bed, her body. He certainly wouldn't have lied.

She said, "I don't understand. How—?"

How does this boy belong to the emperor, my emperor, my Chien Hua? Grandfather, be plain . . .

Perhaps he tried to be, but something overwhelmed him.

"By law," he said. "As Jung does. Unless, unless he belongs to the goddess now. Mei Feng, we saw the dragon, but she kept us safe . . ."

"One thing at a *time*, Grandfather," or they would all of them get utterly lost. She seized the gnarled strong rope-rough hands that were fretting at her gown, snagging the silk as they tried to make her see what he had seen, what he lacked the words to say; she held those hands tightly in her own, realizing suddenly how soft her own were becoming, how little use she would be now on the boat; she said, "What law—Oh. Oh, no . . ."

Unexpectedly, it was Hui—who had claimed, of course, not to be listening at all—who cleared matters up, brisk and kind and declaratory: "I think the little one must be a eunuch, lady."

So did she, now, at last. Had rain and unhappiness made her stupid, or was she always this slow? Perhaps you didn't need to be clever to sail a boat and net fish, net an emperor in a fog . . .

Her grandfather was nodding, and so was Jung. "Yes," she said. "I understand. But how could . . . ? Was it an accident?" Boys were castrated deliberately, even by their own parents, to win a place for them in the Hidden City, where they might rise and rise; but surely not in time of war, of rebellion, when the emperor had fled the palace . . .

Her grandfather was shaking his head. "It was . . . not an accident. A terrible thing."

Something so terrible, he didn't want to say. It must have been something of war, then; she knew that appalled him. Very well. No doubt Jung knew, and could be induced to tell her later.

She said, "Never mind. He belongs here, to us. That is enough. My women will take care of him; the emperor's own doctor shall see him immediately. Hui, will you attend to that?"

"Of course, lady."

"Good, thank you. Jung, would you prefer to be with the other eunuchs," *make friends, make a place for yourself,* "or to stay with the child for a time?" *Be fussed over yourself, no doubt, pretty young man with taking eyes; be better fed and sleep more comfortably, avoid other duties for a while . . . ?*

He said, "Please, lady, I would like to stay with the child." *Sensible young man with taking eyes*—but Jung went on, "He is . . . special to me, to us both. He saved our lives, I think, on the water."

"It was the goddess who saved us," Old Yen said flatly. "The child is her vehicle, no more."

"It is enough," Jung retorted. "Without him—"

"Without him, I would not have sailed; but he was the goddess's promise, her word in flesh, her doing." Which was a grim thing, seemingly, from the way he tried to flinch back from his own words.

"Wait," Mei Feng said, almost desperately. "Jung, can you tell me what happened?"

"Not properly, lady. I was late to this story, as your honorable grandfather has told you; I only saw the end, when the dragon came again."

"Again?"

It was one word and she dropped it like a stone; she could almost not bear the weight of it.

Jung bowed his head, her grandfather lifted his to meet her eye to eye. "I had seen her at the Forge, before. When the pirate Li Ton had charge of my boat and me."

Bewildered, she could only repeat, "The *Forge*?"

"Yes."

"Why would—a pirate—take you there?" There had been a beacon on the Forge, she remembered, smoke still rising in the dawn before the dragon was seen to rise and plunge and rise again. Again and again. Before the bodies began to float ashore, before all the wreckage arrived.

"We were sent."

"Grandfather . . ."

"We didn't know what it meant, to set a blaze on the Forge-top that night. We had no choice anyway, he would have killed us if we refused—but we didn't know about the fleet.

"We did that, yes, we built the beacon, under the pirate's orders. The doctor and his niece, the boy in chains and me. We built it and burned it, and come the morning we saw the rebel fleet on its way to Taishu."

She wished, she really wished he would stop talking now. It had been so hard to see him started, and now he dug his own grave with every word, he built the scaffold on which he would be tortured first. Hui was listening. Whatever was said here, it would be repeated to the empress; and to have in her hand the names of those who fired the beacon, that was power she would welcome. Power she would use. Mei Feng could not see, now, how to save her grandfather's life.

"But, but that was a good thing in the end," she said desperately. "Because the dragon rose and destroyed the fleet . . ."

"She did. Because the boy broke his chains, and hers."

Mei Feng shook her head. Again. This story kept leaving her suddenly stranded, just when she thought she understood. "It was the monks who kept the dragon chained, you always told me that."

"It was; and it was a survivor from the Forge who chained the boy, trying to echo their work. He managed, barely, for a time. She stirred, she was seen, we saw her; but she could not rise. Until the boy Han broke those chains. Then she was free, and any boat abroad on the water was in danger.

"She sank them, she sank them all; and then she came to the Forge. To kill us, I think, but she could not. She was not so free after all. The boy prevented her, and so we were allowed to sail away.

"The pirate made us sail to the mainland," where something

happened, it seemed, that Old Yen did not want to say; "and then he walked us into Santung. He wanted to speak to Tunghai, I think. He thought the doctor might bring him there. But there was . . . trouble, and the doctor died, and the pirate was arrested; and I, I was sent by the goddess. With a message. For the dragon . . ."

"Sent by the *goddess*? Grandfather . . ." She had never questioned his devotion, although she'd never really shared it. When she was a small girl, trips to the temple were fun, whether they involved tramps along clifftops or the tight fascinating streets of the big cities, Santung or Taishu-port. Smoke and bright colors and chanting, a moon-cake for the goddess and a moon-cake for herself: it was a treat to go, and an extra treat to go with Grandfather. By the time she understood that her father and uncles and most of their neighbors weren't so devoted, that most other sea-captains either didn't follow his heartfelt rituals at all or else did so in a perfunctory and dutiful manner—well, it didn't matter. Most other sea-captains weren't such good sailors either. That was what did matter by then: the kick of the living deck beneath bare feet, a taut rope and a batten-sail trimmed to catch the wind exactly, salt water and salt air and the heave and rush of the sea. She watched her grandfather and learned from him. And never quite learned his faith, but never quite learned to match him either at the steering oar or in his simple read of tide and weather: where the fish would be running, where drift would carry the boat, where to marry the two. It seemed . . . fair.

But this, now? He was old and strained and anxious; perhaps his mind had finally toppled over, from dedication to obsession? If he went to speak to the goddess, and actually heard her talking back to him . . .

He was nodding emphatically. "Yes. The Li-goddess sent me. She spoke to me: once in her little temple on the headland west of Santung, and then again in the city."

"She spoke to you. How did she do that—through the priest-

ess?" There was no priestess in the abandoned temple, as far as
Mei Feng knew; they used it as a landmark more than a place of
prayer. Grandfather liked to go up there sometimes, but she used
to stay in the boat.

"Through the children," he said. "There are refugees everywhere, and damaged children, mutes. She uses those. She used this
poor boy," a gesture to the silent child, "everyone heard him.
Everyone in the temple. She spoke to the pirate, but it was a message for me."

He sounded, she thought, entirely mad. She didn't want to look
at Hui, because his face and eye would confirm it. She didn't want
to speak, because her voice would give her away. Even mad, he
would still understand her. He always had.

A silence fell, but only briefly; then the eunuch Jung lifted his
head again, from where he had been smiling down at the unre-
sponsive child.

"I wasn't in the temple, lady," he said, "but I believe the old man
is right. The dragon would have drowned or swallowed us both on
the water today, but something stopped her. She was enraged, but
something stopped her, and calmed the waters. I thought it was
the boy. Old Yen says it was his goddess."

"It was the goddess. These are her waters, and she will not tol-
erate the dragon free. She used the children to say so. To me. It was
my task to say it to the dragon. I thought, I *thought* she meant
I should sail back to the Forge and tell the boy Han that we had
left there. Let him tell the dragon. But the dragon was watching the strait, of course; and she saw us abroad and came for us,
and . . ."

And, poor old man, he must have been terrified. Who would
not be, confronted by the demon of all their early terrors? Every
child on Taishu grew up with tales of the dragon beneath the sea,
and how she was chained. Every fisherman's child feared the day
when she would rise. Just as inland children feared the night and
what lay in holes beneath the earth, creatures of darkness, sea-

children feared creatures of wind and water and storm. Dragons, that is to say: and the one dragon in particular, their own, the one they knew to be there.

After a long lifetime sailing above her head, listening to the monks' great hammer pounding chains like a guarantee that she was safe in her prison below, he had heard its recent silence with dread. Mei Feng understood that. He was a man of faith: he couldn't believe in the goddess but not in the dragon, or in the benevolence of one and not the malice of the other. How he had found the courage to sail deliberately into that maelstrom, where the one must be pitted against the other, she couldn't imagine.

"She rose up from the sea, from the goddess's own waters. I didn't know what to do, except what the goddess had told me. So I cried the message up to her, before she could eat us. And I did, I did wonder if the goddess would be done with us then, if she would allow the dragon to . . . But of course not, she wouldn't treat me so . . ."

He still didn't sound entirely certain, Mei Feng thought. Something had shaken him. Not in his faith, but in his ardor, perhaps, or his tender regard. Something he had seen, and had not loved.

Never mind. She said, "So did the boy," this wordless child in his utter absence, "did he speak to the dragon, is that what happened?"

"No, no. I had to do that. I had to speak to the dragon," which had clearly been momentous, and she really wished she could have been there to see him standing in his frail boat and bellowing in his great sea-voice at a creature that could swallow him as easily as she breathed.

"And, what then, did the dragon listen to you? To the goddess, I mean, to her message?" This was how to get him telling stories, she had learned it long ago: ask the right questions, and let him find the answers one by one.

"She did understand me, I think, but she was . . . infuriated. She meant to kill us anyway, for sailing on her waters, but now she wanted to break the boat around us first, let us watch our own deaths coming . . ."

"So what happened?"

"They're not her waters," and he sounded almost smug in his goddess, almost as he used to. Mei Feng was still sure she could hear a difference in his voice. More awe than worship? Something. "She was furious, but she couldn't touch us, the goddess wouldn't let her. She couldn't come close to us: the water wouldn't carry her, and if she tried to fly she fell out of the air, and even the splash of her falling, even the wave from that never reached us. We might have been floating on a different sea."

"He says it was his goddess," Jung said softly, "but I think it was the boy. He has been like this all the way," slack in the eunuch's arms and slack apparently in his own head, staring in mute disinterest at whatever fell before his eyes, "except just then. He didn't speak, not to the dragon; but he was alert and sitting up suddenly. He watched the dragon, his eyes followed her everywhere—and as the old man says, she could not come near us."

It wasn't quite a quarrel between Jung and Old Yen, whose hand had saved them, but it veered close. Mei Feng knew where she stood; she did want the boy to be more than a puppet, but nothing would allow it. He offered a convenient body where perhaps the goddess needed one—her spirit was too diffuse to work against the physicality of the dragon, unless she could be physical herself?—and so she used him. And then slipped away again, and left him as he was. Discarded, still ruined. Perhaps hurt a little more, damaged beyond recall. She was too big, and he too vulnerable . . .

Raped girls and mutilated boys, the lost and silent might be easier vessels for a goddess to inhabit than stubborn women and strong-willed old men. It was unbearable, but it might also be true.

Mei Feng said, "It is a wonderful story. My lord the emperor should hear it; he likes to know of his servants' adventures, and he needs to learn more of the goddess. And the dragon. He is in council now with the lady empress his mother and the generals, but Ping Wen will—"

"Wait," Old Yen said, startling her. "Ping Wen?"

"Yes. He is . . ." What was he, exactly? Chief of the council, governor of the island? Something, certainly, more than one general among the rest. He sat on her own little footstool in the emperor's absence, and spoke in his name. He was the second man on Taishu, she supposed, in this new dispensation: almost the first, given that the emperor was something more than a man, afflicted with godhood.

"I know what he is," Old Yen said urgently. "He is a traitor. The emperor must not trust him! Nor you, you must not. He will betray us all."

"What? Grandfather!" She did not like Ping Wen, had not liked—or, indeed, trusted—him even before he hatched his plan for war and seduced her proud and gullible lord with it, but still . . . "You must not say such things! Really, you must not." Ping Wen was a proud man himself, and not at all gullible; he might have as many ears in the palace as the old woman did. And pay them better. "How could you know this, anyway?"

"I was there," he said. "Here, in the palace, in the throne-room. It was Ping Wen who put the pirate in command of my boat and sent us to the Forge, to light the beacon."

She shook her head slowly. "No . . ."

"Mei Feng, it was."

She didn't disbelieve him, exactly: she was only bewildered. How could her grandfather have been here at the palace, taking orders of any kind from General Ping Wen? With a pirate? Nothing made sense, except perhaps his accusation. She hadn't lived long in the court, but it was long enough to believe that traitors could be anywhere.

Even in the empress's entourage, there could be traitors. There must be. Ping Wen would have his ears there above all, to learn what the old woman was saying, thinking, planning to do. Just as she would have her ears as close as possible to him.

Mei Feng glanced at the old eunuch Hui under his umbrella, and trusted him not at all.

Hui put a finger in his ear, miming rain and deafness. Well. She could trust that or not, it made no difference. He had heard, and he would use it as he chose. There were perhaps people who would poison him, sooner than let him speak; she was not one of those. Besides, she had no poisons.

Old Yen was urging her to warn the emperor, to have the general arrested, everything sensible and safe and impossible. She had advocated so much against Ping Wen these last days, she had so fallen out of favor with her lord already, he would not listen to her; and she couldn't thrust her grandfather forward as a clear and unbiased witness. His open confession before the throne that he had helped to build that beacon would mean his death, unequivocally.

She was baffled, helpless; she needed an ally, and found unexpectedly that she had one.

If she could trust him.

Hui said, "Lady, I may have rain in my ears, but not yet in my head. If your honorable grandfather will tell us all that he knows, perhaps I can find a way to alert those who should be watchful of his majesty. It ought not to come from you, nor from my own mistress."

No, indeed; the empress was in worse odor with her son than Mei Feng was herself. Those two were probably still arguing across the throne-room floor. While Ping Wen watched and listened and said very little, because the emperor was saying it all on his behalf. Digging the pit himself, perhaps, in which Ping Wen meant to trap him . . . ?

Hui had lived all his life as a palace servant, at the heart of court. If anyone knew how to raise suspicions where they would do most good, he would be that one.

She would need to trust him. That was hard. The second lesson of palace life was that everyone needed a network, allies and servants and spies; the first lesson was to trust none of them.

And then there was Jung, listening. Too late to send him away, far too soon to trust him.

She took a breath, took a step, walked into conspiracy.

Said, "Yes. Grandfather . . . ?"

four

The camp around the city was left standing when the rebel army at last moved into Santung: left to fall over, that is, unattended, like a body abandoned by its spirit.

It had been a city in its own right, populous and distinct. At first it was a city of soldiers, encompassing the ghosts of the city they had killed. Now it was a city of flies and rats under an imperium of cats that couched in shadows, rolled and stretched in sunlight, watched with a wary contempt as humans passed.

For there was still a human occupation: the desolate, the raped and widowed, the ruin of Santung. Those women not wanted elsewhere, not kept. Some of their children, those who could be saved no other way, not saved from this. A few bold or desperate men crept out of hiding, prepared to believe a rumor of amnesty sooner than die in a hole.

Also a few of the rebels' camp-followers, preferring to camp separately from their men. The city proper was no place to be now, where everyone watched the sky in anticipation of the dragon. If she came, it would be brick and stone and tile, the broad streets and high roofs of Santung that drew her—they reasoned, if anyone wanted to call it reason—rather than this squalid tangle of fabric and timber. And until she came, or until people decided that she would not come after all, their men were no good company, no easy company, better no company at all.

Also, necessarily, people passed through: mostly on the roads, east and west. Soldiers in squads, and soldiers on their own; soldiers driving wagons, rarely full and often empty. Other traffic was more limited, more watchful, tending to scurry in or out early in the morning or else in the growing twilight, always at the end of a watch when men were weary and thinking of food and bed, inclined to be slack.

THAT SHOULD have been all: a city of transit, a city of the dispossessed. City of vermin. No one native, no one here because here was where they belonged or where they chose to be or where they had to come.

And yet, and yet . . .

THERE WAS one more stream of people, who did not follow the roads through the camp and did not settle into whatever shadowed hovels they could find against the rain. Who came with purpose, fugitive and nervous. Who turned off the road, to follow a path that twisted curiously around obstacles that were no longer there, huts and tents fallen down or blown away or salvaged. Sometimes the path met the opposite effect, where an abandoned ramshackle structure had collapsed across the way. There a new path was being impressed by slow feet around the blockage, this way or that, but it always came back to the original.

Which led, eventually, to a tent that survived intact, untouched, untroubled. Its pale silk was rain-dirty now, mud-splashed and weary but still standing proud. It still even had its board outside, MEDICINES AND TREATMENT HERE, though few of its current patients could read it.

Possibly its current doctor couldn't.

TIEN STEPPED off the road with purpose in her mind, determination in her legs, a companion at her back.

Or not so much a companion, perhaps. A companion should

more properly walk at her side, not dog her heels. A companion would talk to her, be an equal, be companionable. Have a name that was known and could be used, responded to, even . . .

A servant, then? Not by any choice of Tien's. An assistant would be welcome, in the way that Tien herself had been assistant to her uncle all the months and miles that had brought them here—but an assistant who knew nothing and never spoke? What help she could possibly be, Tien couldn't guess.

Except that it was a help already to have someone with her, another body, legs and lungs working in concert with her own. Tien had never been alone, never imagined having to make her way alone, build her own life among the ruins of other people's.

And now here she was, having climbed through the ruins of Santung to the ruins of the army camp, looking to build a life. If it could be done at all, it would have to be done in the aching shadow of her uncle's death, the cold pit of his loss, the ruin of his life and hers together.

It would have to be done without Han also, with barely a view of the distant jag on the sea's horizon that was the Forge where she had been forced to leave him. Was he still there? She didn't know, and had no way to learn it. He would be lighting no beacons now.

But. It didn't need to be done on her own, and that was a blessing. She was determined, it would prove to be a blessing.

It was the temple priestess—of course!—who had suggested that the castrated boy's mother should come with her.

"She is better, I am sure, without her child. And of course she is welcome here, as you are—but she is not truly one of us, any more than you are. Like you, she needs to find some other way to live. I think you can help her to it, and I hope she may prove a help to you along the way. Will you take her?"

"Will she come?"

"Oh, that I am sure of. Yes, I can promise you that she will come."

AND SO she had, and so—for a while, for the walk through Santung—had the priestess herself and some of her temple sisters. It was odd how protected Tien could feel, in the company of other women who should be just as vulnerable as she was herself. There were soldiers still on every corner, idle and afraid, one eye on the sky and the other on whoever came and went. All soldiers were the same soldiers now, those who had desired her and chased after her and hurt her uncle and driven them to the temple steps before the pirate Li Ton faced them down with her uncle's severed head—but apparently they did not want her now. Not under the eye of the priestess. Rather they called greetings and asked for blessings, or walked a little way alongside: not so much an escort, more as though they themselves craved her protection.

Perhaps they were right. Perhaps she was as immune to the dragon as she was to the soldiery. Perhaps the goddess shielded her devotees against more than mortal harm? Tien didn't know, but she was grateful all the way up the hill.

With all of Santung's burned and bloodied streets behind them, all her broken walls and dreadful tensions, the priestess called a halt.

"We turn back here."

"Oh, won't you come—? Just to the tent? It isn't far now . . ."

"No, my dear. You need to do this by yourself, not with a barrage of nuns all about you. I will send my sisters up when they need treatment; or you can send to us, even come to us if you are lacking something."

She thought she was lacking everything, courage not excepted. But the priestess was implacable, and at last Tien and her—yes, call her a companion—stepped off the road and onto the path that wound so oddly but determinedly through the wreckage of the camp.

Once already it had been the path of her life; now it was again, or it would be. Perhaps.

THEY WEREN'T the first to walk this way today. Tien had come with few expectations, but she hadn't expected that.

At heart, she had come up here to see what—if anything—was left of her uncle's tent and stores. His practice, surely, would be long gone. Tunghai Wang had promised to put another doctor in his place, but that man would long since have followed the army down into the city proper. There could be no constituency here anymore, so why stay?

And why would anyone move in, to fill his absence?

She had come in hopes, but not in hope of this: the tent unharmed, the stir of shadows on the walls, the buzz of voices. The clink of a bronze pestle in a mortar.

A figure in the doorway, coming out. A woman with a twist of paper in her hands, cupped as though it were something precious.

Tien recognized the pose and what she carried, and what it was wrapped in.

That was how her uncle's patients had always seemed, coming out with medicine: supplicant and grateful.

That was how they carried the twist of herbs that he had given them, except that his were always twisted up in muslin tied with string, sealed with his chop.

That paper, that held the woman's herbs today: that was a sheet of Uncle Hsui's writing, his careful notes on treatments and their uses.

She was . . . confused, intrigued, infuriated. All at once. And deeply disturbed on top, because those writings were largely what she'd come for. She hadn't expected honestly to find a practice here, and she wasn't honestly sure that she wanted one. To sit in the silent company of this other woman and her uncle's ghost, to read, to study, to learn—that would have been ideal.

Almost ideal.

If her eyes had occasionally lifted to the sea, to that dark little jag on the horizon, to see if any smoke might rise in a message that was readable—well, that would be understandable, surely? Given that the purpose of her study, her need to learn was there, all there?

And now here was something entirely otherwise, a doctor still in her uncle's place and somehow finding patients.

She let this patient go her way, and walked into the tent with her nameless companion still behind her.

AND FOUND it almost all as she had left it, except for the man who held court there.

The long table, the bench, the waiting people. Not so many as there used to be, but enough. The shelves, the jars, the chest of drawers.

The brazier was gone, and so was the kettle that had always steamed above it. The lamps that hung from the tent-poles were gone; the texts remained, though it was almost too dark in here now to read them. It was surely too dark to read the silk and paper labels on the drawers and jars. It didn't seem to matter.

A man sat bare-chested on the examination table, just reaching for his shirt. Another man stepped toward the chest of drawers in gray robes too long for him, an old set of her uncle's clothes that she had washed and patched until she wouldn't let him wear them anymore, although he wouldn't let her throw them away.

"Your blood is cold and sluggish," the man was saying, "and your kidneys want heat. You must take fu-tzu; make a tea of this," a handful of dry leaves taken from a single jar, "and drink it three times a day. This much," adding a judicious sprinkle more to the folded paper and then screwing it closed at the top, "should last you for a week. Come back to see me then. Do not discard the paper; there are charms written on it, as you see, which will be as efficacious as the medicine."

His patient bowed and was grateful, and handed him a sack-wrapped package in payment, some kind of trade. Food, perhaps; there could be nothing more precious now.

Except their lives. Tien tapped her companion on the shoulder and led her swiftly out of the tent, murmured urgently in her ear and waited for her nod. The woman might not speak, but she understood. Something to be grateful for.

Alone, Tien lingered at the back of the tent, listening while the next patient described sore and flaking skin on her knees and elbows. Then, while the man was bent forward to see the rash in that dim light, she moved swiftly to the shelves behind him. By the time he had straightened and turned, she had already lifted down three jars and was tipping out a measure from each.

"You, girl—what do you think you're doing . . . ?"

"My lord the doctor," she said, as ingratiating as brusque can be, "has undoubtedly seen eczema many times before, and will no doubt offer the same treatment as my uncle did, who was doctor here before. I used often to prepare it for him, so I thought I could save my lord the time." And even while she spoke her hands were working, mixing the herbs and wrapping them in another sheet torn from her uncle's writings.

This supposed doctor was a fat man, which was suspicious itself in a time of war and famine. He was an ignorant and a dishonest man, Tien knew that much already. She was gambling now on his not being a fool as well.

She gambled, and she won. He grunted, took a step back, let his indignation fade.

"Good, yes. Yes. You carry on . . ."

She handed over the herbs with instructions, how to make a brew from them that the woman should both drink and wash with, wherever her skin itched at all. Also, washing her clothes would help; Tien couldn't resist adding that.

The woman reached into those same malodorous clothes and drew out something wrapped in a scrap of linen. Something wet, that had already soaked the fabric through. Tien caught the dark scent of blood: duck's liver, perhaps?

She stepped back hastily, not to come between the doctor and his fee. That would be crucial.

So too was confidence. She waited where she was, between the shelves and the chest of drawers, while the man interviewed his next patient with many a sidelong glance at her. She blessed the weeks and months that she had stood just here, watching and listening, learning from her uncle; she blessed the simple troubles that these people brought, that she could diagnose for herself without needing to count a pulse or look at a tongue; she blessed her own swift eyes and mind and fingers, that could again have the medicine half mixed before the doctor could turn to look for it.

She recited the herbs and their virtues as she wrapped them, as though for the doctor's approval. By the time they treated their last patients of the morning, he had fallen almost silent, letting her question and diagnose as well as prescribing for them. Good: he was quick to learn.

And then the very last man limped from the tent, and they had it to themselves; and now she could let her anger blaze, turning on the fraud and demanding, "Who are you? And how dare you steal my uncle's place, his things, his honor and reputation? You are no doctor, you know nothing, you—"

The slap that answered her was delivered roundly, by a fat heavy hand. It sent her sprawling across the matting floor, to crack her head on the leg of the examination table.

"Who am I?" he repeated calmly, standing over her. "I am master here now, and you will not forget that. Who are you?"

"My name," she muttered thickly, pulling herself back up, "my name is Tien. I am niece and assistant to the man whose tent this is, whose—"

"No," and he slapped her again, just as hard, on the same stinging cheek. This time she was already holding on to the table, and did just about manage to keep her feet, though the blow rocked her sideways and knocked her dizzy. "You are my servant now. If I choose to keep you. If you want to stay here and work for me," which of course she did, it was her sole purpose now; which he was astute enough to see and to seize upon. "You will show me respect, in front of the patients and when we are alone. You will cook my meals and wash my clothes. I will permit you to dispense the medicines, but only under—"

But just then they were disturbed: a shadow at the door, a man staggering in. The same man that she had first seen treated here. He had been calm and grateful when he left; now he was in tears, almost, and bleeding from the nose, in high distress, gabbling incoherently about an assault, a woman, a theft . . .

Tien hastened to sit him on the bench, to bring water, to wash his face and quench the bleeding.

"Master Biao, Master Biao! I was attacked! The woman rose up from the shadows and knocked me down! And then she stole the medicine that you had given me, and ran away with it. And, and, I have nothing more to offer you, but please, I need my medicine . . ."

"And you shall have it, of course," Tien assured him swiftly. "You sit here with Master Biao, and tell him everything you can about this wicked woman who attacked you, so that we'll know her again. I'll mix you another paper of the medicine you need."

She remembered his complaint, she remembered what Biao had given him; she felt Biao's glare on her as she assembled what her uncle would have dispensed, just a pinch of fu-tzu in among a quantity of other herbs. The patient was too sore and self-involved to notice, and wouldn't know when he came to make the tea.

When finally they had persuaded him to leave, still complaining, with his twist of herbs this time securely inside his dress, Biao was clearly about to remonstrate with her, perhaps even to strike her again; but there was abruptly another shadow in the doorway, another person coming in.

A woman, who most exactly matched the description her recent victim had just given.

Who was carrying, indeed, openly in her hand, the stolen twist of paper.

Tien thanked her carefully, wishing only that she knew the woman's name; and took the twist and emptied it with equal care back into the jar of fu-tzu.

Biao had stood gaping throughout. With the lid back on the jar, at last he found his voice; he said, "Girl, is this your creature?"

"She is my companion," Tien agreed solemnly. "Her name is lost; we should think of something to call her. Nurse, perhaps?"

"But she, she assaulted my patient!"

"She did. At my request. You should thank her for that, *Master* Biao. She saved your patient's life." And then, as he stared and gawped again, "I don't know where you stole your little knowledge, but fu-tzu is deadly poison, unless it is mixed in proper proportion with its counter-agents. You would have killed that man with his first dose. What I gave instead will cure him."

"I told you, girl, you will treat me with respect . . . !"

"You said that, yes. I say this, that if you raise your hand to me again—or to my woman here—you will never be able to trust anything that you take from me. Does your food have fu-tzu in it? You would never know. What is in your tea? I will not tell you. I even know what to wash your clothes in, that will have them poison you through your skin when they are dry and you are sweating. You are a fat man, you sweat a lot; you should learn to be careful of your clothes.

"Also," she went on relentlessly, "my friend here is watching you. She would not take it well if she saw you strike me. You have seen what she did to your patient, simply to save his life, simply because I asked her. What do you imagine she will do to you? In the dark, perhaps, when you are sleeping? You should learn to fear the dark.

"Unless," she said, "unless you and I sit down now, over a drink of tea that I will make and we will share quite comfortably among the three of us, and discover a way that we can all three live together, to the benefit of all."

five

So if you hate it here in the hills so much, old man, why didn't you go to Taishu-port with the emperor and Mei Feng?"

"Because—oof!—I am not a fool. This, now, this is uncomfortable, uncivilized, no way for a man to live. Oof! Anywhere near those two just now, with their tempers so foul at each other? That would be—oof!—a life not worth living. Yu Shan, is this *hurting* you? At all?"

"No."

"Let me try." That came from two sides at once, two different voices chiming with one thought at one moment: both female, both full of purpose. Yu Shan shivered, although the day was warm.

He was not as tall as the emperor, but tall enough; a coat measured to the emperor's size was not ridiculous on him. And he was as strong, perhaps stronger. Certainly he made a good test subject, to stand still in the emperor's armor and be hit.

Certainly they could not ask the emperor to do it, and no one else could stand up under the weight of a stone coat against the weight of Guangli's staff, swung with all the effort of his shoulders.

At least, no one else was fool enough to try.

Yu Shan had volunteered for this, in a sense. He had not volunteered to have his clan-cousin Siew Ren take over swinging the staff. She might be a girl half Guangli's age and half his size, but she had stone in her bones and a good deal of purpose in her arms; and on the other side from her stood Jiao. Who had no staff, and was drawing out her tao instead. At that first grate of steel, everything stopped. It was Guangli who said, "No! Wait, you can't . . . !"

"We need to find out if your armor works, don't we?" Jiao said, the very voice of reason. "The emperor's enemies won't be hitting him with sticks. Do you trust this coat of yours, or don't you?"

"Yes, of course," he said, with doubt etched deep into his voice. "Those scales will turn any blade. They'll blunt it, if you're fool enough to keep hacking. They might break it, if he can just keep on his feet. But—Jiao, it's Yu Shan, and—well, I could be wrong, I could have made it badly . . ."

"We'll find out, then, won't we? Better to find out on him now than on the emperor when it matters."

And she swung her blade in the sunlight, and Yu Shan—somehow!—managed to stand still. Jiao favored a long, heavy-bladed tao; he caught the full weight of it across his ribs, as she swung from the shoulders with both arms.

Or maybe not, despite her bravado. Perhaps she didn't put all her strength into it. Her arms were long and tough and practiced, particularly at hacking with a blade; he ought surely to feel more than a light impact, spread across his chest? None of them had expected the blade to cut through the armor—he thought, he hoped!—but the impact surely should have left a bruise.

He really didn't think she was trying.

The armor was an eelskin shirt for toughness and suppleness together, sewn with hundreds, maybe thousands of small overlapping jade scales. It hung to his knees, which would be mid-thigh on the emperor. He was . . . aware of the weight of it, if quite untroubled; just as he was aware of the tingle, the touch of jade, but untroubled by that too. Separated from him by the soft oily eelskin, it barely added to what he had already: the immediacy of jade against his skin, the amulet of beads he wore around his neck; the intimacy of the shard of jade in his mouth, under his skin where his blood could draw on it directly.

Jiao frowned and shook her arms loosely, as if the impact had jarred them to the shoulders. As if she'd put more effort into that blow than he'd felt or realized.

He might have said something, but he couldn't think how to do it without sounding as though he mocked her, which was the last thing he meant or needed.

Besides, there was a blur in his peripheral vision, and that was Siew Ren taking a turn, swinging that heavy staff once about her head for speed and effect—she was good with a staff, she could take pigeons in the air as they came in to roost; he knew, he'd seen her do it—and then bringing it slamming down toward his shoulders.

And bizarrely misjudging her aim, getting it entirely wrong, so that the blow caught him full-force on the back of the head.

There was an eelskin hood that Mei Feng had procured, but that was still in Guangli's hut waiting to be sewn with scales once this test was over, in case she could actually persuade the emperor to wear it.

Yu Shan's head was bare and the staff was hard and Siew Ren had swung it with all the uncoiled tension of her slender body, all the power of mountain-trained jade-enhanced clan muscles.

It did actually jar him from his stance, where he had stood four-square and untroubled beneath Guangli's buffets.

It did also actually hurt, quite brutally. Dizzy with the pain of it, he couldn't actually see Siew Ren's expression. He did hear her voice say "Oops" in a tone of deep satisfaction, the moment after she struck, in that brief stillness before the pain erupted; but then he heard a softer sound that might have been distressful, just under Jiao's shout of protest. And when he felt an arm around his chest to hold him up and fingers gently exploratory in his hair, he knew without need of eyes that it was Jiao's arm that held him but Siew Ren's fingers that probed for a wound.

And, apparently, couldn't find one.

"Don't snarl at me, it hasn't even cut the scalp, see?"

"You still might have broken his head beneath."

"Not his. He always was hard-headed," though she said it with less confidence than the words desired, as if she was astonished not to find him bloody and skull-crushed, knowing just how hard she'd struck, how much harder than she'd really meant to do it.

It was almost pleasant for once to be bickered over, rather than sniped at; but he shrugged them both off—gently, gently!—and tested his own ability to stand.

And could do it, though his head still pounded; could blink away the blindness, though pain still squatted like a venomous toad behind his eyes.

Could look around and smile at them both, and at Guangli too. And shake his head, square his shoulders, say, "Again, then, hit me again. On the armor would be better, probably. That's what we really want to test."

"Yu Shan," Guangli protested, "are you sure?"

Yu Shan smiled. And grimaced at the pain of that little movement, but still, he was sure. "A crack on the head doesn't change anything. We still need to know that this is right, before we offer it to the emperor."

He took his stance again, and nodded to Jiao. Gently. And said, "Properly, mind. There's no point doing this if you're not trying to kill me."

"Sweet," she said, "I've been wanting to kill you for weeks. Hold still."

"Just, not the neck, yes? No higher than the shoulders . . ."

She grunted, which might have been a promise; and went for a belly cut, slamming in hard—and again the blade bounced off jarringly, and again he felt little more than pressure against his gut.

"That'll do, won't it?" Guangli said pleadingly. "That's plenty, to be sure . . ."

"Not yet," Siew Ren said behind him. "I haven't had my proper turn, and Jiao's barely started. You got to hit him far more than we have, old man. Stand back now . . ."

This time she aimed the staff at his ribs, while he lifted his arms judiciously out of the way. The staff thudded into the scales that layered his side, hard enough to break whatever bones might dare to stand against it. It didn't even knock the breath out of him. He could have snatched this end and twisted it out of her grip while she was still wondering why he wasn't lying broken on the floor.

There was the sound of stray tinkling, as a few scattered scales were knocked loose and fell to the ground. They'd need to check the stitching, he supposed, if a few blows could shake them off that way . . .

And then Jiao struck again, while he was distracted. Which of course made no difference to the armor, its attention was absolute; and then Siew Ren, and then Jiao, and he just stood with his hands tucked behind his head and let the women work out all their troubles on his body, because really he wasn't feeling a thing, although the shirt was suffering, shedding more and more of those carefully-sewn-on scales, and—

AND GUANGLI was perhaps trying to stop them again, but no one was listening to him now; and suddenly Jiao's tao found a space where Siew Ren's staff had knocked loose a whole patch of scales, leaving nothing but the bare eelskin, which was tough of course but nowhere near tough enough to turn her blade aside, and—

AND THERE was a slashed hole in the emperor's gift, and Yu Shan was bleeding through it, and that wasn't good. Not by any measure.

HE WAS actually bleeding rather a lot, and it was starting to hurt now. Rather a lot.

SIEW REN made a little mewing sound, and let the staff drop. Jiao was methodically wiping blood from her blade, from instinct or good training or an urgent need to be doing something; which earned her a glare and a hissing accusation, which she only shrugged at. "I've seen this before, you haven't. When the emperor was skewered by one of those assassins we fought here, his wound was worse than this. Far worse. And it just healed up while we watched."

"Yu Shan is not the emperor!"

"No, but he's got just as much jade in his blood. If not more. He'll be fine."

She wasn't half as confident as she sounded. Her eyes spoke against her, watching him with a hollow anxiety.

Himself, he didn't feel fine at all. His tongue groped for the little nodule of flesh in his mouth that masked the chip of jade, as if touching it, pressing against it would initiate the magic. He was too dizzy, though, to remember what he really believed. He thought perhaps he ought to sit down.

He did sit down, right there, in a pool of warmly sticky—oh. That would be his blood, then. He didn't like that, but wasn't sure he had the strength to stand again.

Besides, here was Siew Ren, easing him back, making a pillow of her lap for him to rest on. He did like that. It was the first tender sign he'd had since she arrived, first memory of that easy closeness they used to share.

Jiao was bent over his middle, working the armored shirt up under his armpits to see how hurt he was.

He couldn't see it himself, not with Siew Ren cupping her hand beneath his chin to prevent his looking. All he could do was look at her, then, measure his damage by the depths of her anxiety. And then by the depths of Jiao's relief as she said, "See? The bleeding's stopped already."

"It can't have done. That terrible great slash? It goes right down into his—oh . . ."

"Not anymore, it doesn't. That's what I mean, we can sit here and watch it all knit itself together. He'll be seamed like jade, a little, when it's done, but he won't even have a proper scar. These boys' bodies don't work like normal flesh, there's too much stone in them. Stone doesn't flow like blood does, it doesn't cut like meat. Yu Shan? Does it even *hurt*?"

"Not . . . so much. Not anymore. It did, at first."

"Yes, and then your body remembered not to do that." She slapped his bare flank—the other side, not where she had cut him open—and said, "Do you want to get up and try again?"

Yu Shan opened his mouth to say no, *no thank you,* and was forestalled:

"No, he does not! We've seen enough, we've proved the shirt doesn't work. We'd proved it sooner, when all the scales fell off; you didn't have to keep hacking at him . . ."

"Child, you were the one who knocked the scales off, and I notice you didn't stop hitting him after. You'd have stove all his ribs in before I ever had the chance to cut him, if his bones weren't made of rock."

Just briefly, he'd imagined that their mutual concern for him might have knitted them together, at least a little, in concert with his flesh. No such joy; of course they would blame each other, if they could. His body was what they fought over, after all.

He wished above all that he could bring them to peace. There seemed to be nothing in his body that could do that, though, and his mind was an empty rattle.

Guangli's voice cut across the two of theirs, bleakly authoritative. "Oh, be quiet. There is no point in arguing fault. The boy is hurt, and getting better," and Yu Shan at least could hear his fascination in that, his obsession with all things jade, even under the disappointment of failure. "This is a catastrophe in other ways, in every way. We have spent—I don't know, how many days?—in shaping these scales and sewing them all in place; and it was all wasted. In a real battle, the emperor might as well have been naked. Our work is lost, and we have nothing to show Mei Feng."

"Oh, not all wasted, surely?" That was Siew Ren, looking for hope urgently because she couldn't bear to start again. "Look, none of the actual scales broke, you and Yu Shan carved them so well; it was only the threads that snapped, and then the blade cut the eelskin. We just need to find something stronger to sew the scales on with, and maybe a tougher lining, maybe oxhide, or . . ."

"Oxhide would never be supple enough, and it would cut just the same unless you boiled it, in which case it would not be supple at all and we could sew nothing to it. Besides, what stronger thread do you know, than this waxed silk we have been using? That's the first point of failure. We can go nowhere if we can't attach the scales; and there is nowhere farther to go in that direction."

"Wire is stronger than thread," Jiao suggested.

"Only in pulling. Wire will snap under blows. Any wire flexible enough to sew like thread will snap like thread, but sooner."

"Wait, then . . . How clever are you, Guangli?"

Yu Shan couldn't see his face—indeed, all he could see was Siew Ren's face, where she was still holding his head—but he knew Guangli's expression sight unseen: the eyes half closed, the cheeks puffed out a little, the lips pursed in a silence that spoke loud enough to carry. *Clever enough, woman. Cleverer than you.*

"In your hands, I mean," Jiao persisted, "in your craft?"

"As clever as any in Taishu," he said, meaning *cleverer than any you could find anywhere.* "Why are you asking me these things?"

"I have this bracelet," she said, accompanied by the scratchy sounds of her unclasping it. Yu Shan knew it well. It was more functional than decorative, he thought, like almost everything she carried: strips of thin steel that linked together to make a guard for her left arm, the arm that didn't hold a blade. It reached from the wrist halfway to the elbow, and had dents enough to suggest that it had been useful; her skin would be more scarred without it. Perhaps her arm would have broken, under one or two of those blows. With a broken arm, perhaps she might not have survived that encounter, or what followed. Yu Shan held that bracelet in great fondness in his heart. Just now, though, he didn't entirely understand its relevance.

No more did Guangli. "I see," he said, over soft metallic rustlings as he must be turning it in his hands. Siew Ren's fingers pressed lightly on the softness beneath Yu Shan's chin: not dancing as they used to, only applying pressure. "And?"

"And they are not wired together at all, except the two ends where they clasp. One link grips the next thanks to its shape, that's all; and they are supple in wear, and rigid under blows, and do not come apart. And I was thinking, a clever man could cut scales of jade to do the same, to cling to each other without need of thread or wire or an undershirt . . ."

"Metal can be molded, hammered, shaped . . ."

"I said, he would need to be clever."

"You can let the flattery lie, Jiao. I have my pride, but I am not entirely foolish." Even so he was pleased and interested, engaged, turning and turning that bracelet.

Yu Shan thought about wearing a shirt of jade, nothing between it and his skin, all over; he shivered, with a kind of appalled envy.

Siew Ren felt that and said, "What is it? Are you hurting, bleeding again . . . ?"

"No, nothing. Only thinking. Let me sit up now."

"For what? You will be dizzy, all that blood you've lost . . ."

And he was still lying in it, which would be another reason to move, but he said, "Guangli and I have work to do, if we have to carve that many scales again, to a different pattern."

Different patterns for different places on the shirt, he guessed.

Scales that would link together and cling, not come apart. Jade would not break under blows, that much at least was certain. Hard to mine and hard to carve, it would resist mortal weapons as strongly as dragonhide. Maybe more so: dragons had been slain, from time to time, by mortal heroes or conspiracy.

So had emperors, of course, but not when they were clad in jade. If Guangli could devise the proper patterns, Mei Feng might be pleased with them yet.

six

*M*ei Feng, ever since we came to this rat-infested island, you have been telling me that there is not and can never be food enough to feed us and all those we brought with us. Even if we eat the damned rats. This is a solution, this is the *only* solution, and there will never be a better time than now. Don't you *see* . . . ?"

Sometimes, Chung did very devoutly wish that he had never gotten himself mixed up in the affairs of royalty. He should have been a fisherman, or a dock worker like his father. Then he could have stayed safe, or as safe as war and weather would allow. At any rate he wouldn't need to be here, nervously on his knees, staring down at his fingers while the powers of the palace raged around him.

As far as he could tell, he didn't actually need to be here anyway. But Mei Feng had summoned him and not sent him away, and now the emperor was here and he didn't dare move, not a muscle. Most especially he didn't dare lift his head, because either one of them might catch his eye and who knew what that might lead to? A swift execution for impertinence would be a kindness. Far worse and much more likely, he could find himself called into the argument, on one side or the other. That would be . . . unimaginable, except that he could imagine it all too clearly. Unimaginably awful. Irrecoverable.

Not his soul, but his service belonged entirely to Mei Feng, so should he side with her? And disagree with the *emperor*? Face to face, tell his majesty he was wrong?

It was unthinkable. But so was the opposite, to stand against small fierce Mei Feng who commanded his body and his loyalty, if not quite his soul. Even if he thought the emperor was right.

Chung wormed his way backward, till the soles of his bare feet pressed into the painted wood of the wall. Shen had told him of adepts in the high mountains—nothing, he was assured, like the little foothills that were called mountains here on Taishu—who could pass through crowds or stand alone on a bare plain and be not invisible but entirely unseen in either place. At the time Chung had been defensive, pointing out that his own home mountains might not be so foolishly, unnecessarily high and might not have mad old men lurking in their caves pretending to be invisible when actually nobody was looking, but they did at least have jade at their hearts and jade tigers in their forests.

Now, though? Now he concentrated so hard on seeming a native part of the room—over here there was just floor and walls and corner and Chung, nothing worth noticing—that the argument he was trying to avoid just slipped past him. He was only snagged back into it when Mei Feng turned and marched toward the door, snapping her fingers for her loyal messenger to follow.

Turning her back on the emperor, walking out on him. And taking Chung with her, mute partner in this horrendous offense, under the eyes of so many courtiers and eunuchs . . .

He rose because he had no choice, and tried to scuttle out in her furious shadow; but an unexpected voice snagged them both, as light and sharp and delicate as a fishhook: "Forgive me, majesty, but actually there *is* a way to take the fleet across the water to Santung."

Mei Feng stopped dead in her tracks, and Chung perforce stopped behind her. When she swiveled around, she had to push him physically before he recovered enough sense to move aside, to let her see who spoke.

When he looked—and so much for all his invisibility, here he was side by side with her, inextricably aligned, if the emperor deigned to notice—he saw that it was one of the eunuchs. A young man, a new face. There was only the one new eunuch in the emperor's service, strangely come and oddly accompanied and bizarrely breaking into the discussion now.

That was it, of course, that had always been the killer point: that they could not send an army to Santung if they wanted to. It was Mei Feng's triumphant parting blow, though Chung heard it now only in his memory, groping back.

And the eunuch thought he could deny it. Indeed, the eunuch did deny it simply by being here, even before he said, "We sailed here by the goddess's grace, majesty, and in defiance of the dragon."

"Oh, and can you guarantee that grace again, to sail a fleet back?" It was Mei Feng necessarily who flung the challenge, and now it would be a disgrace in Chung to back away, to dissociate himself from her. He stood boldly at her side, and really wished he didn't have to.

"I believe so, lady, yes. If we take the child."

Mei Feng felt betrayed, and twice betrayed; Chung could see that in her. He could have seen it if he didn't know her, he would have known it sight unseen. She had won this man a place here, for himself and the child that he came with; and now—

Now he was using that against her, the place he had and the child too, and she had no answer to it.

A Chain of Days

one

*F*or once, the dragon's fury seemed not to be aimed at him.

He knew her rage from afar, as he knew her coming; when she landed on the Forge-top, he was there to meet her. There was nowhere to hide—how could there be, when she made shift inside his head?—so he might as well be mannerly.

Besides, he was curious. She had been raging for days, and he couldn't understand it. His mind might be the simplest, easiest thing for her to pick apart; hers was a vast and complex array that he couldn't hope to read except when she allowed it, what she chose to share. It was as much as he could do to sense her feelings and her movements. She was darkly, bitterly angry; that was not new, but the cause was. Something about her freedom to move, something that restricted her almost as though she were chained again, chained differently . . .

He couldn't understand it. What could stand against her now? Except himself, fractionally? When she was first chained, the stories said a magician came to do it with prayers and spells and a monksmith at his back, whom he set on the Forge to keep her chains ever-fresh.

Actually, the stories said that he came with *the* monksmith, that there had only ever been the one in all these centuries. Han no longer believed that. He had seen the man, had seen him die, had seen nothing in him except grace and a sorrowful kindness that had done him no good at all, an apparent wisdom that had none the less not saved him. No hint of age-old endurance, power beyond the mortal, anything that could stand against the sordid folly of his death.

There must have been a magician, once; there must have been a first monksmith to build the forge and make the first chains. They might have been the same man. It didn't matter.

This mattered, that Han had willfully undone as much of their work as he could in what was not quite a desperate random protest. To save Tien, he had loosed his own control over the dragon, or tried to; which was all the control there was, or seemed to be.

Nothing was ever as simple as it seemed. He had cut the chains, and she still was not quite free of him, nor he of her. Despite that, there should be nothing else to hold her. And yet . . .

AND YET here she came, in a surge of hot wet air, and her landing on the peak was almost clumsy. For a moment, he wondered if she would actually topple down the slope. And where he might seek shelter from her temper if she did.

She caught her balance, though, with a bizarrely graceless swing of her long tail; and when her head lunged forward he didn't even try to deflect it. He understood absolutely that for once this was not an attack on him.

She showed him her terrible gape, her teeth, her livid lethal tongue, too close. He smelled the fierce salt of her breath; felt the sheer animal intensity of her that was not at all mitigated by the dreadful intelligence of her spirit; said, absurdly, "What can I do to help?"

He said it aloud the first time, which was like whispering into the muffle of his hands when he stood in the typhoon, when his voice was the last thing he should use.

He should have swallowed the question down, hoped to be lucky, hoped she hadn't caught even a hint of the indignity of it. Instead he put it again in his mind, where she liked to lurk: *Great one. How can I help you?*

It was folly, even to be asking. She was dragon, he was mortal man; she was in every way his enemy. He waited for an answer none the less, and had one of a sort: an echo in his head like the slamming back of great bronze doors, a glimpse of roiling confusion, the raging turmoil that was her mind, vast storms and systems that he could not hope to encompass. There was nothing useful he could draw from that, nothing he could do but wait.

Until now, nothing had been more important, nothing had enraged her more than this negligible human, this mayfly creature who had yet some influence on her. Now, though, she settled slowly into the rock and ash and ruin on the peak there; she snapped her teeth a time or two and gazed at him with eyes that shone like a summoning; she said, *Little thing, there is nothing you will do to help me.* Not *nothing you can do.* He could walk willingly into her mouth, for example, only that he would not. Nor would he put himself within the clutch of her claws.

Tell me, then, he said, having nothing else to offer but a bare curiosity. *Who has upset you, who could aspire so high?*

She hissed, between her teeth. And, unexpectedly, told him.

There is a power, here in the strait. Your kind call her a goddess; I do not know. But she . . . cooperated with those who chained me. She held me prisoner, and claimed these waters. My waters, she claims them for her own.

And what, he said, *you cannot teach her otherwise? Now you are free?*

I said, she is a power. And I am chained to you still, and not myself. I cannot resist her, quite.

No more could he resist the dragon, quite, except in that little way that meant she could not eat him. Her stench made his head swim, unless it was her potency, unless it was the stress of her regard. Her eyes ate at him like acid. He said, *Great one, if you can bring me a boat, I would willingly be free of you.* Not *I will free you,* nothing so impertinent; and *willing* wasn't the word, quite, because he did feel monstrously guilty about it. Suo Lung set the chains on him without his consent, but discarding them would still be his own choice. Which would make him responsible for what followed, what must follow: the dragon free, with all that that implied. Tien would be unhappy.

Han knew the guilt of that, and would not let it stop him. He never had lived his own life, but he meant to do it now.

Bring me a boat, he said.

The dragon said, *I tried, but she would not let me near it. She is not that strong, she is not*—not as strong as a dragon, she meant, her body shifting slightly, crushing rock to dust—*but she makes her people slippery. And I could not shift the water or the wind, to bring the boat here.*

That was the confrontation that had stoked her anger to its incandescence. She had tried to do a thing, and had been prevented. That age-old helplessness, familiar through the long years of her captivity, her new freedom only an illusion after all—no wonder she was angry. The only wonder was that she had thought to come to him.

Bring me a boat, he said. What else could he say? *I am not you, I am not anything like you: I cannot swim, or fly.*

I could carry you, little thing, she said, not the first time but more determined now, or more desperate. If a dragon could know the taste of desperation. *If you only hold still, and let me clutch you.*

He said, *Bring me a boat.*

THIS TIME when she left, she rose in a sudden storm of dust and rock and ash that stung his eyes and skin. By the time he could see again, she was gone. Into the sea or the sun, he could not guess.

Until he reached a moment later for her mind and found her plunging deep, trying to wash fury from her heart as easily as she could the filth from her scales.

He wished that he could plunge like that, suddenly out of the world's skin, this scant scrap of fabric between the deep waters and the wide sky. Here was where the trouble clung; it might be good to be gone.

EXCEPT THAT she was still troubled, whether she swam or flew, and he was maimed and heartsore and so very much not a dragon. He couldn't understand where she might look for her pleasures, in what her ambitions might consist; his own were bounded within simple lines. He wanted to be with Tien, comfortable and settled, far from war. Not frightened, not in pain. Not shackled to a dragon.

It didn't seem so much.

Tien might be a little angry with him, for setting the dragon free. She had strong notions of duty and what was proper, what was owed. His own mind turned more toward survival, for himself and those he loved. He had gotten by, as a river rat and as an inkboy; he had—just barely—gotten by as a pirate brat.

If he could get to the mainland somehow—if the dragon managed to fetch him a boat, preferably with sailors aboard, because Han didn't know how to work a vessel by wind and water, he hadn't been that much of a pirate brat for long enough to learn— he would have more reasons than the dragon's impatience to see the cuffs and collar struck off. Once it was done, it was done. Tien would forgive him, and they would travel inland. Far inland, very far from the dragon and all her harm.

Yes.

Day by day he was getting by as a dragon's brat, but only day by day. It couldn't last. He would go mad, or she would eat him, or find some other way to bring him to ruin. He held the typhoon in a noose of rotted rope, and the bitter end was around his neck. It would break, or it would strangle him, or else it would carry him away. There were no other choices, except that he let go.

two

*I*f Mei Feng sat down to make a list, all those many ways she felt betrayed—well. It would be a long list, and most of her friends would feature.

At heart, of course—at the head of the list, and running all the way down the margins, and neatly closing it out at the tail too— would be the emperor, the fountainhead, the source of all betrayal. Who apparently still expected her to lie in his bed and listen to his snoring, even when they were not at all speaking to each other.

Then there was Jung the eunuch, who had so cruelly misused her foolish kindness by offering the child he carried—a *child*!—as safeguard against the dragon's fury. Which was an offering the wicked emperor was ready to accept, for the sake of his stupid war.

Jiao and Yu Shan and Guangli the jade carver, those she could almost ignore; their failure to produce the simple commission she'd asked for, an armor for her lord the emperor to protect him in his folly, was almost negligible in such a list of blame. If they had been here, she suspected that Jiao and Yu Shan too would be demanding a place in the boats; it was odd to find herself reluctantly grateful for their absence, not to be yet worse betrayed.

The head and the heart of all betrayal might be the emperor, but there was a grand passion in that. She could almost enjoy being furious with the Son of Heaven, being appalled by him. It was the proper way of things, perhaps, that a god-on-earth should be heedless of his mortal possessions, leaving them outraged and desolate.

It was her grandfather who spoiled that high-minded suffering. He made it stink, the whole rank idiocy of it.

He was her grandfather, and if he knew nothing else, he knew her intimately; he *must* know how she would feel about this madness, especially the cruelty of using a child to make it happen. He must know how she would hate that. And yet, and yet . . .

Oh, he probably hadn't volunteered. Likely he had simply been told, *you will lead the fleet,* and what could he do about that?

Not refuse, of course; she knew it. But he had a boat, he had all the sea to hide in; and his Li-goddess held him in good favor, he didn't truly need a child on the deck to ward away the dragon. She didn't think he did. She thought he could simply have sailed away.

But no, there he was in the harbor with a squadron of other vessels grouped around him, too late to make a dash for it now. He hadn't come to see her since it was decided; she'd had to learn from others that his would be the pilot-vessel, he the guide.

Jung the eunuch, of course, would carry the child. He had outfaced the dragon once; it only made sense that he should do it again.

Mei Feng of course had gone to shout at Jung, but couldn't find him. He had already insinuated himself into the palace staff. It was as though there was another secret palace within the one she knew, one that was private to servants and eunuchs and clerks. She couldn't find her way in; she met locked doors, locked faces at every turn.

When she sent for him, still he didn't come. Her messengers said they couldn't find him either, but she wasn't sure. They stood within his world, on his side of the wall.

She could hate Jung, she thought, if only he was visible, physical, available to her fury. It was harder to hate a ghost. She knew nothing of him but his name and his face, the soft shadow of his voice and his betrayal.

The emperor was almost his reverse: impossibly visible and physical, eternally there in her eye, inescapable. And implacable. It might have been Ping Wen's war once, but he had seized it and claimed it, as swiftly and irrevocably as he had her; it was his new delight, the rival she had feared and anticipated and never somehow imagined like this. It was the stranger in their bed, and she could find no way around it. He wasn't even trying to find any way back to her. That was his great betrayal, she thought: not that he would not listen, but that he would not try.

And still it was her grandfather's that sat in her mind like a foul taste in her mouth, like something rotten in her belly: his acceptance of what was unacceptable, unbearable, just wrong. So many ways of wrong . . .

IT WAS her grandfather, then, his utter wrongheadedness, that drove her out of the emperor's bed while he was still snoring. It wasn't so very early, but he slept late always, later if she let him; today, she thought, if he slept till she woke him he might never wake at all.

She slipped out of the bed and out of the chamber, more cautiously than she needed to. If the moment of her leaving didn't wake him, nothing would.

In the room beyond, her women intercepted her. A little astonished at seeing her like this, alone and independent; a little shocked that she dared to sneak away. Even after months she could still surprise them, it seemed. Something to be glad of, on a miserable morning.

She couldn't evade their determined attentions. She was washed and powdered, oiled and perfumed and dressed, and then only let go on alone when she threatened to make noise enough to wake the emperor after all, and blame the noise on them.

As threats went, it was empty, but they pretended to be as cowed as she was pretending to be fierce. Once they knew where she was going, none of them would willingly go with her anyway.

On her own, then, and head high with the bitterness of that—of being so betrayed that there was no one to walk with her, out of all the people who mattered to her, to whom she'd thought she mattered—she walked across the formal garden that separated the emperor's wing from his mother's.

THE DOWAGER empress was not expecting her. Nevertheless, Mei Feng found her exactly where and how she always had: even more formal than the clipped and cosseted garden; sitting erect in her private chamber, exactly as much softened by age as she was by kindness, which meant not at all; a rock that would not weather.

She said, "Well, child? How does the Son of Heaven?"

"He is sleeping, great lady."

"Of course," she snorted, glancing out of a high narrow window at the sun. "And so you have come to seek me out . . ."

"Of course," though it had never happened before. "Great lady, please—can't you stop him?"

"You have heard me try," the old woman said drily. "And these days I thought he was more inclined to pay attention to his new . . . possession, shall we say?"

Black inkstone eyes, the glitter all surface, like a wash of water over the truth beneath.

Mei Feng had no stomach for a fight, nothing to offer except honesty and desperation. "These days, he only pays attention to Ping Wen. Great lady, you *know* that. And Ping Wen is a traitor, and the emperor will not *listen* . . ."

"I have known Ping Wen all his life," the empress said neutrally, "and I would not listen either, if a girl said such things to me." And then a breath and that blank black stare again, before she added, "Without evidence."

"I, I cannot . . ." Really, she could not; if she brought her grandfather forward as witness, he condemned himself from his own mouth. "But it is true. Ping Wen ordered the beacon lit, to launch the invasion from the mainland."

"And thus destroyed the invasion fleet, and left the emperor in his current happiness, planning the rebels' annihilation."

"Yes, but Ping Wen didn't know that would happen, he didn't raise the dragon!" She knew who did, but this wasn't the time. "And he knew about the assassins too, who came to kill the emperor. He was warned! But the soldiers who brought the news, he had them all executed. And instead of passing the warning on to us, he sent us a letter telling us to stay where we were, where the assassins were coming to find us."

"Did he so? And do you have proof of this? I heard that he executed a squad of soldiers for lying to him about the dragon."

"Which turned out not to be a lie at all. But he hides the truth behind that apparent mistake. I might, we might still have his letter, urging us to stay at the site of the new palace, because there were assassins here in the city . . ." But there had been a lot of letters, and time since, and the chaos of flight and the chaos of building-work and servants constantly cleaning up, and the possibility—no, nor even the probability, but utter certainty—of spies in the workforce, Ping Wen's hidden hands. She was not at all confident of finding the letter now. Her only other witness was again her grandfather, who had stood in the throne-room and heard the warning given and seen Ping Wen's response; whom again she could not produce in evidence, for his life.

The old woman shook her head. "Letters can be forged."

That was true too, but so was this: "Generals can be poisoned. He tried to slay your son. And now he wants to lead him into an insane war against the man you've been fleeing all this time. Even if you don't believe me, can you afford the risk? Ping Wen dead will keep Chien Hua safe, here, under your eye . . ."

It was the first time she had used the emperor's name in his mother's hearing. She did it deliberately, but it won her nothing more than a slow shake of the head and a harsh, astonishing laugh. "Do you think so? It would be too late even now, he would insist on his war even without his general. Besides, it cannot be done. I have been trying to poison Ping Wen for weeks. He is too well protected." A little pause, to let that sink in. "Perhaps we should hope that tonight's expedition is not a success. I hate to wish ill fortune on my son, but . . ."

It was tonight's expedition that Mei Feng had particularly wanted to prevent—her grandfather's leading the fleet out into uncertainty and darkness, peril beyond measure—but she had nothing more to plead. The empress would care little for the fate of a fisherman, less for a mutilated peasant child. Indeed, from the old woman's point of view, it would be better all around if the whole fleet foundered and was lost under the dragon's wrath. That would be seen and known, and an end to all hopes of crossing the strait. An end to all threat of invasion, too. The empress could hold her son in safety, content; and beware of Ping Wen's future machinations, and machinate no doubt on her own behalf against him, and . . .

And Mei Feng's grandfather would be dead, along with the child and a few hundred men besides, and she didn't think she could bear that. But otherwise, what? The fleet would sail home in success, immune to all dragons and swollen besides, leaving the enemy in disarray and dread; and the emperor would carry on planning his invasion, under the guidance of a traitor who wanted to see her man dead, and she didn't think she could bear that either.

When she counted all the betrayals of her life, mostly she ended up counting the emperor on every hand. Almost everything she valued had come to her through him; everything she lost now, that too was due to him. And she could stoke her fury up again, stoke it and stoke it, there was so much fuel there—but it was still only a shadow, a mask laid over what she wanted, what she lacked, what she lamented. She had had influence, and treasured it; she had loved to be the core around which the emperor had turned, the fixed sure heart of his world, for those few months that she had sat there. She had loved her man, and still did. Love was a blessing, something to hug to her, in the hollow of her heart. Rage was a flower that embraced it, a false flame that burned away nothing beneath. Being loved, though, knowing herself loved and listened to and yearned for: that had been beyond price, beyond measure, the most of everything that he had taken from her.

What she could, she was resolved, she would take back.

three

I am Chung the messenger, he thought, almost desperately, *I am Chung the messenger! I am not Chung the warrior! What am I doing here . . . ?*

He did know, of course, exactly what he was doing here; he just couldn't quite believe it of himself.

He was crouched in the bow of a boat that smelled of fish and weed and rank salt water, along with far too many other men. All of whom were warriors trained, who carried arms as naturally as he carried a sealed scroll in a satchel; all of whom were watching the setting sun at least as nervously as he was, and possibly wondering just as hard, quite why they were there.

One of them, the man on his immediate right, was Shen. Who was of course the sole true reason for Chung's being there: because if he couldn't stop Shen's going off on some lunatic adventure—and that was a given, that Shen couldn't be stopped—then Chung was most certainly going with him.

Even at the cost of this terror and worse, this bewilderment: this not at all knowing what he should do when they came to land, even assuming that they did survive the dragon.

Shen said "Stay with the boat," but that was . . . not possible. No.

First, though, first would come the dragon. If she came. If she wasn't hunting far away, or lurking deep down, ashamed or afraid after her last confrontation with the goddess . . .

It had all been carefully explained to them, how the little eu-

nuch boy spoke with the voice of the goddess and would keep the
dragon off. They all understood that, yes. Whether they believed
it, quite—that was another question entirely. Shen of course was
from far away and had never heard of the Li-goddess; the same
was true for all the emperor's army, which meant most of the men
aboard the fleet tonight. Chung was Taishu born and bred, he had
lived all his life—he was told—under the goddess's favor, as the
dragon had lived so long under her guard. Under her waters.

Even so, Chung was terrified. And doubtful. Even here on Old
Yen's own boat, the same that the eunuchs rode in, that had already defied the dragon and made the crossing once. The fisherman might be a special favorite of the goddess; she might have less
interest in Chung, none at all in Shen or all these others. There was
no good reason to imagine that she would act to save a fleet, just
for the sake of one old man and a child.

Which was why the emperor was sending just a raiding party, of
course, this first time out. If the fleet was lost, he wouldn't lose his
army.

Nor most of his bodyguard, nor any of his close friends. Shen
had volunteered, and still had to argue his way aboard. Where
Shen went, Chung followed; that was understood. He was only a
messenger anyway, he was expendable.

Mei Feng might not think so, but hopefully Mei Feng would not
find out. She wasn't here, of course. She hadn't even come to the
dockside to see them sail.

The emperor had been there, almost alone by imperial stan-
dards. His bodyguard stood all about him and General Ping Wen
was at his side, but no Jiao, no Yu Shan. Perhaps they'd taken Mei
Feng's side against this whole affair, and stayed away as a gesture
of support. Perhaps they were sulking, because they wanted to
come and the emperor wouldn't let them. It was odd not to see
them there, but Chung was grateful; they were more eyes not to see
him, not to carry the news back to Mei Feng that her own personal
runner had run off on this desperate folly in defiance of good

sense and her explicit order. In defiance of his own instinct too. He squatted in the bows and gripped Shen's sleeve and really really wished that neither of them had come. They would fetch home nothing good, he was sure of it. If they got home at all, with the sea and the enemy and the dragon all working to see that they didn't.

It was evening under a clearing sky, with the sun just lowering into the last of the day's clouds. The Forge was a silent, sullen shadow off the port bow, all wrong: no spark of fire at its peak, no hint of hammer-blows rolling over the water. Chung really wished the old man had not chosen to sail so close. Let the others watch the wide open sky, or peer fretfully into the water; Chung watched the Forge.

And so was first to see its shadow stretch and rise. When something else rose, rather, from its shadow. How had he known? He couldn't say: only that the Forge had been at the heart of the dragon's story all his life, so where else should a man from Taishu look to find the dragon?

SHE ROSE, and her undulating flanks glittered and sparked in the low sun. A low breath of wonder rose in response from the flotilla, even as all the overloaded boats shifted closer together, packing as tight as they could around Old Yen. Taishu and the emperor could ill afford to lose any boats at all, but if they must, these were the ones they could best do without: low and leaky for the most part, half held together by residues of ancient fish.

The men would be a greater loss. They were close enough to swamping their paltry vessels simply by their numbers; closer now in the rush of their fear, their rush to come within the saving shadow of the boy's grace, of the goddess. They must cluster and press, barge others out of the way. Boats rocked dangerously into each other, bounced in one another's wakes, came close to tipping over entirely. Men clutched and yelled, cursed and prayed; few had the sense to sit down and bail.

Perhaps it was the kindness of the goddess, that none of the boats did overturn or sink. Perhaps it was the luck of fools at sea. They gathered close and no catastrophe occurred, but catastrophe was coming none the less. What would a few lost boats matter, after all, against the dragon, who sank entire fleets in her temper . . . ?

She swam in air, as it seemed, more eel-like than birdish, wingless as she flicked her way toward them. Until she stretched her legs down, with all their talons showing. Then she was bird-cruel and malign.

The babble was frantic and futile, curses and imprecations and pleas addressed to the dragon or the goddess or the absent emperor, some other distant treasured god or lover, mother, anyone. What struck through it all was the old man's voice, Old Yen at the steering oar, chanting his own prayers as though no other man were saying anything. His was a faith Chung was ready to believe in, or at least to cling to: like wreckage, if it could only keep him afloat. Him and Shen together.

Clinging to Shen and gazing back toward the fisherman, Chung saw two other figures emerge from the boat's cabin, toss back the hoods that hid their faces, look around . . .

Chung yipped, he couldn't help it; and thrust his way down off the foredeck, hauling Shen after.

There were men everywhere, surging mindlessly to and fro or else static and staring, watching the dragon come. Chung kept his eyes on his target and plowed relentlessly aft, until at last: "Jiao, Yu Shan! What are you *doing* here . . . ?"

It was the wrong question, of course, an idiot's question. They didn't answer; they didn't need to. They had sneaked aboard against the emperor's order and hidden out of his sight below because they didn't want to be anywhere but here this night, they couldn't bear to be left behind.

The tall bandit woman glanced upward, nudging Yu Shan to do the same. There was something about Yu Shan that was odd, not himself but the shirt he wore, that rippled and gleamed in the shadows; but his head tipped back, his eyes turned to the sky and dragged Chung's with them, because in the end nobody could avoid looking at the dragon.

She loomed in the sky above them, like—well, like nothing they had ever seen. Too dense and deadly for the blackest of thunder-clouds, too vast and solid for the most extravagant of kites, too ultimately real for a dream. *Like death,* Chung thought, suddenly trusting not at all in the rumor of a goddess he had never seen, when the dragon was so entirely and absolutely there. And had been the death of many, many men in boats gathered together just like this, just a few short weeks ago.

And meant to be the death of many more, here and now, by the way she coiled and poised like a snake about to strike, if snakes had ever been so monstrous large, so toothed and clawed, so casual in air, so bright and cold and deadly.

She hung for a moment, and the men in the boats all around were screaming now. Here on the fisherman's decks, they were mostly screaming at the eunuch where he stood in the stern with the little boy in his arms.

"Lift him up! . . . Let her see him! . . . Let him speak to her! . . ."

Some few were screaming at the fisherman to bring his goddess forth, but Chung thought that was just as pointless. The goddess was there in the child, or else she was there in the water or the air or wherever a goddess might choose to linger, or else she was not. Whether or not they cared about mortal lives, gods did not come to mortal call.

The old man paid no attention. He shifted his oar automatically, stared up with the rest of them, wheezed out the monotone of his prayers.

The young eunuch who held the boy, his shaved head was glistening with sweat and he was whispering urgently in the child's ear, talking either to the boy or to the goddess, who could tell? The child didn't speak, the goddess didn't reveal herself by any other means, the dragon didn't go away.

THE DRAGON struck.

OR TRIED, at least, to strike. Tried to snatch: she came slamming down out of the sky with one foot reaching, claws extended to seize a boat by the bows and shake the crew out of it, or else carry them away still clinging.

And she failed. She missed; or her leg slid off some barrier that no man could see, that wind and water flowed straight through but dragons apparently could not pass. Her clutch found nothing, and her body plunged into the deep.

It was the fools aboard who cheered. The dragon was at least as dangerous underwater. Maybe more so, because you couldn't see her coming. Actually that might not make a difference, but water was her element as much as air, that was the point. She was somewhere beneath them, and she hadn't at all gone away.

The fleet knew it too. At least the captains and masters knew it, and the men learned it soon enough. On this boat they learned it from Jiao, who leaped up onto a barrel, spread her arms wide and bellowed: "Hold tight, hold hard, you fools! Do you not realize she's *coming back up* . . . ?"

They snatched hold of ropes or spars or anything fixed that they could reach, and stared down between their feet as though decks and hull were all transparent and the dark sea too. Unless they were expecting to see her eyes burn through wood and water and all. Perhaps they were. Perhaps they would . . .

Don't think about it. He took his own hold—on Shen, the most solid object within his reach, who had already bonded himself to the mainmast—and tried not to stare between his own feet. There were Shen's eyes to gaze into instead, until he scowled and shook his head and nuzzled into Chung's shoulder. After that there was at least Yu Shan's curious shirt to look at—like a snake's skin, made of so many interlocking links and what were they, not steel but . . . no, surely not, they couldn't be . . . ? —until, indeed, the dragon rose.

DECKS TOSSED, water threw up white between them, that close gathering of boats was torn apart as she came up like a whale through a spinning school of fish, mouth agape to seize and swallow.

And yet, and yet . . .

She rose like a spear through a ring, as the water bore the boats apart to make a hollow circle that she exploded through; and so she missed them all another time.

And hung overhead again, and if a creature that was half god and half reptile could look baffled, then Chung dared to think that perhaps the dragon did. She was almost half-hearted, as she plunged to strike again; he was almost not surprised when she missed again.

This time she veered so sharply from her line, no one could think it deliberate. It was as though a wind had struck her, a wind of solid storm, so hard she toppled in the air and twisted as she fell, and met the sea side-on and a long way from the fleet.

The great splash of her falling raised a wave that might have flooded some of the low boats, but that it never reached them. The sea flattened somehow, between her and here; all they did was rock gently in the distant whisper of that shout.

This time the hand of the goddess was manifest, and awesome. This time no one cheered or cried out; there was a terror in seeing the power of an immortal so close, even when it worked to your own good. People were wordless, breathless almost, staring first at the sea and then at one another and then at the rear of the boat, where the old man stood with the eunuchs at his side.

Did Jung go to lift the child high, feeling that massed gaze on him? And did Old Yen still him, with a hand on his arm and a shake of the head?

Chung wasn't sure, it was hard to see through the surge of men around him as fear of the dragon was consumed by fear of what had forced the dragon off. Someone had voice enough to cry "Will she come back?" without being exactly clear whether he meant the dragon or the goddess. Not even Old Yen had any answer to offer. The only possible response was to sail on and see. The fisherman's boy Pao elbowed his way through the throng, shrieking for space to work, to help the sails find their lost wind again. Old Yen called across the water in a strange hooting voice, presumably saying the same or something like it to the other boats, *give me room here, room to sail, fall back and follow me . . .*

Jiao seized Chung's arm and hauled him into the cabin. Shen followed by default, because Chung had not let go of his sleeve. Yu Shan came after, and closed the door behind them.

That privacy was a kindness, perhaps, as Jiao unleashed her lashing tongue at Chung. "You asked us—us!—what we were doing here?" When they were both hung with blades, when Yu Shan was hung with that extraordinary shirt, when the answer was obvious. "You, though, what are *you* doing here? Little running-man? Not too much room to run, is there, up on deck? And no one will be sending messages to Tunghai Wang, at least not the sort that anyone needs to carry . . ."

It was true, all true, and it had all been running through his head already, even down to the same acid loading. He had no defense to offer, but didn't need one; Shen reached around him from behind and folded his arms tight about Chung's chest, and that was defense enough.

Except, "I came," he said, "Shen didn't bring me." Just in case it should look that way, that he'd been pulled aboard like a mascot, without a say in his own folly. It was important, apparently, to assert his own folly. Unless he only wanted to excuse Shen's.

"Oh, and the difference would be what? Exactly?"

She knew the difference, exactly; she was only tormenting him because she could. It didn't matter anyway, because he was here now and so were they and no one was going back. Just then the boat rocked beneath them, and Jiao sat down neatly on the cot as it rose up to meet her; and reached out an arm to pull Yu Shan down beside her as it fell away again, and the gesture would have looked entirely normal and natural two months ago, but now all it did was raise another question in Chung's head, *where's Siew Ren?*

Which was impossible of asking, but would have lurked in his head regardless if Shen hadn't lashed back at her, "At least we weren't hiding, out of the emperor's sight . . ."

Jiao sighed. "No, you weren't, were you? But then you didn't have anything *to* hide, except your own selves," *which he utterly overlooked, of course,* which she managed somehow not to say and so of course didn't need to.

For once, Chung was quicker than Shen. "That shirt, Yu Shan. Is it really jade?"

Yu Shan nodded, as if words were too much for him altogether. Perhaps they were. Chung wasn't wearing the thing, hadn't so much as touched it yet, and still felt overwhelmed just to be in the same space as such a treasure. Such a forbidden, impossible treasure . . .

He had seen Yu Shan's jade necklace, often and often; he'd touched that, by permission. He had seen the emperor's rings. He'd seen the Jade Throne itself, and once the emperor upon it. He'd never been so close to so much, so intimate with the stone; and Yu Shan, Yu Shan was *wearing* it . . .

It was dim, almost dark in the cabin there. He wanted to go closer, to drop down onto his knees and peer with his nose just a finger's-width from the shirt. Lacking consent—lacking any freedom of movement, any movement at all, with Shen's arms still locked around him—all he could do was ask questions. "I don't understand. How can it be yours, Yu Shan?"

"It isn't," though it had to be Jiao who told him so. "It's meant for the emperor, of course. This is just—oh, call it a trial. We need to be sure that it does what it's supposed to, and that a man can wear it all night and still run around in the morning."

"But, but why would the emperor want to wear a shirt of jade?" He was the Man of Jade, but that didn't mean he had to dress up in stone . . .

"Oh, he doesn't. The thought hasn't crossed his mind. It's Mei Feng that wants this."

"I still don't see . . . Ouch!"

That was Shen, rapping his skull with hard knuckles. Then rubbing it better, a little more vigorously than he might. "Chung. *Think*. Which is harder, your skull or a stone shirt?"

He tried to break Shen's nose, by slamming his hard head backward; but Shen was ready for it and his head met only those knuckles again, patiently painfully rapping. So then he did think; and, "Oh. Yes." Jade would turn a blade, and the emperor had been stabbed once already. It would surely stop an arrow, maybe stop a club with no more than bruising for the man who wore it, and he wasn't sure that the emperor could bruise. "But can you run in it? Really?"

"Yu Shan can. Really. And fight in it, and climb trees. And swim if he has to, though he says it drags him down. The only thing he can't do is talk, but at least that means he can't argue."

"I can talk," Yu Shan said, as though to assert that he could argue too, only that he chose not to. His voice was odd, as though thinned by distance: the other side of a mountain, say, or swallowed at the bottom of a mine.

"How does it, you know, how does it *feel*?"

Yu Shan only shook his head. It was Jiao who laughed.

"You can't ask him that, Chung. You can't ask him anything. Afterward, he'll tell you that it hurts, except that it doesn't hurt at all. Like being wrapped in fire that's cruel but not actually hot, he might say, or wearing an ice-shirt that isn't really cold, although it is. His blood is so thick with jade, I think it clogs his thinking. I don't know, maybe the shirt is the real brain. That much jade all linked together, it's got to be smarter than he is. The shirt talks to the stone-dust in his blood, and the dust talks to him, and he just has to listen . . ."

Yu Shan smiled peaceably. Jiao rolled her eyes, and tucked her arm through his; and that must be a consequence of his being lost in jade, because he would have jittered away from her and looked around for Siew Ren else. At which point Jiao would have either hit him, or more likely just stormed away and brooded behind the dark shadows of her eyes.

Perhaps it was Siew Ren they had been hiding from, as much as the emperor? If she knew about the shirt, she would surely have been here alongside them. How Jiao had sneaked him away, Chung couldn't guess and didn't mean to ask. Really, he wanted to ask more about the shirt, but she was no more help than Yu Shan . . .

"Never mind, sweet," Shen murmured in his ear. "It's only stone," *and this is flesh,* the pressure of his body against Chung's back, entirely discounting their own scant shirts on this hot damp night. "Let's just sit in the corner here, and talk again about what happens when we land. How you stay in the boat here, yes? And guard Old Yen, and the boy . . . ?"

THAT WAS Shen's plan, it had never been Chung's. Chung had pleaded his case for coming—rather fluently, he thought—by virtue of his childhood at the docks; he knew boats, he knew how to sail, he would be a useful hand on the return voyage. In truth, though, he only meant to stick to Shen. If the dragon swallowed one of them, she would have to swallow both; that was how close he meant to stick.

Now that the dragon had swallowed no one—well. It meant a night aboard this crowded boat and then a morning of steel and flame, blood and death no doubt, fear and sweat and screaming.

It would be hard to keep both eyes on Shen, but Chung meant

to try. And he held the hope that through all the blood and the screaming—which would be Shen's task, largely, because that man knew nothing whatsoever about boats—Shen would at least occasionally think to keep at least one eye on him.

THE CABIN filled up as time crept past, as slowly as the boat seemed to be creeping across the strait. Men were coming in damp, though there was no sound of rain; indeed there was no sound of anything on deck except an occasional muffled voice, Old Yen calling to his boy or to another boat. The men still out there were as quiet as those who came in, who seemed not to want to talk at all.

After a while, Chung pushed to his feet and tugged Shen up after. As wordless as anyone, even in his own head; not knowing what he wanted, only that it was not this. Shen followed dutifully, out onto the deck—

—AND INTO a thick fog, word-swallowing, world-swallowing. It explained the silence entirely, in the men as well as on the sea; Chung shivered, and groped blindly behind him.

The physical warmth of Shen's body, the solidity of bone and muscle, the resilience of skin; he should have felt comforted, that those at least had not dissolved into chill vapor. Shen still had his voice, even, for now. Ignorant northerner. But all these men were ignorant northerners, all bar a handful; and all bar Shen had been silenced already. And this close to his ear, Shen's voice really should not sound so flat and fading as he said, "What, then? Will your old fisherman lose his way in the fog? Will he miss the mainland altogether, or are there rocks . . . ?"

Of course there were rocks, but Chung shook his head, wondering if Shen could even see him do it, as the fog flung itself between them; and groped for his own voice now, and found something scratchy and thin, and used that to say, "The dragon's breath . . ."

"What?"

Here was a breath of wind to stir the blanket, to show them Old
Yen lighting a lamp at the stern; here was a place to sit unexpectedly, on coils of rope laid ready. "It's what we call the fog. We've always said it, that the fog is her breath rising, where she could not
rise herself."

"What does it mean?"

The words, or the fog? Chung was too fogged to ask. Right now
it only meant that he was frightened, and wanted to sit here holding on to Shen until the stars came back.

NO STARS, but Old Yen's droning prayer was a comfort in itself,
like a rope to cling to. They faced aft, to where the old man
worked his oar, sooner than stare into the blank nothing ahead; it
was better to see the blurred glow of the lamp, the occasional
glimpse of another light beyond.

On this boat, only Pao moved, and that not much. The wind
had died as the fog had risen, so the boy had little enough to do:
tighten a rope here or there, let drop another sail on the foremast
more in hope than expectation of another breath to catch.

Still, they made headway. Chung could tell, by the way knots
and twists of fog flowed backward in the lamplight. Tide and current must be carrying them onward. They had time enough, plenty
of time to cross the strait before first light. They'd only set off so
early because they'd wanted to dare the dragon in daylight. Chung
wasn't quite sure why: either the goddess would protect the fleet or
else the dragon would destroy it, and either of those could happen
just as well in the dead of night. But people seemingly preferred to
see their doom approach. And to see her baffled, of course, to see
her splash out of sight and not rise again.

But now she was down there, plotting, and it was only her
breath that rose; and if the northern men didn't know it, those
from Taishu would be sure to explain it to them.

It was a threat, perhaps, or just a reminder. It was aimed at
them, perhaps; perhaps at the goddess.

It was not, in the end, something to be feared. The dragon was defeated; the goddess would not let her touch them. What did it matter, if she wreathed the sea in a sulky fog? The chill of it might bite bone-deep; the dreary weight of it might lie heavy on them all, dulling their minds into wordlessness. If this was the worst she could do, this was their victory. They had the best man imaginable at the tiller, a man who knew these waters by their smell and feel, and was a favorite of the goddess besides; he would see them to land.

So said the men, at least, when they managed to speak at all. Chung said nothing more, but only leaned into Shen and waited for this to pass, the fog and the night and all. None of it, he thought, portended any good.

Also, he watched the cabin door.

Time and distance: both crept by. Or seemed to. Perhaps the dragon swallowed them. Perhaps the dragon had swallowed every-thing, and the goddess hadn't saved them after all. She might be like this inside, all fog, endless, inescapable . . .

The cabin emptied suddenly, a stream of men coming out, laughing. Laughing. Those same men who had sidled in there, damp and shivering, with all the warmth and courage sucked out of them. Jiao had done something, said something, set them on fire. Not Yu Shan: people liked to be with him, Chung had seen that again and again and felt it too—this very night, when he first saw them, he had made that dash across the deck, and not for Jiao's black eyes and sour smile—but Yu Shan was always quiet. Even without the weight of jade on his shoulders. It was Jiao who was the talker.

She must have recovered her voice in the crush of the cabin there, and deliberately stoked up passion in men who had been ut-terly cold and numb. Even now she called out over their heads, a suggestion so lewd and unlikely that it made Chung gape. Every now and then, this company he kept would just casually and incidentally make him feel awkward and provincial, the little islander he was; he could still be shocked just by the idea of Jiao—a mercenary, a pirate, a *woman*—even before she opened her mouth. When she did, he could still be appalled.

Hard-traveled Shen chuckled at his side. Someone in the bows roared back a counter-offer, and she invited him to come down and demonstrate. Loosening her tao in its scabbard as she did so, with a loud and deliberate scrape of steel.

Someone else started to sing unexpectedly, what must be a northern marching song, that must have helped to carry them all these thousands of miles from the far fabled Hidden City. Now they had turned, they weren't running anymore; Chung shivered as Shen joined in, as they all did, as the men's voices rolled out across the deck and down into the fog and the dark.

Other voices came back to them from other boats. Ashore they might have been more raucous, but they could never have been more needy or more welcome. In the still and the chill of the fog, boat sang to boat, a small army sang together. Not all their songs were about women, and not all of them were coarse, which surprised Chung almost as much as Jiao's first filthy outburst; and among them at last they sang up a wind that blew the fog to rags even as it collected in their sails, as it helped the tide to carry them across the strait toward Santung.

ALMOST, NOW, he didn't want the sun to rise.

Sound reaches over water and Old Yen said the coast was close, so they had stopped the singing; a lingering collective warmth still overhung the boat, though, and reached out to embrace the clustered fleet. The warmth of packed bodies was a different thing, immediate and welcome, taken from strangers and given back. The warmth of Shen's body was different again and more than welcome, needful and desired and right there; and Shen's voice in his ear, just that low occasional murmur was another nature of warmth, something that happened deep inside and radiated outward.

Chung was happy, in this shifting state between one thing and another: between night and day, between Taishu and the mainland, between one fear and another.

Sunrise meant arrival, and he would rather not arrive. Traveling was better, safer, warm.

But light was sneaking up already, staining the star-black night like spilled ricewater soaking into cloth, as insidious as fog and bringing the same kind of chill with it. This was why they'd come, of course, it wasn't really to test the goddess against the dragon, or the child as a good-luck charm. It was for this exactly, the light and the land rising together, the bar of black below the taint, the threat of coming sun.

It was for this, the grunt from Old Yen and the clattering rise of bamboo-stiffened sails, the sudden kick of the deck beneath them as they stopped idling and turned purposefully to land.

It was for that, ahead: the first faint distant sparks against the black, fires being lit on cold beaches, where Tunghai Wang's abiding army was already building and equipping a second invasion fleet.

For this, then: where the ramshackle flotilla split into war parties and swept in with tide and wind and the first touch of sun, to strike at a dozen separate beaches at once. To catch the boatbuilders off their guard and unguarded, because Tunghai Wang was the hunter here, the man who chased. The emperor was the boy who fled, who had never yet dared to stand; who could guess that he might strike now? Who would ever imagine that he could, when a dragon patrolled the strait . . . ?

Chung watched the other boats move away in lines and little groups together, shadows drawn on shadow. The men around him shifted and muttered, rubbed bare arms against the sudden chill that promised action at last, touched blade-hilts, touched one another.

He felt Shen's hand slip away from him, some at least of Shen's attention going with it. He wanted to protest, and bit down hard on the impulse. Shen was a warrior here, one among his brothers, dragging a long chain of hard miles and bitter memories behind them. Chung was the extra hand, the hanger-on, the danger: inexperienced, unbonded. Not driven by the same cold fire, the absolute need to strike back.

Shen was the better fighter, of course, that was understood: tougher and more vicious, trained both in the yard and in the field, on the road. Shen had killed people. Still, he was not invulnerable. Not wearing a jade shirt. Sometimes even the greatest fighter needed someone else to watch his back. Which was why Chung was here, why the unfamiliar weight of a tao was pulling at one hip, awkwardly unbalanced against the knife on the other side.

If he had a need to use them, he would find a way. If he could get by without, he would do that willingly; he had no wish to be a bloody-handed warrior. That was important to Shen, whom he loved, but it bewildered him. All he wanted of today was a swift engagement and a safe return. With as many of these men as possible, all of them if possible but one in particular. One was not negotiable.

THE BOAT tossed awkwardly as it drove into the shallows, as the beach shelved beneath the hull. There was a dragging hiss when they struck sand, wind and water and momentum still carrying them forward against the land's resistance.

If there were shouts from the beach, cries of astonishment, challenges, alarms, Chung couldn't hear them for all the shouting aboard. Men lost their footing as the boat stuck at last, and shouted; men leaped over the side and found the sea farther or deeper or colder than they had thought, and shouted; men shouted simply for the sake of it, to tell the enemy and the world and the attendant gods that they had arrived, they were here, they had braved the dragon and the ocean and come through.

When they had shouted, when they had glanced over the side and seen their brothers struggling in dark waters, they mostly made their sensible way to the bows and jumped from there.

Shen did, if only because Chung had held him back from any wilder leaping. There had been . . . an exchange of eyes about that, which Chung had possibly won simply by being uncowable, not giving ground.

Shen moved forward then, to the bows and so down into the surf; and once he was gone—almost immediately, indeed, but not quite—Chung followed.

AT FIRST it was impossible to see anything, anyone. There was no hope of finding one man in the surge. Nor of hearing any one voice in all that noise. Was warfare always so loud?

The surf was loud enough, breaking with a roar on that same bar where the boat had beached, then hissing all the way past his feet and higher. Perhaps the men shouted simply to be heard above it. But no one was shouting orders, or indeed anything that needed to be heard. It was just shouting. Or shrieking, as often as not. He might not have guessed that hard men could produce such shrill sounds.

He ran stumblingly among them, disoriented and bewildered, only because everyone around him was running too. Up from the chill and suck of the water and along the sands, where at least it was easier going; they ran into yet more noise, noise like a wall, yelling and screaming and the clash-and-scrape of steel on steel, the wetter thud of steel on flesh.

They'd found someone to fight, then, and something to fight toward: a beacon of flame, a blazing brazier on the sand. Chung saw it intermittently, obscured by the shift and tumble of bodies, black shadows, any one of which might be Shen. He was not, he was *not* going to cry the man's name, not distract him when he might be just a blade's edge from death.

Apparently, he was going to run. Toward the fire, toward the light, just like everyone else: which meant, of course, toward the fighting.

He supposed that he should draw his tao, and perhaps his knife too. He had no idea who was friend and who was enemy, but if anyone came at him with a blade swinging, then he'd know.

Besides, they gave him something, two things to hold on to in the dark, in the hurly. It was good to keep both fists clenched as he waded into the chaos ahead, to feel the weight of two blades probing before him. They almost had more purpose than himself. He only wanted to find Shen and watch his back; his blades, he thought, were more lethally inclined. He needed to be careful with them.

Logically, anyone with their back to him should be a friend, advancing down the beach. That would work, wouldn't it? If he just didn't stab anyone in the back . . . ?

But the melee wasn't like that at all, there was no hint of advance or retreat: only a twisting mess, a morass of men, bloodied and frenzied and so *loud* . . .

One man came reeling out of the swirl, like a spark thrown up from the brazier, so random; and there was no confusion suddenly, no possibility of mistake. This was no one from the boat, from any boat. From anywhere on Taishu. He was too fat. And too old to be a fighter, and half naked, as though he had been sleeping somewhere on the beach here and had woken at the first screams of assault and was perhaps still not properly awake, still bewildered by what was happening here.

Except that he had something in his hand, a wicked curved blade on a long handle, which was likely a boatbuilder's tool of some kind; and it was a steady hand that held that dreadful blade, and a strong arm that brought it sweeping down. Chung even thought he could see stains on the steel, as though it had already bitten deep into others before it reached for him . . .

And really he had no choice except to fling himself inside the swing of it, too close to the fat man for the hook of the blade to find him. Too close to back away now, almost eye to eye and the man was screaming like every man else; and Chung was too close to do anything, really, except let his own hands do what they had trained for, his own blades do what they so very much desired . . .

AND THEN the fat man was quiet, quiet at last: quiet and still and hacked open at Chung's feet, and the wet sands drank what they could of what he had spilled out.

And Chung just stood there, staring down at what he had done, his first time, strange and terrible and not at all what he had come for; and he didn't even lift his blades in defense as another man ran at him, screaming. Perhaps he couldn't, perhaps they were too heavy for him now. As though they had drunk more than the sands, drunk and drunk of blood and life and spirit. As though they were over-full now, too much for mortal man. Too much for him.

So HE only lifted his head as the man came at him, only stared in mute bewilderment. He did see the darkened steel of a long straight sword, he did understand that it meant to gut him; perhaps he thought he deserved that, it was his turn now, as he stood in the strewn guts of the fat man. It might have seemed a pity, perhaps, to die so ugly in the half-dark and without Shen's hand to hold, but Shen would find him afterward, perhaps, and take his body home, give his ghost rest . . .

A sudden flower erupted from the man's chest even as he ran, a flower of dark heart, a solid thing that just kept coming even after the man had entirely stopped. Not a flower at all, then, but he still needed time to understand it as a length of bamboo, sharp enough to be a spear at need. A spear thrusting outward meant that it had been thrust in from behind, but Chung couldn't see at all, he couldn't see anything until the man at last fell down, was allowed to fall, because Shen let go the spear.

And of course, yes, it was Shen: who had seen Chung and his danger, and was swift enough to save him. And then swift to curse him out for being there, for being stupid, for putting himself at risk: "Didn't I tell you to stay on the boat? Why are you here, what did you think you could do, all useless . . . ?"

I killed a man, but that wasn't a useful answer.

Thankfully, this wasn't the time to debate it. There were other men to kill. And there was other work to do, the fleet hadn't sailed here just to kill boatbuilders in their fat bewildered fury.

Someone had kicked the brazier over, or else it had just been tumbled in the melee. Glowing charcoals had fallen beyond the stone and sand it stood on, into a stack of rolled sails. Canvas and bamboo were blazing suddenly, spilling light all down the beach: light enough to work by, until the sun at last came up to see what had been done here.

Light enough to show that there were not so many left to kill now. The beach was a boatyard, not a barracks; Tunghai Wang had certainly set soldiers here, but they were to watch for thieves and deserters, to keep the men at work and their work on shore till it was needed. Not to fight off raids from the dragon-guarded sea, an unimaginable assault from the coward army they had chased so far.

They weren't ready, and they weren't enough. Mostly they were dead already, and the men they'd guarded slain beside them: boatbuilders and apprentices, doubly doomed for being here and for being what they were. Everyone on the beach would die, because there was no time to sort between them; but anyone with the skills to make or repair a boat, they would die because that was the most loss that Tunghai Wang could feel. He had soldiers and to spare, but he could only build another fleet if he had the men to build it.

The men he had, these dead men had made a strong start, a new beginning since the ruin of his first invasion. Spaced along the sands was a line of hulls, some whole and some half finished, some old wrecks under repair.

Now Chung could snatch Shen's hand and tug him down to the first of those beached hulls, a river sampan standing proud on a new keel, refitted for sea.

"She'd sail," he said, "just as she is," except that all the sails were ablaze behind them and they had no time to rig her anyway. They knew that, they had always known. A rope from her bow to the old man's boat and a couple of men with oars, they could handle the crossing if the goddess was kind. And why would she be anything other, why save them from the dragon only to drown them now?

The next was just a hull, but she would float; she too could be towed and rowed.

The next was not even so finished as that, only a few timbers shaped around a frame. Not worth the taking, but enough to leave burning at their backs, with all the loose timber and the tar and everything too heavy or too awkward to carry away. Ropes and stores were coming on the boats, as much as they had time to snatch and stow; the rest was for the fire. Iron was coming if possible, or else it was to be tipped into the sea if it could be moved at all. Steal, disrupt, destroy . . .

SMOKE AND flame and screaming: the city would be alert already. Soldiers would be coming soon, in numbers.

It was hard work, swift work, hauling every seaworthy hull down into the water—not far, blessedly, as high tide coincided with the dawn: Old Yen had known, of course—and flinging ropes from one to another. Running up and down the beach with blazing torches and buckets of pitch, to set fire to whatever they could burn. Dragging crates of nails and fittings to the water's edge and tipping them into the bobbing hulls for ballast first and use later

on Taishu, along with tools and chains, more rope, the boatbuilders' meager stores of food and tea. Recovered weapons, of
course.

Now Shen really should be glad of Chung's help, there was so
much that needed doing and so little time. At least he'd stopped
cursing: no time for temper, only to heave and haul, to make quick
judgments and quicker dispositions, *take this, burn that*. No point
breaking up stone forges, they were too easily rebuilt, but the iron
plates and fitments, yes, take those; an army always wanted iron.
The emperor did, and so must Tunghai Wang. Take from one to
feed the other: a double benefit.

Which was the point and purpose of this raid, entirely. Tunghai
Wang wouldn't see it as a prelude to anything. Weakened as he
was, he must still be the huntsman in this chase. The emperor was
a stag in flight, not a tiger turned at bay; in Tunghai's view he
would want boats for his fishermen, not his soldiers. He would be
seeking to delay and discourage a second invasion, not to launch
one of his own.

So said General Ping Wen, at least, and the emperor at least was
persuaded. Mei Feng was not, but the emperor wasn't listening to
her any longer. Chung knew.

He and Shen flung a bundle of bamboo spars into a sampan
that wanted only a mast, that could surely be paddled all across
the water by herself if need be. A cry from the beach behind
them, an arm thrust upward showed them men pouring over the
headland. Armed men, a stream that would be a flood soon
enough.

Time to go. They could have done more, if they'd been left to
do it; these soldiers would know they could have saved more, if
they'd only gotten here sooner. War was probably like that, Chung
thought, small achievements and small frustrations, more often
than it was the triumph and devastation of stories, history on the
march.

He and Shen threw their weight against the hull of the sampan, felt it give and check and give again. More men joined them, urgently; at last it was sliding, and there was water around their feet.

Water to their knees, and the sampan floated free. They piled into it and seized paddles and oars—raw timbers, even, if nothing else came to hand—and drove them into the surf, forced the boat away from shore.

Didn't look back to see who had been left behind, dead or wounded or plunging after, whether they could swim or not. It was every man's last task to save himself; no one could afford to wait.

Which was why Chung had heaved Shen's legs aboard before he'd clambered up himself; it was orders, his duty, absolutely.

THEY CAME up alongside Old Yen's boat, like a high, wet, rocking wooden wall. A rope was dropped down and tied off; most of the men scrambled up it, but Chung shook his head and let the sampan drift behind, taken in tow when there were only himself and Shen still aboard. It was all they needed, to fend off other craft and bail her out if a wave swamped her; and, "If you want to yell at me some more," he said, "at least you can do it in private."

"I don't want to yell at you." Indeed, Shen was sinking down to squat at Chung's feet, amid all the gear they'd flung aboard. "I want to know where you got the idea that you could fight beside us, that's all."

"From you, of course. You trained me."

"Not with blades. It was horrible to watch, you don't even hold them right. Kitchen boy. You stick to your cleavers next time, and cook supper for when I come home."

"No. I'm not letting you go off without me. You'd best teach me how to use a tao, if I'm so hopeless. You can start when we get home. What's the matter with you, why are you— Gods, Shen, are you *hurt* . . . ?"

"Mmm." Slowly, carefully, Shen was peeling his sodden shirt

away from his shoulder. That dark soak was not all seawater, and not all the blood was other people's; there was a deep slash from Shen's shoulder, running down over his ribs.

Chung let his paddle fall onto the boards beside him. "When did that happen?"

"When we were fighting, idiot." He was trying to be amused, condescending, as he so often was. The light was on his face now, and he looked as gray as the sea, under a slick of sweat.

"But, but then I made you do so much work with me, just to stop you fighting . . . Why didn't you say?" *Why didn't I see?* was the more honest question, and they both knew it.

"Because then you would have fussed, of course. As you are." *Because I didn't let you see.* They both knew that, too. There wasn't much they needed to say between them, though Shen seemed to think this one thing was important, lifting his good arm to touch Chung's, to say, "Shouldn't you be rowing, or something? We're going to hit that big boat if you don't . . ."

Chung glanced up, to see the high stern of Old Yen's boat about to overshadow them. He stood, legs spread, and fended them off by hand; and scowled down at Shen and said, "Why didn't you go aboard with the others? People up there could help you. And you'll be no use to me down here, bleeding everywhere, getting under my feet . . ."

Shen lay between his feet, sprawling now that he didn't have to hold himself up anymore, and grinned up at him. "Truly? I didn't fancy the climb. I think that sword broke my collar-bone. Besides, there's more room here. And I can be with you . . ."

So did Chung think that collar-bone was broken, now that he took another look at it. But the rest of the gash was no worse than ugly; it would scar, but Shen had scars already, and the salt sea had already stanched the bleeding. And yes, he too would far rather have Shen in his boat and under his eye than out of sight somewhere on the crowded boat above, one among dozens, with no one particular to care for him.

"Lie still, then," he grunted, and picked up his paddle again, to give them some distance from the fishing-boat. Shen's shirt was ruined already, so he could use that for a pad and bandages, as soon as he had hands free to dress the wound. If he sacrificed the sleeves of his own, he could knot those into a sling to support Shen's arm, not to let the broken bone grate and shift around. How the man had fought and run and hauled so much with a bleeding wound and a broken bone and Chung hadn't even *noticed* . . .

HE WAS tired and shaken, but guilt was a lash. He did two men's work as best he could, keeping the sampan handily out of the big boat's wake while he patched Shen up and saw him settled. They could hope for a swift and untroubled passage back across the strait, but not quite yet; Old Yen was hugging the coast, sailing westward rather than out to sea.

Ahead and behind, smoke was rising in the clear air, from other raids on other boatyard beaches. The fleet had to reassemble with all its gathered trophy craft; it might not actually be needful—perhaps the goddess could protect a hundred scattered boats, perhaps she could hold the dragon back altogether—but nobody actually knew. It would be a brave man who would sail the strait alone, or anywhere other than in Old Yen's immediate shadow. A brave man or a foolish one, or both. This fleet was full of brave men, but few of them were foolish in that way. Chung thought that every one of the raiders would find their way to the rendezvous, though it would be a long drag for some.

The old fisherman had nominated a particular creek as a meeting point, farther west than any of the beaches they were raiding. Nobody worried about Tunghai Wang launching boats out of Santung to attack them; the generalissimo had few enough to start with and had lost a lot today, he wouldn't risk those that he had left in the city docks. Even so, this diversion added time and work, opportunities for trouble.

Chung's own trouble lay on the sampan's boards and smiled up at him as he stood in the stern to row. Pain was in Shen's eyes, the tight contracted pupils; in his face too, another kind of tightness about that mobile mouth and in the way the skin had stretched across his cheekbones.

His voice was as pale and shadowed as his skin, almost but not quite unrecognizable. "You do that very well. Water rat."

"When, when I was a child," it was harder to speak, seemingly, when he wasn't the one who was hurting, "when my father worked at the docks, some days he would take me with him. I could row him across the water, he taught me how; and if there was cargo, sometimes I could ferry it from ship to shore. Sometimes it needed both of us, an oar each, but . . ."

"But you learned, and you grew, and so you have a skill I didn't know about." Shen was mock-scolding as he used his good arm and the boat's rising side to haul himself up until he could sit and see where they were going and at least pretend to be comfortable, with his back set firmly against Chung's one leg and his arm curled for bracing about the other.

"I haven't touched an oar for years," or been in a boat at all since he was taken into the palace kitchens; and he was feeling it now, already, a dawning ache in his shoulders although this was easy yet. He was mostly working with the towrope, just to keep the sampan from knocking against the other tows or wallowing too much in Old Yen's wake, not to let it jar Shen's broken bone.

He could be a stable support, too, his runner's legs set wide and solid, giving a little to the movements of the boat but shifting not at all; and when Shen turned petulant anyway because he was so sore and didn't want to show it, when he said, "Why are we going this far out of our way, where's that mad old man taking us?" Chung could be as calm and deceptive and unforthcoming, as supportive as the sea itself beneath them.

"A creek, he told us. I don't know why, it's something that matters to him. It'll be fine. We'll get you home soon enough, and I'll take you straight to the doctor."

"You won't need to do that."

"Oh, what? You've been badly cut, that needs cleaning and binding properly, better than I can do it; and someone needs to look at your shoulder too, see if the bone needs setting . . ."

"Leave it alone, it'll all heal. We've seen worse on the road; there are worse this morning, they need care more than I do. But what I meant was, you won't need to take me anywhere. They'll be waiting on the quayside when we dock."

"Who will?"

"Mei Feng, with doctors."

"No, sweets." *You're delirious,* but he wasn't going to say so: kept his sudden worry to himself. "Mei Feng doesn't want anything to do with this. And how would she know, anyway, that you were hurt . . . ?"

"Not me, but she'll know there will be hurt people in the fleet; and she'll need to be sure that her grandfather's come back safe. And she'll know by now about Jiao and Yu Shan, even if the emperor doesn't. And the child too, she'll want to be sure about the child. So she'll come, and for excuse she'll bring the emperor's own doctors. And she won't tell him, but one of his servants will, so we'll either come early and have the fun of seeing him chase after her, or—more likely, seeing that Old Yen is taking us all this far out of the way—we'll come late and he'll be there already and they will have had their fight without us. But there will still be doctors waiting, and them too. So don't you worry about me . . ."

IT WAS too late, of course, not to be worrying about him. Worry was just there, like a weight against his one leg, like an arm wrapped tight around the other. But when he checked, he didn't think that Shen was bleeding anymore; he might even be a better color, in the better light. And Chung had bound his arm up tight and Shen was being good, not shifting it inside that binding. He said the shoulder hardly hurt at all.

Then again, he also said that pain didn't matter, that it could be set aside and stepped away from. Which was so obviously nonsense, Chung reminded himself not to listen to anything else the idiot might say. He would make his own judgments, and bring Shen to the doctor as soon as possible.

As SOON as he was allowed, that meant. For now seemingly they had to keep sailing along the coast here, even though the long stream of boats behind them suggested that the fleet was all together already and there was really no need to go on. Progress was steady, but uncomfortably slow; at least, Chung was uncomfortable in this little sampan and Shen had to be, although he swore not.

A man with a fast horse might keep pace with them along the coast road. That shouldn't matter, because no horse could bring a man to sea, but even so he didn't like the thought of being tracked, watched, perhaps worked against. He didn't like the sea much either, how it lay there threateningly still, brooding as darkly as the dragon.

She must be somewhere in that water, as she seemed not to be in the sky. There was no certainty that she would not erupt again; nor any certainty that the goddess would protect them again. She might be angry that they used her—or her child—like a good-luck token, like a guarantee, back and forth across the water. Perhaps she had only meant to allow them one safe passage. Perhaps they should have been grateful, taken the dragon as a warning and her protection as a gift, never dared to look for it again . . .

Old Yen would not say that.

Perhaps.

He at least was confident of his goddess. But old men always are sure of whatever it is, diet or work or worship, that has allowed

them to become so old and sure; and old men too can be overtaken
by calamity despite all their certainties, let down at the last by
their miracle herb or their hard-set bodies. Or their goddess, not
so potent after all. Or not so kindly, not so well disposed.

Old men can be wrong.

Also, they can be perverse.

They can lead a fleet of weary sailors, carrying a cargo of
wounded and exhausted men and trailing a second fleet of boats
not fit to sail; they can lead them not home but along an enemy
coast to one particular creek, one narrow inlet below a headland;
and there, where no one could see what kind of force the enemy
might be mustering landward, they can toss out an anchor, ignore
the fleet entirely, demand a boat ashore.

OLD YEN hauled on the towrope, drew the sampan up to the high
side of his own craft and let himself down into the bows. All without warning, without even a word called down to Chung.

Then he cast off the rope, made his way to the stern and said,
"Take me to the shore."

Chung said, "My friend is hurt, he can't . . ."

"He doesn't need to. You know how to handle those oars, I've
been watching you. Or do you want me to take them?"

Chung's shoulders were on fire and his arms were leaden
weights, but no, he didn't want that. Not with Shen listening,
watching, right there.

Nor did he want to go ashore. It was all delay, when they should
have been halfway home by now. He said, "The emperor will be
angry, when he hears that you wasted time and kept his men in
pain for longer than you had to." His own anger was meaningless,
but the emperor's—well, the emperor was a god too, as well as a
forceful youth. He might be one to set against the Li-goddess, in
the old man's head. Especially with Mei Feng at his side, equally
angry with her grandfather.

But Old Yen said, "It is the emperor's order," and then there was nothing more to say, nothing to do but row.

ACROSS THE narrow span of water to the inlet's gentle flow, to the western bank below the headland. As soon as he felt the bows grate on shingle Chung was over the side, into waist-deep water. Except that he had to separate himself from Shen first, and so he was not after all so quick, and the old man was ahead of him: plunging in and wading forward, laying tough gnarled hands on the bow and hauling with a will.

With Chung's urgent help, the sampan was safely grounded above the water's reach before Shen had pulled himself awkwardly to his feet aboard.

A path led upward from this stony beach—or at least, there was a route where men might scramble up the cliff, where others had done it often enough before them. One-handed, it would be hard; one-handed and in pain at every jolting step, it would be dreadful. Shen looked at it and stiffened, set his lips thinly, said not a word.

Chung spoke for him, to the fisherman: "Why are we here, old man?"

"There is a temple, up above . . ."

Chung nodded; he had seen it, a small square build against the softer shapes of nature. "And, what, you want to make an offering to your goddess?" Would that buy them another safe crossing of the strait?

"Not that, no. Not that alone," although he did have a satchel on his shoulder, and his hand touched it lightly at the thought. "There are . . . people, a few, I had to leave here before. A woman, and her two daughters. We are to fetch them now. It is an order," stressed again.

Very well. A woman, and a pair of girls. Chung looked at Shen and said, "Stay here with the boat. We can do this very well without you."

It was a swift unspoken conspiracy between them, that Chung would say that and Shen would believe him. They both knew Shen could not climb that cliff and achieve anything at the top, except a strong antipathy to climbing down again.

"Be careful," he said. "A woman, after all . . ."

"And two girls. I will be careful, I promise. You, too. Watch that boat, watch the water; watch for trouble, and call out if you need me."

"And you," Shen said. "If you need me."

They smiled at each other, reasonably content, each knowing the other's anxiety and thinking it foolish, thinking that this at least should be easy.

CHUNG HAD meant to go first, but Old Yen swept by him at the foot of the cliff, impatient and imperative. The old man was sure-footed on that crumbling slope, and his knotted calves drove him upward at a killing pace. Chung was breathless and sweating before they reached the top, his legs burning to match the cruel iron ache left in his arms by miles of rowing.

Old Yen seemed untouched. If he waited for Chung at the top, that was only his native manners; if he waited longer to let Chung recover a little breath and a little composure, that was an effort of manners, made explicit by the old man's long-suffering silence and his folded arms, his manifest aspect of waiting.

At last he nodded beyond Chung's shoulder, to make him turn. There stood the temple, its red clay roof-ridge adorned with gods and dragons—their paint long since peeled away, but their figures still clear beneath the sun—and its corners rising to peaks, topped by further dragons.

And there beneath the roof, on the top step, stood a woman, with one girl at her side. Still a child, that girl, despite her solemnity; it would be a good thing, Chung thought, to take her to safety. Before the war came to Santung a second time. If there was

safety anywhere, it ought to be in the emperor's shadow, on an island the enemy couldn't reach.

Why the emperor would want the girls, or their mother, Chung
couldn't imagine. Imperial motives didn't matter, though. He
could guess at Old Yen's, and that was enough. Tired as he was, he
could help three slight females down the cliff and into the sampan;
and then he could row more, as much as he had to, if only he could
row home.

To the temple, then, under the wary gaze of the woman and her
daughter both; and pausing one step below for the fisherman to
say, "I have good news. What you asked that first night, that I
should take you and your daughters to Taishu? I have the emperor's consent to bring you across today."

The woman was small and sour, and unmoved. She said, "I
think we have the goddess's consent to stay."

Old Yen blinked, and hesitated; and went on less certainly, "Perhaps I should have said, I have the emperor's order."

"Perhaps you should. It makes no difference here. Do the emperor's orders reach across the strait? I think Tunghai Wang is in
command on this side. And I would not listen to him either, if he
spoke against the goddess."

"I would never speak against the goddess. I do not. How could I?
It was she who brought me safe across, she has kept me safe all my
life. She would not force you to remain here, when war is coming . . ."

"Is it so? I have seen war, old man, but it didn't find this house
before. The goddess kept it safe. You told me to shelter here, do
you remember that? And I have, and she has kept me safe and my
girls too. More, she has taken my daughter to be one of her own,
while we take care of her and the house together, don't we,
Shola?" The little girl nodded, entirely serious, entirely responsible. "I think the goddess can keep us safe again, if men are stupid
again, if they can find anything left to fight over. Come inside,
you, and let me show you what we have done."

"I have seen already . . ."

"It is different now. Come."

Inside was smoke and incense and the soft red glow of temple lamps, to set against the bright hard sun outside. And statues, of course, and a few hangings that were not so faded, that Chung thought were new to the temple. And people, too. A girl—or a young woman, almost: husband-high, they would call her on Taishu—knelt before the altar at the front, in the clouds of burning joss, rocking gently and humming beneath her breath. Two men sat shyly against one wall, with a sack of produce at their side. They might have been farmers come to market; likely they were worshippers come to make an offering to the goddess or the priestess, or to both.

They looked relieved, almost, to see more men come in. Even strangers, even with the weary stink of battle clinging to them. At least, Chung did still smell of blood and smoke. Old Yen smelled of the sea.

Men know how to deal with men. The woman and girls, perhaps, had overfaced them, here in the house of the goddess; now they got to their feet and bowed tentatively, warily, and still looked nothing but relieved.

Old Yen nodded back, and turned to the woman. She said, "You see? They took me for a priestess, and the goddess has made it true. Perhaps I should shave my head and be a nun, but it would upset my daughters," meaning, clearly, the one daughter, the one who rocked and hummed and took no notice of these new arrivals. "Change is difficult, we like to be settled, we like routine," *she does;* "so I keep my hair, for now, and we stay here."

There was no challenge in her, no confrontation. She said it simply, as a thing that was. Was so, was inevitable, simply was.

Old Yen had trouble with that, seemingly. He said, "That first night, you begged me to take your daughters at least, if I couldn't take you. I can do that, I think. They would be safe on Taishu."

"They are safe here, now. Under her protection."

"No. You know what happened to her temple in the city."

"Of course, but this is different. No one touches her here."

"Only because this was abandoned and forgotten. If you have brought it back to life, that makes you less safe here, not more."

"This is her home now," the woman said, as stubborn as the fisherman, "and ours too. We will not leave it, no."

"You must. She must, at least," with a nod toward the girl in the smoke. "The emperor has need of her."

"Need? Of my daughter? The *emperor*?"

"Why not? He is a god too," echoing Chung's own thought from before. "The goddess has used her to speak to us, to *me*," with a little shudder on the emphasis, as though that was a cursed moment as well as a blessed one, "and now the emperor has use for her. Perhaps he wants to speak back to the goddess, through her. How would I know? I am not his confidant, I am his servant. His messenger. He sent me to fetch her, and I will."

"No." She meant that to be flat and final, all too clearly; and all too clearly, the fisherman was not about to accept her refusal. With orders from the emperor, how would he dare?

Chung's easy trip up to the temple and back had suddenly become a great deal more complicated. When the two worshippers glanced at each other and took a pace or two toward their priestess, he wished avidly for Shen—a healthy Shen, a whole Shen, not the drawn and suffering one he'd left down in the sampan—or failing him any other man from the fleet, any of those hard dangerous men so inured to fighting, so heedless of death. A blade looked so natural in their hands, they'd likely not even need to draw one.

Chung himself was hopeless with a blade in his hand. Here, that wouldn't be a problem. He'd slipped the awkward tao out of his belt while he rowed, and hadn't remembered to replace it; his knife he had lost somewhere on the beach, in the battle.

Unarmed and alone, he stood behind the fisherman and tried to look dangerous, imposing, so much of a threat that no actual threatening was needed.

Old Yen said, "I will let you stay here, then, for the goddess's sake, but the girl must come with me. And she will need her sister too; it's the little girl who looks after her, isn't that right? I know it is, I have seen . . ."

"She said no, old man." That was one of the local men, stepping up beside the woman, standing between Old Yen and her daughter. Both her daughters, as he shepherded the little girl behind him.

"You should go now," the other man said, "and tell your emperor that he cannot have these girls."

They were . . . just men, country men, peasants: built of the land, soil and stone. Strong as a tree is strong, strong to endure. Chung wouldn't care to wrestle either one of them. The two together, he thought they would probably tear his head off.

Except that they wouldn't need to, they could simply cut: what peasant went anywhere in his life without a tao in his belt? Neither one was drawing a blade—yet—in the sanctity of the temple, but if the fisherman pushed this . . .

Something in his stance said that the fisherman did not want to push it, that he liked nothing about this errand; but he had his emperor's commission and he wasn't backing down.

He said, "He is the emperor of us all, and you cannot refuse him. You dare not."

And he went to push past the men, toward the altar; and one of them seized his shoulder and pushed back.

He was an old man, sure, he carried that in his name; but he had grown old on the sea, he had salt in his bones and his own knotted, tangled kind of strength. He wouldn't be pushed, not easily.

And so they wrestled, the fisherman and the peasant; and, what, should Chung only stand and watch as the woman did, when the other peasant went to join in with his friend, to hurl the old man out of there? In defiance of the emperor, and in full sight of his own goddess?

Chung hurled himself into that battle and was carried out in the general tumble and the turmoil of it all, to roll bumpingly down the steps and onto the stony grass beyond in a tangle of limbs and heads and breathless cursing.

The peasant men picked themselves up first, and gazed down at the other two with a kind of slow satisfaction, reckoning presumably to know victory when they felt it, defeat when they saw it.

Then they lifted their heads and looked out over the strait, and their faces changed abruptly.

Chung almost felt that that moment paid for the bruises and the mud. Almost.

He stood up slowly, sore in every joint; reached down an arm to help the old man up; turned to look the way that everyone was facing.

Saw what he knew was there, what the peasants were staring at, what he had not felt the impact of till now, till it was needed: all the fleet spread out across the water, the empty boats and the barely-manned making it look larger even than it was.

"Yes," Chung said, improvising furiously in the peasants' faces, "yes, those are our friends there. That is the fleet sent by the emperor, to escort this woman and her daughters; that is how much he wants, how very much he values them. The old man and I came up alone to fetch them, as a kindness; must we go back down to fetch a dozen men? Two dozen? Two of us you can roll in the mud, perhaps, but must I fetch enough to roll you right off the cliff-edge . . . ?"

"No." That was neither of the men; the voice came from behind them, from the temple steps. From the woman standing there. "No, you leave them be. If the goddess will allow it, we will come."

She sounded weary, as though all fights were unavailing, victory as useless as defeat.

Chung thought she was right. And went in with her none the less, the old man at his back, silent and filthy and breathing hard. Mud in his beard.

Both girls were standing in the altar-smoke, hand in hand. When their mother beckoned them, they went to her; or at least the little one went, tugging her elder sister behind her.

She looked from one adult to another, and no words were needed; in her mother's too obvious surrender, she found her own.

"Are we all going?" That was her only question, and it was meant for her mother, *are you coming too?*

The woman was desperately uncertain, looking from her children to the altar and back again, setting her own peace against her daughters' futures. She said, "I think, I think we should ask the goddess. If she wants me to keep her house here, then I must; but—"

It was her elder daughter that she looked to, as though in hopes of hearing the goddess speak through her. Old Yen had said something much the same. The girl was silent; Chung thought perhaps she was an idiot. Or just too much hurt, like the eunuch boy on the boat.

Like him in other ways, seemingly, a mouthpiece for the goddess when she chose to speak. Not now. In the face of her silence, the mother seemed lost, utterly unable to decide. It was Old Yen who found her a solution.

"Stay," he said, more gently than Chung had heard him yet, "and I will bring her back to you. I will bring them both. The emperor will not want to keep her long."

That might not be true. Still, Chung wanted to believe the old man, as much as the old man wanted to be believed. If it was a conspiracy, the woman seized the chance to join. Seized it slowly, reluctantly, but seized it none the less; nodded and said, "Yes. He would not take a daughter from her mother without great need. When the emperor needs, and the goddess does not forbid: yes.

Take her, take them both. Take care of my girls, and bring them back. I will be here. I am sworn to this place now, and these people are sworn to me."

She was trying, Chung thought, to sound like a priestess, all unpracticed. Perhaps she had been a mother too long.

HE HIMSELF, not used to girls, he left them to the fisherman.

Stepped out of the temple, thinking only of the steep climb down—a little of what help the girls might need, and mostly of Shen who was waiting at the bottom—and not at all of the men they had left out here, the peasants staring at the fleet.

And so found himself staring at two drawn taos, with determined men behind them.

"If you don't live to run for help," one said, "your men won't know to come."

"Don't be foolish," Chung said instinctively, "my friend's waiting in the boat. If we don't come down . . ."

"He'll come up, and we can finish him too. Or we can go down and do it, when we've done you."

"And, what, you think the fleet will just sail away without us? They'll come looking."

"We'll be long gone by then. We'll take the priestess and her girls, keep them safe, your men will never know where to look for them."

Chung could have said *no need, we're leaving you your priestess,* but they didn't give him the chance. They just came at him, there on the steps, while the others were only shadows in the doorway at his back.

Unarmed, against men with blades: Chung suddenly remembered every one of the bruises, nosebleeds, black eyes and concussions that Shen had given him during weeks and months of training in his difficult empty-handed skills. More, he heard Shen's sharp instructions, almost literally, inside his head:

DUCK UNDER *the blade as it swings, so, and be glad the man is no warrior who faces you. Root yourself and strike back, hard and upward, here between his belly and his ribs, where he has no notion of protecting himself. See him double over with the breathless pain of it—and as his head comes down, catch him in the temple with your elbow, so.*

Good. As he falls, he lets his tao drop; leave it lie, you're no good with a blade. And here's the other man, hewing at you already. These peasants hack as if they were cutting paths through the forest, of course they do, it's the only speed they know. You work at a different speed, they won't come near you. Step back beyond the fall of his blade, then swiftly in again and kick. Not the arm that holds the blade, nothing that moves. Kick for his hip, shake him where he stands. Then step inside his reach and use your hands, both hands, swift and hard, no mercy: do you want to live, or not? He wants to kill you. He knows nothing, but he'll still kill you if he can. If you let him. That would be a shame. You know nothing either, but at least you're trying to learn . . .

EVEN IN Chung's head, in his imagination, Shen still had that sneering whip to his voice that could drive Chung beyond his own limits, past pain or fear or reluctance. His hands hammered at the peasant, at ribs and shoulders and belly. The man had no room to use his tao, so his arm came swinging at Chung like a club; Chung blocked it with his forearm to the wrist, and saw the blade fall from suddenly numb fingers. And knew how that felt, exactly, and punched while the man was still staring down at his dropped weapon, wondering perhaps how to retrieve it.

Chung's fist broke his jaw, perhaps. Something, at least, shifted in the man's face; and in his head too, some shift of understanding.

NOW A *knee to the groin, now the elbow again, and a kick to the head as he falls . . .*

It was Shen, almost, more than Chung; he felt little more than a puppet in another man's hands. That made it easier, perhaps. Especially afterward, when there were two men lying broken and bloody on the ground and one of them might never stand again; when even the fisherman was looking at him askance, stepping out of his shadow; when his voice snapped to hurry the girls to the path down, and the little one looked at him with a kind of hatred mixed with fear, and he could tell himself that that too belonged to another man, who would not care about it.

four

Apparently Mei Feng could be angry at the emperor in a whole new way, for a whole new offense, without in any way affecting all those other earlier reasons she had to be angry with him. Angers could accumulate, layer upon layer, all sliding over one another like these awkward and ridiculous silks he obliged her to wear—and yes, even she did know and acknowledge that was unfair, that he would far sooner see her in the scruff-clothes she wore at their first meeting or indeed in nothing at all, if he only ever actually looked at her again. But he didn't get the choice and neither did she, and so it was entirely his fault, like everything that had happened this morning.

It was afternoon now and laying toward evening, but these were the morning's troubles just coming into harbor now, safe at last. Or safe for now, at least. Safe until the emperor chose to send them into danger again, his chosen children: into dragon-haunted waters with war beyond.

The war had made her angry first, but now it was the children. The little eunuch boy had inflamed her, but he was apparently only the start. He had been brought to Taishu in hopes of finding shelter, and was being used to wage war; this new girl had been fetched, deliberately fetched, for the same stupid purpose.

And Mei Feng's own messenger had helped, apparently, but she wasn't really angry with Chung. If she shouted at him anyway, it would only be to relieve her feelings, because she did need to shout and it was getting harder to shout at the emperor. These days, he was inclined to walk away. To seek out General Ping Wen, as often as not. She and he used to plan their palace together as a way to escape the stifling emptiness of the court; now he planned his war as a way to escape her.

And with Ping Wen, who was a traitor and meant to destroy him, and she still had no way to alert the emperor that would not betray her grandfather. She had tried, sinuously, to embed doubts and suspicions in him, but what would have been easy a season ago was suddenly impossible, because he was not listening to her.

Which was another reason to be furious with him, as he walked blindly to his own calamity. The empress his mother had tried also, and failed also. They needed to be less subtle, perhaps, but simply talking, telling him wouldn't do it now. They wanted proof, a witness they could safely bring before the throne; and Ping Wen had been careful so far with his witnesses. There was only her grandfather, this side of the water and surviving.

The war, Ping Wen, the children: Mei Feng was exhausted, almost, by the effort of being so angry. Worse, now she was angry and provoked. She had come here to the dockside for the children, to claim them into her own particular care, and the emperor had taken them away from her.

There was the eunuch boy, with the perennial Jung carrying him in his arms; and then there were two girls, a young one leading an older as though she were blind or slow in the head. And because the emperor and Mei Feng were not talking, because what he did used to be what she did too and now was not, therefore he had contrived to take possession of them all with a word and a snap of his fingers, a flurry of palace servants like a flock of birds about the children, wafting them away up the hill.

Leaving her standing, stranded, alone on the quay.

Not alone for long, because there was Chung her runner whom she could compel with a snap of her own fingers, and shout at to her heart's content—except that he was coming off one of the little boats with his friend from the emperor's guard, and Shen was pale and hurting, with one arm bound up tight.

Mei Feng had never understood those two, from the first day when they tried to kill each other and came perilously close to achieving it. Now they were inseparable, when she would allow it. Occasionally she had valid need for her own personal runner; more often she used Chung because he was her own and she felt a need to assert it, to have some moments, places, people in her life that were not subsumed by the emperor; the rest of the time he might as well have been in the emperor's guard himself, living side by side with Shen and sharing his duties and his training, his food and his blankets and his time.

She might not understand it, how they had gone from that to this, from swift hatred to a swifter love; but she knew pain and distress when she saw it. Shen was in pain and Chung was distressed, and now was not the time to shout at either of them.

She was really growing very good at swallowing down anger. She stopped them with the gentlest hand imaginable, just as though they were any other pair of soldiers disembarking. "How is he hurt?"

Chung seemed not to have the words; it was Shen who managed a smile somehow. "Not so badly as he looks, thank you, lady. My collar-bone is broken, and I have a cut to the ribs . . ."

". . . Which is worse than you want me to know, and not as bad as Chung imagines. I understand you perfectly." It would be sweet if she weren't still so angry, swallowing it like bitter bile. "See where the lamps are burning, along the dock there? I brought doctors," the emperor's own, ordered down before the emperor could think of it himself. "There will be a wait, other men have been hurt perhaps worse than you, although Chung will not believe that; but they will see you as soon as they can."

A nod of thanks to her, an odd smile that passed between the boys—something said already, that could not be said to her—and they moved on in that slow cautious shuffle, young survivors bringing their hurts home, still wary of the world and each other, wrapped entirely in the joys and pains, the relief and wonder of that survival.

She watched them go, still bewildered, thinking that men were so strange, so very strange; and now there was only her grandfather worth shouting at, and he would be a longer wait, the last man ashore. In the meantime, there were others coming down the quay. Some she knew and some were hurt, they were all exhausted; now that the emperor had seized his children and gone off with his generals, there was only her from the palace to speak to them, to walk with them a little way, to leave them feeling better than they had been.

So she drifted slowly away from her grandfather's boat, just to the foot of the quay. When the flow died to a trickle, when it died altogether, when she looked back and saw just two more figures coming down the gangplank with her grandfather still stowing ropes while his boy washed down the deck behind them, then it was time to go and speak to him, perhaps to shout, if she could still find the energy; but she knew these last two before she saw their faces, just from their size and the way they moved, and they ought not to have been anywhere near this mad expedition, she was sure they hadn't had the emperor's permission to go—more, she was sure they hadn't asked for it—and now perhaps she might shout except that she didn't really want to, it was all too much for her, though she might yet want to hit them.

"Jiao! Yu Shan!"

"Ah." They glanced at each other, as guilty as children caught in mid-crime. The mercenary woman, bored and wanting an adventure; the boy from the mountains, the jade-eater, unnaturally strong and fast, wanting to test himself against the world. She understood them both, she thought. And why they would need to sneak away, to avoid both the emperor's gaze and Siew Ren's.

There was something more, though: something in the way Yu

Shan was standing, trying to shadow himself behind Jiao. He wasn't hurt, not him, she wasn't sure he could be hurt anymore. Something, though. And something in the way they glanced at each other, unreadable, a secret not for sharing . . .

Except that they could swallow all the secrets that they chose, but they couldn't hide what Yu Shan was wearing, some new kind of armor it looked like, though why that boy in particular would ever want to burden himself with armor she couldn't imagine. He looked uncomfortable in it even now, sweat-sodden; and the lowering sun caught it strangely, made it seem . . .

"Yu Shan, no. Tell me that's not . . ."

It was, though. She could see it, she knew it from intimate experience these days, though even that stray thought was a soreness, a bruise tonight. He wore a long sleeveless shirt of linked scales, and every one shone with the true deep-sea green of imperial jade, the emperor's own stone that no one else might wear, that they should not even touch except to mine it or to work it or to haste it on its way to the Man of Jade.

No wonder these two had been lurking aboard until the emperor had left the quay. That was death, right there on Yu Shan's shoulders: the death they'd both escaped before, and this time even the emperor's friendship wouldn't save them. It couldn't, in the face of such extravagant defiance. Mei Feng had seen most of the emperor's treasures by now, much of the beauty that had come from the Hidden City; she had seen nothing remotely like this, wearable jade, a marriage of craft and artifice and wonder . . .

She said, "I ordered that for my lord the emperor. Not for you."

"Well, but we had to test it. Before we could let Guangli—or you—give it to him. Didn't we?"

Perhaps that was right, perhaps they did. She should be grateful, but it was hard to remember how; all her good feelings had been rubbed away. She took a breath, took a step back from her anger, said, "Tell me, then."

It looked . . . magnificent. Imperial. A work of astonishing

craft: supple and substantial, almost liquid in the light as Yu Shan
shifted his shoulders and the stone shivered all down his body. But
she hadn't wanted it for beauty, or for an exhibition of its maker's
skill. They had plenty of those already, jades left almost natural
because no carver would touch them, others cut so intricately they
were like portraits of other cities, older days.

Jiao grinned, took Mei Feng's wrist and pressed her hand
against the shifting scales. It felt unexpectedly warm and yielding
beneath her fingers; no wonder Yu Shan was sweating, on the inside of such a skin.

No doubt the emperor would sweat too. She used to enjoy making him sweat. Such a treasure as this, such a toy, she could have
found inventive ways to do it, better than sending him to war . . .

That was no longer her interest. She frowned and said, "You
feel like a snake, Yu Shan. It's almost soft to the touch." And
smooth like polished jewels, warm like gold; it seemed to tingle
just a little against her skin. She didn't know how a dragon felt,
but it should be something like this.

She didn't want to think about the dragon. She was still too
angry with all of them, for chancing their lives and one another's—
and the children's, those especially—against the dragon.

She said, "That's not what matters, though." Not the beauty,
not the craft, not the feel of it. No. None of that. They might be at
odds, but he was still her emperor; it was her duty, to see him safe.
Where she could. "Does it work in combat, is it effective?"

Yu Shan smiled, and gestured vaguely at himself. He was still
breathing and apparently unhurt, unmarked; but she had seen him
survive a fight without benefit of armor. He wasn't a warrior, he
didn't have skills like Jiao, but he was lethal none the less. *Did you
test it properly, did you stand still and let them hit you?* That was
what she really wanted to ask.

Apparently, Jiao knew the question, all unasked. "Here," she
said, still holding Mei Feng's wrist and guiding her hand to one
patch of scales, over Yu Shan's breast. "Here is where a flung

dagger-ax struck him, point-first. It should have skewered him. Can you feel where the point broke through the scales?"

"No." The shirt felt immaculate, there as everywhere.

"No. Here," a tug on her wrist and then the pressure, *touch again,* low down on his hip, "here is where someone cut at him with a shipmaker's blade on a long handle. It could have cut through oak. He's no fighter, this boy, never saw it coming; and I couldn't reach him in time."

"You? You stood and watched."

"I said, I couldn't reach you. What should I do, then, turn away?" It was—almost—like the byplay of old, tussling in words, when they were intimate friends. Perhaps they were friends again, back end of a battle. Mei Feng was envious: *may I come and fight with you next time, will that buy me the right to tease my lord and see him smile at me again?*

But she was angry, and didn't want to tease him. Nor to fight. Nor did she want to be jealous of her friends. She could be happy for them, at least until Siew Ren came to find them.

In the meantime, Jiao stroked Mei Feng's fingers over the flowing warmth of the stone shirt and said, "Feel where the jade has chipped and shattered, under that blow?"

"No," she said. "No, I don't feel anything . . ."

Not a mark, not a scratch. She wondered how they made the carvers' blades, what could cut and scrape this stone. Yu Shan would know, no doubt, but it didn't matter now. She said, "Yu Shan? How does it feel, is it hard to wear, hard to fight?"

He shook his head, pushed his hand through his hair, said, "You feel it, but it's not like weight. Not dead weight. More like muscle, an extra skin, more power. It's . . . wonderful." He sounded like he didn't want to take it off.

Perhaps Jiao thought so too. She reached over and pinched a sticky tuft of hair between finger and thumb, squeezed out an accumulated drop of sweat. "Hot, though."

"Yes. Hot. Tell the emperor that," grinning again, looking like a boy again, dressed up in soldiers' clothes. "Tell him not to wear anything underneath it. I put a shirt on first, and that's sodden . . ."

LATER, IN the late of the evening when old women and young girls do not sleep—perhaps for one reason and perhaps for another, but sometimes because their sons and lovers are hatching war with dangerous men elsewhere in the palace, and so they are perfectly free to hatch conspiracy themselves—she sat closeted with the empress in her shadows and unwrapped the folded wonder of the shirt and showed it her.

Even an empress, even a woman who has schemed and manipulated for the throne and all but stolen it entirely before the end, even she will apparently hesitate before she handles a coruscation of jade, before she lets it shimmer and run through her fingers in the transitory lamplight.

Even she will shiver afterward, and wonder perhaps quite who she is in league with here, quite how bold this girl will be.

". . . Yes," the old woman said at last, as though the weight of her own silence had dragged it out of her like a jewel on a chain. "Yes, this is a gift fit for an emperor. If it will fit him."

"Oh, it'll fit. Yu Shan says Guangli can add as many more scales as it needs, to make it fit; he has them all cut and ready. I don't understand how they hold together, but it's like links in a chain, he says, he can add them or take them away until the fit is perfect."

"And if my son will wear it."

"He'll wear it." She was just as certain about that, only this time it was her own certainty she offered, not someone else's she had borrowed for the occasion. "You know how he is about jade, great lady," *you made him so*. "He'll love it. And it will keep him safe. Safer. On the battlefield." Everything was contingent, diminishing, regretful. "Please, what can we do about Ping Wen?"

An armored shirt was no protection against treachery; and he would be far from either of his palaces, far from the watchful regard of his womenfolk, exposed and vulnerable. She couldn't bear to think of him as vulnerable, but it was true.

"Child," the old woman said, "leave Ping Wen to me. He will be here, left as governor despite his protests; his people are clerks these days, not soldiers. They will be . . . distracted, perhaps, and war is dangerous to everyone."

"Are you saying"—her fingers reached for the shirt again, and not just to have something to play with while she fumbled for a handful of obvious, difficult words; it was astonishing, how hard it was to give it up—"are you really saying that you can have him killed?"

"I could do that, perhaps. Men do die, in wartime. And the Son of Heaven would be safer if he did. But I might not. Women too can die, old women insist on it sooner or later, and if the council thought that I had helped Ping Wen out of this world—well. I am allowed to interfere, but not that much. Half those old men would be afraid and mistrustful then, and I would not survive that.

"Besides, we have said the general is treacherous, we have told the emperor to be watchful of him. If he simply dies, all that work is lost, and my son will simply turn to another adviser. If we are shown to be right . . ."

"We have no proof." No proof that they could bring forward; she would not, would *not* expose her grandfather. Whatever the cost elsewhere.

The old woman smiled. "Anything can be turned up, in war. A man can be found, perhaps, who will confess to sailing with your pirate, Li Ton I think was his name? Summoned by Ping Wen and sent to light that beacon, to bring the invasion here. There are men in the army who have not forgotten me, I think, nor my man who was emperor before yours. They will do as I ask, if I give them a reason. A prisoner will confess to anything, under the right persuasion, and my son will believe it when he hears it directly. Of course he will; it is true. The Son of Heaven can be deceived, he is young yet, but truth will shine at him when it is needful, like jade through common rock."

And yet she was talking about deceiving him herself with false confessions; and about destroying another man, a stranger, an unknown prisoner, simply as a tool toward the destruction of Ping Wen. This was the palace, this was the life Mei Feng had now. This ancient spider was what she should aspire to, her best hope of life and influence.

And yes, she would plot with the empress to make this happen, to betray one man with another, because it might prove to be the only way to save her lord. And she would give him the jade shirt—somehow: they had yet to agree how best to do that—before he went to war, because that too might prove to be the one thing that would save him. She would guard against treachery with treachery, and she would guard against war with the gear of war, and it still wasn't enough.

She was still as angry as ever she had been, but that made no difference here. He was her emperor and her man, and she was furious with him and would save him despite himself, despite her temper and his own best efforts, if she could only find a way to do it.

Outside, storm battered at the roof and the shutters. Mei Feng shivered; she did not believe in omens, but she did most definitely believe in the dragon. And in the dragon's temper, which was worse even than her own.

Stone and Water

One

She saw them before he did.

Indeed, he saw them first through her.

If the fog was her breath, a heavy cloak that she laid like a claim across the water—*mine!*—then the typhoon was her temper, the vicious lash of the winds and the dark deep howl that they rose up from, the chill still stare of the eye and then the fury again, worse than before.

All his life, Han had known that the typhoon was her temper. Once it had been because she was chained, and he had been inland at the limits of her reach: rising rivers and cascading rains, roofs ripped from houses and boats left far from water, old men sucking air through their teeth and saying it would be worse on the coast, if any fool were fool enough to be there.

Then she was free, and her temper was an eruption against him alone because she was not free after all, because he rode still in her head and could twist her out of true if never bend her truly to his will.

They were still trying to learn how to deal with each other, for this little time until they could each be freed; and she was still not free at all, because there was another power in these waters and they were not hers after all. She could not break those paltry humans in their eggshell boats when they dared to chance the open strait, because she was not allowed to.

And so she sent the typhoon, or else the typhoon came because she was so raging; and for weeks nothing did sail on the strait, because nothing could.

She sailed on the wind, as though to claim it for her own, storm-empress; he sheltered as best he could in rock-caves filled with curses. When she came to him, he said, *Bring me a boat, and weather I can sail in,* and ignored the fact that he didn't know how to sail.

After the storm was over, she was still angry, and disturbed; she still rode the wind and glowered down on Taishu-island and its boats. He knew. He was in her head, and saw them packed like seeds in all the ports and harbors.

The storm's wake had brought clear skies, strong seas and a steady, whipping wind. Almost, Han thought the dragon was abroad for the simple pleasure of it: soaring high and then plunging like a stone, stretching to cleave the sea as she struck, sinking deep and thrusting up again, she might have been a youngling at play, thrilling in the power and precision of her body, nothing more.

Almost.

Almost, he thought it was true. After so long in chains, small surprise if she chose to exult in freedom. Even if it was limited, circumscribed, deceptive.

But, when she was high, he knew she was looking down, seeing all those many boats that packed the harbors like great seeds afloat. Seeing how they all fared forth like seeds in the wind, boats on the water.

When she plunged, he knew this was yet one more attempt to assert herself, her authority, her possession of these waters.

When she struck the sea, he knew this was yet one more failure, one more spite, something to hate.

Some two things to hate, because the fleet was divided: she struck at one and could not hit it, she tried to rise up beneath the other and could not.

She tried to bring back the typhoon, he thought, to sink them all in open water, and could not do that either.

He ran up to the height of the Forge to watch the fleets go by, one on the one side and one on the other; and, of course, to wait for her.

two

The Man of Jade was going to war, going to reclaim his empire, and even the dragon had turned out to see him sail.

So it seemed, at least: a parade unimaginably honored, an enterprise blessed before its launch. With such an omen, such tribute in the sky above him, it was inconceivable that he should fail.

ALL DAY the dragon coursed the strait, spotted time and again by the watchers on Taishu. Now she patrolled the island's coastline, as though she mapped every bay and headland, every crag and jetty, every kink; now she lifted high above the silent monument of the Forge, a bare dot in the scrubbed pale blue, an eagle in possession, wherever her eye fell or her shadow touched; now she came to Taishu-port itself, hung in the air above the docks and peered down at wharves and shipping. She seemed intrigued by the many boats crowded stem to stern, so close that an agile and carefree child might run and leap—as many had, in defiance of anger and solemnity and import, prognostication, in defiance of it all—from one harborside to the other, as though the sea itself were wooden now and bridged itself.

If it would, if it could only do that, the army might march to Santung and save these boats, this journey.

Not save itself the peril, under the dragon's eye; but boats were perilous in themselves, the sea was a threat on its own and the weather too. The typhoon—the dragon's wind, they called it: and some swore that they had seen her aloft at its height, rejoicing, dancing in it—had blown for too long, weeks, till the sky itself was exhausted. Now there was a tug in air and sea that promised handy sailing, but no one trusted it. Not with the dragon so very present, ready to whip up the storm again.

Trust the Li-goddess, the old man said, though he said it bleakly. The old man was the emperor's touchstone these days, the man to whom the emperor himself would trust himself; and where the emperor trusted, who would dare to doubt?

Besides, there were the children. Gifts of the goddess, like living charms: they could charm the dragon, charm the storm, charm the wind and water.

With the emperor to lead and the old man to guide, with the goddess to bless, with the children to ward away all harm: then, yes, even the dragon could be seen as a luck-token, a sign of fortune, a promise from the immortal realms.

AND SO, all day, fleets had assembled and men had boarded while the dragon watched.

Last of all, the emperor had come down with his people, his guards and company, his council of the wise. There had been priests and blessings and formalities, good omens and bold oaths.

His woman, his girl, his concubine: she had come down separately, with just a eunuch for her servant and an elderly man for companion, a man from the jade quarter with dust under his skin. They had made the emperor a presentation, no part of his plan. His mother had appeared on a balcony to watch, and he hadn't been looking for her either.

It was strange to see the emperor surprised and then surprised again, more than surprised by what his girl gave him. It was a wonder, a marvel of man and nature and the gods all hand in hand: a shirt of jade, an armor and more, a statement; more, a proclamation: *this is the empire,* it said, *this is the Jade Throne, I am the imperium itself.*

He stripped off his imperial yellow there and then, before his people; stripped down to his trousers and donned that stone shirt slowly, formally, in full sight of crowded decks and wharves and streets. The Man of Jade dressed in a shirt of jade, stone on skin, and there was a shout that might have split the sky if the dragon hadn't been up there to stitch it all together, weaving and weaving through the air.

three

Yu Shan watched the emperor discard the long yellow of his robe, watched him pull the rippling green of the armored shirt over his head, stone on skin—and felt a shiver of longing, a physical twitch in his own skin, as though it yearned to carry that weight again.

His tongue touched the little nub in his mouth, where flesh had overgrown his stolen splinter; his hand reached to his neck, where beads of jade lay openly against his throat. Those were gifts of the emperor, both the beads themselves and license to wear them: a sign of his generosity, a sign of his possession. *I own your life,* they said, *that is truly my gift to you,* and it was true. Actually, though, privately, Yu Shan thought that his life belonged to the stone. He thought it always had.

At his side now stood his clan-cousin Siew Ren, who thought his life belonged to her. She always had, it seemed. Once, she had taken him for granted; now she took him as a birthright, fiercely.

Jiao was elsewhere, on another ship. Yu Shan might have preferred yet one more, all three of them apart, but they went where they were told to go. Obviously the emperor's own sworn guards—Siew Ren among them—would sail with the emperor. Jiao swore loyalty to no one. If half the guard thought of her as captain, that was strictly unofficial, unacknowledged by the emperor or herself. As witness, she was not here. If she were asked, she would say she went where she chose to go, where she could be most use. It wasn't true, of course, but she might somehow manage to believe it.

Yu Shan would sail with the emperor, then, because the emperor would not let him out of his sight today. Siew Ren would sail with the emperor because she was sworn not to let him out of her sight. If that kept her at Yu Shan's side too, it was a happy chance. For her. The eunuch boy would sail with the emperor because he belonged to the emperor and the goddess both together, and their claims could not be divided. The girl belonged to the goddess alone, and would sail on an old jade ship at the head of a second fleet.

If the goddess could speak through separate children in separate temples, she could surely protect two separate fleets. They thought.

No one knew, of course. No one even knew for sure that it was the children who guaranteed the protection of the goddess. When they spoke in her voice, it had been in the old man's presence, both times; perhaps he was the lucky charm, the object of her interest.

Jiao was sailing on the jade ship with the girl.

Yu Shan looked, and couldn't even see her. There was a pack of soldiers at every rail on the high-sided junk, a swarm of sailors clinging to her masts and rigging. Jiao might have been anywhere, on deck or above; she might have been with the girl, wherever she might be, on deck or below.

Was he turning to look for her, or turning away from the emperor, not to watch him in the wonder of that shirt, not to feel the hunger of it in his own yearning skin?

He didn't know. Neither did Siew Ren, but she probably had suspicions. Her hand slipped determinedly into his, *I am here and you are mine.*

Best not to argue; easiest, perhaps, if it were true. Certainly he could pretend things were that uncomplicated. For a while, for a day or two, till they met up with Jiao again.

On the quayside, Mei Feng was kowtowing formally to the emperor. Here at last was something truly easy: to fail to hide a grin at the sight of it, to wonder conspicuously how long it had been since she'd done that. To feel Siew Ren's nudge in his ribs and know that at last they stood in entirely the same place again, thinking entirely the same thought.

THE EMPEROR left Mei Feng on the boards of the wharf there, and came aboard Old Yen's boat. That in itself was a procession, and a procession must needs be met; Siew Ren left Yu Shan's side, and went to join those who ushered him watchfully into the cabin. When she took on a duty, she took it seriously. She'd been happy, he thought, in their valley with their people, happy in her prospect of him; now that she'd left it for his sake, and found him not the prospect that she'd thought, she needed something other to make sense in her life. Her little touch of jade made a potential soldier of her; training and enthusiasm and determination vindicated it. And a reason to be close to the emperor kept her close also to Yu Shan, whom she would not give up.

There was a sudden flurry of movement on the dockside, as the moorings were cast off. Of course the emperor would lead his fleets to sea. Besides, every captain else meant to follow Old Yen, so long as there was a dragon in the sky. Not all had sailed across the strait and back, to see the dragon defied; not all who had seen it believed entirely that the eunuch boy had warded her away; there was not a captain in either fleet who would stray far from Old Yen's wake this crossing. It might have been the boy, and the girl might have that same magic, but who knew? It might all be the goddess's kindness to her favorite fisherman. Best stay close, press at his stern, one fleet all the way . . .

All around the harbor, then, ropes were flung from wharf to deck, boats jostled for space, men cursed as they tried to ply poles and oars until they could get out to open water and the wind. What magic the fisherman had, Yu Shan didn't know; perhaps it was only that other captains gave him space, for his own sake or the emperor's. One way or another he found room for his steering oar, he found a current that gripped the keel, he even found a wind to fill a sail and draw him neatly out of harbor.

Everyone else on deck was looking forward to the sea or upward to the sky, anxious about the dragon or the war to come, or both. There was only Yu Shan looking back at who was left behind them.

The great jade ships took longer to unmoor, or else their captains were wise enough to wait until a waterway was clear. Or . . .

Yu Shan was, perhaps, still looking for a glimpse of Jiao. That ship above all seemed to be lingering, as though the captain waited for something specific. For someone . . . ?

The emperor's farewell party had paraded back toward the palace. His mother had disappeared from her balcony. There was only Mei Feng left, suddenly very small and alone despite the eunuch who stood with her.

They seemed to be walking the wrong way, farther down the wharf. Then they disappeared behind the bulk of the jade ship. Yu Shan watched sailors scurry about her decks; when he glanced back to the wharf, there was a eunuch, scurrying off alone.

No certainty that it was the same eunuch, they all looked alike in palace dress at a distance. No certainty of anything, but Yu Shan was smiling to himself as he turned away from the rail, as he looked to see where Siew Ren had gotten to, whether she might be willing to put up with him.

four

*W*ell, what? Should I just sit quietly with all the other women—"

"Mei Feng, he doesn't *have* any other women."

"With his mother, then. Does anyone think I should sit there in the women's quarters with his *mother* and just wait to hear news, eventually, when someone dares, someone *deigns* to sail across the strait and bring it to us?"

"Yes, of course. That's what everyone thinks you should do. Everyone who doesn't know you," Jiao amended hastily.

"They're going to be disappointed, then, aren't they?"

Disappointed was hardly the word for it. Surprised, astonished, outraged: those came closer. But only the people who didn't know her, and why should she care about them? Jiao did understand, entirely. Which was why she had bribed the jade ship's captain with promises of imperial favor hereafter. Those promises could yet turn out untrue—when the emperor found out about this, he might be angry to the point of executions—but they had been made in good faith, and Jiao was easy about them.

Besides, she had left broken promises in her wake before, and men dead because of them, and had never yet been haunted by vengeful ghosts.

She said, "His mother will likely think you've dressed up as a man and sneaked aboard with the soldiers."

Likely, everyone would think it. Mei Feng still kept her hair cropped boy-short—the Son of Heaven liked it, apparently: though that might only be because he had no experience of long hair, or because he liked her however she came, or because she liked it herself and therefore so did he—and she was infamously more at home with sailors than with courtiers, and had wickedly seduced the emperor into spending weeks and weeks in the forest with a camp of unschooled fighters. Where else should they look for her now, but among those same fighters on their way to war?

Jiao still thought she would look better with the soldiers. Not all of them were men, though the women were almost entirely among the emperor's personal guard, where Mei Feng dare not go. Jiao was an exception; Mei Feng might have tried to be another. She looked far less comfortable, more out of place here in a cabin, with a flurry of more or less reluctant women.

Which Jiao very carefully did not say to her, because no good ever came of that kind of honesty. Instead, she said, "When the time comes to take the girl on deck," *when the dragon comes* was what she meant, "will you be staying down here out of sight?"

Oh, the glare! That was what she'd worked for. She didn't need the words that came with, the torrent of denial, "No, I will not be staying down here out of sight! These are my responsibility," with a nod sideways to the two girls, the big one and her younger sister who was so very much in charge, "and when we take them up to outface the dragon I will be going with them, standing with them, whatever may come of it. And . . ."

And actually that was when Jiao left the cabin, grinning as soon as she dared, as soon as her back was turned to the still-ranting Mei Feng.

LANDSFOLK HAVE no place on deck when a ship is leaving harbor. Jiao knew that better than most. Down, then: down to one of the holds, where these ships had ferried load after load of jade, year after year. Raw jade and carved jade, jade-dust and polished jewels: the air down there was heavy with the memory of stone.

The memory of stone and the presence, the immediate presence of men.

Too many men, packed too close. If the ship could carry its loads of stone, surely it could carry this load of bone and muscle; but this hold could not contain them. They were too nervous to be kept in the dark, swayed to a rhythm they couldn't read, jostling one another as they slipped and snatched. Men couldn't be stacked like jade, stored until wanted. They would be fighting soon; there would be blood and deaths before they ever crossed the strait, perhaps even before the dragon came.

It was the dragon, of course, they were afraid of. Regardless of goddesses and magic children, regardless of imperial promise and imperial risk. They had likely all bought amulets and charms that offered immunity from dragons, and still none of them would actually believe it until they saw her veer away, plunge into the sea, miss all the fleet entirely. Stowed away down here, of course they could see nothing. They stood or sat or squatted in the dark and waited to die, and were afraid and edgy and flung about by the sea's heedlessness—where was that goddess when Jiao wanted her, to settle her waters down?—and any minute now, there would be trouble.

It was a hatch that Jiao flung open, so that she was gazing down into the mass of men. The fall of lamplight showed her a rise of hopeful, upturned faces. For the moment, she had their attention; a sudden toss of the hull or a careless elbow and a snarled curse would seize it from her.

She sat on the edge and let her legs dangle, booted feet just a little above their heads. Any other woman would be taking a chance: a fuck would do as well as fighting, to distract them from their fears. If the fuck was an effort, if the woman screamed and struggled, all the better. But these men knew her, or at least they knew who she was. No one down there would touch her without an invitation.

Which only added salt, of course, to her goading.

"Well, look at you," she said, her voice pitched to carry to the farthest corner of the hold. "Packed like fish in a jar. Are you comfy down there, lads?"

A few voices called her down to join them, but the effort was half-hearted.

"Steady, now. If I had time, I'd take you all—but not all at once, and trust me, there is not time enough to give each of you the attention you deserve. A hero deserves a hero's portion."

A voice asked about Yu Shan, his heroic qualifications. She frowned, and reached as though to close the hatch; a dozen voices forestalled her, and there were sounds of a scuffle below.

"Ohé! Stop that, you let him be . . . Is that the man who doubts Yu Shan's . . . capacity, is it?"

A mumble from the man himself, any number of others more assertive: yes, this was he, the fool, the disparager.

"Well. This is the hero who's prepared to fight Yu Shan, is that right? To prove a man is better than a boy? Don't you lot knock him about, that's not fair. He needs to be fit when he faces my *boy* . . ."

A gale of laughter, all but drowning out the man's humiliated, desperate pleas: no, he didn't mean that, he didn't mean anything, he didn't want to fight Yu Shan . . .

"I don't suppose you do. I don't suppose any of you do. You'd need to, though; you'd need to best him first if you wanted to bed me. I'd insist on it. Tell you what, though," she went on, in the face of their sullen silence. "Rather than fighting him, why not fight with him? Prove yourselves better, outpace him, outslaughter him? He's only a boy, after all. And not a warrior."

She let them ponder that, until, "We can't fight with him, he's with the other fleet!"

"He is, he's with the emperor. So let's race them to Santung, get there first, be in the city before they are. Then you can fight side by side when he arrives. You can do me a favor, show him how to use a blade, teach him some tricks maybe; he's not stupid, but he's no use with a tao. All he's got is strength and speed, and he stole those from the emperor . . ."

While she bantered, the shift and sway of the hull had changed

beneath them. They must be out in the open strait now. There
would be less work on deck, less urgency, more tolerance for passengers. And a far greater chance of dragon. Almost a certainty.

Men like to see the thing that's like to kill them.

She said, "Meantime, we've a long night to get through. What
say we get up on deck before the light goes and the rain comes, before the rest of you ugly types spill out of the other holds? There's
no sleep tonight, and no one's going to mind if we burn some lamp
oil, so long as we keep out of the way. I've a flask, and so do half
of you; and you're all holding cash, and a curious yen to lose it to
me in a game that I can't possibly be any good at, being a woman
and all . . ."

They had a ladder to climb, but few of them troubled to use it.
Jiao backed away, and the hatch-rim was suddenly aswarm with
hands as men leaped up and hauled themselves out. It was the best
she could manage, one squad pacified and brought to hand; one
squad that would fight with her all the way, watch her back, die
with her if necessary. Not die for her, perhaps, not yet. That too
might come, if the fighting turned bad.

If they ever came to fighting.

First, there was still the dragon.

And then—if they weren't all eaten or drowned—she could
play these men all night, bond them to her like a pirate crew, land-
pirates.

And come the morning there would be fighting, war. That
would keep her busy.

AND NONE of it, nothing of it could substitute for Yu Shan, or
squeeze him out of her head. He lurked in her blood as much as
her mind's eye, his absence a constant dull ache that had her rubbing her arms although she was not cold, a hollowness in the air
that had her always looking around although she knew he was not
there.

It would not kill her; it would not even distract her when there was work to be done, fighting or ducking dragons or bonding with her men. Nor would it leave her, ever.

It felt, just a little, like the way he said he felt in the absence of jade. Needful, hungry, unsatisfied.

She was too old for this, and far too wise. And here none the less, caught somewhere between desert and desperation, a lack in her body and a yearning in her head.

five

*A*ll his life, Old Yen had sailed above the dragon's head and barely given her a thought, except to be grateful to the monks of the Forge as their hammer pounded out their promise to the world, that she would be kept in chains.

Grateful too to the Li-goddess, of course, always that. These were her waters, where the dragon lay.

Now he sailed back and forth across the strait under the dragon's eye, and she was never out of his mind.

He believed—who better?—in his goddess, and in her protection. He had seen it demonstrated again and again, even before the dragon rose; he was her living proof.

Her advocate, that too. He had made promises in her name, and even the emperor believed them. Even the emperor's advisers, who had allowed the Son of Heaven to sail with him.

If that cautious council could trust in her, who had never offered a moon-cake at her shrine or seen her hand on the waters; if they could trust the precious body of the emperor to his promises, then certainly he should trust in them himself.

And he did, of course he did; and yet, and yet . . .

Old Yen might not doubt the goddess, ever, but he could still doubt himself. He was no priest; he might be mistaken. And the goddess—he had learned, newly—was not the kind and gentle lady he had worshipped for so long. She had, no doubt, purposes of her own. In this mood, he could no longer imagine why she should want to save the fleet, or the emperor, or himself. If she was not well disposed, inclined to listen to an earnest prayer, then he had no idea what she was or why she would ever lend a hopeful fisherman a hand.

Nothing to do, then, but pray and hope, reach for a lifetime's faith and never try to understand it. Certainly not try to understand her; she was beyond him, as she always had been, only that he had been too slow to grasp that. He had thought they were friends, as a kitten might think it was friends with an emperor.

HE HAD thought his own beloved Mei Feng was friends with this emperor, but he wasn't so sure of that now either.

The emperor stood out on the stern deck with him, only to show his men that he was not afraid of any dragon, so long as he stood under the shield of the goddess; and Old Yen had to ask, of course. It would not be true to say that he was not afraid of any emperor, even on his own deck, but this particular emperor was a boy, and almost a friend of his, and almost family. And the generals and advisers who had come aboard with him were still in the cabin, out of earshot; there was no one but the emperor himself to be offended, if a fisherman spoke to the Son of Heaven.

He said, "Majesty, I saw Mei Feng on the quay there, giving you that, that," that object so extraordinary he had no word for it, a shirt somehow made of scales of jade that clung to one another and to the emperor like a second skin. The emperor himself seemed hardly to believe it; he kept glancing down, shifting his body to feel the weight of it and the way it moved. Reaching to touch, to run his hand over the hard glimmering smoothness of it.

"Yes?" The emperor's eyes, lifting to find his: they too were hard and glimmering and smooth, as darkly green as the shirt and as impenetrable.

Old Yen had been hoping for a smile on the face of her boy, at least a little warmth in his voice, perhaps a little wonder. She was wonderful, and two men who loved her ought perhaps to talk about her a little, when they were tense and anxious and uncertain.

Instead—well, he couldn't falter yet, although he wanted to. One step more: it felt uncomfortably bold in the face of that blank regality.

He said, "Majesty, how is my granddaughter?"

"You saw her. I believe she is well enough," and apparently even the gift of that shirt was not enough to mend whatever had broken between them.

Well, it was a hard gift in a hard season. There would be time later for reparations, perhaps. In his triumph, if it came to that; or else in his defeat if he survived it. He might lose the battle and retreat again, if he could find a boat to carry him back to his mother. He would need Mei Feng then, then above all, but there was no way to tell him so.

Perhaps he knew already. He touched the shirt again, was suddenly all boy and not at all emperor; slid his eyes sideways and murmured, "Has she always been so *angry?*"

Which gave Old Yen the chance to smile, to nod, to stroke his beard and say, "Yes, indeed. She was born furious, and nothing has softened her yet."

The emperor sighed. "I thought she was furious like a kitten, fierce and delightful. But now she is like a river in spate, a mountain river, cold and angry and unforgiving . . ."

"No, majesty," daring to deny the emperor his insight, "not unforgiving. Relentless, say rather, until she achieves what she wants. It's something that we love in her, that she will be angry at the world until it changes." At the world, or at a man; he didn't need to say that.

The emperor almost seemed to hear it anyway. He shivered visibly, though he couldn't be cold and Old Yen didn't think he was afraid. "Well," lifting his head, staring forward, "she cannot change this. Except . . ." He laid his hand flat against the shirt almost as though it might have been her hand. "She thought of this, you know, and had it made. Even, even in her anger."

"Yes, of course. Her anger is always practical, majesty; she doesn't only shout and steam, she looks for ways that she can make things better." Better to have an emperor and a man to love, than not; better someone to be angry with, than the other thing.

His thin words couldn't bridge the gulf they'd torn between them, and besides, he was probably speaking to the wrong one; but he could at least point out where a bridge might lie. He'd need to bring the emperor safe back to Taishu first, or it would be him Mei Feng was angry with, and no hope of forgiveness. She was . . . not always reasonable, where she had suffered an irredeemable loss. Her mother's death she had always blamed on her father; that was why she made such a willing crew for Old Yen, so young. It was a way to escape her father and a way to spite him, both at once.

Youth and rank are famously not receptive to wisdom. He had preached hope and patience, as carefully as he could; now he had nothing more to offer. They stood each of them caught in the other's silence, nowhere to go from here except onward into ocean, night and war. None of which seemed to matter as much as that silence did.

It was almost a relief when the dragon came.

She came in low, gliding over the water like the dusk, a darkening shadow; and rose to skim—barely—above the highest mast in the fleet, which was the jade ship's. There was someone up there at the masthead, Old Yen heard the whoop faintly in the wind of her passage; and was already smiling in recognition before he remembered that no, Mei Feng was not with this fleet, she was safe back on Taishu.

Likely that was Jiao, then, whooping in some folly of excitement under the dragon's belly. For sure it had sounded like a woman.

For sure it had sounded like Mei Feng, and the emperor had looked around also at the call.

And then, never mind whoever had whooped: that was the dragon and she was here, and now they would learn—again!— whether they were safe indeed under the goddess's blessing.

THE DRAGON rode the air, low above the fleet, and then climbed higher. She hung overhead like an omen, like a raptor, like a promise of doom. *When your goddess turns away,* she seemed to say, *you will find me here. Waiting.*

six

Tunghai Wang had slept well all his life, even as a soldier on campaign. Especially, perhaps, as a soldier on campaign, when his bed was a blanket if he was lucky, under a roof if he was lucky, more often on ground that was dry if he was lucky, under a sky that—if he was lucky—might not rain on him.

As a general he had rated a tent, a wagonload of furniture and men to erect it every night, take it down and pack it up next morning. His bed was a rice-straw pallet on a frame, and he had still slept well.

On the long march from the Hidden City, the year-long chase across the empire, when sometimes they were so close to their quarry that there was no time to pitch a tent and he had simply lain down among his men for what few hours' rest they could afford to snatch—then, yes, with all the noise of an army camp around him and all the tension of the hunt, then he had slept exceedingly well.

Now, though? Now that the chase was over, now that his hopes were in abeyance, now that he had four close walls and a solid roof, a good mattress on a good bed, warmth and comfort and company too if he chose it, a guard outside the door to ensure that he was not disturbed whether he was alone or not?

Now he slept badly, those nights that he slept at all. The doctors said his body was out of balance with his soul; they prescribed teas to drink and prayers to recite, gifts to various temples, exercise and particular foods.

Nothing helped, which surprised him not at all. He thought it was the dragon in his dreams. Certainly he had slept well before the dragon came, even the night the beacon flared, the night he sent the fleet.

The dragon destroyed the fleet, and Tunghai Wang had not known an easy hour since.

He consulted the doctor on the ridge, but that fool was no better than any other. It was his assistant, the girl working as his servant who offered hope, but not there. She would need to study, she said, certain books, certain scrolls that might be in the city, in the palace he occupied himself, if she might have his consent to search . . .

Anything, of course. He had hopes of that girl, though none of her master.

THE MORNING of the beach raid, he had heard its noise and smelled its smoke before any man thought to come and tell him. Sound and smoke both travel, far and fast; they can outstrip any news of war, to find a wakeful soldier.

Walking on one beach after another, amid sprawled bodies and smoking ruin, the stinks of blood and ash intermingled in the sand beneath his boots, he said, "This was desperation, no more. They saw our fleet and knew they could not stand against it; they knew we would build again, come again; they came to do what they could to forestall us, to delay us a season if they could. No more."

"The dragon, though, general," an aide murmured, his eyes shying at the sky. "They dared the dragon, to do this . . ."

"I said. It was desperation. What else?"

NOW, THIS morning, he knew what else.

He had been sure, so sure they would not come again; and now they had.

The typhoon had come and gone, the endless storm that was said to be the dragon's temper. He had taken that as assurance that they would not come again. If their first raid stirred up such a fury, a second must bring destruction on their heads.

Besides, there was nothing more to raid. It would take a year to build another fleet; they would know that, knowing how much damage they had done, how many craftsmen slain, how many hulls stolen, how many burned. Why should they chance the dragon again until they had to?

But now they had. He was called again, privately from a sleepless bed; he had ridden up to the headland. In the clear light of an early sun, he saw a stain on the water to the east, a stain to the west. Boats, his runners and riders told him; ships, they said. Fleets. Invasion. Oh, he was bold suddenly, this emperor boy . . .

PERHAPS HE had reason to be.

High on the wind above, drifting from one fleet to the other as they parted, rode the dragon. A weapon, a conscript, an ally . . . ?

Whichever one, it really made no difference. She made all the difference in the world.

Already the men here, his most reliable men, were wanting to retreat up the river valley out of Santung, to head inland as fast as they could go. They might have fought an army here, even depleted and anxious, as startled and unready as they were; but who could fight a dragon? Who would dare?

seven

*B*iao was master in the doctor's tent because Tien allowed it: because it flattered him and did her no harm. Her uncle might have been angry, but he was beyond this world now. She did not, she most determinedly did *not* believe that the ghosts of beheaded men were cursed to wander for eternity, sundered from heaven. No.

Her uncle had believed it, but—well, right or wrong, his faith could make no difference. None at all.

No.

The space behind the tent, the slope down to the river belonged to the eunuch boy's mother. She drew water there and washed clothes and dressings and sometimes patients too, just as Tien used to do. She cooked meals there, again as Tien used to do. When it wasn't raining she spent all her time out there, crouching quietly bereft in those brief times when she could find nothing to do.

Lacking any name for her else, Tien called her Mu Gao, because she was tall and lean and her son was far out of her reach now, and again it cost Tien nothing.

Except her space, perhaps. She had lost what she used to have, and had not gained what used to be her uncle's. Between Master Biao and Mu Gao she could have felt entirely squeezed. Except . . .

Her proper life was still in healing; her practice was still in her uncle's tent. It was she who diagnosed the patients and dispensed the medicines, though she worked behind the puppet figure of Master Biao. Everyone knew. It was her they trusted, though it was his fat hands they paid. She had her place and the respect that she was due, though it was all veiled by a conspiracy of deceit. She and he pretended that Master Biao was the doctor here, and the patients pretended to believe it.

Still. He was master in the tent. That was agreed between them. The rest was Mu Gao's, by right of seizure. Which left nowhere for Tien, except . . .

EXCEPT THAT Tunghai Wang had come to consult the doctor, because he was not sleeping. She wasn't sure whether the generalissimo remembered her face, whether he knew she was her uncle's niece; but he saw soon enough who could help him.

Every morning, then, before sun-up, she would take this walk: away from the tent and from Mu Gao, who would be already awake—Tien was not entirely certain that the dour silent woman ever actually slept—and nursing a slow fire into life, ready for the day, while Master Biao snored on inside the heap of his blankets, never ever ready for the day however late it came.

With no more than a cup of something hot inside her—"white tea" they called it but it might be anything except tea, brewed from whatever fresh leaves they had picked yesterday unless there had not been time to go harvesting, in which case it would be nothing but hot water—and the pearl glow of the sky to guide her, she would follow the steep road down into the city.

Shadows along the way would resolve themselves eventually, reluctantly, into people—they might be soldiers on watch or soldiers on patrol, they might be soldiers at liberty, they might be civilians hungry or hopeful or sick, they might very well be patients on their way to the doctor's tent even though they knew the doctor would not be seeing patients for hours yet—who would greet her with respect because everyone knew her and what she did.

The high square shadows of the city streets would enclose her, with their little groups of soldiers always gathered at the corners like rubble fallen from the walls. Here now there were no greetings, only the falling silence and that awareness of being watched as she hurried by, knowing she was safe enough because these men knew her too. Which might not have been enough, except they knew also that she had the sanction of the generalissimo to come and go at will, which was like having the sanction of the dragon: exactly like, as both the dragon and Tunghai Wang had lost one battle, one, and the dragon had come back from that, she had risen into her power again, and so why not Tunghai Wang?

At last, here was the governor's palace that Tunghai Wang had claimed for his own, where she like a little mouse half-hidden and half-ignored had nibbled off a corner for herself.

The guards at the gate knew her, and let her by; so did the guards in the first courtyard. Indeed, they waved her through more briskly than usual, as if she mattered less than ever, as if their minds were thoroughly elsewhere.

In the second courtyard, she glanced briefly toward the gateway to the third, where the generalissimo would ordinarily be bathing and breakfasting and briefing his generals at this time. Today there lacked the usual bustle of horses and litters and guards, but busy or not, she would still not go that way. She did not need to speak to him, to see him, to examine him again. She knew what ailed him, what kept him wakeful. There was no cure for it this side of the strait, except by poisons that would harm him night by night even as they numbed him into sleep, that would kill him quickly by carelessness or slowly by constant repetition. Either way he would be dead too soon, unsatisfied, his ambition unrequited. That would be no use to her, and possibly a danger.

Left, then, to a guarded doorway, where again she was let through unchallenged.

Here was a hall, dark-timbered, dark; she stepped over the threshold and reached to the left, where a lamp was always burning on a shelf. Waiting for her, set ready. Sometimes she wondered if the generalissimo filled it and lit it himself in his restlessness, in hopes that it might guide her to a cure.

If he did, he was doomed to disappointment. Another disappointment. He was a disappointed man already, which was why he could not sleep.

With the lamp cupped between her hands, she walked to a smaller door, a side-chamber, her little miracle, the space that she had made her own.

No one else came here. Tunghai Wang did not read, assuming for a moment that he could. A man might have the gift of it, she supposed, and still choose not to use it. If he was a warrior, say, if he thought he could win all his arguments at the edge of a blade; or if he was a commander of men, say, with his eyes on yellow silk and a green stone throne, who could order others to read to him, and then most likely only messages and treaties.

Where Tunghai Wang chose not to lead, not a man in his long shadow would push ahead. *It took a girl,* she liked to think, *not sworn to him, a lucky chance,* though the luck was all her own.

Not even his looting, raping soldiers had found this room, or troubled with it after it was found. Shelves and boxes full of books and scrolls: why bother? They would be good only to start fires, and Tunghai Wang slew firestarters out of hand.

Tien was careful with her lamp, though not from fear of Tunghai Wang. It would be her tragedy to start a fire here, whatever the consequences. It would be burning out her own heart.

Whoever made this room had worried themselves about fires. Here was a niche set into the wood of the wall, rough stone to stand a light on and bright polished stone to reflect its light out into the room. She put her lamp in the niche, opened shutters in anticipation of the day, sat at the reading-desk and reached to the shelf below. Here was the scroll she had been looking at yesterday. A slip of polished bamboo marked her place.

It was no doubt a terrible thing to be deceiving Tunghai Wang, and terribly dangerous too. She ought to be ashamed; she ought to be afraid. But she did already know the cause of his insomnia, and there was no cure to be found outside himself. She had told him so, as best she could, and given him advice that he was not following because she was a slip of polished girlhood and he carried the marks of a hard lifetime on his body and had no idea how he might listen to her.

Besides, he didn't want to change his soul, his life or his ambitions. He wanted a draft that he could swallow down and so sleep, and so rise again the same man but better rested.

And—who knew?—perhaps she would find the recipe for such a draft, somewhere in this library. No cure, but a treatment, yes. It was not what she was looking for; she might not believe that it existed; it might turn up none the less. There were records here from a thousand years of medicine and magic. She had not tried to count the many hands, the many minds whose work had been brought far and far across the empire. She wasn't cataloging the collection—although she could, and someone ought to—nor trying to put it into order. It had an order already, like a map of its first owner, a network of ideas and connections that Tien tried first to trace and then to understand.

If there was a path to what she wanted, here was where she would find it: here if anywhere, if she was able. Where else could such a library have collected, an aggregate of wisdom on the two subjects that most concerned her? She was not the first to wonder, to worry, to need. Her uncle had studied as best he could, without notice or resources; she could do better. She must do better.

What she lacked, of course, was time. She read hastily, skimming anything that didn't seem useful, dwelling only where she found mention of the dragon or control. Which was unlucky perhaps for Tunghai Wang, but she consoled her conscience with the thought that control was what he needed too. Coupled perhaps with a modicum of insight.

She had brush and ink on the desk there, and a sheaf of little papers supplied by Tunghai Wang, or at least at his order and supplied by his men, which meant that they were torn from any other source of paper that they found. Often there was some part of a painting on the reverse, and she hated that. Using those, she felt as guilty as the hands that had torn it: as though the desecration, the destruction of art, continued beyond the destruction of the thing itself.

Perhaps that was why she was less inclined to copy what she needed, more inclined simply to tear it from the book or from the scroll, to slip it inside her shirt and steal it as she blew out her lamp, as she left the library to the light of morning, a little less every visit than it had been when she came.

Perhaps she wanted to be as guilty as she felt.

Or perhaps she only wanted to be practical. Master Biao had torn so many pages already from her uncle's books, it was just easiest to hide new pages, needed words among the discards and the ruin where no one would ever think to look.

No one would ever look in any case. It was herself she hid them from. Who else? Master Biao read no more than Tunghai Wang, whether or not he could, and Mu Gao surely not. There were no thieves came sniffing around their tent; one at least of them was always there, and they were known to treat thieves and rogues as well as honest folk. Instead of honest folk, perhaps. There were no honest folk, in this grim city these grim days. People survived by thieving, one way or another.

Perhaps that was why she had taken to it herself, because theft was the currency of the times. Or else because the knowledge was stolen, so the paper might as well be also? Or something deeper, perhaps, and more determined. Whatever she took, she kept from other people. If there was an answer for Han here, he would have to come to her . . .

Or it might only be that there was a pleasure in this, scuttling out of the palace in the early day with secrets crinkling against her breast, past guards who knew nothing of them, away from Tunghai Wang who had no notion what she was taking from his seize;

climbing the long hill out of the city with something at least to compensate her, something achieved against the desperate cruel failure of the streets around her, that could not feed or shelter or protect their people; coming to the tent with something that Master Biao could not touch, Mu Gao could not interrupt, no one could have anything to say to it but her.

Perhaps that was why she stole these pages, to give her sole possession: to let her feel, just for once, *this is mine . . .*

Hers and she was holding to it, her whole little stack of knowledge, speculation, fantasy and lies. In there if anywhere was the gem of truth she sought, that moment of recorded wisdom. Set down for the ages, and hers now if she could only find it.

Lost forever, perhaps, if she couldn't, if it needed other wiser eyes. She should feel guilty; she did feel guilty. More than that, she felt determined. It would be here somewhere, and she would find it, and save so many lives and hopes . . .

MEANTIME, HERE was a queue of the early sick, and Master Biao livid with her for being absent, again, when he was wanting her.

"You, Tien—where have you been? Again? Always sneaking off when you know you will be needed, when you know mornings are the busiest times, when people bring the diseases of the night to us and I want you most urgently and you are never here, and . . ."

She stood calm beneath his onslaught, because it was only words; he wouldn't strike her again. These days, he didn't even shout: hissed rather, as though all the roughness and sharp edges, all the volume of his voice had been rubbed away by a too long flow of words. She waited for that flow to check, and then bowed low, an insolent submission that he would know to mean nothing.

"Give me one minute," she said, "to change my clothes, I have the mud of the road on me; then I will be here to help you serve your patients, *Master* Biao."

A screen of silk gave the thinnest illusion of privacy, but it was enough. If he eyed her silhouette as she changed, whatever soft shadows the light might cast against the screen, that was only his lust and she was accustomed to it, accustomed not to worry about it. If he was harvesting snatched glimpses of her body—the thrusting peak of a breast, the slim roundness of a buttock—he wouldn't see what mattered more, what her hands did besides shedding fabric from her skin.

Her dress she set aside for washing; Mu Gao would find it, before Tien had time to see to it herself. She was accustomed to that too. Her stolen papers went into the bottom of her chest, in among a sheaf of other pages. No one would find those, until she had time to come back to them.

Then, with her hands empty and her mind too, with the light shivering kiss of clean silk against her skin—just where Master Biao would like to set his hands, and dared not—she stepped back into the open tent and bowed to him, and then to the first of their patients sitting waiting on the bench.

AND THEN had no time for anything except medicine: the mental practice of it, listening to Master Biao's drilled questions—she had him following her uncle's formula now, when he could remember—and the patients' replies, halting or shifting, wary or confessional or urgent like a flood; hearing the words and the manner of them both, and seeing how their bodies also spoke, how they sat and stood and gestured, how they breathed, how they sweated; hearing Master Biao's counts as he took the pulse of heart and liver and spoke each of them aloud; drawing on everything she knew from her uncle to make a diagnosis, irrespective of anything more that Master Biao might say.

And then the physical practice of it, the weighing out and wrapping of ingredients—not in the pages of her father's books now, but in scraps of silk or linen that she garnered and Mu Gao washed—and giving them to the patients with careful repetitive instructions, making allowance always for what they would forget or ignore or be unable quite to follow. Clean water was hard enough to find; sleep could be harder. Even Tunghai Wang couldn't find sleep.

She was busy, then, entirely: so much so that the first sounds of soldiers passed her by entirely, and it needed a woman's scream to alert her.

A woman who might have been a patient coming or going but was hardly likely to be anything other, here in this abandoned camp above the city. The screaming was supposed to be behind them, over, done; but here it was again, all fresh, and now, yes, she could hear men's voices baying like hunting dogs, the rush of feet, the clash of steel on steel.

And that before the first man appeared in the doorway of the tent, filthy and blooded, his tao bare in his hand and his grin just as bare, just as lethal.

There was terror in the tent then, a quantity of screaming. He looked around, a little dazedly, as a man might who found himself unexpectedly in a palace treasury. With, perhaps, time to loot. Pockets to fill.

No treasures here, in terms of gold or jewels; but there were food and spirits, taken in payment from Master Biao's patients, which are always treasure to a soldier. And there were women too, just the same. He hardly knew where to start, except that the food and flasks would wait and the women not. Also the food and flasks were as silent as they were patient, which the women were not; and there were men too, with whom something must be done, and—

AND HE had not finished raising his sword to begin to threaten that something, before someone was moving forward through the terror, and that was rather bizarrely herself, Tien, which was alarming; and she was talking already, quite calmly really although she at least could hear the thread of tension in her voice vibrating like a gut-string as she said, "Are you hurt, sir? Please, come in. Master Biao will tend to you directly. In the meantime I have hot water and clean cloths, we can wash the blood away at least; and there is food if you're hungry, water or something stronger to wash it down. We draw no distinctions here, soldier or civilian, rebel or imperial guard," said that way because he was surely the emperor's man, though she wasn't quite sure immediately how she knew that, "anyone in need of healing is welcome in this tent, and I hope you will say so to all your brother soldiers . . ."

eight

From first light, every morning now, Ma Lin stood on the cliff's height and looked across the sea for her daughters, where they were, on that low slip of darkness they called Taishu.

She was not made to be solitary. And never was, for one full day together; people came with offerings and prayers, food for the goddess and food for her. She was scrupulous these days, now she could afford to be, now she had no daughters to feed. She never touched what was meant for the goddess.

Sometimes it was as much as she could do, more than she could remember, simply to eat what was meant for her. There was an ache in her that no food could satisfy, she could eat and eat and still be hungry for her daughters and her man and her city and her lost life and oh! her daughters, so why should she trouble to eat?

This lonely vigil did her no more good than the food; she stared and stared and still got never a glimpse of her girls coming back to her. It seemed important all the same that every morning's sun should find her here, as still and erect as the temple at her back, a priestess greeting the day. Except that actually and honestly she was no priestess and she was only looking for her distant daughters.

She could bear the dead one, she thought, more easily than this. Death made sense to her, at least. Sometimes she thought a little ghost-girl caught at the leg of her trousers, tug-tug, and she wished that Meuti had found a better rest; but little girls did die in times of war.

Girls were stolen too, of course, by soldiers and such, but not like this. Not to be the voice of a goddess, to speak perhaps to the emperor himself . . .

It was good to stand with her back to the temple and all that that implied, like a character of denial. Ma Lin could not read, but she knew how to write an emphatic *no!* with her body flung in silhouette against the sea and sky.

She was doing just that today when the light-stain leaked from sky to sea, to show her angular shadows against the dark glitter of the water, black ink written over spilled ink, boats crossing the strait.

At first, she thought *they are bringing my daughters back to me.*

But there were too many boats, and some of them great ships too large for girls; and they landed and landed, they landed men and men, an army of men, and all on the other side of the creek.

She thought, *they have used my daughter to do this, to keep the dragon at bay; and now they have done it, they will bring her back to me, and her sister too.*

But when one boat did at last come to her side of the creek, and land people at the foot of the cliff, it was only men they landed. One of them was the old fisherman who had taken her girls away, so she might at least have hoped for news of them; but another was a young man dressed in an extraordinary shimmer of light. He glittered as green as the water below, as green as the eyes of the dragon overhead. And that was the emperor, and even Ma Lin had no courage to do anything but kowtow as she was told to and then play priestess as he brought his offerings of gratitude for safe passage to the temple, and none of those was either one of her daughters.

nine

The emperor and his fleet had turned westerly, to land at first light and follow the coast road to Santung. The jade ship had turned easterly with its fleet, to strike as hard from the opposite direction. The idea was to trap the rebel soldiers between two unkind hammers, to pound and pound, to drive them one way and the other, disoriented and defenseless . . .

It was more or less the same idea that Tunghai Wang had used, when he took the city in the first place: except that Tunghai Wang had been expected, waited for, even a little bit prepared against. The remnants of the emperor's army had built barricades and fought as best they could, for as long as they could. Fought and died, as they had expected to.

The plan said that Tunghai Wang would be unprepared, even now: that any defenses he'd thrown up since the raid would face the beaches and the sea, but that there would be no serious defenses anywhere. His enemy was across the water; his enemy had been running and running, the emperor was a coward boy under the influence of his coward mother, he would lurk and lurk until the rebels forced the fight. Even when his men had so unexpectedly struck the beaches, it had only been to burn and steal boats, to delay the inevitable, to win himself one more season of life . . .

So the plan said they would be thinking, this side of the strait.

Did Mei Feng believe it, this wonderful plan? Not for a moment. It was hatched by Ping Wen; she had no doubt there was treachery in it.

Which of course was why she had to come. But the emperor would of course not bring her and not license her, and the only other way she could contrive was this, hiding herself among her women as they tended to Jin, the voice of the goddess, who would see them safe across the water.

Which meant necessarily the jade ship, which meant that she was safe from being seen by either the emperor or her grandfather; but the jade ship was the wrong ship by definition, leading the wrong fleet, taking her as far as she could be from the people she cared about. The emperor went west and she came east, and she couldn't watch over him at all until the two forces met up again. Hopefully victorious, at Santung-river, with the rebels in full flight—or dead in a river of blood, she supposed, but she'd rather see them running away.

Even that might be too late. Whatever Ping Wen intended, it might be timed for early in the day. It might have happened already. Mutiny on Grandfather's boat, perhaps? A swift knife in a sailor's hand: not turned against the emperor, not in that magnificent jademail coat, but to slay the child who spoke for the goddess and kept the dragon away. That way he could slay the entire boatload all at once, the entire fleet indeed. Himself included, but there were men who would do that, swallow their own deaths to achieve something that mattered more than life. And then that same magnificent jademail coat would drag the emperor down swifter than any, and they would all be lost.

Or Ping Wen might have a way to signal the mainland with all their plans and artifice; and the emperor would find his force met with a stronger, right there ready at the beachhead. He and his men would all be slaughtered in the surf, and no mail would help him then.

Or if not there, then on the road.

Or if not on the road, then in Santung before she could fight her own way through to find him.

Or just at that moment, just as she did finally reach him and recognition would be in his eyes as it used to be, just for that one brief moment he would be bewilderedly delighted to see her, and right then would be when treachery struck and death took him and she would see him die and it might even be her fault.

Or, or, or . . .

HE WAS out of her sight, out of her reach; there was nothing she could do to help him, only count the ways that he might die, and that helped neither of them.

She did it anyway, meticulously, because there was nothing else she could do. The jade ship might be so much larger than her grandfather's boat, but she still floated by the virtues of wood and moved by wind and tide. Mei Feng knew her by touch and feel and sound, by long experience, by dead reckoning; she could count a dozen ways in which to make herself useful aboard. An easy dozen, just by looking around the deck. And she could offer herself for none of them. She was caught in the logic of her own scheming. She was a servant attendant on the strange silent girl who was the goddess's oblate, not quite a nun but might as well be; or else she was the emperor's consort, vainly trying to follow her master to war.

If she was the servant, then she might as well be a nun herself for all the work she would be let do with the sailors: *tend your mistress, girl, don't fuss about hauling sheets and tripping over stays and getting yourself underfoot.*

And if she was Mei Feng—well, she might be out of favor with her lord and the generals aboard might even know that, but they would still preserve her intact for the emperor's later judgment. She would be all but locked away, certainly kept far from any fighting. Which would mean far from the emperor too, likely sent back to Taishu with Jin and the women as soon as any craft returned.

So. After her first wild, reckless scramble up the mast, her whooping at the dragon's belly—a stupid indulgence, but all the crew was cowering in the scuppers and someone had to shriek resistance into the wind, they couldn't all dance attendance on the silent Jin—she had had nothing to do all the long dark of the crossing but sit on the deck and watch others sail the ship, when she wasn't listening like everyone else for the waft of dragon overhead or the surge from undersea, looking for a great body to occlude the stars. Waiting for the goddess's protection to fail them here, or else for it to fail them *there,* westerly, where her lord had gone, where she could see first the clear lights of her grandfather's boat and then the smudgy lights of his boat in among so many others and then a single blur of distant light and then nothing at all, no sign of them, no news.

And the dragon came and went overhead all night, which might have meant anything at all or nothing at all, depending; and with first light the jade ship's captain finally turned her bows toward the land, with all the fleet around him.

AND HERE they were, safely landed. There was no opposition, no one to see except a handful of gawping peasants. If there had been a watch kept on this bay, it was a watch that was running or riding now, swift as it might, back to Santung to make report.

And if that report was redundant, if Ping Wen and Tunghai Wang were in conspiracy, then of course there would be no one to challenge them here. All Tunghai's men would have gone to face the emperor, the only one they had to kill. The generals might think the plan was working, but generals never budgeted for treachery. Mei Feng expected nothing else.

Mei Feng had her own problem now, as secret as treachery: she had to get away. Away from the other women, except for the one she meant to take with her; away from the jade ship, away from the beach and the bay. All unnoticed by anyone who might want to stop her.

THEY HAD brought the girl Jin out onto the foredeck when the dragon first came swooping over, in case the girl had to see the dragon or the dragon the girl, in case the voice of the goddess had to speak. Apparently not: but when the light came and the jade ship dropped anchor in the bay, when she started to unload her troops, when the sky was empty Jin still wanted to sit out on the deck. Her sister sat with her, of course, and so did the other women, Mei Feng among them. They watched the soldiers disembark, and if there was no reason for anyone to chivvy them back below, nor was there any reason Mei Feng could think of, why they would or how they could argue for a trip ashore.

Until—bless her lost heart!—Jin gave them one.

Unless it was the goddess, of course. If Jin ever spoke on her own behalf, Mei Feng had never heard it. Nor had she ever seen the girl so direct and purposeful, unless perhaps it had been the first time the dragon flew above them, when she turned her head upward to stare and stare while all the women around her flinched and cowered, while Mei Feng shimmied up the mast. One glance she gave now, that seemed to be aimed directly at Mei Feng, with a biting integrity; and then she turned to her sister and said, "I want to go ashore."

Perhaps the voice was only dusty with disuse, caught with splinters. To Mei Feng it sounded more broken than that, as though something altogether too big and too strong were trying to use it, as awkwardly and damagingly as a soldier's hard callused hand might rip a fragile and slender glove in trying to draw it on.

The words, though, they were clear enough; and the will that drove them.

The little girl blinked up at the bigger, startled almost beyond measure. Then she asked a little-girl question, as though just for a minute she could shrug off the cloak of competence.

"Why?"

"To give thanks," Jin said—if it was Jin, which Mei Feng doubted more and more—"for a voyage safe completed. There is a daughter-temple in the village, where we may burn joss to the Li-goddess."

Was there a village? It wasn't to be seen anywhere in the bay. Mei Feng might climb the mast again and still not see it; wary of pirates and sea raids, people here tended to live a mile or more from the coast.

A glance at the little girl, a wide-eyed shake of her head: neither she nor her sister knew anything about villages hereabouts, or the temples they might hold.

How did that feel, Mei Feng wondered, to find that someone you loved had been taken for use by a god?

Much as it might feel, she thought, to find that the boy you loved was emperor and hence a god himself; or the other way around, perhaps, that the emperor-who-was-god was also a boy and could be loved, however difficult he might make that sometimes, however high he tried to sit aloof on his uncomfortable throne of stone.

However many stupid risky wars he dragged her into . . .

A gesture brought Dandan swiftly to her side. Officially one of her women, a servant, just a few years older than she was; these lonely days, something closer to a friend. A friend who could read, which mattered more today.

"Go to the captain, at the stern there; say that the voice of the goddess wants to go ashore to pray. Two boats, tell him: one for us and one for an escort." He would certainly send an escort anyway, so she might as well demand one now. "Be . . . expectant. You know." As though there were no possibility of a refusal.

Dandan knew. But, "It might be easier if I could say the consort of the emperor expects it."

"It would. No, though."

"You are here now . . ."

". . . And they could just as easily send me back. Or hold me here with the ships, far from everything," far from her lord, her straying love, the idiot endangered emperor who wouldn't listen to her. "The voice of the goddess should be enough." More potent even than her own, if the captain had any gratitude in him. Or any sense.

ONE OR the other. Dandan returned with promises, and five minutes later there were boats, and men to man them. Men sufficiently refined—or browbeaten, more likely, just in those few minutes, *the goddess herself will be watching how you handle her women, so mind your manners, if you can find them at all*—to help awkward feet and nervous hands on the ladders, to see everyone settled more or less comfortably before they pushed off and rowed away.

Ashore they found a road, or at least a track, rising up from the sands of the bay. Before it bent into a stand of bamboo beyond the dunes, Mei Feng turned for one last look at the bay, at the sea, at the bright morning and the fleet that filled the water; and so she might have been first to see the flicker in the sky which was the dragon back again.

Everyone else saw her soon enough. The dragon swooped, low over the beach; men screamed and ran. If Jin had kept her at bay before, she wasn't doing it now, even from this little distance. When Mei Feng checked, the girl hadn't even turned to watch; she was still following the track, alone now but for her sister.

Perhaps the goddess knew it didn't matter. The dragon sank no ships, swallowed no men.

All she did, she seized a boat where it was drawn up high on the shore there.

She was gliding so low, it was barely possible to make out what she did within her own undulating shadow: but Mei Feng saw the stretch of one long clawed leg, the seize, the rise that followed with a boat like a trophy gripped below.

There went boat and dragon, and here she stood with so many others, staring, bewildered, too far away to be afraid.

At last she remembered the emperor, and what she really did

have to be afraid of, as he was too stupid to fear it himself. She shook herself and turned to see Jin a fair way farther down the road already with her little sister trotting anxiously along beside, clutching Jin's hand because she shouldn't go alone but casting longing glances back because they shouldn't go alone together and she couldn't stop the bigger girl at all.

Mei Feng organized her women and the soldiers too, called them back to their duty, led them in a hurry behind.

ten

A city defended once can be defended again. Its reputation will speak through its stones; it has a memory of resistance, walls that say no, gates that refuse to yield.

A city that has fallen once will fall again. That is . . . inherent. Shame sinks to its foundations, weakness and loss and surrender lie like characters to be read in the very dust of its streets.

What the city knows, its people know. Give them time enough, and they might forget the reason; they might not remember why they keep to the walls and shadows, why they slink out of the light, why they walk with their eyes cast down and talk in mumbles, all sidelong and wary. Why it embarrasses them to be who they are, or why they are afraid of strangers.

They don't understand how other people can be so strong, so confident, so open; they know there's something lacking in themselves, and they can't put a name to it, and they're afraid of that absence too.

Or give them no time at all, let them be the ones who took the city; let them remember how easy it was for them, how impossible for those they took it from, how indefensible the streets and slopes and alleys truly are.

Let them crouch within their hopeless barricades, and wait for war.

WAR IS always coming, where it has come before.

A city that has fallen once will always fall again.

TUNGHAI WANG walked the streets of Santung and knew, he *knew* that he could not hold it.

In his head it was treacherous underfoot, slippery with blood and greasy with fear because he had made it so. In his head, his hands could find nothing to hold on to.

In fact, it was his men who would not hold. Who were already not holding. They thronged the streets and muttered, turned their heads away when they saw him and muttered more. They watched the ridges east and west, the rising smoke of battle, almost more nervously than they watched the sky, where the dragon had been almost a constant in the hours since dawn, coasting between one low horizon and the other.

East and west, where the emperor had landed armies. Unlooked-for armies, that should have been impossible and were not.

The runners who brought reports of it arrived barely ahead of those soldiers who should be building barricades and harrying those armies; who had seen the fleets and the numbers of men and the dragon too, and had tried their utmost to outrun their runners.

Already they were infecting all his army. He had lost this battle before it was fought, lost Santung before a single imperial troop set foot in it.

Those troops were at the margins of the city now, and meeting precious little opposition. He and his generals too were learning how it felt to be weak, to order men where they would not go. To be helpless in the face of defiance. He might as well throw name and reputation into the stew of what was lost. Already men were streaming up the river road, northward. Already, he suspected, his generals were joining them. If he went too, if he mounted up and rode off now, he could at least keep his army intact and organized. Retreat was not defeat, not yet.

eleven

This, now: this was how a woman ought to live.

When that woman was Jiao, at least. When her arm didn't feel rightly balanced without a blade in it, when her long legs needed to stretch and strain, when her skin felt better sweating under leather than silk.

When roads were for running down and doors for kicking in, when the glazed light of morning found her unslept and already filthy, an ache in her shoulders and a stiffness in her neck, a twitch in her muscles and her eyes sore from jabbing into shadows.

No blood on her naked tao, not yet, but that couldn't last. With that certainty came the rising tang of fear that she felt like steel in her bones, chill and stiff and something she could use, a strengthening. Some people were disabled by fear, but Jiao seized it gratefully, like a gift. If she wasn't afraid, what would throw her into the noise and stink of battle, what would drive her arm to kill strangers as innocent, as uninvolved, as mercenary as herself?

She felt no passionate commitment to the emperor, that was sure. She hadn't gone to Taishu in support of his cause, nor followed him here to achieve it. Neither did she feel hatred or contempt for Tunghai Wang and his rebels. They were soldiers, just as she was; just like the baying pack of men at her back, who would have fought as easily for the rebel cause if they'd happened to fall in with Tunghai Wang's recruiters instead of the emperor's . . .

They might have wished for that, every day during their long retreat. They might have longed to be rebels instead of imperial troops, to be the ones who chased. One thing, though: that year on the road had taught them to be proper soldiers, her kind of soldier, pirates of the road. Let others charge ahead, let them race to be first to the city, first to the fight, first in the emperor's favor. Let them chase fleeing rebels down the road, across the paddy, through the forests and all the way to the hills. She led her troop in a slower pursuit, checking every hut they came to. Searching empty granaries and busy temples, scouring woodland, looking for the spies and assassins, the ambushes that she would certainly have left behind.

Looking and not finding yet, finding only priests and peasants who cowered or wept or were sullenly silent, who gathered close their idols or their children, their ducks or their little stores of rice in helpless protective gestures. Not a man at her back who would touch the idols, or the children; pirates could be as superstitious as they were sentimental. Besides, there was no more value in a broken statue than there was in a dead peasant.

Hungry peasants mattered less. Barely a man at her back who didn't have a duck in his bag now, or a sack of rice at his belt. Every pirate-soldier is a looter too, and Jiao herself reckoned herself wealthier by two days' food, though she had one of the men carry it for her.

Here was a barn that might have been heaped high with rice-straw at this season and was empty, sign of a bad harvest or a harvest not gathered in, lost to war or weather. The barn smelled of nothing but its own shadows and dust, dried dung and rot. Nevertheless she sent men climbing into the roofspace to find who was hiding in the rafters, who had disturbed the cloud of bats they'd seen issuing like smoke before they came.

A shriek, a plummeting body landing with a brutal thud: he might have broken bones after such a fall, he must have bruises. Just a boy, though, scrawny and bare-legged, empty-handed, no threat to anyone. Jiao laughed, and nudged him with the toe of her boot.

"You, boy—do you want to be a soldier of the emperor?"

Slitted and shrunken with pain, only his eyes moved, indeterminately. She laughed again.

"Wise boy. You lie there and think about it. If you do, come after us and ask for Jiao; I'll see you fed and dressed. Armed, too. Otherwise, run and hide, be bare-assed and hungry and free. Your choice."

If something had broken in him, of course, he would do neither, but only lie there until he died. The way he squirmed, though, when her foot poked at him, she thought he'd do well enough. The emperor didn't really need more soldiers, but every troop could use a local boy. Give him a tao to carry, he'd never realize he was just a servant. Give him food and trousers and a tao, he wouldn't care anyway. Give him a sense of belonging, and the emperor might really have another soldier regardless.

A cry hailed her out of the barn. One of the men she'd left to watch the road: she found him doing that exactly, looking back the way they'd come with his eyes shaded against the rising sun.

"What is it, Jing?"

"Runners, coming after us. Should be ours, must be; messengers, I guess. But . . ."

"But?"

"But they're women. In skirts. And one of them's not much of a runner."

If there had been other fighting women aboard the jade ship, or anywhere in that fleet, Jiao didn't know it. And no one would choose to go to war in a skirt. Nor would anyone choose one woman in a skirt to run a message, let alone two of them.

Jiao grinned and said, "All right. These are for me. Got any more of that chewing-leather on you?"

Other men carried dried meat to chew on; Jing's preference was fruit, sliced and left to hang in sun and wind until it was dark and shriveled, almost indistinguishable to the eye.

He reached into his belt-pouch; she said, "Not for me. There's

a boy in there feeling sorry for himself. Go in and make him glad
he didn't break his skinny neck in falling, would you? Give him
something sweet to suck on, leave him with a good memory of
us," and perhaps there'd be someone else to come chasing after
them. Boys enough would be ruined today, one way or another; it
would warm her soul a little, to save just one.

She stepped out into the road and lifted a hand, to stop Mei
Feng and her woman.

"*What,*" she asked, entirely redundantly, "are you *doing?*"

"I need to reach the emperor." As if it was obvious. Which, Jiao
supposed, it was: if you were Mei Feng, or if you knew and understood her.

What was odd—if you knew and understood Mei Feng—was
that she'd brought one of her palace women with her. Jiao
couldn't remember her name, had never troubled much to distin-
guish among them, might not have recognized her anyway in this
sweating, disheveled, gasping creature who had no notion how to
run.

"I thought you went to all this trouble," with a gesture at the
plain clothes, the improbable skirt, "to hide yourself from the emperor?"

"I'm here now," as though she could not be sent back again—
which might be true, even. There were only two children they
thought could guarantee safe passage to Taishu. A wise emperor
would play the wise general and keep both at hand, in case of
need.

Which would not stop him shutting Mei Feng up under guard,
somewhere safe and far from him. Jiao would do exactly that, she
thought, if she were emperor.

In the meantime, though, it would be necessary to keep Mei
Feng alive; which apparently required Jiao to be scathing now.
"And what is it exactly you can do when you reach him? If he lets
you stay within reach?" *He is the Man of Jade,* she was saying,
with his magical jade armor that you gave him and his strength

and speed that he gets from the stone itself; what can you do, compared with that?

"I can watch his back," she said stubbornly, "against those who ought to be his friends."

And no, that was not Jiao she was including in her glower, unless Jiao stood against her. It was Ping Wen, of course, whom Mei Feng believed so devoutly to be a traitor, against whom the emperor would not hear a word.

That was good enough for here, for now, for an encounter by the road a mile short of the war. Jiao gestured with her head, *join us and welcome, then. You and your woman too. If you can keep up.*

SHE LED her troop on at a lope: not following the road now, taking a farmers' track that ran parallel, to surprise any hidden rebels who might be hoping to surprise imperial soldiers on the road.

This way was muddy, a little awkward, a little overgrown. A glance back showed both young women trailing behind, impeded by their skirts. They'd just have to catch up at the next halt if they could—except that the next time Jiao looked around, there was Mei Feng at her elbow. With her skirts rudely slashed apart and knotted up around her hips, her bare legs already slathered with mud. Jiao supposed it was decent, by a very crude and basic measure of decency. To judge by their calls and whistles, her men approved thoroughly, by any measure of very crude approval.

Mei Feng called something even cruder back over her shoulder, and then grinned up at Jiao.

"They say there was a boy in the barn back there. If I'd thought, I'd have gone in and stolen his trousers."

"He didn't have any. I expect we can find you trousers, farther on. And a tao."

"I don't want—"

"How are you planning to guard the emperor's back, without a blade?"

"I've got a knife," Mei Feng said, slapping the hilt of it where it hung inappropriately from a dainty belt. "That'll do."

Jiao grunted, and jerked her head backward. "Your friend—"

"Dandan."

"Yes. What's she for? You should have left her to look after the girls. She'll only slow you down."

Indeed, she had clung to the decency of her skirts and was making heavy weather of the path, falling farther back now that Mei Feng wasn't beside her to nag or drive her on.

"Jin and Shola will be fine. They have women enough. And the village priest too, now. I left them in the temple, charming him with gifts. Dandan's for the other end. When I reach the emperor. It'll be . . . difficult anyway, but he'd be furious, he'd be *ashamed* if I just turned up alone, after running all through a city of war on my own. I can't do that anymore. I can't do that to him. So I thought I'd best have a companion, a chaperone . . ."

It was thin cover, and not likely to help much; but the Mei Feng of even a month ago would not have thought even that far ahead, would never have seen the need for any cover at all. Jiao thought the girl might be growing up, at least a little.

PAUSING ON a sudden hill, she saw a pillar of smoke rising to the north, solitary and unforthcoming; and on the path behind, farther even than Dandan was a jag, a speck, a tentative shadow following.

Jiao called a halt, and picked four men to investigate the smoke. "Mei Feng," she added, "you go with them. See what's what."

She already knew what was what, or could make a fair guess at it. So could the men. This was an aspect of protecting Mei Feng, to introduce her early to the taste of war. It was a kindness in a way, Jiao's way; if it was short of mercy, that was Jiao's way also. She didn't envy Mei Feng the discoveries at the foot of that pillar of smoke; nor pity her for what she would learn there. She had chosen to come to the war. Let her see it, then, for what it was. She would need to know, before they reached the city.

Meanwhile, Jiao's squad could sit and grunt and murmur in the shade, soldiers seizing the chance, knowing that the day would shift and change before too long; and she could watch those figures on the path back there and calculate how long it would take the boy to catch up with the woman, how long the two of them to reach the squad here.

Too LONG: she saw the one join the other, but Mei Feng and the men came back before the pair together made the foot of the rise. She wouldn't wait.

The returning men told her everything she needed to know: empty hands, the jerk of a head, *move on*.

Even so, she looked to Mei Feng. Make her say it all aloud, give her nowhere she could hide, even inside herself.

Mei Feng's hands weren't empty, nor were her legs still bare. Jiao thought she was already doing better than anyone could fairly expect.

She said, "It was, it was nothing. *Nothing*. Just a hutment in the paddy, a few folk living there, nothing to fight over. No one did fight. They were just . . . Someone slaughtered them, that's all. There weren't any soldiers, just peasants. Dead peasants. Nothing at all . . ."

Jiao nodded. What did she expect? This was a day for slaughter. And bodies didn't always tell the tale. There might have been soldiers, rebels, who saw an imperial squad on its way and fled before it reached them. That squad might have seen the running men and suspected a trap, an ambush. Suspicious, frightened soldiers were inclined to slaughter on the off-chance, just in case.

No need to say so. Mei Feng needed the lesson, not the reasons behind it. Besides, Mei Feng had a peasant's trousers on her legs, and had stopped to wash the mud off before she dressed. And she

had an armful of other clothes salvaged from the fire. That was
piracy, the pure thing. Jiao was pleased with her, and secretly impressed. "Be kind, then, and take trousers to those two," where
they were still toiling upslope through the mud and their own
soreness and exhaustion. There was nothing broken in the boy,
bones or spirit; she thought he'd do. Soldiers like to keep a pet. Especially one who can be trained to wash clothes, fetch water, run a
hundred little tasks at day's end in an army camp. Mei Feng would
look after her woman her own way, but, "Give the lad a drink, too.
And see that he washes, next time we cross a stream."

Be kind. Let the boy see that there was kindness in the emperor's army, a little now and the promise of more to come.
Clothes and water, something to chew on the road and a little
touch of mothering, *mind you wash your feet now.* He'd thrive on
that, and sell his soul for more.

SOME SOLDIERS—or their commanders—didn't understand the
recruiting power of kindness, and so burned harmless hutments
and left peasants dead in the mud.

Some didn't always have the time to think about it, or else they
didn't take the time. They were surprised, or they flung themselves
forward without looking, or they were sent or driven or led too
far, and . . .

Jiao had been there herself, time and time again: when the air
was filled with screaming and some of it might be, might well be,
might as well be your own; when your blade was wet and heavy in
your hand, and fear pierced your bones like spikes from deep in
the bitter dark, and all the world was closing in around you like a
tunnel, a mouth that would swallow you whole; when there were
bodies hurtling at you and bodies trying to flee you and you
hacked at both simultaneously, indiscriminately, and only wondered later which was which and whether it might matter.

Here on the ridge at the city's edge, with the streets running
down toward the river and the dark alleys twisting away to either

side, their walls unforthcoming and every one of their gates a
threat—well, it was no surprise if the first squads here had been
just like that, slaying whoever came in reach.

Here were broken barricades, the wreckage of them, dragged
aside along with the wreckage of the men who had defended
them; those bodies intermingled with others who had surely not
been defending the barricades. Sheltering behind them, rather:
women, mostly, because the men of Santung had all fled or been
killed before and not many would have found their way back yet.

Slain without orders—she hoped—and only in that fearful hot
frenzy, they were still just as dead. At least none here would know
them, unless perhaps the boy did. He was trailing behind still,
with Mei Feng and her woman; Jiao only hoped that none of them
would look too closely. Bodies were worse, always, when you
could put a name to them. Names summoned ghosts into the
dark, into the dreamtime, the space behind your eyes. Bodies
could be ignored, shrugged off, forgotten—once you were used to
them, once you'd learned the ways—but ghosts not. Jiao knew,
she'd borne a few ghosts of her own for long enough. Perhaps she
still did.

Despite the bodies, though, despite all the signs of warfare, the
city was oddly quiet for a battle-site. Jiao nosed warily past half a
dozen alley-mouths, listening for screams or the clash of blades—
for anything, really, that would speak of soldiers and fighting,
trouble, war—and hearing nothing that mattered, nothing to fret
her piratical soul.

At last she stopped a man, a runner with the imperial yellow
sash. He should have been inviolate, untouchable at any time, let
alone in a city of war where the emperor himself was fighting; but
she stepped into his road, and when he tried to duck around her,
she seized his arm and held him.

"Tell me, man—where has the battle gone?"

He gaped at her, stuttered, "You, you cannot delay me—"

—and was promptly shaken hard enough to jar the teeth in his skull. "Oh, can I not? Tell that to the emperor—but make sure I'm standing there beside you, because I'll enjoy the laugh you get from him. I can delay you as long as I choose. That woman who follows me so closely? She is his chosen concubine, and *she* could flay you alive and take your skin back to make a cushion for the Jade Throne, and he would not speak a word against her. So forget your own importance and listen to mine, just for this little minute. Where is all the fighting?"

"There is none," he muttered. "Tunghai Wang will not fight. That is my message, that I am carrying back to the ships. The rebels are running out of Santung as fast as they can go, all along the river roads. Climb up onto a roof for the view, and you could see them do it. Now let me go, Jiao. I know who you are, and Mei Feng too."

There is power in names, even the names of the living; names can summon trouble, which Jiao could just as well live without. She wished the man fair running and let him go.

There was a high building just on the corner of the street there, with a flat roof and an outside stair. She ran swift-booted up, and yes, the runner had been telling simple truth. There were people streaming away from the city, both sides of the river. At this distance it was all movement, but it was a movement she'd seen again and again throughout her life, there was no mistaking it.

She had seen herds of animals, deer and cattle being driven, but this was different.

She had seen pilgrims in progress and refugees in flight, and this was still different.

This was an army, soldiers in retreat. Disorganized and afraid, armed men still move together in ways that set them apart from civilians. Jiao watched them run and knew how they felt, how they sweated, how they smelled. How they watched each other, how they watched the road ahead and the road behind, how some little corner of their minds was always hoping to find more men around them. A civilian might long for open spaces, room to run, but a soldier knows where his best protection lies. Being faster than your brothers can prove as deadly as being slower. Massed bodies packed about you, that's a shield and defense if anything can be.

Sometimes, nothing is. Sometimes absence is the only survival skill. But still: a running army is a roadful of individual soldiers, and most of them—the wise ones, the veterans, the ones who carry scars on their skins and scars in their heads—are pressing inward, jostling for cover as they run.

Which leaves the recruits, the ignorant, the innocents on the outside, most exposed and barely even knowing it, glad perhaps to have space enough to stretch their legs, even to outspeed their elders. Drawing attention to themselves every way, making themselves first target for spears or arrows or a horseman with a blade . . .

LET THEM run. She'd always rather see an enemy's dust as he fled than his face as he charged. Almost always. Some men needed to die, but not so many; and those apart, it was always better not to fight.

Almost always.

If there was a tingle of disappointment in her arm, she could ignore it. And thrust the long-bladed tao into her belt, to make the point more clearly to herself how strong-minded she was, how she could step back from that offer of war, let the bite of fear drain out of her bones, never miss it . . .

If there was the enemy, clear to be seen, where was the emperor's army? Still in the streets or on the riverbanks, harrying the rearguard and giving chase already . . . ?

Hundreds had gone ahead of her, hundreds more would be coming in from the opposite direction; Santung must be swarming.

It was hard to see down between the city's buildings and into its streets. Easier to look across the river, see this side reflected on the opposite slope, see how soldiers like ants poured down the wide streets and into the darkness of the alleys, imagine how they howled . . .

Not imagine, so much. If she listened, up here, she could hear it after all: that distant noise of battle, the yells and screams, the clash of steel on steel.

There was fighting, then, just no resistance. She felt for the rebels, almost; it was so hard to fight and flee, to doom your rear-guard, your friends . . .

In search of friends, she scoured the ridge across the river, hoping for a mass of yellow which would be the emperor's personal guard, perhaps a flash of sun-on-green which would be the emperor himself in that ridiculous jade shirt. That's where she ought to find him, high on the hill there, angling for the best view just as she was herself. Him and all his party, perhaps, on a building just like this, somewhere in that patterned maze that made one half of this city above its river, like a butterfly with its wings spread wide: she stood on one and the people she wanted stood somewhere on the other, and she couldn't quite see them yet. Now that she was explicitly looking it was something she needed, a sudden seize of worry, and she wanted to leap onto the roof's parapet for that extra step of height, but it would be quite a stretch up onto glazed and sloping tiles and she wasn't a fool, she wasn't going to risk the momentum of her jump carrying her over the edge.

Just in the corner here was a stack of spare tiles and a mound of what she guessed was the clay used to make mortar, under a length of old sacking. A step onto that and a foot on the parapet, she'd be rock-solid and sensibly safe . . .

. . . EXCEPT THAT as she stepped onto the sacking, she felt the mound give and shift beneath her weight. For a moment, the briefest of blinks, she thought that was fresh mud underneath and her foot was going to sink right into it.

Except that the mound gave only a little, only enough to startle when she thought she was stepping onto something solid and hard-baked.

Then it resisted.

Then it rose, it erupted beneath her feet and flung her off-balance, flung her all the way over onto her back so that she sprawled helplessly before him as the man beneath the sacking hurled himself up to loom above her, his hand already reaching to his blade.

THIS WAS it, of course, what she'd been looking for, why she'd been so wary all the day: this was the stray rebel soldier, abandoned or trapped on his own, trying to wait out the daylight till he could slip out of the city and away.

Too late now.

No time, no point even trying to scrabble her tao into her hand; by the time she had it halfway drawn, his steel would be in her heart.

She'd always sworn that she would go down fighting. She had also always sworn that when the end came, if it was clear and inevitable, she wouldn't struggle against it. She'd have dignity enough to look death in the face and laugh.

It hadn't occurred to her till now that those two vows might work against each other. She could reach for her tao anyway, although there was no point; or she could gaze up at his and laugh, although there was no dignity in this sprawl on a stranger's roof, and precious little that was funny either.

She would be dead either way, dead in moments, it didn't really matter; except that it did to her, it suddenly mattered exceedingly, and she didn't quite know what to do.

Which might be why she turned her head aside—not to avoid the sight of that blade stabbing down, only to give her a moment undistracted, time to think—and so saw a shadow reach across the roof toward her, which was a figure on the stair, which was—

—MEI FENG, almost the last person she'd want to see there. Any of the men would have been better, genuinely a threat, maybe a distraction to this man who hadn't quite killed her yet. The boy would likely have yelled for help and gone hurtling back down to ground again.

Mei Feng, though: Mei Feng might yell but would certainly hurl herself at the rebel, try to help, and so die too. Perhaps do it first, deliberately, try to buy Jiao the time she needed. It wouldn't work, because the man would have time in plenty to slay Mei Feng and then Jiao while she was still struggling to her feet, struggling with her tao; but Mei Feng might do it anyway.

Which would be noble and heroic and pointless, and both women would end up dead at his feet. Which they were going to do in any case, and that was just sad, when there were so many other ways for their two stories, their two lives to go on; and other people who cared and would be sorry, and . . .

AND YES, Mei Feng launched herself at the rebel, and it was perhaps Jiao's fault that he had already seen her, she had looked that way and he might have followed her eye. Or he might have caught a glimpse in the corner of his own, a flash of movement, the stretch of her shadow. It didn't matter either way because there still wasn't time enough to do anything, though Jiao of course was doing what she could, drawing up her knees—too slow, too *slow . . . !*—to kick out at his ankles, in vague hopes of toppling him over the parapet, inevitably too late for Mei Feng and probably for herself too even if she believed that he would so conveniently go over, which she didn't, but at least she'd answered her own question, what to do. Of course she would fight, helpless and hopeless and empty-handed, empty of head and empty of heart and . . .

AND *SOMEHOW* is a weasel word, but somehow Mei Feng was impossibly fast to cross that roof, so fast it wasn't possible but there she was, before Jiao could bring her boots in line, before the rebel could raise his sword.

And Mei Feng didn't have a sword, of course, she wouldn't carry one; and she wasn't a fighter anyway, she wouldn't know how to use it if Jiao had forced one on her. All she did was barrel into the man, batter his blade aside and hurtle him over.

Not over the edge, even, only to knock him sprawling; but that was good, that was plenty. Jiao could deal with him now, she'd be up before he was and blade in hand, ready to skewer him as he had meant to skewer her, only she wouldn't linger so long . . .

LONG ENOUGH, apparently, long enough; swift as she was, she was still too slow.

By the time she was on her feet, she didn't need the blade.

She was sorry, almost, to slam it back into her belt-sheath; sorry to crouch beside her friend and peel Mei Feng's fingers one by one away from the handle of her knife; sorry to need to do this, to wipe the blade and draw the girl back from the seeping pool of blood where she was kneeling, where she had dropped to her knees and slit the rebel's throat as he lay helpless.

It might be—must be!—the first man Mei Feng had killed, the first whose blood she had splashed on her own clothes, her skin, her hair. Whose reek she would carry with her for the rest of her days.

Jiao had seen this often and often: the stillness afterward, the self-absorption, the trembling doubtful wonder. She knew how to deal with it, but only in boys. In raw recruits, who could be bullied and teased, intimidated by a woman so much more at ease with this than they were. Comforted by roughness because their lives were rough, they would turn—when she would let them—to their comrades, their cohorts. Lads their age would be awkward and awed, asking how it was; older men would be mock-casual and celebratory, telling them how it had been for them, their first time; both would do them good.

Neither would be any use here, now, for her. Mei Feng was entirely the wrong person to be first this morning with blood on her blade. Jiao could wipe the steel—on the dead man's clothes, according to all tradition—but she couldn't wipe her friend's mind, which needed it more.

She slid the cleaned knife back into its sheath on Mei Feng's belt, with a brief, "Well done. Thank you. You'll want this." *Give it a hone tonight, or it'll lose its edge*—but that was instruction for a boy, not fit for her. Not from Jiao. She'd have one of the men say it later. Right now, because she simply had to know, she said, "How did you ever move so fast?"

Mei Feng shrugged, tried out her voice, found that she had one still: "He was going to kill you. I . . . hurried. That's all."

Suddenly voiceless herself, lacking any words to say how far that fell short of all, Jiao kissed her, and then drew her to her feet—

—AND THEN let her drop down again because she had to, and held her shoulders while Mei Feng vomited helplessly, sailor-like over the side.

twelve

*R*ight now, Yu Shan thought, what the emperor needed most was Mei Feng.

Or his mother.

Someone he might at least listen to; someone he used to listen to, at least, even if he was out of the habit now.

Failing that—as it must fail, as it had, because he would listen to none of the generals who had battered words at him, again and again, like seawater splashing uselessly against a rock—then probably what he really needed was someone faster, stronger, more determined than himself, to physically restrain him.

Which of course meant Yu Shan, if it meant anyone at all. There was no one other, and even that would be a hard wrestle, a close match. Yu Shan had a sliver of jade in his mouth, and he thought that might give him the edge; but the emperor had an entire shirt made of scales of jade, and hadn't taken it off all night, all day.

Yu Shan wasn't sure. And, in any case, was not going to make the attempt. For fun, yes, and at imperial command, he would wrestle with the emperor. On a battlefield, though, in sight of half the imperial army, in the height of war? And for no fun at all, but purely to prevent the emperor from doing the thing he wanted most?

No. Mei Feng would do it, any way she could: by argument or by command; by holding on with both hands to his ankle if she had to, if there was no other way. More likely by leaping onto his

back like a monkey, wrapping arms and legs around him, covering
his green eyes with her palms, making him look ridiculous in the
mocking eyes of all the troops he was so eager to lead. That would
work, perhaps. But Mei Feng was not here, and not in favor anyway. Yu Shan couldn't even invoke her name as an argument, *Mei
Feng would not be pleased*. That might have worked before, but
now it would act only as a goad.

His mother would do it, simply with her own frail body set determinedly between him and what he wanted. There was only one
person who could induce the emperor to stand up to his mother,
and that was Mei Feng, who was not here. Which was an irony of
sorts, Yu Shan supposed, except that the dowager empress was not
here either.

Of course, the emperor had brushed them both aside, in his determination to have his war. That was a special case, though, the
influence of Ping Wen and the urge to strike back after so long
running, the call of history and the need to live up to his father, to
make his own legend.

Besides, he was a boy, and boys will fight. In despite of all their
womenfolk. Yu Shan understood that, in a way that Mei Feng
never would.

If his womenfolk were here now, though, and seeing this—well.
The emperor would not be brushing them aside, they wouldn't
have it.

In their absence, what he needed was someone as bold as his
womenfolk to stand up to him, to stand in his way, to tell him no.

Not Yu Shan.

He had the strength—perhaps—and he had the privileged position, here at the emperor's elbow. He had the insight, he saw the
need. He still would not do it.

Instead he watched older and wiser men, senior generals, baffle
themselves with pleas and arguments that did no good at all. He
saw them wish that they could just call up a sergeant to wither this
idiot young man into obedience, if emperors were only susceptible

to sergeants, or to withering, if there were only one man in all the imperial army bold enough to make the attempt.

He saw them wish that Yu Shan were that man. And wished it so himself, somewhat, but wishing didn't make it true.

So the army still plunged on down the slopes of Santung, looking for the war that it had come for; and the emperor ran on in the fore of that army, blade in hand, while his officers panted and sweated behind and even his personal guard was lagging and Yu Shan was the only one who could keep up, the only one who could match him for speed and endurance both, certainly the only one who could stop him.

And would not.

No YOUNG man—certainly no young man in armor, with a blade— would want to hold back, to watch a battle from a distance, to give orders and see other men die in pursuit of them.

Even so, emperors should learn to do it. This emperor in particular should have learned by now.

What it was, Yu Shan thought, was that this very particular emperor had been in a fight already, face to face and hand to hand. He knew the taste of it, the bite, the smell and effort, and the shivering rush that came afterward like wind in the veins, a flow of chill through all your body's tissues as you walk away with your enemies dead on the ground at your back.

The emperor had fought and killed, seen his friends die and survived it. He probably thought he was immortal.

So did Yu Shan think so. He'd seen the emperor felled by a blow that should have killed him, a tao slash at the emperor's ribs that should have cut through shirt and skin, through flesh and bone together, to pierce to the heart of empire, the emperor's heart itself.

He had seen the emperor fall bleeding. He'd seen that dark flow stop too soon, as if there were no heartwork left to pump it: as if the blood lay still in the emperor's veins, and the emperor lay still in the hands of death, as he ought.

But the emperor's eyes had shown nothing but a bright bewilderment, which was more or less how Yu Shan felt also, because that tao had only glanced off his bones and not cut through at all, despite having enough fury behind it to knock him clean off his feet.

Jade in his blood, to stop it gushing; jade in his bones, to give them the stone's strength against steel. What could kill him, then, what possibly?

And that was when the fighting caught him unprepared, all but undressed, only a shirt to wear. For this battle today he wore jade mail. Yu Shan had already seen one arrow strike that and shiver into flinders. He thought any blade that reached so far—tao or dagger-ax or spear, any blade at all—would do the same exactly, try to slide harmlessly off stone and find itself too much harmed already, shatter from the force of its own blow. While the emperor just stood there, unshaken, untouched.

It was unfortunate that the generals had also seen that arrow strike the emperor. They must also have seen it break and fall, but that was negligible, against the simple fact of its impact.

"The shirt protected me, that's what it's *for*."

"Majesty, yes, but if the arrow had struck your throat, your eye . . . ? Your majesty should stay back with us where he ought to be, where he promised his mother to keep . . ."

". . . Then I might as well have stayed in the palace on Taishu, and not come to the war at all!"

Which was no doubt how the old men felt too, and what they must most devoutly be wishing right now, though none of them quite had the nerve to say so. Yu Shan himself snorted softly, the least possible reaction, and caught a swift sideways glare from the emperor: which might have mellowed into a self-knowing giggle under other, almost any other circumstances. The emperor was always privileged to laugh at himself, often with the connivance of his friends.

Not here, not now. The emperor made a gesture that said *step aside!* to those generals who had actually dared to stand in front of him, to block the road down to the river; at the same time it said *gather round, and stay alert!* to his imperial guard, men and women both, where they dawdled watchfully, trying to achieve distance from the argument while keeping protectively close to the Man of Jade; at the same time, briefly, it said *keep up if you can, if you must* to Yu Shan.

All in that one little moment before he dodged around the slowest of his generals and went running like a carefree child down the hill.

There was a longer moment of hectic, cursing scurry: and then they were more or less as they had been, running order, with the guards in their proud yellow ahead and behind and to either side, the emperor in his green between, Yu Shan at his shoulder.

Siew Ren one with the guards, in yellow of her own, why not? She was here by right, as a fighter. Yu Shan could neither deny her place nor keep her safe; she would have been furious if he had tried.

The generals here and there, keeping up or left behind, as they would. The laggards had their own guards, and would not be left exposed; besides, there was hardly any danger, in an all-but-abandoned city with hardly any war in it.

Which was another reason, perhaps, for the emperor to be so on fire with the need for speed, to race down to the river before all the rebels could slip away, to catch up at least with his vanguard—those bold soldiers who had run ahead of their master—and so engage at least with Tunghai Wang's rearguard, if he couldn't arrest the traitor generalissimo himself.

He wanted something to show for his day, Yu Shan thought: something more than an empty city too easily regained. He wanted to be a warrior, scars on his armor and blood on his hands. His own hands, not just his fighting men's.

So this, the hard hunt down to the river: and there were bodies to run by, but none too many of them and some of those were only

stray civilians by the look of it, killed by one side or the other because they were foolish or unlucky or simply there where the blade
or the arrow chanced to be. There were broken doors and scattered barricades, but all the men—the living men—in the street
were their own. There must still be rebels cornered and in hiding,
there might yet be an arrow or two or a shrieking fanatic leaping
from shadow; but the war had marched ahead of them like
weather, it wasn't here in Santung anymore.

Which ought to have been all that he wanted, all that they had
come for; they ought to settle for that. Even Yu Shan—who knew
all about fighting to defend a friend or a mine, a clan's hold on a
valley, but nothing about waging war—felt sure that they ought to
stop now.

Here at the city's edge, with the river valley bending ahead of
them and the last of Tunghai Wang's fleeing army still in view, he
said so.

"Majesty," he said, because there were generals listening and
some of the emperor's less courtly soubriquets should really be
kept for more private occasions, when no one could hear but the
imperial guards who had invented them, "do we need to go farther? You have chased Tunghai Wang entirely out of Santung; his
army is divided, disorganized, utterly in retreat," both sides of the
river, they could see that quite clearly; utterly unready to offer any
resistance, the rebels had seen their doom coming and simply fled.
It was a triumph. "It is your triumph," he said, making the emperor a gift of his good fortune, just as some wiser courtier might
have done. Given his audience, Yu Shan felt proud of that.

"But?" The emperor was ready to make him a gift in return, in
acknowledgment, because they were friends of a sort.

"*But* I think it would be wise to stop here." *Your generals are
right,* but there were better ways to say it. "Your army is not organized or equipped to chase him farther; we came to fight, not to
pursue. The empire is vast," and never mind that Yu Shan had seen
almost none of it, that this was in fact the farthest he had ever

come from home. "If they scatter as they run, your army will scatter too, trying to hunt them down," like dogs in a field of rabbits when you had gone out to hunt deer. "What if the rebels turned to fight after all? You could lose half your men before morning," and whistling through the woods wouldn't bring them back again.

The emperor laughed and clapped him on the shoulder, wouldn't listen: "Not these men. They have spent a year running from Tunghai Wang; now this is their chance to make him run. I couldn't call them back now if I tried," meaning *you can't call me back now, though I hear you trying,* "and I wouldn't try. Strategies of war, Yu Shan: you didn't have lessons half your life, you didn't have to read all the books there are. Any city that's fallen once will fall again, and Santung has fallen twice this year. We took it, yes, but we couldn't keep it; not if we left the rebel army out there. Tunghai would draw them together again, if we gave him time to do it. He would march them back, and we would have that fight we came for, only we'd be trapped against the sea again, and there is no way to defend this city. There'd be nothing to do but flee again, and carry our losses with us. That would be catastrophic; one bad decision and I would turn a victory—my triumph, did you call it?—into a defeat I could never recover from.

"Come on," he cried, embracing them all now with his voice, with his wide-spread arms, with his bright and startling eyes, "when they're running, would you leave them to run alone? Besides, there are our friends," right there where they could see them but not reach, the other half of his army on the other side of the river, "don't you want to meet up with them again? There is no bridge in Santung and the ferries are gone, but a mile higher up the valley we can cross the river and be one army, at least for a little. Then we can organize, Yu Shan, for the pursuit." *And you can see Jiao again, be sure she's safe, don't you want to do that?* "For now, tell them to do what we do, to chase along that bank as we do along this."

Flags and trumpets would carry that message, but he wasn't

waiting to see it done. He could see his war still retreating from him, hear it in the too-distant sounds of fighting, and his feet wouldn't hold him still any longer.

It had never occurred to Yu Shan that so much of war would be running. Or trying to slow the emperor down, to remind him over and over that the two of them could outrun their friends without trying and it would be a really, really good idea not to do that.

thirteen

*M*ei Feng was not actually being as stupid as her friends believed. She knew as they knew that she could never fight her way through to the emperor's side, cry *I have come to protect you, lord!* and expect to be taken seriously.

What perhaps they had forgotten was that she knew Santung at least a little. Specifically, she knew on which side of the river stood the governor's palace.

Finding Jiao on the road had really been no part of her plan. Following the older woman up to the roof and so having the chance to show her that she could look after herself—yes, and her friends—just with the little blade she carried had been an unexpected gift, a blessing. A touch of the goddess at work, perhaps. Yes.

At least that incident and the all-but-empty city together had allowed Jiao to relax her watchfulness a little. Which allowed Mei Feng to let her and her troop get just a little ahead, and then just a little farther, and then . . .

AND NOW she could grip Dandan's arm with one hand and the boy's with the other, tug them both swiftly into an alley and lead them away before anyone looked back again to find them.

"Mei Feng, what . . . ?"

"Shh, don't talk yet. Just run . . ."

BY THE time she heard a yell of alarm, it was some distance behind, and muffled by the rise of walls between them in this tangle of lanes. She wasn't sure if Jiao would send men after, or come herself; either way, she hoped to have lost them already. If not, if luck or judgment or some more mystical skill kept them on her tail, she still thought she had speed enough to stay ahead.

Like Jiao, indeed, she was surprised to find just how fast she could run when she needed to. Sailor-girls grew tough muscles, but she was better used to endurance than speed.

Ah, Chien Hua, lord of my body—what have you been putting into me . . . ?

Apart from the obvious, of course, the blushworthy, though that hadn't happened for a while now . . . ?

He did occasionally feed her a bite or two of his own food; that might make a difference. Or else it was the simple constant, the physical presence of him. After so long in his company, so immediately there to be kissed or caressed or just incidentally rubbed up against, small wonder if some fraction of the magic invested in him should have rubbed off on her. Skin to skin, just a hint of jade-dust.

Or maybe it was just her fancy, or Jiao's, or both. Dandan too was frequently around the emperor, but apparently took no benefit; she was gasping already, stumbling and dragging back. At last, too soon, she grabbed hold of a gatepost and couldn't be moved, not yet.

"Mei Feng . . . Where are we . . . where are we *going*?"

"Up there," with a jerk of her head to where the governor's palace frowned down over the city.

"Whatever for?"

"Because Tunghai Wang will have been living there, all the time he was here. And he won't have taken anything away, all his papers will still be there; and you can *read*, Dandan, you can help me search . . ."

Dandan shook her head, breathed a little, at last managed, "If the papers are there today, they will still be there tomorrow, Mei Feng. What's the *hurry*?"

The hurry, of course, was Mei Feng herself. She would not be free like this tomorrow. She might be back in Taishu, or locked at the emperor's side, or locked somewhere far away from the emperor. She needed to bring him something, to justify herself; she hoped to bring him something to justify her accusations, Ping Wen's guilt.

She had to find it now, but Dandan wasn't moving. And if Jiao was coming after them, she might be getting close . . .

"Dandan, I can't wait. You know where I'm going. You, boy," she still hadn't learned the boy's name but demanded his obedience anyway, "stay with her. When she's fit for it, bring her to the palace. You know the way, yes?"

He nodded, mute and nervous.

"Good boy. If our friends find you first—well, bring them too." It wouldn't be so bad, having Jiao and her troop arrive; just so long as Mei Feng had time enough to find something first. She had to justify herself to everyone these days, apparently. To everyone who loved her, who ought to trust her . . .

Perhaps that was war, or it might just be adulthood. She remembered when life was easier.

No matter. She left them there, her two unlikely allies, like a stepping-stone for anyone who tried to find her. She'd do well enough without Dandan, if she had deserved any grace at all from the goddess. She had at least learned the characters for "Ping Wen." If his name was on a sheet of paper, she would find it. If she was only given time . . .

THE GOVERNOR'S palace stood on a sudden natural bluff above the river, where it could look as though it had been lifted by the swift hand of the gods above the common people and their business. She had known it all her life, but only to stare at from way down below.

She had no doubt in her mind that Tunghai Wang would have lived in the palace, for these short months that Santung was his

city. And where a general, a governor, a city's lord lived, there he
ruled from; there he met his ministers and kept his clerks and gathered all his papers. If there was any proof that Tunghai Wang and
Ping Wen had been in conspiracy together, there she would have
the best chance to find it.

Best proof came in written documents. She had hopes. The two
men couldn't meet or speak directly; short of sorcery, then, they
must have written, unless they trusted verbal messages to their go-
betweens.

Conspirators are not a trusting breed, and generals do not rise
to power by being open with their underlings. Mei Feng thought
there would be papers.

There were no bodies at the palace gates. Of course not: this
wasn't a last stand, desperate men backed into a corner, defending
what they valued more than life. Tunghai Wang wouldn't let himself be trapped here in the city. He would have heard the first rush
of the invasion and been away, leading his men upriver as soon as
it was clear that they could not stand.

He might have thought it out already, ahead of time. If the emperor did somehow manage to come against him, he must have
known they could not stand. A good general would surely have a
plan of retreat. Even against the most unlikely of circumstances,
the running boy turned warrior at last, the rabbit that bit back . . .

Mei Feng astonished herself with a smile, just as she walked between unguarded open gates. Even once she had saved his idiot
life, exposed the traitor and won his love again, she thought perhaps she would not tell the emperor that she had envisioned him
as a rabbit. Even a most ferocious and deadly rabbit with jade eyes
and steel teeth, a bold and courageous hero-rabbit leading an
army of . . .

No. Not that.

A tiger, jade tiger, yes. That he'd like. Blessed by the mountains,
by the stone itself . . .

She could wish for a tiger herself right now, proud and lethal, padding at her side. Rumbling, perhaps, deep in its wonderful throat, as a warning to the watching world.

If you were a tiger, of course—a jade tiger, most rare, most wonderful—the world would always be watching for you. Best, probably, to assume the same was true for her, here and now. Tunghai Wang had gone, and taken his soldiers with him; that didn't mean the palace was empty. Or safe. There would be servants clustering in their own halls, anxious, waiting for the new dispensation. Tunghai Wang would not have left his soldiers, but he might have left his clerks; they might be hiding and hoping, sitting it out till nightfall. She knew how dangerous a clerk could be, with a knife in his belt and nothing to lose except his life.

There might even be assassins, dressed as clerks or servants and told to wait in hopes of the emperor's arrival, the emperor's inattention, the emperor's throat suddenly at their blade's edge . . .

The emperor's woman would be a lure to such a man. Mei Feng needed to be careful. Frightened and abandoned men will kill without thought, without reason; she might find both within these walls. They might find her.

She needed to find someone. Everything was risk. She would be careful, she would be as sensible as she could, and in the end she would still have to accost a stranger and ask for help.

Pardon me, sir, can you read? Oh, and can you read your future, can you see how very good for you it would be to help me now, and how very bad if you refuse . . . ?

She really could wish for a tiger, just to help her make the point. Or a man, a big man or two; there were times when being small was nothing but a handicap, when she wanted to be imposing and make demands. Perhaps she should have waited with Dandan and her boy; perhaps she should have run a little less fast or a little more obviously, and let Jiao and her troopers catch them up . . .

Too late now. And no point trying to sneak in here like a thief, however much she wanted to sidle along the walls and keep to shadow.

Boldly, then, she walked across the paving of the first court and up broad shallow steps to the vast bronze doors of the palace. One leaf stood ajar. She allowed herself one moment to be just Mei Feng, which meant nervous and utterly out of her depth here, a little fishergirl abroad and lost in the affairs of state, of emperors, of war; then she took a breath, wiped her sweating palms on her borrowed trousers, and stepped inside.

First and foremost, it was dark in there. Great halls and wealthy houses were all like this, she had learned: as though the air, the light itself darkened with the costly woods that made the floors and furniture. They turned inward, on their private courts. If there were brighter rooms, they would be farther in than this, looking out onto the gardens behind the palace. Likely, though, even the gardens would be dark, with narrow paths between high and gloomy trees, cramped pavilions overlooking murky lily-crowded ponds. If she had missed any one thing more than any other since the emperor brought her ashore—apart from her grandfather, of course, and her freedom, and the strait—it was the light and space of her childhood. Which meant the strait, of course, which meant her freedom. Which had been all bound up in her grandfather, until the emperor took her away.

It was as well for that boy that she loved him.

Here was an audience hall, empty. As empty as the streets, as the city. The city was irrecoverable, she thought. It was no doubt too convenient to let go; there would always be a city here, to handle trade with Taishu and fetch back jade. But whatever they called it hereafter, it would never again be what Santung was. That was gone.

No wonder if the streets were empty and the halls abandoned. If she had been a servant here she might have left herself, sooner than stay to serve another master in a city of ghosts.

Still, there had to be someone. She *needed* someone, and so there had to be at least one lurker left. Yes. That was how the world worked; she decided it.

She didn't want to run through the palace, calling; she didn't want to skulk. There had to be a way between those two, a calm and mature means to locate someone useful, preferably literate, perhaps a little cowed . . .

If there were any such person—if it were her—they might well be lurking in the more private corridors of the palace. Here in the great hall was too obvious, too open. Yes. She'd find them somewhere that was harder to find, even if they weren't exactly hiding.

She knew the way that palaces worked now. She knew exactly where to look for a door and a swift way through. Over there, behind the screen in the corner, farthest from the public door and closest to the dais where the governor's chair was set . . .

She was halfway across the hall floor when someone walked around the screen ahead of her.

Limped around the screen, rather.

His crutch and the way that he used it—with an awkward wincing skill, leaning into it in a way that would have cost no thought if it didn't cost him pain at every step—both said that this was no fresh injury, no damage of the day. He had limped for a while at least, likely for a long time. Long enough to find himself the perfect prop, just the length and weight he wanted, with a grip for his hand and a padded rest beneath his armpit.

He might, perhaps, have been expecting to see someone else. Some other kind of person altogether: a soldier, say, or perhaps an officer with a troop of soldiers at his back. Rather than a single stub of a girl, oddly dressed and oddly bold on such a day, in such a place as this.

He recovered quickly, though she could see that a recovery was necessary: a hesitation, a falter in the swing of his lopsided stride, a moment where she thought the crutch might slip, he might lose balance and fall and be altogether helpless at her feet.

A moment, and no more. Then he stood magnificently recovered, magnificently still, waiting for her to come to him.

It was still dark, but her eyes were adjusting. Besides, she was used to this being in vast and shady halls with looming men. This one at least didn't loom so much as the emperor, he wasn't so tall by a distance. That might have been his twisted leg, bending him down. He did have the face of a northerner, with all its inherent height.

Could he have come—could he have been brought—all that way, chasing the emperor with Tunghai Wang? For sure he was not the emperor's man—unless he'd been left behind in the evacuation to Taishu, in which case he was probably not the emperor's man any longer—and she would bet that he was not a Santung native either. If the generalissimo had gone to the trouble of arranging a carriage or a litter, carrying him in the army's wake for a year and more, this must be someone of value.

He didn't dress like a general, nor like a senior official. Besides, he hadn't fled with Tunghai Wang. He had been left behind—again?—or else he had chosen to stay.

Mei Feng's hand was on her dagger-haft, her every muscle was alert; she was hoping devoutly that she really was infected with the emperor's jade-strength, his jade-speed and startling eyesight. She might need them now. Twice in one day . . .

The man spoke, and his voice was rough and raw; he said, "Well. What are you looking for, young woman?"

Instantly honest, just to see what effect it had, she said, "Tunghai Wang's papers, if he has left any behind," *as he seems to have left you.*

The man smiled, with all the bitterness that comes with wisdom. "As he has left me, you mean? Well, well. Can you read?"

"No." That wasn't a confession, she didn't say it sulkily, caught out; nor was it an appeal, though she might ask him for help if he came close to offering it. For now, this was an exchange of information. "Are there papers?"

"Yes, yes. Of course there are papers. He has not taken the time to pack." *Neither his papers nor me,* he seemed to be saying; and, *pity me if you dare.*

"Can you show me?"

Actually, that might be an appeal; but he seemed to be treating it as again a simple question of fact.

"I can show you where to go," he said meditatively, in some way—some very polite way—drawing her attention to his crutch although he neither shifted it nor glanced at it, nothing so crude. "There are a great many stairs."

"Oh. Is there, um, somebody else? Someone who might come with me, and read what the papers say?"

"There are other people, yes. Some no doubt can read. Why do you wish to have these papers read?"

If there was a stress on one word in that sentence, it was as mild as the twitch of his eyebrow: not an insult and not contempt, merely a part of the question, a piece of information that he lacked. An officer of the emperor might well be interested in Tunghai Wang's abandoned letters, but a girl so young, so rudely dressed . . . ?

He wasn't rude himself, and nor need she be; but neither need she be forthcoming all at once. It was a trade, almost a game, this posing question for question: *one answer at a time . . .*

"The generalissimo has been in touch with someone on Taishu." The crippled man's gesture said, *Of course.* Well, yes: of course. But, "Someone high," she went on, "high up in the emperor's counsels. I . . . wish to know who that is, and have hopes that his papers may tell me," *and never you mind who I am.* It was, perhaps, not something to be noised abroad too loudly, at least not here and now: where she was keeping company with a man who might be lame and slow but was still entirely proficient, who quite possibly had fitter colleagues within call, who might have need of good currency and see it suddenly in a hostage, one who stood by her own claim high in the emperor's regard . . .

"I know a man," the man said, "who can tell you that, as clearly as any paper would."

Did he mean himself? She was doubtful and hopeful, both at once. She said, "A man I can take before the emperor?"

"If you can get him there," said judiciously, almost an examination, another way to approach that question he had not yet asked, *who are you?*

"That," she said firmly, "I can do."

"Well, then," the man said. "Perhaps you had better come and meet my man."

HAD HE been negotiating right from the start?

Yes, of course he had. He was a cripple, left behind; whatever relationship he'd had with Tunghai Wang, it had left him in obvious peril. Mei Feng might be a girl, she might be dressed like a peasant; neither she nor her body nor her dress could disguise—apparently—the fact that she had purpose and knowledge, which suggested some manner of influence. Which suggested, apparently, some degree of hope to hobble out of here, if it could be bargained for.

They were, apparently, bargaining. Sight unseen and all unknowing, ignorance on either side.

She said, "May I ask your name?"

Yes, of course she might ask; that was in the rules. He might even answer. If he did, it would be honestly.

He said, "My name is Ai Guo. And yours?"

"Mei Feng."

If he knew the name, he didn't show it. Ping Wen might have told Tunghai Wang this or everything, if he had a way to do it.

She didn't know. She did know that they were bargaining, because he was taking her down further stairs, crutch notwithstanding. Presumably he did also mean to climb back up, which meant his first refusal had been a negotiating position and not a confession of weakness after all.

Well, she was learning.

So no doubt was he, but he was good at this; she couldn't tell what he knew already, what he learned or guessed or only hoped.

Stairs and stairs. This was stairs enough to be significant, dungeon-down. Ai Guo might be a swift and subtle negotiator, but he paid a bidding-price with every step. He could put his crutch down first and lean on that, he could hop down onto his good leg and try to keep the other from any contact, and still the jar of that halt-and-hop glossed him with a bitter sweat, it set his mouth in a hard thin line and stilled his tongue entirely.

She might have talked for both of them, but she was afraid of giving too much, winning too little. His silence was no use to her, and she was unconvinced about this man he wanted her to meet. Papers with Ping Wen's chop on them, those were what she wanted. She had a man already willing to swear to his treachery, only that she couldn't produce him, for fear of what would happen if she did. Another such would be no use to her.

Still, she followed Ai Guo. Three flights of steps that grew increasingly narrow, though oddly well lit; there were lamps already burning in niches all the way down. She supposed he could hardly manage a light and the crutch together, given how often he grabbed at the wall with his free hand. He must have been ready for this, waiting for someone to come. Waiting to betray Ping Wen—she hoped!—to whoever came along.

To her, as it happened. Which might convince him no more than it convinced her, but she was what he had . . .

Down, then, to the dungeon level; along a passage that was chill and gloomy and unhappy, the walls sodden with ten thousand miseries.

He brought her to a door that was locked, to which he had the key; he unlocked it and swung it open and gestured her within.

She expected a prisoner in chains, naked and brutalized, because what else would you find in a dungeon, locked away?

She found a man in a cell, yes, but with a lamp of his own; and a robe too, and a pallet on a frame to keep it off the dank floor. The robe was scant enough and the lamp was bright enough to let her see that his skin held words, characters she couldn't read and really wished she could.

He glanced up at the open door, saw her and stood effortfully, bowed with an edge of irony that she could appreciate, that she would have liked to applaud.

Then he nodded at Ai Guo and sat back down with an air of expectation, like a man waiting to be questioned. Again.

Very well, then. She jerked her head and said, "Who is he?"

Looking at the prisoner, a question for him; jerking her head toward Ai Guo.

The prisoner didn't even quirk an eyebrow. Very simply, he said, "That is Ai Guo, who is Tunghai Wang's torturer. Who are you?"

One answer deserves another; they were playing that game again. With honesty, again. She said, "I am Mei Feng, the emperor's favorite," because that was information that could win her more than it could lose her, now. She thought, she hoped. She gambled.

A suck of air but that was behind her, that was Ai Guo, making calculations; which was fair enough, because she was doing the same herself. Tunghai Wang's torturer: a man skilled enough to be worth bringing all this way, dispensable enough to be left behind. Bitter enough or desperate enough to make a trade, his promised safety for—what? For this, perhaps, a prisoner delivered?

She waited, and soon enough Ai Guo at her back completed the introductions: "This is Li Ton the pirate, who used to be Chu Lin the general, who can tell you all about Ping Wen the traitor."

The man's eyes seemed to spark at that, even as her own heart lifted; but what he actually said was, "Never mind Ping Wen, let me tell you what else you need to know, what this man . . . persuaded me to tell the generalissimo."

A tortured man tells true: that was fundamental, inherent to the ways of justice. She blinked, at the thought of anything mattering more than the exposure of Ping Wen; and said, "What? What is that?"

"I had a boat," he said, "command of it, with an old man as captain. He took me to the Forge, at Ping Wen's word; and then he brought me here, to the mainland. I should have gone back with him, except that I was taken prisoner here. Tunghai Wang . . . learned the truth of this," with a glance at Ai Guo that was not at all accusing, all revealing. "I don't know, but I suspect he sent someone else in my stead."

"Wait," Mei Feng said, "wait . . . This old man. What was his name?"

"Old Yen, everybody called him."

Oh, Grandfather . . .

"Keep him," she said to Ai Guo. "Keep him until my friends come, a woman and a boy; they will be here shortly. They may have soldiers with them. Then say that Mei Feng has given orders that the two of you should be brought to the emperor, as soon as may be."

The one man was crippled, and the other had been his guest, his tortured guest for weeks; neither one of them was in any state to move fast, and now she really had to.

A Dragon in the Wind

one

*I*n, she said.

In that? he said. *I will not.*

She hissed at him, and he stood firm. It was a folly, a nonsense, a joke. It would not serve.

She said, *Little thing, get in.*

Or what? he demanded.

Or I will bring rain to this rock: so much rain that it will drown all the little plants you eat, and all the little animals you chase. It will drive away all the birds you try to snare. I will have it rain so long and so hard that it will wash all the soil from the stone, and take the trees with it. And then you will have nothing, nothing at all, and so starve under my eye; and then I will eat your bones and be free. Little thing. Get in.

In honesty, he had no idea why she had waited so long to threaten this, because there was nothing in the world he could do to resist it. If she meant it, it would happen; and she did very clearly mean it.

Even so . . .

Han sat on a rock, and began to bargain.

two

Truly, if Shen had not been so impossibly angry about it, Chung would not be here. He was Chung the messenger, not Chung the warrior. Shen's training and his own diligence had given him a fighting skin, the superficial skills of it, but not the heart at all.

Perhaps all warriors were the same, hiding some other self beneath a lethal bluster? Perhaps. He might have liked to think so, but he couldn't persuade himself. Chung couldn't know the heart of another man, but he knew Shen as well as anyone could hope to, mind and body and blood; and he didn't believe that Shen was hiding anything. That man was a soldier all the way through.

Which was what made him so difficult now, when war was here at last and Shen could not fight it.

"I thought you'd be glad," Chung said once, risking more than he knew. "I thought this was every soldier's dream, to be excused duties for a while." *To lie in the grass*, he meant, *with food in your belly and a bottle at your elbow, someone who loves you kneeling beside, your wound healing well, an impressive scar to show people later and every little foul-tempered convalescent whim catered for in the meantime . . .*

"Not when his friends are going to fight," Shen snarled. "I should be there, with them."

And you're the one who's stopping me. He didn't say that again, he didn't need to; it was writ large on his body, in his scowl. It wasn't true, of course—it was the doctors, the *imperial* doctors who had taken one look at Shen and ruled him unfit to fight—but Chung had been saying the exact same thing beforehand, *you're not fit to fight*. So had everyone, the emperor included. Chung said it first, though, and most heatedly; and it was Chung who fetched the doctors, thinking that a medical opinion might carry more weight than an imperial or a loving one. Not so, apparently . . .

"It'll go just as well without you," Chung said now, trying to reassure, heaping error on top of error. "Even you're not indispensable," trying to tease his ego, *my arrogant little soldier*, error upon error upon error. "One more sword, what's that? In an army?"

"One more sword that knows the right place to be, when it's needed," Shen spat. "Not indispensable, no—but someone will die because I'm not there. One of our friends, most likely. That's how battle goes. You know."

He did know; but not even shared experience could save him now, when he wanted to use it on one side of the argument and Shen wanted to use it on the other.

At first they only argued, Shen was only angry because he couldn't go. Later, when he understood that Chung was even thinking about it—oh, then had come the fury. Hard hands, hard words; a cold back turned until Chung sought out another place to sleep.

Even then, the right word from Shen—it didn't even need to be a kind word—would have changed his mind, in so far as he had made it up at all.

All he got was savagery, intercut with the logic that he could already use against himself, no use to him at all.

"You? You're a messenger, not a fighter. You only know how to run."

"Yes. They will need runners."

"You're Mei Feng's runner, not the emperor's. She's not going; why are you?"

I'm not, not yet; I only think I should. "The emperor may be glad of me. And I do know how to fight, you taught me. I can handle a blade, even, better than before, after all this practice. I could be really useful."

"You could be really dead. Fool."

Then Shen took it into his head to behave as though Chung were dead already, a ghost already, to be ignored or else cursed and driven away: which only drove him into the strong grip of a decision. He would go, then. Not to be Shen, take his place, no: that would be ridiculous, it was one of the ridiculous accusations that Shen flung at his head along with bowls and stained bandages and one time a used chamber-pot. But to be himself, Chung the messenger, following his emperor and being with his friends. Fighting if he had to, for something that he thought he might believe in, if he could only pin down quite what it was.

He had actually been glad to step on the boat at last, to be committed, a part of the great invasion. Nothing he could do then but be the best soldier he could manage. He fancied himself going home with tales of glory—*I saved the emperor's life, I saved the day, I ran the message that brought the victory, we would have been lost without me*—but he knew those were just fancies. Mostly he only wanted to be sure of going home.

At least he had the emperor to follow and people he knew around him, the imperial guards he had trained with in the forest. They had adopted him, he thought; he was more a pet than a colleague, but a welcome pet, a mascot for the troop.

They must have been seen from the city like a rising horizon, a darkening on the edge of vision, an encroaching storm. Not quite running except when the emperor did, they never quite caught up with the vanguard: only the signs left like a trail, bodies by the roadside now and then, blood-wet. Some of them might have been rebels, trying to delay the emperor's men, give others more time to flee. They might have been rebels too slow to run; they might not have been rebels at all, only peasants unlucky on the day. The emperor glanced the first time, stiffened his face and hurried on. Chung tried not to look, but that was harder. The bodies danced in the corners of his eyes.

The emperor's entourage worked hard to keep him behind the stormfront, and that not far, never far enough. He was emperor, and this was his day of vengeance, long delayed; he wanted to taste it for himself. If he couldn't have Tunghai Wang at his sword's point, he wanted someone at least, anyone, any rebel. And was frustrated, because the city was empty, near enough. Emptying as they watched, wherever they had sight of the river, where trails of retreating men showed on either bank.

Even the emperor could not have everything he wanted, even on his day of triumph. They chased as straightly as possible down from the ridge to the river, as fast as possible until an arrow hit the emperor's jade mail. There was serious argument then, the sweating generals demanding that he take himself back out of danger; he resolved that by stepping quite neatly around them and running on. He would have gone alone if others hadn't scampered to keep up, to keep ahead.

Chung ran easily enough in his wake and thought, *If Shen could see me now, he wouldn't mind so much. There's nothing here. One arrow, what's that? Not worth crossing the channel for . . .*

THERE WERE more arrows, but none that came near the emperor. There was no real resistance, no barricade that had not been swept aside already, no holding out to the last man. Skirmishers on the flanks, who fired arrows from cover and flitted away before a squad could find them: nothing worse than that. Nobody, it seemed, was prepared to die for Tunghai Wang.

And here was the river, broad and full; and over there was the other arm of the imperial invasion, advancing just as fast, finding almost no one to fight.

There was no bridge, there were no boats, it was too far to shout. Still, the soldiers could wave at each other. Chung did that cheerfully, though he hardly knew anyone over there, and couldn't see those few he could have named. Jiao should be there somewhere; if she were standing among the men on the bank she would be standing out, so she wasn't there.

He hoped she wasn't hurt. He hoped nobody was hurt, or as few as were hurt over here.

He hoped they could stop, now that they had the city and the river, but he had small actual hope of that. The emperor had come for a battle, and he wouldn't be happy without one.

Besides, the running rebels had been close enough to see, from higher on the ridge. Who could resist a chase?

NOT THE emperor, that was certain.

He hadn't stopped to wave, only to give swift commands to his trumpeters and bannermen. That done, he was setting out to run again.

"Majesty, *wait*!"

"For *what*?"

"For your own safety, and for our peace of mind." The general bold enough to shout at his emperor was bold enough to snarl a little also. His arm came perilously close to gripping the imperial shoulder hard enough to give the imperial person a brisk shake. "Majesty, do you not *see*?"

"I see a clear path along the river, with my enemies retreated out of sight; I see my men eager to pursue them, on this bank as they are already on the other. I see the shadows growing shorter, good time passing. That's what I see. Tell me, Meng Yao, what do you see?"

"I see an old godown in disrepair," his stabbing finger pointing, "where a hundred men might lurk for exactly this, the chance to catch a fool young emperor unprotected." His hand might have stopped a fraction short of shaking his fool young emperor, but his voice did not. "Beyond it, I see another," that stabbing finger hard at work, "and another, and another. If I were Tunghai Wang, I would have spent a thousand men that way, because you are young and want to hunt."

If I were Tunghai Wang, he seemed to be saying, *you would be dying now, or soon now, if you were not dead already.*

And he and Tunghai Wang had been colleagues, no doubt, for decades, friends perhaps, debating tactics over flasks of fiery spirits late into the night. They would know each other's minds from a thousand battles fought in talk, a thousand games of elephant chess. He was a man to listen to, at least.

And the emperor knew it, that at least; he sighed and stood still. "If he had time," he said—perhaps a little hopefully?—"if he could organize his men, then yes, he might have done that . . ."

"Majesty, Tunghai Wang has been a soldier all his life. If he only had five minutes, he could organize his men. Enough to spring a trap on his pursuers, at least, to delay us while he makes a good retreat. If that trap happens to catch the emperor, that is his luck and my failure, that I have allowed my emperor to run headlong into it." Which he would not do, his voice and body said together, if he had to trip his emperor over and sit on him.

"Or perhaps his luck lies in knowing you are here with me and saying this, making me listen; and so he does not need to spend his men, because you will still creep cautiously from one godown to the next while he makes his getaway with all his men intact."

The emperor wasn't really arguing, though: only standing resentfully acquiescent while the general organized his own men to search the godowns. Not the imperial guards; they stayed grouped around the emperor, talking to one another, talking to Chung a little.

Not talking to the emperor. This was different from the camp in the forest, where he was almost—almost!—one young man among many: where they could laugh and sweat and sleep and eat with him, where he could let slip the overlord and be more communal than regal, more human than godly, more like them than unlike.

Not here. The companionship of generals was . . . inhibiting, keeping comradeship as far at bay as it kept wariness close at hand. And here they had to prove themselves, they had to keep him alive or what purpose did they serve, what had the camp in the forest been for, and all that training? They were daunted by that arrow, the memory of it; and they were daunted too by the jademail shirt, which could keep them at a distance even more easily than a general did.

Its relentless shimmer was a constant reminder that this young man was not as other men, nothing after all like them. It was his birthright, his immeasurable fortune to wear an immeasurable fortune that they were forbidden even to touch. They stood back from the shirt, more than from him; so he stood on his own except for generals who had only ever seen him in terms of his throne: to be shifted their way when possible and not at all when he was stubborn, but stone either way. They wouldn't think to talk to him, and so nobody did.

Chung couldn't have been the only one who noticed. He did think of stepping out of line, putting himself forward, going to stand with the emperor; and of course did not, and nor did anyone else.

They watched Meng Yao and his soldiers make their way along the waterfront, from warehouse to boathouse to shabby broken warehouse. They saw gates levered open, doors kicked in. Building after building they saw men edge inside, heard voices call.

Saw a few lurking refugees herded out at swordpoint. No rebels, no resistance.

Only time passing, measured by the current in the river: how it swirled and bubbled, how it turned and backed up as the tide came in.

STILL NO rebels.

AT LAST the emperor's impatience reached combustion, just as even his general's caution was exhausted. The one strode forward so fast he was almost running already, so eruptively that his many escorts did have to run to catch up to him; the other waited by the roadway, bowed low, said, "Majesty. I do believe the riverfront is safe."

"I do believe," the emperor snarled, "that if Tunghai Wang is also safe, it will be because of this!"

No, Chung thought: of course the emperor would blame Meng Yao, but it was not the general's fault. It was Tunghai Wang, playing them, knowing them. Knowing that they would have to search the godowns regardless, he had left them empty, saved his troops, still bought himself an hour.

No, not so long as that. Meng Yao had been swift and efficient, the tide had been on the turn, it had only seemed an hour. The sun said otherwise.

No matter. It had been long enough to infuriate the emperor; long enough to let the rebels run far out of sight.

Now he chased. Which meant that half his guard had to chase harder, to stay ahead; and Chung was a solid, ready runner. He found himself in the forefront without at all meaning to, shoulder to shoulder with men who had followed the emperor—or preceded him, like this—all the way from the Hidden City; and with men and women fresh from the jade clans, who had never been this far from their valleys and never expected to be so.

He ran with his tao drawn, as the others did, so as to be ready; unless it was simply so as to seem one of them, though he wasn't sure whom he might be fooling. Not himself, not them, not the emperor. Not Shen. Even in his absence, not Shen.

They came past the last of the godowns, past an old wharf for a river ferry where there was no ferry, either side of the river. The road ran on, barely more than a muck track for farmers. There was nothing to be cautious for now, no buildings to alarm the general, only the inevitable paddy rising in terraces both sides of the valley—

—UNTIL THEY came around a bend in the river, and saw the bridge.

The bridge already broken, deliberately so perhaps, to stop them corresponding with the other half of the army. It was a wooden structure that arched across the water in dolphin-leaps, what were really two separate bridges from this bank and from that, meeting on a little island-rock between. At least, it should have arched in dolphin-leaps. It used to.

The leap from the island to the farther bank was gone. The bridge rose from its footings just far enough to say *I was a bridge!*—and then its timbers frayed into empty space, a leap that vanished, as though pressure of time and use had worn it entirely away.

Chung didn't believe that for a moment. He believed rather in what he couldn't see, rebels crawling among the timbers beneath, knocking out the vital pins that held its span together. The sudden fall that followed, dark and heavy lengths tumbling into the busy, hurried water.

There would be no pause here, no reunion across the water. It didn't matter for Chung—Shen was far away, across another water altogether—but Yu Shan might have appreciated the chance. Or the emperor or his generals, for more tactical reasons; or any number of the troops, only because those were their brothers over there.

Their brothers were to be seen, massed on the bank there, waving. They were yelling too, only their words couldn't reach so far; the waters were noisy here, squeezed either side of that island and again at the bend, high and urgent in their hurry to the sea.

There were figures to be seen on the island too; and angular shapes that were not natural, frameworks with arms that moved in sudden awkward flurries . . .

And now there were dark specks rising from the island, not birds but something hurled, like rocks. It was in that moment that Chung understood: those were actual living rebels on the island there, and they had machines that threw rocks, which was probably what the soldiers on the other bank had been trying to say . . .

Not rocks. They rose so slowly, he had time to see how unnaturally round they were: worked stones, perhaps, but there was something more. He thought flickers of light accompanied them in their flight. When they rose above the horizon of the valley wall, he was sure he saw thin trails of smoke hang behind them as they arched across the sky.

One more glance across the river, just that moment he could snatch his eyes away; beyond the gesticulating soldiers he could see stretches of the riverbank seared black. And, yes, something piled that might be bodies, burned almost to charcoal . . .

He opened his mouth to yell a warning, but there was no time. They had seemed so slow to climb, those dark barrels with their trailing fuses; they were suddenly in a dreadful hurry to descend, as though they wanted to outrace their own surprise.

He wasn't the only one to understand. People were gasping, shoving, trying to scatter; but the roadway offered little space and too many bodies, while the paddy was a soft slow clinging wade, impossible to hurry through.

Chung looked back, to where some few bolder guards were pushing closer to the emperor. Shen would have done that: not so much to offer his own body's protection, but only to be there where it mattered, at the heart of things.

Chung was too late, too slow. He looked up again and here they were, hurtling now, impossible to duck or dodge. Impossible to do anything but stare.

Down they came, smoking, fizzing. Their falling made its own noise too, like the sound of wind contained in a pipe, but Chung was sure that he heard fizzing.

ONE FELL into the river. A splash, a moment of floating—just long enough for Chung to register the baked-pot look of it—and then a swirl and a gurgle and it sank.

ONE FLEW over his head, over everyone's head, fell into the paddy and was lost in a great eruptive splash of muddy waters.

APPARENTLY, CHUNG'S mind was keeping count, all unawares: *two more . . .*

ONE FELL on the road ahead.

The track might be muddy and little-used, but there was stone beneath the mud, generations of farmers building it up to take the weight of their carts and wagons. The projectile fell like a barrel, and smashed like a pot; he thought it was a pot, that brief moment that he saw it whole. A huge pot of unglazed clay, spilling blackly across the roadway.

Spilling black fire as it seemed, as flames erupted.

Chung felt the heat even from distance, even as his counting mind thought, *too far to hurt, which means three misses, which means . . .*

ONE MORE.

ONE THAT fell behind him but not so very far behind, not far enough.

He heard its fall, he heard the soft explosion of its flame; he heard the silence first, and then the screaming.

He turned then, his body a great reluctance but he had to know.

Not the emperor, no—but close enough.

Close enough to splash.

A gout of fire clung to the emperor's back, to his jade-scale shirt.

That was the first Chung saw, the first he looked for, the closest flame to him.

The emperor was ignoring it.

Beyond him, others were burning. Screaming. Writhing.

Roll on the ground, Chung wanted to call, but no one would hear him.

Besides, the ground was aflame, a great blaze of fire leaping up to divide the emperor and his nearmost guards from all those who came behind, those he had outrun.

Screams were cut off by splashes as those who were burning leaped over the wall into the paddy.

Those who didn't jump were thrown in bodily, by the emperor and Yu Shan working together.

Slow to turn, slow to start moving, but when Chung did, it was with a perfect resolution.

The *emperor* was *burning* . . . !

THE EMPEROR was tall and solid, stronger than he looked. Hard to move. Also, weighted now with a shirt of stone.

No, Chung would not try upending him into the river. Or the paddy.

Instead he dropped his tao, bent as he ran, scooped up a double handful of wet mud.

Which he hurled onto the emperor's back as soon as he was close enough, as close as he dared come to that flare of fury. Not close enough to slather it on by hand, he wasn't brave enough to thrust his hands deliberately into a furnace; close enough to feel his skin tighten and his muscles flinch. How the emperor endured the heat of it so perilously close to his own skin, just the thickness of a fine stone scale away, Chung couldn't imagine.

If the emperor had chosen to ignore the fire, he certainly didn't ignore the mud. That might be because the last of his burned guards had gone into the water, and he was alert again to the world around; it might be because a gobbet of mud missed the fire and landed in his hair.

He half turned toward Chung—which meant he half turned his back toward Yu Shan. Who stooped and rose and flung his own handfuls of mud; and meanwhile Chung had crouched again for more, crying, "Majesty, turn around, let me . . ."

"It doesn't burn," the emperor said calmly. "At least, it only eats itself. I don't even feel heat—"

It was eating the mud, perhaps, if it couldn't eat the jade. At least, handfuls of mud had no effect; the fire blazed as brightly despite Chung's efforts, despite Yu Shan's. The emperor might claim to feel nothing, but it had already singed his hair.

Just then a voice cried a warning, an arm flung up to point: more canisters from the island, already in the sky. The emperor cursed, grabbed an arm in each hand—almost at random, it seemed, except that one arm was Yu Shan's; the other, as it happened, was Chung's—and flung himself forward.

The jerk of it almost pulled Chung's arm from his socket. The mud fell from his hands and he was dragged along like a reluctant child, like booty, like prey. He had to stutter a few desperate steps before he caught some kind of balance, before he could find any speed of his own.

Even then, there was nowhere to run to. The earlier missile's fire still burned, the one that had fallen short, all across the roadway from river to paddy. They would have to wade, unless they swam.

Chung glanced up and saw stark black shadows in the sky, already falling.

And the emperor was still on fire.

Perhaps he thought he could run straight through the blaze ahead, and the flames not harm him? Perhaps he thought he was untouchable?

Perhaps he was right, but it wasn't true for Chung. One desper-

ate glance at Yu Shan, behind the emperor's back, through the sear
of flame—and Chung swung himself forward on the emperor's
arm, thrust a leg out, and tripped the Man of Jade.

At the same time—as though they'd discussed it, as though
they'd rehearsed it—Yu Shan drove his shoulder into the emperor's, so that all three of them went sprawling in an ungainly,
rolling tangle, over the road and over the edge and down into the
river.

Down and down into dark roiling waters that snatched Chung's
breath away, that tumbled him end over end until he had forgotten
entirely which way was up.

Growing up in the docks, on the wharves all day long, he had
been in the water and out of it, wet more often than he was dry; he
swam like an eel, sinuous and native. Until today, when the jarring
shock of the fall and the rough battering current almost made him
forget how to swim at all.

He thought he was lost, a nonsense soldier fallen to a stupid
death in this unfought war, dead before the enemy could even be
brought to battle.

He thought how angry Shen would be, which was a sorrow he
could almost smile at if he weren't being hurled against rocks on
the river bottom.

But he opened his eyes, at least, at the thought of Shen; didn't
want to shame him by going into death like a coward, all courage
washed away.

He opened his eyes and saw a light that was momentarily
yellow, flame beneath the water, and he thought *the emperor's
still burning, it must be sorcerous, that wicked fire the rebels
throw* . . .

But the yellow died, not so strong a sorcery after all; and then
the light was only a glimmer of green, a frog in a pond.

And that was still the emperor in his shirt, and Chung did try to
swim toward him. He still had no breath, and couldn't hold his

lungs empty for much longer; but he kicked against the current and struck out with what strength he had remaining, and . . .

AND THEN a hand gripped his neck and dragged him startlingly upward, and his head broke surface and he crowed a ragged breath, and then another; and that was Yu Shan's head in the water beside him, breathing easily, almost amused.

When he could talk—it took a while, it hurt a lot and was little more than wheezing with a shape to it, but he had to try—he managed, just, "The emperor . . . ?"

Who had still not come up for air, anywhere that Chung could see. Which ought not to be possible, but a lot of that young man's gifts were not strictly possible for mortal man. They did clearly lie within the grasp of a god. Or a man of jade, given that he did seem to share them with Yu Shan.

"Gone that way," Yu Shan said, nodding upcurrent. Of course. Where he couldn't run because his path was blocked by fire, of course he'd swim it. His victory was in peril, his chase was delayed; did anyone think he would wait calmly until he could consult with generals, fetch up men and boats, assault the island and its garrison like any normal commander . . . ?

Chung was a fierce swimmer if he had to be, but this current was fiercer. He couldn't swim against it. Yu Shan could, though; and still could, even with Chung clinging to his belt.

They swam underwater as much as possible, and close to the bank. The surface was all broken anyway where the river rewove itself after the island had torn its single flow in two, but still better not to chance being seen, two heads breaking water in mid-stream.

They made their way swiftly—at least, Yu Shan made their way, while Chung clung and kicked and tried to feel useful, not too much of a drag—up to the bridge and into its shadow; and there, yes, there they found the emperor.

Waiting with as much patience as he could muster, not much:

clinging to a dank timber and gesturing to them for silence, caution, speed.

HIS JABBING finger showed them why. Higher within the arch, shadow had substance: other figures hung in the framework, waiting.

Waiting surely until they heard footsteps on the bridge above, soldiers running over to attack the rebels on the island. So few men, holding up an entire army while Tunghai Wang ran farther and farther away: of course the vanguard would hurry across the bridge, as soon as they found a way to reach it. And then a few mallet-blows on appropriate pins and the bridge would disintegrate beneath their feet, and those who didn't fall into the urgent river would find themselves stranded on the island, just a few helpless men in the face of a triumphant defense; and the rebels would still be free to carry on hurling their fire until they had no more, by which time their comrades and commanders might be hours, even days ahead . . .

Not if the emperor had any say, they wouldn't. He went climbing softly up the bridge's wooden girders with Yu Shan at his side, their noise covered more or less by the noise of the river beneath them.

Chung stayed below; anything else would have been ridiculous bravado. He knew he had no place in this exploit. He really had no place with them at all, Yu Shan should have seen him safe and left him on the riverbank for the guards eventually to find him.

Here he was, though, and glad of it, thrilled; and saving it up to make a story, something to tell Shen. Something not to spoil with absurd heroics, trying to overreach himself, getting himself killed and maybe others too, maybe even the emperor too . . .

He did lift himself up out of the constant frothing tug of the water: partly to feel safer, partly to see better. To have more to say, not to spoil the story.

He would swear that jade shirt shed a light of its own. Perhaps it only caught the reflection of daylight off water, but it shone in the shadows and he thought it was deliberate, inherent, something of the stone.

Something to see by, however it came: a strange and greenish light as though the emperor were still a frog as he crawled long-leggedly, long-armedly through the network of crossed timbers that supported the arch of the bridge.

Yu Shan stayed close enough that Chung's eyes could follow him too, a figure of shade, green shadow in a green light.

Those above them might have been asleep, or daydreaming, or listening very intently overhead, because they seemed to notice nothing beneath them. Not till the last possible moment, when that greenish cast embraced them too, and one of them glanced down in puzzled wonder.

And screamed, so that there was no secret anymore; the sound echoed and echoed, trapped in the shadows between wood and water. Chung's head turned away instinctively from the man's naked fear, his naked shame—

—AND SO he saw the other two men who had been crouched deep in the footings, where even the emperor's jade-bright eyes had overlooked them.

Two men swinging with the ease of practice through the frame of beams, long knives between their teeth; and only him to stop them, disarmed and awkward and dripping wet . . .

He set his jaw, just to stop his teeth from chattering, and began to swing himself slowly up the climb of the bridge and out over the water.

They followed, casual and unconcerned, competent and lethal.

Up, and out.

Halfway up, a man fell screaming by his ear; fell into the water and was lost, a sudden silence, an absence.

Another man fell with no sound at all, only the sudden shadow of his plunging body, there and gone, dead already.

Not the emperor, not Yu Shan. Chung didn't even need to look. They wouldn't die like that, swift and meaningless and gone. He'd seen men die just that way on the beach raid, and still didn't believe it of those two. Besides, neither one of them would scream.

Perhaps those two swift deaths whipped on his pursuers; perhaps they thought he was climbing up to seek help of his friends. Perhaps they realized that his friends might actually survive that strange quiet fighting overhead, now that the odds were more in their favor.

They came after Chung more urgently then, which only meant that he needed to do something a little sooner. Otherwise he would climb up into that higher fight, get in the emperor's way, bring two more rebels up beneath Yu Shan just at the wrong moment . . .

So he locked his legs around a horizontal beam and let his body drop down like a child hanging from a tree branch: drop and swing with his arms at full stretch, suddenly and unexpectedly within snatching range of one of the climbers below.

He had to arch his spine painfully to do it, but for a moment at the height of his backswing there he was, just an arm's length away. The rebel was startled, clinging on with both hands, helpless; and Chung could simply reach out and grab that heavy knife the man held in his teeth, seize the handle and jerk it away.

Teeth wouldn't grip on oiled steel, against that abrupt sideways tug. Now the man was disarmed, and Chung had a weapon.

That was all he'd meant. He swung himself back up again with a terrible effort of his belly muscles—Shen would have laughed, and then made him practice the move over and over, again and again, week after week till it was easy—and went to put the knife in his belt.

And saw dark streaks on the blade, and for a little moment wondered how he'd cut himself.

But of course it wasn't his own blood; that blade hadn't come anywhere near his skin.

A quick glance down showed him the man he'd just left, still clinging to the beams, lifting his head as though to stare after Chung, to accuse or just to protest, *why did you do this to me?*

One brief glimpse in the shadows; that was enough. Chung turned his own face away, not to see what he'd done, that had left a blade so darkly marked and so easily wiped clean.

The knife was double-edged and sharp as the wind. Jerked savagely, heedlessly out of the man's mouth, it had cut through his tongue and the flesh of his cheek, the muscle and bone of his jaw; he gaped slack-mouthed and always would, half his face hanging open to the world.

He had a comrade, a friend perhaps, who was suddenly being as slow to chase as Chung was numbedly slow to get away. Who had stopped to listen to the slow keening that arose from that ruined mouth, to touch his companion's shoulder in some hopeless gesture of sympathy, of pity, of promise.

Who lifted his own head now to find Chung looking down at him watchfully, unable after all to keep his face turned away.

The rebel took his own knife from between his teeth then, in a deliberate gesture; gripped it fist-tight and began to climb again.

This time, when Chung swung, he used his hands to grip the beam. It was his legs that drove in toward the rebel. Who needed one hand to grip, and could only slash wildly with the other while he clung to a perilous balance on the dank and slippery woodwork.

Chung felt that blade score across his leg, but he had too much impetus for so fine a cut to divert him. His feet slammed against the rebel's chest, knocking him back against an upright, knocking all the breath from his body, knocking him from his stance so that now he was only hanging by that one desperate hand.

Chung bent his legs at the moment of strike, so that his body went on swinging in toward the rebel. In the moment that he had before he must swing away again, he let his legs slip around the man's waist and lock behind.

Then, with his own body's weight and a great jerk, all the muscles that he had working with him, he pulled the man off the
bridge.

And swung back, unlocked his legs and let him fall.

One last despairing clutch, the man's hand trying to snare
Chung's ankle; but that ankle was wet already and slick with
blood now, it offered no safe grip. Chung felt him slide away, didn't
listen for the splash. He gathered himself for another effort, to
haul his body up into the safety of the bridge's frame; felt a burning pain in his leg just at that worst moment, and wondered if he
was actually going to make it—

—AND A hand reached down to seize his wrist, lifted him up into
that reassuring woodwork. He found himself safe—entirely safe,
no question—in the irresistible strong grip of the emperor.

"Are you hurt?"

All instinct and courtly convention told him to lie, to say *No,
majesty,* and allow the emperor to let it go, not to concern himself
in the least.

But his emperor was his commander too, and this was a field of
battle; and Shen had trained him better than that. What was right
at court was wrong in war. He said, "A cut on the leg, majesty."

"Can you stand?"

"I . . . think so." It hurt more, now that he was thinking about
it. His trouser leg told him nothing, being sodden already from the
river; he was trying to test the leg itself there on the cross-beam,
but the emperor was still supporting his weight, and how did you
tell the Man of Jade to let go?

"Well, perhaps another swim will help."

"Another . . . ?"

You weren't supposed to question the emperor. Everybody did
sooner or later, but that was in camp. At court, they tried not.
Here in battle, Chung was fairly sure that he shouldn't. He bit that
one off half asked. And glanced up into the green-shaded shad-

ows, trying to see past the obscuring glow of the jademail shirt; and said, "Are there . . . ?"

And choked it off again, but the emperor smiled and said, "More rebels up in the arch there? No. This bridge is safe, until our people come."

Which would be soon now, surely, an imperial guard without its emperor. But there were still those terrible fires on the riverbank, the guards must still be under attack, more canisters hurling at them; maybe not so soon after all. Maybe even time enough for the rebels to send more men under the bridge to bring it down . . .

Perhaps the emperor meant that the bridge was safe because he and his companions were there now to protect it. Chung said, "Yes, majesty. So . . ."

"So where is Yu Shan?"

Chung nodded.

This time the emperor didn't smile. His eyes were bright and compulsive, and Chung couldn't look away. A proper subject keeps his head low and his gaze lower in the presence of his emperor, but they had learned other manners in the camp. This was neither court nor camp, and even so Chung had no wish to stare, nor to be stared at by majesty, but he wasn't being offered the choice. Something deliberate was happening here, and it was the emperor's decision, and . . .

And it wasn't that Chung heard a noise below, even now, when he might have been listening for it. What he heard instead was a silence, an end to noise: the breaking-off of a sound that had been low and persistent and sharp enough to cut through the constant noises of the river, only he'd been too busy to give it any attention.

The emperor heard it too, or heard its ending. And still didn't release Chung's gaze, but only said, "Yu Shan is . . . attending to the last of the rebels."

That must mean the one Chung had left with a ruined face. That missing sound could well have been the moan of a man helpless in extraordinary pain; so Yu Shan had gone to help in the only way that would suggest itself, the way of war.

Chung didn't try to look.

Yu Shan came gracefully up to join them, and the emperor said, "The three of us, then: Chung is hurt, but he thinks not badly and a swim will help his leg if you and I help him, Yu Shan . . ."

"Majesty?"

Here he was asking questions again, but he was too bewildered to hold himself in check and the emperor didn't seem to mind.

"Yes, Chung?"

"Where must we swim to now?"

"The rebels will be watching the bridge," Yu Shan said, "as well as our friends across the river. If they see us—well, there are only three of us, until our friends catch up. We don't know how many they are. And if they throw fire at us as well as swords, even the emperor may not come through it."

The emperor thought he was fireproof like his shirt, but he nodded cooperatively.

"We can't just sit and wait," he said. "Our people will come through, but they might have to wait till night, or till they can fetch boats up; and more of them will die in the meantime, perhaps many more if they keep trying to reach us through that firestorm. We need to prevent it."

"The rebels are all busy looking downriver," Yu Shan cut in. Interrupting the emperor was a great offense, greater than staring, greater than questioning: so impossibly forbidden that there could hardly be a law to forbid it. No matter. He might have learned it from Mei Feng, who did it all the time. "Shooting their fireballs, killing our people. We're going to swim up to the north end of the island; that way we can surprise them."

If they don't see us in the water, if they don't have a watch on that end of the island; and we'll still only be three, and what if . . .

Arguing with the emperor, once he'd made up his mind? Pointless, even if Chung had any way to measure how very much it was forbidden.

BACK INTO the water, then, briefly and anxiously aware of more flames, more shouting on the riverbank; anxious too about what lay ahead, how he might possibly help.

For now he was a hindrance, but at least not an awkward one. Yu Shan and the emperor could both apparently swim one-armed and underwater, utterly untroubled by towing Chung against a current that would have swallowed him and never spat him out again.

They could hold their breath too, far longer than he could. They ran him to the ragged edge of his control again and again, and still clearly came up each time sooner than they needed to.

Once, they came up under the bank and he could see across the water to the island. He saw no rebel watching the water, no alarm, no men running for weapons. What he did see was order, regularity, the discipline of soldiers. They hauled down the arms of their flinging machines, loaded a projectile—carefully!—into the basket, lit the fuse and heaved on ropes that caused the basket to hurl upward, the projectile to fly away. They watched how it flew, where it landed; perhaps they made an adjustment to the line of the machine; and then they did it again.

And there were four machines and many men, and every one of those projectiles meant a fresh blaze falling on or around the imperial troops. Chung couldn't see what harm his friends were taking; there was smoke and flame and no time, the emperor wouldn't let them linger with their heads out of water.

The last time they rose, they were in mid-river and there was no island where he looked for it, to the side, where it had been. The emperor and Yu Shan hung in the water, motionless except for hands and feet, as though this was the sea at the slack of the tide; Chung still needed to cling to Yu Shan's body as he turned around, as the current sucked at him. There was the island: a strip of rock that stood proud of the water, just wide enough and flat enough to take the footings of two bridges, just long and wide and flat enough to hold four machines and their busy crews. And a stack of projectiles, Chung could see that now too, built up like barrels at this near peak of the island where the rock narrowed like a jade ship's cutwater, where it slit the river like a blade slits a run of silk.

No watch, no guards: who could come this way, except by boat? And there was nowhere here for a boat to tie up, only blade-sharp rock rising sheer and slick from the river's swirl.

Barely anywhere for a swimmer to clamber out, unless that swimmer had jade in his blood, in his bone.

The emperor approached the black wall of rock, reached up and found a handhold, another . . .

Once he'd pulled himself up out of the water, he paused and stretched down an arm. Chung found himself lifted bodily by Yu Shan, passed into the emperor's grip.

Looking at that dark rock face as he was raised past it, he could see no handholds, nothing his numbed fingers might have gripped. He watched from above as Yu Shan scrambled up after, and it looked as though he simply smeared his skin to the rock. Perhaps the stone in his blood reached to the stone outside and clung . . . ?

They had come up into the shadow of that stack of containers. Briefly, even the emperor let them crouch and rest there, let the weight of water drain out of their clothes, let them peer around the wall of pots to see just how many men they had to face.

They couldn't wait long, though, while those machines still hurled fiery death at their friends, his troops. Nor could they stay undiscovered long, while men came to the pot stack again and again . . .

Soon, then, a man came and lifted one more canister from the heap, and found himself abruptly facing the emperor he had rebelled against, whose troops he was raining fire on, whose own body perhaps he would have liked to set aflame.

He never got to do that.

He might have had a moment to realize, to understand that this was indeed the emperor and that there was a long list now of things he never would get to do.

Then the emperor's blade pierced him, and he fell.

In falling, of course he let the canister fall too.

If it was fused, at least it wasn't lit; but who knew what sorceries were in that black stuff that the pottery sealed? Perhaps it would flame in sunlight and the fuse was only a precaution. Perhaps it would ignite every one of these gathered canisters, and they would all erupt at once. Not even the emperor would be proof against such a fire . . .

Chung had time to picture that, all of it, in the moments that the canister took to topple out of the toppling man's hands: the terrible slow flickering start, the creep of black, the eruption.

He had time to picture its aftermath, the end of empire and his own less significant end, in the little singular moment that the toppling canister needed to crash onto that brutal rock beneath.

Except that what he could picture, so could another man.

Yu Shan, in this case.

Whose hands caught the canister a perilous finger's-breadth above the rock as he dived forward, as he rolled and held it somehow safely all the way, as he rose to his feet again in the same moment still with his arms full of unexploded death . . .

. . . AND IN full view of all those rebels manning the flinging-machines, who reacted with a roar of discovery, an abandonment of their ropes and pulleys, a snatching-up of swords and dagger-axes . . .

No POINT staying crouched now in the shadows, nothing to hide from.

Chung and the emperor stood up, blades in hand: the emperor with his long broad-bladed tao, Chung with no more than the knife he'd taken under the bridge. It didn't seem to matter much. In standing up he'd seen beyond the machine crews, to the footings of the bridge.

To the squad of men who had been crouching there, ready for whatever troops came across the bridge if it didn't fall beneath them.

Who were standing now, turning from that to this, from the fight that hadn't come yet to the one that was here now.

Who were—well, too many to fight. The emperor might be fire-proof, but he was not invincible. He'd been wounded once already in battle, in his first battle, against assassins in the forest; and had survived it because his jade-hard bones wouldn't let steel cut through them. This many men could overwhelm him; and then they could hack him apart, cut him into many pieces, and even the jade-magic couldn't draw him back together.

At least, Chung thought not.

Hoped not, truly, although that might be treason or heresy or some such. A piecemeal emperor, surviving disarticulation . . . No. Please, no.

But he didn't see how the emperor could survive this forest of blades, unless he dived back into the river. Which Chung just knew he would not do.

Chung tried to move, to stand in front of the emperor, a little proper gesture of *you shall not pass*.

There was an impossible, an imperial chuckle in his ear; an ir-resistible hand on his shoulder, nudging him gently aside.

"Thank you, Chung, but you should probably take shelter be-hind me."

That would be sensible, but not actually possible. He couldn't survive where the emperor didn't; they would kill Chung in relief, in celebration, just in passing. And he couldn't dive into the river and hope to survive that. He'd be drowned and dead before ever he reached calm waters.

So he shook his head and said no to majesty, moving to take a position at the emperor's side.

Yu Shan looked back, rolled his eyes at them both, turned to face the onrush of rebels—

—AND HURLED the canister he held. The man he'd caught it from, the man the emperor killed, he'd been using both arms just to lift it; Yu Shan lobbed it one-handed, high and looping.

HIGH OVER the heads of the advancing rebels, who were perhaps amazed that he could do that, knowing as they did just how heavy it was; and then perhaps relieved and contemptuous, just for that little moment when they realized it had missed them entirely.

UNTIL THEY heard it land behind them, among their abandoned machines, between them and their friends at the bridgehead.

THEIR FACES, some of them: their faces were terrible, in that moment before they turned to see the truth of it.

How that canister shattered on the rock, right there between one machine and another.

How the black liquid it contained splashed out between the two; and how it was hard to tell whether it caught fire from the one side or the other, because both machines had an open flame there to light their fuses, and it really might have been either one. Or the sun, of course, or some kind of sorcery.

There was surely a sorcery in the fire that leaped up. Chung knew about oil, all manner of oils. None of them would yield a flame this furious, a heat this vicious. It seemed to seize whatever fuel it could find, clinging to wood and flesh with equal greed; where it found nothing but stone—on the bare rock of the island here, on the emperor's back before the river doused it—it only sat and waited, burning nothing but air, seeming not to burn itself out, not to drip or drain away.

The machines were largely bamboo and twisted rope, with leather slings. They blazed mightily, going up like grass.

The men were lucky, on both sides. The squad from the bridge hadn't reached quite so far yet; the teams working the machines had all rushed forward to face these invaders from the river. There was no one left to get caught in that sudden conflagration, no monstrous death to watch or listen to.

And no way for the bridge squad to reach their colleagues through the flame; no way for their colleagues to retreat, unless they went into the water. The fire bisected the island entirely, trapping them at the peak here with these impossible saboteurs . . .

There were still many of them, all against three. Chung might have felt dangerously outnumbered if his two companions hadn't been the men they were, men of jade, immeasurable.

He still worried for them all, because a blade could still kill any man or all of them together. He worried most for the emperor, who refused to understand that, who thought he was fireproof. Who was jumping onto that great stack of projectiles right now, balancing on a liquid hell if any one of the rebels had a spark of fire on him. Or if the wind carried a spark from the inferno at their backs, or . . .

The emperor held his arms up, and bizarrely, unaccountably, the rebels stopped their charge. A few short paces separated them from where Yu Shan and Chung stood, at the foot of the heap now, blades drawn to make some show of guarding the emperor above their heads.

Perhaps the rebels were glad of that sudden excuse to halt. Chung saw more fear than fury in them. Not fear of the blades they faced, that would be ridiculous, but perhaps of the men who bore them. At least of Yu Shan, who could pick up and hurl one of their projectiles one-handed.

More, though, they were afraid of that fire. Nervous glances measured how far it was behind them, how the sparks carried, what it could find to burn from there to here . . .

This must be why they had not destroyed the second bridge till now: not to maroon themselves with a stack of these volatile weapons, not till they must, hoping to leave themselves the chance of an escape.

They should have brought a boat, he thought; they should have thought that little bit farther ahead. Tunghai Wang should have thought it for them, when he was planning this, when he was ordering machines built here to guard the river roads. For certain sure he had not arranged it all in an hour this morning, caught up in a great retreat . . .

But they were here now and so was Chung, with his friend Yu Shan and the emperor also; and there was no boat, and there was an engulfing fire between them—between them *all*—and the bridge away.

Perhaps that was why the rebels were prepared to listen to the emperor. Who looked down at them as if they were his own people—which they were, of course, even though they had sold themselves to Tunghai Wang—and said, "Put up your blades. There is no point in dying here now."

Not a man did what he was told, but more looked back or looked sideways, looked at one another. Now that they'd stopped, it seemed there wasn't one ready to hurtle forward again. Likely it looked very bad to be first, even with a crowd behind you.

The emperor waited just a little time, then said, "Yu Shan, one of those machines isn't burning yet."

Indeed, it was the one nearest to the rebels—*nearest to us!* Chung thought, and tried not to let his face so much as twitch— that was only smoldering along the side that faced the fire, that was still waiting to burst into full flame.

Yu Shan laughed, and slipped his tao into its scabbard. The relaxed way he did that was almost threatening in itself, so dismissive of the men he faced.

Then he picked another of those canisters from the top of the heap, reaching for the very one the emperor was standing on, making him dance to the side, laughing in his turn; and he looked at the machine that wasn't burning, and the gathered crew of rebels that stood nervously between him and it—

—AND THEY backed abruptly, silently, without any discussion to one side and the other, to leave him a clear passage through.

They thought perhaps that he would carry it toward the fire, if he was entirely mad; or else that he would throw it as before. Either way, all too clearly, they did think him mad. There were fire and sparks all around, and he had seen directly how these pots would burst and flame, and yet he still lifted one and stood ready to hurl it, and they wanted nothing except distance, more distance than they could find on this little rock.

In fact, he rolled it. There was a natural crack in the rock of the island that made a gutter all along its spine, whose two edges gripped the pot and steered it just where Yu Shan clearly meant it to go, the smoldering side of that nearest machine. Where it bumped and jostled against a leg of the machine, and sat and smoked a little; and they waited, watching, the rebels edging back and farther back, and Chung wondered if the pot's seal would give way before its contents were hot enough to burn, and if not then what would happen, and—

—AND THEN it did happen, and it was an explosion beyond anything Chung had ever seen or imagined. Not even the rebels could have expected this, surely. A flung pot broke on impact, before the fire caught. If they had seen this before they would have been screaming at Yu Shan, ducking for whatever shelter they could find behind one another, not just that nervous sidle out of range.

If they'd seen this before, they would have known they were not out of range, nothing on this island was out of range.

The flask exploded and fire gouted up, flame enveloped the machine in a moment, but that wasn't the worst of it.

The worst was how the air was suddenly lethal, a blast of heat and wind with a vicious whiplash sting to it.

Chung saw a man's eye gone, just gone into a hole, and he could have sworn that smoke came out before the welling darkness.

He saw a man's throat opened, but not from a sword cut, nothing like that, it didn't seem to bleed, not soon enough; at first it only gaped like a second mouth while he gasped for air and couldn't find it.

Chung himself felt a whip-cut across his face and ignored it while he could, while he was occupied with gaping at the fire, at the rebels so strangely injured out of nowhere. At the emperor, who was gazing down at his own chest—his jademail shirt, rather—with an expression of puzzled wonder, reaching to pluck something from between two scales.

He looked to Yu Shan at his side, and found him unharmed but also staring, but not at himself. At Chung.

"You're hurt. Did you know?"

He did know; it did hurt. Like a burn now, more than a whip. He reached a hand up—and snatched his fingers away again, biting back a yelp. No fire, but the flesh burned to the touch none the less, flamed like a brand where he touched it.

"What *happened*? Why doesn't it bleed . . . ?"

"It is, it's starting now."

So was the man with the open throat, starting to choke on his own blood. Twice doomed, Chung thought, no hope for him.

The emperor jumped down, and showed them something on the palm of his hand: small and sharp and blackened, vicious as a wasp but inert, clay, a piece of pot.

"I felt them bouncing off the shirt," he said, "but this one caught between the scales and stuck. The pot shattered when it exploded, and all its little pieces . . ."

All its little pieces had flown like sparks in all directions, and struck like flecks of steel. Chung would be marked for life—*not so pretty now, Shen, will you still love me? when I carry this mark that says I was here, where you were not?*—and could count himself lucky; others would be blind or dead.

Others would be thinking they had found a new weapon.

Not the emperor, not yet, but he would talk about this, of course, and some of his generals would see what he did not.

Now, though, he looked at Chung, and then at Yu Shan; and nodded, and turned to the rebels and said, "We need to go now, we still have a war to fight. If you wait here and do no more harm, you will suffer none from us. But my people will be coming over that bridge soon. They will want revenge, because of what you have done to our people ashore, and you have nowhere to go. You need someone of ours, to speak for you once these fires burn out. Which is why we will be leaving Chung here—"

"Majesty, no!"

It should properly be death to interrupt the emperor, but everyone was doing it today.

This time, the emperor overrode him. "Yes, Chung. Yu Shan and I could carry you ashore—and what then? Shall we carry you all day? You're hurt, twice hurt, and you can't keep up with us. Here, you can be useful. Protect these men. Will you do that?"

In truth, he had no choice. They all knew that. His emperor ordered him to it; besides which, his emperor could jump into the river and be away, Yu Shan with him, and what could Chung do then? Jump after them, splashing loud enough—sinking loud enough—to be sure they noticed?

Well, yes. Shen would do that, no doubt. Not Chung.

Chung scowled, and nodded, and watched his emperor dive neatly into the river with his friend a moment behind.

And then turned to face a pack of rebels, who could kill him in a moment if they saw a reason to; and lifted his chin, lifted his voice, said, "Your weapons. Take them off, put them down. Make a heap of them, over here," an open space next to the stack of pots.

Nobody moved, so he moved himself: went to that space and dropped his knife deliberately in front of them all. "I'm not your captor, didn't you hear the emperor? I'm here to speak for you. They're more likely to listen to me if you're not armed."

"And what if they're ours? If they find us surrendered to one unarmed man?"

"Listen," Chung said: and yes, there were sounds coming through the fire. Sounds of combat, of one squad as it might be fighting to defend a bridgehead against an army. "If your men fight back there, they're going to die; that's all the imperial guard trying to come over the bridge at once, to find their emperor."

They still took a little time for thought, for muttering among themselves, but not much now. One by one, they came and dropped blades, belts, spare knives at his feet.

One said, "Was that really the emperor?"

Chung nodded.

"And the other one, what . . . who was he?"

"A man of jade," Chung said, "out of the mountains. Half the imperial guard comes from the mines, as he did." Which was true and deceptive, both at once.

"The emperor is the Man of Jade."

"Yes. But the miners have a . . . special relationship with the stone, just as he does." *They're not all jade-eaters, but I won't tell you that.* "They all wear a piece of jade next to their skin, he gives them that license," *because they get sick without it, but I won't tell you that either.*

"Only the emperor can wear jade!"

"Yes. But this emperor allows his chosen people to wear his sign."

"And you?"

"Oh, no," he said, "not me, I'm not from the valleys. Just a wharf brat who grew into a runner, me. I was a kitchen servant before—"

—before I was a friend of emperors he might have gone on to

say, but he should probably not have said any of that, and he didn't get the chance to finish.

He had too many prisoners under his guard, who had just seen their friends hurt and killed among them. He was as unarmed and as trapped as they were, and he was alone; small surprise if one of them seized his words as a confession of weakness. Perhaps the man thought it was an insult, that the emperor left someone so weak to watch him and all his colleagues.

Whatever he thought, he struck out suddenly, with no warning, his great fist flying at Chung's head.

EXCEPT THAT Chung's head wasn't quite there anymore, because actually there had been a warning and Chung wasn't quite as relaxed as he might have been pretending, and Shen's training did have some purpose after all.

A little shift in the man's eyes, a shift in his feet: Chung knew that punch was coming, and where it would land. Where it was meant to land.

Reaction was instinctive. *Trained,* Shen would say. By the time the man had comprehensively missed his mark, Chung was already swaying upright again. His hands were already reaching to grip the man's thrusting arm, to pull him even more off-balance; all his body was twisting beneath that arm, lending a more organized strength to its effort, doing nothing but help here . . .

HELPING TO the effect that the man flew high into the air over Chung's shoulder, came crashing down helplessly onto bare rock, might well have slid off into the greedy river if Chung hadn't still kept a cruel locking grip on that arm.

Chung didn't even look down at him. He looked at the man's cohorts and said again, "Just a kitchen servant, until the emperor's favorite picked me for her messenger. And she only did that to save me from a fight that I was losing."

Every man there could see this message, and understand it. Slowly, one by one, they stepped back, they let the tension ebb out of their bodies.

Chung relaxed his grip, released the man at his feet, reached down to help him stand.

Then, "I don't know how safe all these pots are," he said, "how hot that fire's going to make them—but I think they'd be safer in the river, don't you? While we're waiting?"

All except one, which he sat on to be sure of it, while the men busied themselves—quite eagerly, he thought, for conscripted labor—hurling the stack of projectiles into the water.

When one of them turned to him with a gesture, *that one too*, he shook his head.

"I want to keep this," he said, "to experiment with. And if any of you knows how the contents are mixed, what goes into it, whether there's any sorcery . . . ?"

three

*M*ei Feng went straight to the river, and there was no way across.

Over there she could see, she could actually *see* imperial troops, any of whom might have told her just where the emperor was and how to reach him fastest. Any of them. If she could only *get* there . . .

All her life long, there had been ferries plying this river, back and forth all day and all night too; and if all the ferries were full then a boatman would always take a girl across for a smile and a coin, perhaps for the smile alone. Or she could run down to the docks and find a fisherman, any fisherman. Everyone knew her grandfather, and most of them knew her. The river had never been an obstacle. Till now.

Now there was no way over, below the twin bridges. The ferries were long gone, absorbed into one invasion fleet or the other. Any boatman still on the water when the imperial army's first outrunners were seen on the heights must simply have fled the easiest way, straight upcurrent, away from war and danger.

Another day, another time, Mei Feng would simply have swum it. Today, now, she had the fate of the emperor in her hands, in her head, she'd never been so urgent; and today, now was the worst of the tide with black clouds scudding in, the river still flood-high from the dragon's long typhoon and the wind still stiff in sympathy, even starting to rise again.

Which meant that salt water driving in was meeting fresh water pushing out, making for cross-currents and whirlpools all across the breadth of the river, and waves tossing white in the wind. It would be death for anyone to swim in that. She was desperate, but not stupid. If she threw herself away, she threw away the emperor besides, and she would not do that. She would *not* . . .

Instead, she set out to run upriver.

One comfort, small thread though it was: this was the way the army was tending, either side of the river. So this would be the way to find the emperor. Alone, hopefully: alone with his guards about him to keep him safe . . .

She could have laughed at herself, if she hadn't been so busy running. He had plunged into this war, would surely be looking to fight in the front line, whatever his generals and advisers would demand—and she worried that he was not safe?

But yes, she did worry; and no, he was not safe. If anything could kill him, it would be the blow struck in secret, the coward's stroke when his back was turned, his armor off and his guard down, his guards outside the door . . .

Barefoot and heedless, then, she ran to save her man.

If she was too late, if the emperor died: well, then perhaps she would just not stop running. She could run and run, far from San-tung and Taishu and the sea between; she could run this soft palace skin off her feet entirely, grow new tougher stuff at the same time as she grew new muscles, as she grew a leather hide about her heart.

WHARVES AND godowns, mud and pools, inlets and bridges and water-gates and men. The men were imperial soldiers, not a sign of a rebel except the dead ones here and there, dragged out of her way along with their hasty barricades. That her way was every-one's way, that the dragging-aside might not have been directly for her, that didn't mattter.

What did matter, some of the men tried to stop her, either be-cause they knew who she was or else because they didn't.

At first she snarled at them, and just kept running.

If they knew her name, mostly a snarl was enough.

If a man's hand grabbed, she dodged it; she'd always been quick. And they were mostly hurrying themselves, eyes fixed on a different target, a distant war, grabbing just because she was a girl and there. When they missed her, they let her go.

Those few who wanted more, who wanted to drag her off the river road and into any one of these abandoned buildings, who wanted to abandon their own duty and their comrades too—those she showed more than her teeth and her determination.

She took to running with her dagger drawn. A blade made a great discouragement, the way it caught the sun and caught the eye and brought the two together, *this is bright and sharp and clean, cleaner than any part of you. Do you really want to see it closer? Closer yet . . . ?*

Only one man she actually cut: because she had to, because he wouldn't see or hear or understand anything less. He had seized her wrist, the arm that held the knife, and thought that made him safe. He was startled when she pulled free of his grip, startled by sailor-strength in a girl, but stupid too; he grabbed again, this time for his own blade, and never got it out of the sheath. Her knife pierced his forearm, pinned it to the belt across his belly.

He stood very, very still then, gone a grubby color, slick with sweat. She explained to him, very briefly, what would happen to him if she gave the emperor his name. That did nothing to improve his color. Then she advised him to sit down, just where he was, and to stay there until she was long out of sight. He might use the time to bandage up his arm, she suggested, as best he could with one hand. If he was lucky, one of his comrades might stop and help; but he really shouldn't think to come after her anytime that she might turn around and see him.

She waited for his slow, careful nod of agreement. Then she slid her knife out of his arm. Blood followed, but not the spurting gush that would speak of a ripped artery; he'd live, then. Probably.

She shrugged and turned away, and ran again.

"MEI FENG!"

The city was behind her now, and there was the river's bend ahead; the bridges should lie beyond it, where the river narrowed, where they had been possible. No man had stopped her so far. No man could stop her now, but apparently her own name could.

Her own name in a woman's voice, on this road of men and men and more men.

She twisted around, knowing the voice even before she found the rangy figure striding down from where she and her men had been crouching, resting on an unexpected mound beside the road; before Jiao's long fingers had closed on the back of her neck and given her a monitory shake.

"Mei Feng, always—*always!*—stay with your people. Going off by yourself is stupid, and dangerous to you and to the friends who have to look for you; and even if you don't run into the trouble you deserve, you still end up isolated among troops who don't know you, who can't tell if you're one of us or one of them or just a civilian, just prey . . ."

She knew it, she knew it all, she had seen most of it played out in this last hour, and wasn't about to give Jiao the satisfaction of saying so. Didn't have time to apologize, to explain: or wouldn't take the time she had, which might be all the time the emperor had left. Didn't have time to argue either, to say that there had barely been any rebels left in the city, or that she'd found the only two who actually mattered, who might have been entirely missed otherwise until it was entirely too late . . .

She knocked Jiao's hand away and said it flatly, "No *time!* Jiao, I have to get across the river."

"Can't help you there," Jiao said. Trying perhaps a little too hard to sound tolerant and amused, not to look surprised at how easily she'd been batted off. "The bridge is down. They were flinging fire at us earlier, the whole army was backed up here, but it seems to be moving again."

It did. Mei Feng looked at the stream of men hurrying onward, only really seeing it for the first time now that she was standing apart, while only her mind was running on: *bridge down, bridge down and of course no boats; there's a crossing higher up, more running, more time, farther to go . . .*

"I need . . ."

"I know, you said. You need to cross the river. And *I* said you need to stay with us. So we'd best get started, yes?" She whistled to her men, gestured with a broad sweep of her arm, *that way . . .*

So Mei Feng found herself running at the heart of a pack, which was probably better. If anyone could get her across the river against the odds, that would be Jiao. And no man now would trouble or delay her; and this steady military jog she could keep up all day; and it might seem slow but it would eat up the distance, she did understand that . . .

And even so it was intolerable to be trapped here, the wrong side of the water, when she could look across and see so easily where she wanted to be. She could almost, *almost* shout across, give them a message for the emperor, a warning; but the river was just that little too broad, that little too noisy. Even if anyone would listen to the screechings of some crop-headed ragamuffin in irreverent trousers.

There were the two bridges, one of them broken, all but gone; there on the mid-island, on their stepping-stone were the residues of a fire, smoke and ash and a huddle of men crouching on the bare rock.

Here on the one bank, there on the other were great scorch-marks, where fire had run all across the road from the river to the paddy, although there was nothing obvious to burn. Nothing but people, at least. There were bodies by the roadside, blackened and twisted like iron in flame, ill-wrought . . .

Too close to the bodies, too hurt to shift, were burned men who were not dead, or not yet. They were worse: keening or screaming or lying unaccountably, dreadfully still.

Jiao and the troop just kept running, and so necessarily did Mei Feng: glad for once to be so short among these big men, to be able to drop her head and watch their bare feet and nothing else, listen to the heavy squelching tread of them and nothing else.

UNTIL THE men in front stopped dead and she almost went hard into the back of them, it was so unexpected, she had fallen so deep into the rhythm and strain of running.

She caught herself just in time, or else just too late, her hands coming up instinctively to clutch at sweat-slick flesh. One man gave her a look that might have come differently if she hadn't been who she was, if he hadn't known it.

What she gave him back was pure impatience and a nudge aside, which most certainly would have brought consequences *if* she hadn't been who she was, *if* he hadn't known her to be untouchable. But she didn't have time for games, for folly, for outrage. She pushed through to where Jiao stood, at the head of her men and peering forward; she put a hand on her friend's shoulder for what advantage she could steal and stretched upward, went on tiptoe and still couldn't see over the heads of all the men in front who had backed up and packed together, blocked the road.

"What is it?"

"I don't know. Another hold-up. Not fire this time, nothing I can see. Hold tight, word'll come back to us."

Perhaps it would, but rougher sounds came first: yelling, screaming. Not much steel-on-steel. Whatever that was, it wasn't fighting. It sounded like slaughter.

Whatever it was, they couldn't reach it; nor apparently could it reach them. Jiao's troop colonized the mud bank of the paddy, taking the chance to rest. Jiao went with them, to stand on that high bank and see what she could make out; she sent the smallest of her men to squirm ahead, all elbows; Mei Feng went the other way, to the river.

Looking across was like looking into a mirror: the narrow road that flanked the river on that bank as on this, the steep terraced paddy consuming all the valley else, rising to the ridge. The men who packed the roadway, all that cramped space between the river and the paddy. As there, so here: and so too the sudden obstruction, that sense of hurry stalled.

It was easier to see, across the water. She could look right up-river and see the cause of it, a sudden dam across the road. No, dams were for water; this would be a barricade. And it ran clean across from the paddy to the riverbank, high and strong as a wall, fixed and certain; and there must—she was sure—be another one on this bank, just as purposeful. Those weren't thrown up in retreat by desperate men, no. Any more than fire-throwing machines were built in desperation.

Tunghai Wang had planned for this retreat, however unlikely he thought it. He had envisioned his men fleeing along this narrow valley, up the river to just this point. Which meant . . .

Which meant that this was a trap, she might know nothing about war but she knew that; and looked up, urgently up, and yes: there they were, long lines of men emerging, erupting all along the ridge. All those rebels who had fled along the river road, crossed the barricade and doubled up to the ridge, doubled back . . .

She could see how well the barricade was defended, how thickly men thronged it with spears and bows. Her view of its foot was obscured by the churning mass of imperial troops. That was just as well; she really didn't want to see how those troops clambered up over the bodies of their own comrades, and died, and were clambered over in their turn.

The dead will always outnumber the living, but she didn't need to see that played out for her instruction, the slow relentless wearing away of the imperial army as men hurled themselves against an impenetrable hedge of steel.

Her eyes were treacherous, in league with her imagination. They kept coming back to the men on the ridge. If she couldn't see quite how dreadful the slaughter was at the rampart, if she refused to imagine it, there was no such relief higher up. She could see quite clearly how they came in good order, rank after rank of them down through the paddy, one terrace after another, so fast. It wasn't possible to wade that fast through the clinging mud of a paddy; they must be following paths already laid out, stone built up almost to the level of the water. Many, many paths, to take so many men so swiftly.

They were ready, the good general Tunghai Wang had been *ready* for this . . .

As over there, so over here. Words rising in her terror, caught by some constriction in her throat. She didn't need to scream a warning, not to Jiao, or to any man here; they knew already. This was what they did. What they would have done themselves if they were good generals, with good troops under their command.

As far as they could, they were organizing. Still trying to breach the rampart ahead, to uncork this bottle-trap; sending word back to the city, calling for help but not along the river roads, not to make things worse; seeking whatever shelter there was against missile weapons—precious little on that low and narrow flat between the paddy and the river, in places barely road-wide—and preparing to meet the rebels as they came down from above.

Jiao wasn't content to hold a place in the line, to stand and wait while doom filed down toward them. A few sharp words, and she was leading her men up onto the paddy wall and away, across this lowest terrace to the next and so up again, a series of broad flat steps until they met the rebels coming down.

And then . . .

Well, there were a great many rebels, and they would have all the advantages. More soldiers were following Jiao now, more than her own men, but even so . . .

Not all Jiao's men had gone; half a dozen were staying down on the road. Making a fine job of calling order to the other men around, posting a look-out up on the paddy wall, bemoaning the lack of archers; but they made a point of calling order to Mei Feng too, putting her tight in against that same wall "where nothing's going to hit you, coming down; only as soon as it's men that are coming down you get right back over by the river there, get in the river if you think you can swim for it." She wasn't fooled for a moment. This wasn't their own concern. It certainly wasn't their choice to stay down here while their mates went up high to fight. This was orders from Jiao, *you stay here, look after Mei Feng, keep her safe. Whatever it costs. Your lives don't matter to the emperor, but hers does. And to me. I care a lot about her, and not a jot about any of you, so mind you keep her safe. I'm the one you'll answer to first, if I come back to find her dead and you not, any of you . . .*

Mei Feng wasn't too proud to be kept alive. What she doubted was Jiao's chance of coming back alive. She watched her long-legged friend stalk off; she watched a wolfish pack of men following, lean and dangerous and not enough; this close to the wall she couldn't see the rebels coming down, but a glance across the river could estimate their numbers and measure their enthusiasm. No one could survive that, she thought: not the waiting army trapped below, and certainly not the bold few souls—they looked so few, that side of the river, compared against the weight of men above them—heading up to fight among the terraces.

Mei Feng might have gone after Jiao, if she could only think of a reason that would outweigh all her better reasons for staying down below. Friendship was good, but not enough; stubbornness was recognizable, likely even, but stupid. In the end, it was a simple case that she could work out on her fingers. If she climbed up the terraces in pursuit, she couldn't keep Jiao alive; if she stayed on the road, she might yet save the emperor.

If she could find a way across the river.

It really was as simple as that, as heart-rending and as binding.

She stood still and watched her friend climb up and out of sight, sent a silent wish of luck after her—that kind of impossible luck that battlefield survivors brag about, that no one could work or plan for, no one could achieve or carry—and then she turned away, turned to the men about her, looked for anything she could do to help.

No archers, but more than one of the men had a sling. Quickly, then—before they could shout at her—she scurried around gathering up stones from the road, anything small enough to be slung, loose enough to be picked out with her fingers.

WHEN IT came—when at last it came, when she was bizarrely almost impatient for it, *now that we all know you're coming, please will you hurry so that we can have the battle done with and get on?*—the first hail from above was of stones, not steel. Stones bigger than the ones she'd been rooting out for slingshot: ripped from the terrace walls, she guessed, that lifted one paddy above another. Ripped out and hurled down: too big to sling but they needed nothing more than muscle and their own weight to bring them slamming down from height.

Mei Feng covered her head with her arms and ran for shelter, what little shelter the paddy wall afforded, less now that it was crowded with a thousand men doing the same.

The brave ones, the ones with slings and nerve enough to step out beneath that fall of rocks, tried their luck with a stone or two in reply. Or a succession of stones, in fact, as many and as fast as they could spin and hurl them.

If they had any joy, Mei Feng couldn't tell. All she knew was the other thing, joy for the rebels, as one by one the slingers fell: not to the stones, which must have been tossed more or less at random, but to aimed and lethal arrows.

There were archers up and down the line, if none in Jiao's squad. They replied as best they could, but it would always be harder ducking out of cover and having to shoot high above them, while the rebels were set and ready and shooting down.

Sounds of fighting came down with the arrows; Mei Feng drew some comfort from that. And men were still running to join in, scrambling over the wall despite the arrows, preferring the risk to the wait.

There was no comfort to be had across the water. There she could see what must be happening on this bank too, played out for her instruction: the steady descent of the rebels, one terrace after another; the thin streams of imperial troops running up to face them; the line of contact, where those who survived that far skirmished and fought and died.

Died, mostly. In places they broke the line and surged forward, but there were always more rebels coming down. Mei Feng could see isolated pockets of soldiers still fighting, entirely engulfed by the rebel horde; she couldn't see any hope for them.

Nor for these, the men she stood among. Over yonder, the men waiting on the road were dying individually, unhurriedly, picked off from above. Sooner or later the rebel advance would arrive there, and drive them all into the river. Which they would not survive today, because nobody could.

The men on either side of her were ready.

So was she.

When they decided there was no point standing and waiting to die—orders or no orders—so did she. She couldn't swim the river, there were no boats and no bridges now, she couldn't fly. She had no way to reach the emperor, no way to send him a message. Sooner or later—if he survived—word would reach him of what she had done, and there was perhaps a message in that; and if she was lucky, if she was careful, if she didn't let them drive her into the river, perhaps her body would be found and there was most certainly a message in that if he could only read it.

When they leaped up onto the paddy wall to face whatever was coming, blade in hand, so did she.

She was only a beat behind them because she couldn't leap a wall so high, she had to climb it. Blade in her teeth to free her hands: she could have laughed at herself if only she'd had the time, the courage, someone to tell the emperor what she'd done.

She scrambled up the bank of mud and stone, peering for handholds and for any man above who might reach down to help or else to knock her back.

Because her head was tilted back, she could see a lot of sky.

Because of that, perhaps, she saw the dragon.

IT WAS only a glimpse, but Mei Feng knew what she was seeing: the impossibility of it, the great appalling body that flew without wings, without law.

Today she flew on the wings of a storm, it seemed. As though she dragged cloud like a curtain behind her, great banks of it in sick and heavy colors, yellow and green and gray, as thick as congee. Perhaps the sky was protesting at last, massing up in refusal of a power that would always be alien, never familiar however often the dragon flew.

As Mei Feng watched, that bad sky swallowed the dragon whole.

In the last moment before she was gone, Mei Feng saw that she carried something gripped in her front claws, like an eagle with a fish.

OR AN eel, more like, a clawed eel: a monstrous clawed eel with a monstrous great . . .

A great hand reached down and scooped Mei Feng under her armpit, lifted her up onto the top of the retaining wall and shook her, shook what she had seen almost out of her head, almost.

She took the long knife out of her mouth and drew breath to tell it anyway, before someone else could; and he shook her again and said, "What are you *doing*, Mei Feng? Didn't you hear Jiao? Stay below, I will leave some men with you . . ."

"Who will be no more inclined to stay below than you are," she said, "or me either. I can fight," waving the blade in her hand to prove it, driving him one step backward, *don't you shake me.* "You cut off their heads, I'll cut off their kneecaps. Or, no, better: the other way around. We'll wait at that wall," the next step up, the terrace wall to a higher paddy, "where you can cut them off at the kneecap because that's as high as you'll be able to reach when they're standing on the wall; and then they'll fall right at our feet, and I can cut off their heads."

He stared for a moment, and then he laughed; and he was still laughing as he died, as the arrow slammed into his neck and knocked him back onto the road like a broken puppet, loose-limbed in the wrong way, no control.

For a moment she stood there staring, and a second arrow could have taken her too. Then she saw that he'd dropped his tao, and stooped to retrieve it. If there was a second arrow, it went over her head. A third would never have found her, because she'd already jumped down into the paddy.

Water to her knees and the soft mud beneath, where the rice was rooted; she had always hated this at planting time, when all the village turned out to help. She could be wet all day and all night at sea and never worry, but clinging ooze between her toes was vile.

There were bodies, too, half floating, half buried in the mud. Stray hands grasped at her, stray eyes watched her with the lost passion of ghosts. She plunged blindly on till she came hard up against mud and stone, the next terrace rising above her.

She stalled there, hearing men fight overhead, lacking either the courage or the folly to scramble up between their legs; but one man fell down, dead or dead enough, and another jumped down after him.

WHICH OUGHT to make that man a rebel because an imperial soldier should be fighting his way upslope, not coming down.

That was all the thinking time she had before the man caught his balance in the water, looked around, saw her.

Saw her and raised his tao in an instant, snarling his contempt, seeing her perhaps as a boy or perhaps as a woman but barely worth the slaying either way, although he would.

Only he wouldn't, because her blade was swifter and her wrist was stronger or else she was just more ready. She knocked his tao ringingly aside and took his throat on the backswing, and he fell down to bleed out into the paddy.

And then—not wanting to linger now, not wanting his ghost-glare in her eyes or on her mind—she was apparently bold or fool-ish after all, because she did haul herself up to the next level. Men were fighting on the wall and on the paths, all through the paddy. It was hard to tell which were imperial troops and which were rebels, in all the mud and the noise and the confusion. Mostly, she hoped the imperial troops would know her.

Perhaps all battles were like this, trust and hope?

There was a storm coming; here was the rain, first fall of it, warm heavy drops as thick and hot as blood. It wouldn't stop this man coming at her now, trying to kill her; it wouldn't stop her either. Nor would he.

Always run to meet trouble. His arm was high, his blade was swinging down, he was a fool expecting her to shriek or cower or back away.

She hopped nimbly forward, inside the reach of his arm and lunging. Never mind where his blade went, so long as hers struck home . . .

Which it did, through leather armor and skin and belly, and when had it become so easy to kill a man?

In and out. She pulled her blade free and watched him fall and looked around, saw a man she was sure of, one of Jiao's in trouble, and went to help.

Two to one, and that was easy too, so the two of them went on together. And found another that this man would vouch for, and then they were a threesome.

The rain was coming hard now, making everything harder. Footing was treacherous even on the paths; the grip on her tao was slippery. Sighting men was still easy, there were so many, but telling one side from the other . . .

Most were in the water, churning up the paddy, ruining the crop. A blade lashed out, trying for one of her companions—*cut him off at the knees*—but hers came down first, steel grating on steel, skewing that thrust aside. Her other man hacked down, half split the rebel's skull for him. If he was a rebel. She thought so, probably . . .

And this one too, heaving himself up at her, trying to knock her off her feet, off the path. His shoulder caught her knee, and it was only storm-trained muscles that let her take that, let her catch her balance and keep her feet in the mud. And then he was sprawled across the path and only something to be stepped over. A nod of thanks to the man who had killed him; there should have been more acknowledgment, but breath was short and precious where most of what her mouth could catch was water.

Here came wind too, snatching at what little air she had, trying itself to blast her from the path. She was doubly glad to come to the next terrace wall, glad just to cling to it, to feel her two companions drawing in on either side and clinging too.

It couldn't be this dark, this time of day; the rain must be knocking the light out of the sky, washing it away . . .

A glance up showed her worse clouds than the dragon had brought, black thunderheads from horizon to horizon, tossing lightning-flares between them. No hint, no hope of sun. Except around the margins, where bright day still shone, north and south . . .

"Typhoon!" a voice shrieked in her ear, and what could she do but nod?

She'd never been at sea in a typhoon, Grandfather was just too wise a sailor. She'd never been anywhere but in their little house, hugging whatever came to hand—a puppy, a cushion, a coat: it just felt better, something soft and warm to hold on to—while the wind hurled the rain against the walls and the roof creaked and tried to lift away, tried to lift the whole house away but that Grandfather had built it too tight and too heavy, too well fixed in the earth. Nothing came in, not the least whisper of water, not a stir of the air: only the sounds of the storm, that her child-mind used to picture as monsters stomping and grabbing, spitting and slobbering and utterly denied.

Now the wind could have her, if it wanted her. The rain had drenched her already, and had hopes of drowning her. She thought she'd rather the dragon came to swallow her quickly; or just a rebel, any rebel, there were enough of those around. One quick stab, surely better than this slow pounding to death, or the wind lifting her up and taking her away, set her to fly against the dragon who must still be up there somewhere, still causing this . . .

The wind made a vicious lash of the rain, and every stroke of it stung her to tears, but she could look.

She saw men doubled over in the paddy, she saw them blown over entirely and struggling to rise, struggling not to drown in that little churn of muddy water. Some would make it to their feet, she thought, some not.

What she didn't see, she didn't see anyone fighting now. Who could? Who could conceive of it, even, in this?

She gripped the arms of her two companions, pulled them close and bellowed in her best imitation of Grandfather's fog-voice: "We need to go back! Back to the city!" There could be no war in this, no victory for either side, only destruction for both. And this was only the fringe, first breath of the typhoon; there would be worse and far worse to come.

She didn't tell them that. Two tough men and her own unexpected whip-strength to back them, perhaps they could hold to each other and walk, just about, through this. If they could reach solid shelter before its strength grew, before the waters rose, they might be safe. Perhaps . . .

four

*I*n a boat he could not sail, Han flew—miles above the ground, dreadful impossible miles!—in the grip of a creature he could not trust.

It was a nonsense, an absurd thing. He ought to be dreaming; he ought to wake up. When he clenched his hands this terribly hard on the boat's frame, when a stray splinter from where her claws had pierced the hull drove deep into the ball of his thumb, his only thumb: surely then he ought to wake up?

Except, of course, that he was not asleep nor dreaming, and had never imagined that he was. She was all too monstrously real, and always had been. How could anyone hope to sleep, with a dragon in his head?

It was still absurd to be here, sailing the sky in the grip of a dragon's claws, with no better guarantee than her promise.

As absurd as a man, a boy making bargains with a dragon, say . . .

BRING ME *a boat,* he had said, and she had done so.

Get in, she had said; and then lifted it, carried him across the strait. She might have dropped him, it and him together, at any time, although she gave her word; she might have let them fall and swooped down and swallowed him, swallowed it and him together if he clung. They were both of them agreed, that would be an end of his chains and her troubles, both at once. An end of him, of course, that too.

That did not trouble her.

But she kept her word, for whatever reasons might have been her own. At least, she had kept it so far. Safely across the water, she had brought him; and now—

Now THEY hung over the land, too high to look down except he had to; and what he saw was a typhoon from on top, a pocket-typhoon that filled the river valley and ignored the world beyond. It looked like a turbulent fog, from above: an ink-fog, dark and stirred up, swirling. Nothing at all like water, rain. The wind of it was evident in that wild, twisting stillness, like a top so caught in motion that it hung unmoving, humming, all power contained; here the power was contained within the valley walls, and he knew exactly, he *knew* just what it must be like beneath, and here on top was the only place to be, and still he said, *Take me down.*

Really, little thing?

This was their bargain, their new bargain; he had demanded it in exchange for what she wanted. And had been rather astonished when she said yes, when she complied. She had done it and he should be satisfied, she could demand her own satisfaction now but seemed content to wait. And he had brought this on everyone below, and he thought he ought to be there, if only for a moment.

Really. Take me down. Then, I promise . . .

You have promised already.

So she took him down into that wicked swirl of cloud, and he thought he knew typhoon but he had never known anything like this: the wind that gripped like madness, like steel fetters, that would have lifted him straight out of his boat if he hadn't been holding on quite so tightly already, his legs wedged deep beneath a cross-beam; the rain that was not like rain at all but like walking—sailing—flying into a wall of water, a wall that fell and fell and fell on him, that flooded this folly of a boat in moments and would have drowned him right there in the sky if the dragon's claws hadn't already done so much damage to the sprung timbers of the hull that the water drained away as fast as it could fill.

He could see nothing through the water that engulfed his head, though he left it hanging hopefully over the side until he genuinely thought the wind might rip it off as a bauble. He couldn't breathe, could barely move: only to draw back into the unshelter of the boat, the unsafety of the dragon's protection, huddle his head beneath his arms and hope to survive this. He couldn't imagine how much worse it must be for those below, those not gripped in the security of a dragon's clutch. He couldn't imagine anything, his mind would not move beyond its own immediate miseries.

Take me away from here.

He had wished this on them, on all of them, the two fighting armies below. He had brought it down on them, and he couldn't bear it.

And he still thought he was right.

Take me away meant *now we do what I promised you:* it meant *take me to the beach, where the smiths are,* where he could get these chains finally struck off and set her entirely free. If she chose to eat him then, it would be her choice and nothing he could do about it, but he didn't think she would. Not now.

She flew low along the river, letting everyone see her, letting them all know that this was her storm, her mastery of the sky's temper. Actually he thought it was his storm, the price he'd demanded for her freedom: *see where all those tiny people are contending,* two armies at war, impossible to misunderstand even from above; *do something, anything you can to stop them fighting . . .*

Tien would be grateful, he thought, when he found her.

Other people would survive because of it, maybe thousands of others, but he did it for Tien, for the thought of her.

WHEN THEY reached the city's edge, the rain failed; the wind turned its back on them; the last water fell away through the holes

in the boat's hull. He could stand again, hold again to the side and
peer over.

Even with his back turned to that great storm-shadow, Santung
looked strange from the air. It was no great wonder; everything looked strange from the air. The dark winding of the river
that looked so like a road from up here, stony and still, except that
it was too wide and too empty, like a spill of ink across a page; the
streets that were straight like needles, the lanes and alleys that
wound between them like thread, like an inextricable tangle of
thread; the people who were nothing but fragments of movement,
vanishing stitches up and down the streets, in and out of shadow,
in and out of buildings.

And the buildings like boxes, square or stretched or twisted,
roofs that were only blocks of color, one shade or more than one;
if he knew the city intimately, if he'd had years of living there, he
still didn't think he'd be able to map his way around it from above.

In any case, the dragon wouldn't give him the time. She was fast
through the air, astonishingly fast, as she was astonishingly huge
on the ground. There was the sea already, an incomprehensible
vastness of water; and between the city and the sea were the narrow yellow shavings of beach, and she was dropping down already
to make landing, and—

—AND THERE was no point, because the beach was empty. There
was the run of smiths' forges, one or two even leaking a little thin
smoke still, but no one was attending them. Han had lived days
and weeks in pain and fear, to and from this beach, dragging whatever metals he could find and carry and keep; its busyness then
proved as fugitive as that life of his, now that he had fallen into
this other.

Of course the smiths were gone. If they'd had a choice, it could
only have been to have died here, under the blades of imperial
troops. At the first rumor of invasion, they would have fled with

Tunghai Wang and all his rebels, out along the river roads and up into the hills.

She said, *Little thing. You promised me men, with hammers.* A wealth of threat in so few words, such a small accusation to carry such an infernal weight of danger.

I did, he said, *and we will find them. Take me to the western ridge, above the city.* Smiths were craftsmen, not soldiers; one of them might be lurking in the camp there, hiding while the invasion front passed through, hoping to establish himself with the emperor after. More likely—Han thought, he hoped—he would find the doctor there in his tent, not hiding, confident in the gifts and use of his profession.

The doctor and Tien. She would know if there was a smith to be found. If not, for sure she could find a man strong enough to wield a hammer, to break a few chains and work a collar off.

They would need tools. Han scoured the line of forges, found hammers and cold chisels in swift time, bundled them up and hurried back to the boat, where the dragon had set it on the sand and now lurked above it. Scowlingly, he would have thought, if her face had had anything human about it, if her spirit had. She was always fearsome, but her coiled body, the pose of her neck, her eyes above all as they glowed at him: everything about her spoke of suspicion, distrust, doubt. All of that on top of her common mood, rage barely contained. She never had been anything other than furious, since she broke free—no, since he broke her free of her long sea-prison bed.

Mostly she was furious with him. He ought to be too terrified to move; and yet here he was, hurrying almost heedlessly toward her, anxious only not to drop the awkwardness of his burden, angular sliding weights of wood and metal . . .

He let them all fall into the bottom of the boat, checked that they wouldn't fall out through any of the various holes, and barely had time to scramble in himself before she had seized it—more holes, her talons punching through the timbers as though they were paper—and lifted it, lifted herself and him too into the wind again.

He fell, in the jerk of that lift-off; and lay sprawled painfully on his back across the thwarts, gazing up the length of her scaled leg toward her vivid throat and astonishing himself with a smile. Not for her, of course—what use would she have, for his smile?—or for her sake, but a smile none the less. Insensible, incomprehensible, rising from somewhere deep and dark and mysterious within him, when he had thought all smiling lost or locked away, gone for now if not quite gone for ever.

Now HE did have to navigate himself and her, from mid-air. Hanging over the side, spinning directions like a thread in his head—*yes, follow this road to the height*—or was it that one? *No, no, this, I'm sure this*—and wishing he didn't need to, wishing she could just reach into his mind and take out what knowledge was there, whatever she needed. It would be so much simpler than this struggle to see and explain. Her eyes and her understanding were both so much greater than his own, and she was so used to knowing the world in this layered way, from above and below and all around . . .

If there had been a window to his brain, *I make you free of what is in here, all of it,* he would have done it. So long holding out, and suddenly he would have surrendered utterly.

No need, though, or not for this. *There now, see it? That pale sprawl among the hutments there, where the only smoke is rising? That is the doctor's tent, and Tien's little fire behind it. I can find what help I need there. Soon now, soon, I swear it. Let me down. Let me down here, at a distance. If you try to land any closer you will hurt someone, or scare them into a fit . . .*

IT WAS strange, the strangest of ways that he had found yet to come to her, stepping out of a boat on a high dry ridge with barely a view of sea or river. The dragon made everything strange, though, or perhaps she made everything normal.

He stepped out of the boat and gathered up his tools, struggled again to find a way to carry them, ended by lifting up his shirt hem and making a sling of it. Which he had to hold in both hands, rather grimly, when he could only grip thoroughly with one; which made a hard struggle of his walk through the abandoned camp. He had been seriously cautious in where he'd had the dragon set him down, half a mile from the tent, and he was filthy and sweating and probably ridiculous when he ducked through the tent's doorway and found himself eye to eye with a stranger.

A man, middle-aged, with none of the doctor's lean significance. He was packing knives and bottles into a bag; perhaps the doctor had taken on a servant? He would be needing all the help he could find, sure, with all the hurt there must be now—again!— in the city and beyond it, the injured struggling to find some way back out of the impossible rain . . .

"What is it you want, lad?" the man demanded sharply. "I have no time, unless your errand is urgent?"

Unless your errand is well paid was what he meant. Han knew that phrasing, that particular look. And frowned, and said, "Sir, I was looking for the doctor."

"I am the doctor."

"No, I mean Doctor Hsui . . ." Could Tien's uncle have taken on a partner, rather than a servant?

"Doctor Hsui is unfortunately dead. I am master here now. What is the nature of your business? Any need you have for a doctor . . ."

Dead.

It happened, of course. Around armies, around broken cities, it must happen too often, too early. Around doctors too, perhaps, exposed as they were to their patients' diseases.

And Doctor Hsui had not been a young man; and even so, Han was shaken by the news. Shaken physically, so that he nearly dropped his tools again. And could only shake his head to the new man's questions, and was still trying to find a way to frame one new question of his own—*where is Tien, is she dead too?*—when the flap at the back of the tent opened and she came in.

"Master, are you ready yet? And did you see that shadow that came over? It was gone by the time I looked up, but I think the dragon's back. We need to move, down to the temple. And we should—"

AND THEN she saw Han, and her momentary frown, her swift recognition, her sudden awful stillness were all marvelous to him, marvelous to watch.

And then she was hurtling across the space at him, seeming almost to pass through the benches and chests that stood between them. He couldn't fend her off, with his hands full of bundled shirt and that great weight of wood and iron stretching the fabric; he had no time to find a place to stow it.

In the end he simply let it all fall, dangerously between his feet and hers, so that they both had to dance a little to avoid bruised toes; but then he had his arms again, and her slender solidity inside the circle of them. And her arms around his neck, her face against his chest, her hair in his mouth and no words, no words anywhere in the tent until the man—she had called him "master," which seemed odder even than his calling himself a doctor, and that was odd enough in here, where Doctor Hsui's ghost overstood every shadow—rasped his throat impatiently and said, "Who is this, Tien? And what has happened to your hurry? You were all urgency to be away, down to treat the soldiers; and now . . ."

And now she lifted her head away from Han, which was a wrench, it tore at him; and she turned her head, which was worse, except that he could look at her for a little, at this little part of her, the black top of her head and the way her hair was combed and knotted; and she spoke, and he could hear her voice again and she was still not speaking to him but that didn't matter at all because his name was in her mouth anyway, she was speaking about him.

Tien said, "This is Han, master. I told you about him, he's the boy who chained the dragon."

Which was all wrong, entirely and deliberately so; and entirely and deliberately cruel, Han saw, as the man paled behind her. It was the second time she'd mentioned the dragon in as many breaths, which was neither accidental nor innocent. She meant to do it; but her mind was moving on already, he could watch it at its quick work: looking down at all that ironmongery about their feet and then up at him, at the iron around his throat, feeling the cold weight of chains that pressed against her body, imagining the cold weight of dragon on his mind . . .

She said, "Han, you look terrible. Have you been eating? At all?"

"Yes," he said smilingly, "of course . . ."

"Not enough, and all the wrong things. And there is pain in your face, that hand of yours has been bad again, I think; it drains you, even if there's no poison in it anymore. And the dragon, she drains you too, she does you damage every day. Sit, sit—don't *argue* with me!—and take that shirt off. I will brew a tea for you, a medicine; and when you've drunk it I'll put my needles in your neck, and take that pain away."

He had known her needles before; he remembered the dreamy drifting state they brought him to and tried to hold out against her insistence. "Tien, I need to shift these chains first, I promised . . . The dragon is waiting . . . It won't take long, and then I am all yours, but I must . . ."

Apparently he must sit down, her firm hands offered him no choice. "She has waited all this time, she can wait one little hour more. You will still be here; I cannot vanish you from the tent and steal you away from her. But while I've got you under my hand, right *now,* I am going to give you the start of what you need, Han," and indeed she was pulling the shirt off over his head, giving him no chance to do it himself. "Look at you, all bones . . ."

The doctor said, "Tien, if the boy needs feeding, we can spare

him some food. We can leave him with the food for all I care, let
him eat all he can and watch the rest until we return. But we
should go, do you hear me? *Go*. There will be men, perhaps
women too, at the temple, hurt far worse and in far more need of
your medicines than he is . . ."

He was fidgeting at the very door of the tent, carrying those
bags he'd packed, more like an impatient servant than a master,
casting worried glances out into the air as he spoke. *Don't fret,*
Han could have said, *she is a dozen miles away upriver, playing
with her storm, herding your soldiers this way and that, flicking
lightnings at them like a whip, like a playful child with a whip,
while she rolls on the wind and waits to be freed utterly, waits on
my promise.*

It was Tien's to settle, though, however she chose; and she startled them both, the man and him, by snapping, "If you're suddenly so keen for it, go doctor the soldiers yourself. Watch out the
dragon doesn't eat you on the way. I'm staying here."

The man's hand lifted and he took a step toward Tien as though
it was natural, as though he could beat her as he chose. But a step
toward Tien meant a step toward Han also, and brought Han's
face into his eyeline. What did the man see there, just a cold threatening fury—*touch her if you dare, I have a blade here that will
take your hand off if you do*—or something more, a hint of the
extraordinary, *I have a dragon in the air*?

Whatever it was, it paled him again, it stayed his hand and stole
his will; he stepped backward through the tent door, "Yes, yes, I
will go down. You follow, you will find me . . ."

And then the flap was falling behind him, and he was gone.

After a moment, Tien said, "Will your dragon eat him?"

Han didn't suppose so, no, but he couldn't, wouldn't speak for
her. He only felt confident to say, "She hasn't tried to eat any of
the soldiers yet, or anyone on the ground. And she isn't my
dragon," chains or no chains. Sometimes he thought he was her
human, her boy. Soon they'd both be free now. Soon now, soon.

It felt good to be sitting, better to have her hands on his body, on his skin. It was a loss when she left him, a hurt that was almost physical and very immediate, something to be indulged in, almost a pleasure because he knew that she would be coming back so soon, with a kettle hot from the fire; he could enjoy the anticipation of that even before he enjoyed the thing itself, watching how she moved, seeing and cherishing the little ways she'd changed since he saw her last—her hair was a little longer and a little more rigorously controlled, she was a little older and a little more rigorously controlled, as though she had grown a steel core in their parting—and loving how she kept glancing back at him between scoops as she mixed her tea, a little out of this jar and a little out of that.

She brought him the draft, black and steaming, bitter in scent and sour in the mouth. She frowned at his sipping and said "Swallow it off, all of it. Oh, never mind if you burn your mouth, it'll do you no good cold in your belly." Her hands were gentler than her words but just as determined, tipping the bowl at his mouth so that he had to swallow and swallow or else let it run down over his chin.

And then her hands were in his hair, rumpling it, tangling it between her fingers as she looked into his eyes. He wasn't sure what she was looking for, exactly, only that it was something that needed searching for deep; and it meant that he could look back into hers, which suited him exactly. It was like a plunge into inkpools, into the words of her, where she was written deep in the book of the world's soul; and if he felt the dragon stir, well, no doubt she was just anticipating her freedom, stretching her winglessness against his chains . . .

And then Tien's hands were gone from his hair because they were at her belt, drawing out her slender bamboo tube of needles.

And now they were on his shoulders, urging him to lie down: on his belly, which was odd if she was going to put needles in his hand and his neck as she had before, she had done that face to face; and frustrating, because it meant he couldn't quite see her anymore. But he could feel her, he knew just where her fingers were, feeling out his ribs and spine, tapping through skin to find blood and muscle and tendon, tapping her first needle home. And there was a lovely liquid warmth stealing through him already, as silver as the needles and as sharp, nothing like sleep at all but it left him helpless in her hands, helpless and trusting . . .

More needles, pinning him to the bench there as thoroughly as they might have pinned a butterfly.

Now she was mixing something again. He heard the rustle of papers, the chime of glass, the grind of a pestle in a mortar. If it was another draft he didn't think he could drink it, he had no strength to sit up or swallow, though he had the dragon's strength to fly, he could feel the wind beneath his scales. Her scales. Whichever: they were the same, as they always had been.

A stutter of pin-pricks on his back, and then another. No matter. Perhaps she was sewing wings to his skin, so that he could fly beside the dragon.

LITTLE THING, *what are you at?*

HE WAS at nothing at all. He was at lying still, perhaps; at trusting Tien. That was a place to be. Here was another: he was at the dragon's side. She seemed to know it; it seemed to worry her.

SHE SOARED, and he went with her. He was on her neck and rode her like a horse. She tried to shake him off; he had penetrated her scales, he was under her skin like a worm. She would have scratched at him, but he was in her head: an invader disguised as an embassage, telling lies . . .

LITTLE THING, *you promised . . . !*

Hush, he would have said if he could speak. If he could find words, anywhere in his head, to give a shape to anything he meant.

I keep my word; I want my freedom too. Freedom from you. The chains come off, as soon as Tien is done . . .

WHAT WOULD they call her, what had they ever called her when she was not the Dragon-in-Chains? When she was free, long centuries ago, hereafter . . . ?

WHAT WOULD she do?

WHAT WAS Tien doing, busy there with her needles on his skin?

JABBING, JABBING. He could feel a trickle down his spine, not the rain that washed the dragon's scales, though it was hard to be sure when he flew the storm with her. Was he bleeding? Why would he bleed? What could make a dragon bleed? The songs said they bled in gold, but he wasn't sure. This didn't smell like gold. Nor blood. Nor tea, though she had been brewing something.

TRUST IS a needle, jabbing, jabbing.

DOUBT IS a dragon, hurling herself about the sky; hurling herself about inside his head and somehow not finding him, finding him elusive, too slippery to seize or crush. As though he were a boat on the water under the goddess's protection, when all he is, he's a boy, with a girl jabbing needles in his back.

TRUST IS a needle, jabbing deep.

HE DIDN'T wake, he hadn't slept; but his body came back to him slowly, and his back was terribly sore. And his mind, now—the dragon was battering at his mind as though she battered at a closed door, although he had not closed it.

She was an open book; he almost thought he could read her deeply.

He stirred, tried to lift himself, both hands on the bench. Tien was there to help him, smelling of herbs and herself, her own weariness and something sharper, something that was not quite fear—not fear of him!—but something close to it. Perhaps she smelled of confession, anticipation, guilt.

He looked at her and loved her, and wondered what she had done to pierce his trust so completely, leave it flaccid and empty, like a purse that has spent all its riches.

He said, "Tien, what did you do?"

She said, "The dragon's words, that you wear on your chains; I tattooed you, so you wear them on your skin now. Not with ink, quite: with a brew I learned from an ancient recipe. That and the tea you drank, that bound your mind to hers more tightly. We can strike off the chains, they don't matter anymore. You can't free her; she can't escape you. She would have eaten everyone, if you had let her go."

five

There are degrees of silence, degrees of pain.

The wind had stolen words; the rain had not washed but scoured away all talking, the skin of conversation.

They were in shelter now and had nothing to say, or else no way to say it.

All through the jadehouse it was true. The place was packed with soldiers staring at one another in the wonder of their survival, beaten down and beaten back but here. Here especially, in this particular room, lamplit and busy with expectation, pendulous as a drop of water hanging from a hair—here there were silences and silences, layers and currents of silence, silence in drifts and shoals and catastrophes.

Here at least, here in this corner, where Yu Shan crouched with Siew Ren, there was catastrophe. Speechless, unspeakable, beyond any reach of language.

THE JADEHOUSE was no palace, no fit place for the emperor to rest. It was a fortress, rather, a strongroom built too big: a great square block at the waterside where the jade ships landed, where for centuries they had unloaded their treasures for transport up-river and overland to the Hidden City. Doors of steel, walls of stone, no windows.

No palace, but a fine fit place for an emperor and his guard to wait out a typhoon. If he would only not keep going out into the weather for news of his army, one more sight of stragglers coming down the road, one more assurance that the rebels were not following. This was not a retreat, it was a drowning, and Tunghai Wang's men were as drowned as his, as storm-tossed, as scattered. Worse so, as they had no city to fall back on. His generals had told him so, his own common sense had reinforced the news, and still he had to see for himself, see it and see it.

Yu Shan should have been with him, but Siew Ren . . .

SIEW REN had been behind the emperor when the fireballs struck the bank. Behind but not far, not far enough. Separated by that wall of flame, Yu Shan hadn't known; and then there had been the swimming and the fighting and the swimming again, trying to organize half an army in a bottle-trap, trying to fight an enemy that came down from a height; and then there had been the rain, the wind, the dragon.

On the road back to Santung—with the battle left behind them, half fought, abandoned by both sides—he had stopped to help some guards struggling with their wounded. And asked at last after Siew Ren, where was she, ahead or behind: and so was told. And so left the guards, left the emperor, surged through typhoon and terror until he found her and brought her here.

She would not die, she was too hard for that: jade-hard in her spirit, jade in her blood. Some, not enough. Not to make her fireproof.

She had been badly splashed, appallingly burned. One arm was a shriveled, blackened thing, useless to her; and her face . . .

Well.

She had both eyes still, that would be a blessing, except when she chose to look in a mirror. It was really only her beauty that was gone; her mouth, her jaw still worked.

Only that she had nothing to say, nor he to her.

She had screamed, a little, when he carried her in. Since then the pain had ebbed, a little, or else she had mastered it. Now there was only the silence, that had them both in a grim and unrelenting grip.

WHEN THE emperor came in at last, he was just as grim and just as silent.

He had been supremely happy, Yu Shan knew, earlier this day. Running, swimming, fighting: winning his personal victories, leading his army, seeing his enemy retreat.

He had lost that mood entirely, as soon as he understood that he had led them all into a trap. That Tunghai Wang could so neatly turn evident defeat into probable victory—above all, that Tunghai Wang should have been *prepared* for this, for his extraordinarily unlikely invasion—was a bitter blow, and not one that the emperor could swiftly recover from. He didn't know how. Nothing in his life, nothing in his training had taught him resilience.

He would have fought, no doubt, until all his army was dead around him. Even he couldn't defeat Tunghai Wang on his own, when the generalissimo held all the advantages; he would have fought and lost and died at last, and been rapidly forgotten in the new dispensation.

But there came the dragon, there came the rain: a hammer of rain, a shatter of rain, a crush that bent down even his powerful shoulders, a pounding that went on and on. And with the rain the wind, such that even he staggered a little, even he found it hard to keep his feet in the little furies of the paddy.

By the time he turned, he had no enemy to turn from; the rebels were dead or fled, pulled back to a higher terrace, following their brothers over the ridge in a desperate search for shelter. They knew that no one would be coming after them.

So too did the imperial army know it; they too had already turned and left the field, clinging to one another for support, driving one leg forward and then the other, again and again and once more.

The emperor was the only one who didn't know that the battle was over. His guards stayed with him, those who had survived this far; so did Yu Shan, of course. They didn't need to call him back, only to wait: until he had no one to fight and nowhere to stand in the lashing, churning lake of the paddy, as the terraces above over-flowed into this one with a force like a river, building like a water-fall . . .

AND THEN the long way back, and the search for Siew Ren. Yu Shan had snatched up his clan-cousin and run with her, as best he could; and hadn't thought about anyone else from then till now, but here was the emperor and it was hard not to be aware of him or of his mood, his silence.

He had thought himself mid-victory, and had that snatched away; he had faced defeat in the heat of a furious defense and seen that too snatched away, saved by the weather, there was no comfort in that. And no safety here, in Santung: any city that has fallen once will fall again, and as soon as the typhoon died—as soon as the dragon moved away, Yu Shan thought, for this was dragon-weather—no doubt Tunghai Wang would lead his army back again, and no one here could resist him. Back to the boats, then, away to Taishu with nothing to show but loss and humiliation.

Right now, the emperor was humiliated in another way, fool-ishly and boyishly embarrassed among this influx of his seniors, his generals, his guards. He'd been trying petulantly to strip his sodden clothes away, and he couldn't shift his mail.

Yu Shan felt a moment's mocking pity for the boy so pampered he'd never learned to undress himself. *Just pull it over your head, boy*—but then one of the generals said that or something like it, a more respectful version, "Majesty, so many supple links, that shirt is marvelously flexible; surely if you raise the hem, it will invert it-self as soft as silk, and—"

"Sure it would, General Tso, if I could only lift the hem at all; but see, I can't get my fingers underneath it, it won't come apart from my skin . . ."

Did stone stick to sweaty, filthy men? Yu Shan's own clothes had been practically washed off him; so much water had run down inside, he thought he'd never been so clean at the end of a hard day. Perhaps the shirt was so well made, so tightly fitting it had allowed no access to the rain. Stone was impervious, after all, even ordinary stone, and jade was special in so many ways . . .

He might have gone to see. On another day, he might have gone to tease the emperor into a better mood, a mood that would be kinder to everyone, *see, majesty, this is how we take our clothes off, we humble poor* . . .

But today could only be the day it was, and he could only be here: squatting at Siew Ren's side with no freedom to move, holding her hand against the pain because there was nothing else he could do. Nothing she could do either but lie here and hurt, squeezing his hand tight enough to snap fingers if he hadn't been so much more jade-enhanced than she was, so that he could feel that pressure and not break beneath it.

Never mind the distance or the buzz of voices across the room, he could pick out very specifically when the general said, "Majesty, I—I don't understand this. It ought not . . ."

"No," said the emperor, with that blatant courtly patience, "it ought not." *I believe I said that.* "And yet it does." *Are you an idiot?*

Apparently yes, the man was an idiot. He went on scrabbling at the shirt's hem, at the emperor's skin, trying to separate one from the other and inducing his fellow generals to join in. There was nobody in that room, Yu Shan thought—or at least nobody who knew her—who was not longing for Mei Feng to be there, to slap them all away and take charge of her man in his trouble.

In her absence, it was unexpectedly the eunuch—what was his name, Jung?—who stepped forward from the lamps' shadows. Yu Shan had barely been aware that he was there, except for the general sense—the sense of the generals, by and large—that eunuch-and-child had protected them all across the strait, so eunuch-and-child should protect them all here on land also, so eunuch-and-child had been fetched up from the harbor.

Eunuch without child, eunuch who had left child nested in a heap of blankets in the corner, Jung said, "Majesty, I have oils here, perhaps I could ease the shirt away from your body, if you would allow it . . . ?"

Majesty allowed it; at that point, Yu Shan thought, majesty would have allowed anything that held out the least hope of working.

The least and slowest hope. Yu Shan heard occasional grunts and protests; he saw more and more, as the generals and officials grew bored or embarrassed and so backed off, found reasons to be elsewhere, to walk among their men or record the day or whatever it was that functionaries did when there was no battle to be fought, no errand to be run, no doing anything in the midst of a typhoon storm.

He saw the eunuch bent over the emperor, working his hands with infinite care under the fabulous mail shirt.

He could measure the progress, how far beneath those hands could reach, how far they had to go.

He could stop worrying; clearly there was progress, and there would be more. They could worry later about why the emperor's shirt had clung so determinedly to his body. Yu Shan could let them worry and never trouble about offering his own answer, how his own sliver of jade had settled into the skin inside his mouth and melded into his body, become a part of it entirely, not to be cut out now.

Perhaps all that rain had kept the shirt from doing the same thing, eating even deeper into the emperor's body, singing to the stone in his blood, joining with that same irreparable strength. Perhaps. At least it seemed that the eunuch could separate the two, part the emperor from his shirt eventually, leave him still visibly human. Not wearing scales.

Yu Shan held Siew Ren's hand and worried about her, and gave the emperor as little attention as he could spare, just a glance and a thought, just a listen now and then.

His own pain he could ignore: it was a nothing, only a horror of the future, her future, which was unknowable. And *where is Jiao?*, which was unaskable.

At last there was a cry of triumph: from the eunuch, not his master. Yu Shan glanced across to see the glittering green shirt peeled at last from the emperor's shoulders, pulled over his head and tossed heavily aside.

And then—because his gaze lingered, for no better reason than that the smooth compelling beauty of the emperor's unmarked skin was far more attractive than Siew Ren's ruined face—he saw how the eunuch reached inside his own shirt to draw forth a knife, glitteringly sharp and curved.

How he brought it stabbing down clean and swiftly, into the emperor's unprotected back.

YU SHAN was already diving forward, perhaps the only person in the room who could react in time, except that he couldn't because Siew Ren had her eyes closed and hadn't seen it. She still had hold of his hand with a grip that delayed him, that drew him back even as he dived, so that he had no hope of getting there before that blade had bitten home.

He had no hope, but he dived anyway; and the tug on his hand checked him anyway; and then Siew Ren opened her eyes to look, and perhaps saw, and let him go, but it was too late anyway.

THAT BLADE, that point, he saw them driving down. All undelayed by his howl of protest.

HE SAW the point strike home.

HE SAW the point snap off where it struck the emperor's skin, the blade shatter.

HE SAW how the men around and about, all those spare generals and officials and clerks fell on the eunuch assassin as he failed, how they seized him too late and tore him away from the emperor.

WHO SAT there mostly naked, gazing around in bewilderment, *what happened . . . ?*—in just that moment that Mei Feng hurled herself in through the door, with Jiao in hot pursuit.

She was running with water as they all were, as everyone was who came in from outside; she was running out of breath, gasping hard, as though she'd tried to run even through the typhoon, but she still had air enough to croak a warning, "Chien Hua! Chien Hua, beware the eunuch, you can't trust the eunuch Jung, he . . ."

Her voice died away as she stopped in her hurtling progress, as she took in just a little of what she saw: the emperor confused, the eunuch struggling but contained, the event over.

THEN, YU SHAN thought, she saw nothing but the emperor.

And went to him much more slowly, those last few little barefoot steps across dusty stone; and absurdly, the first thing she said now that her warning was redundant—now that she'd come too late, but she might not realize that for a while—was, "Why's your skin all green?"

He glanced down at himself distractedly and tried to rub it off, muttering "Dust, I suppose, from the shirt," *the jade shirt you gave me*—but his skin was oily, and it really wasn't dust. It was a greenish cast that looked internal to Yu Shan, as though it was rising from below like a blush, jade in the blood. Jade risen in response to the shirt, perhaps?

And how long was it since he'd tried to take his jade rings off?

And would that green subside now that the shirt was off, and what did it mean that steel could no longer pierce the emperor's skin, and . . . ?

AND Jiao came over to Yu Shan, and there was nothing he could do but leave all those questions lying and lead her back to where Siew Ren lay in her corner, in all her pain and damage.

They sat—shockingly—with their backs to the room, to the emperor, and he felt himself wrapped in his own sorrows like a quilt; and even so, the jade in his hearing still wouldn't let him miss what Mei Feng said. What she muttered, rather, after the eunuch had been dragged away and most of the entourage had gone or been sent after him; after she and the emperor had retreated to a corner of their own, as much privacy as they could seize, just not quite private enough to escape one sharp-eared friend's overhearing.

"CHIEN HUA?"
"Mei Feng?"
"I think . . . I think I might be pregnant."

about the author

DANIEL FOX is a British writer who first went to Taiwan at the millennium and became obsessed, to the point of learning Mandarin and writing about the country in three different genres. Before this he had published a couple of dozen books and many hundreds of short stories, under a clutch of other names. He has also written poetry and plays. Some of this work has won awards.